Making It Home
The Friends Group Series Book Two
Ana Blessing

Contents

Book Cover Design by 100 Covers

Proofreading completed by Shelby Perlis (Fiverr @shelbyperlis)

Ebook ISBN: 979-8-9997462-2-1
Paperback ISBN: 979-8-9997462-3-8

Second edition 2026

To my favorite second chance romance, I'll be forever grateful our paths crossed again.

To my boys, for giving me the grace to follow my dreams.

To all the readers looking for happy ever after.

Chapter 1: It's Not All Golden

-Annie, Age: 25-

Six years later—November

I am sick of California, as only a Midwesterner can be. I miss waving to my neighbors without getting a glare in return, driving to a place on an open highway without 24/7 traffic, and my family being within driving distance. The beach has been a highlight of being in California. I'll miss the freedom on a bad day of going to listen to the waves rushing in and out, but the waves don't outweigh my wish to go home. Or at least as close to home as I can get, knowing that Oklahoma doesn't have a major league baseball team. I've enjoyed the experience of being here in LA and getting to help cover the baseball teams here. I am the secondary sideline reporter covering the visiting team at either ballpark. It's been an experience adjusting to the pace of being at so many games, but I've learned a lot here. I love covering baseball, and it's what I was meant to do.

The Series ended yesterday, and I mostly ran background support for the sportscaster team, as neither of the local LA teams made it to the finals. As a baseball fan, it was nice to see the KC Griffons make a run for the pennant, and they played a heck of a season, coming up just short in game seven. The sportscasters on the team think they'll take it all next season if they make a few adjustments, and I am in total agreement; getting some strong pitchers and bats would get the club in a good position to take another run into the playoffs next fall. After the long baseball season, I am planning to head home for the holidays. I get be home from Thanksgiving until just after Christmas. This will be the longest amount of time I've been home since the summer before college, and I am looking forward to time with my parents and my brother Miles, who moved back to our hometown a few years ago after his college graduation.

I've gotten approval to be in Oklahoma longer because I am interviewing in both the Texas and Kansas City markets for the new positions the network has in those districts. My producer here in LA, Mac, gave me a little inside scoop during the Series coverage that I should be on my A game. He followed it up with the intel about the network getting new reporting opportunities. Mac tells me he's learned that the key markets expanding with exclusive sideline coverage are Arizona, Missouri, and Texas. Mac is like my work dad here in LA, and I think he's noticed I am a little out of my element here. Not in the work but on the personal side of life: I don't go out and socialize much, and I'm 100% focused on every extra assignment the network offers me.

I clearly have no external plans to interrupt, so they ask me to do extra assignments like I've done for the Series this year. So, it seems fitting that he'd be the one to let me know about the possibilities of getting out of the big city and back towards my roots. I told Mac he is my hero for the information. He gave me a little pat on the back and said it was the least he could do for his favorite reporter. He made the universal sign of 'shh,' placing his finger over his mouth, before telling me I couldn't tell the other reporters. I made sure to tell him that his secret is safe before heading back to work. I will miss him if or when I move on to the next opportunity.

A few days after the initial scoop, Mac finds me at my little desk reviewing player stats. "Annie, so glad that I've caught you—I may have more information about that exclusive part of the new reporter gigs." "Thanks, Mac, what you got for me?" I reply, curious not for the first time about the details. "Looks like it's going to be with specific teams, for all home and travel games. You'll be responsible from Spring Training to the Series if your team makes it all the way," he says. "Well, that sounds like an experience, doesn't it?" I say, knowing that learning one team and the players on it feels exciting. "Yeah, as I said, one of the teams is your Griffons: you'd be great since you're already an encyclopedia of Griffons history," Mac says, giving me a kind smile. "Yeah... Between you and me, I'm interested in the Missouri or Texas jobs," I tell him. "Annie, you just tell old Mac which ones you apply for, and I'll get with my contacts in those markets, give them the word on why Annie Campbell is one of a kind," he finishes and gives me a little wave before he leaves.

Before looking at any job listing or the actual teams in each market, I know I will be true to my word with Mac. I've ruled out Arizona; Drew still plays for the team. I haven't seen him in six years, and I don't think showing up to Spring training with the requirement that he has to see me every day seems like a better job. Plus, Arizona is still too far from home, which is why I'm looking to get out of LA. I fight the urge to pull up Drew's stats, now thinking about him in Arizona. I've followed his career progress over the last six years because I can't help myself. I watch his progress to validate that all the pain I caused has been worth it.

Watching him climb his way up the minors has been the validation I've needed to dull the heartbreak. Dull is the key word because I can't help thinking about him; my brain brings him up in the most random or, in this case, logical ways. I just can't erase him from my mind. Last season, he'd gotten his call-up to the majors, just like I'd always known he would, and he'd been the key player in Arizona's lineup the rest of the season.

He'd even been nominated and won his division's Rookie of the Year award. I'd recorded his first pro game because I was covering one of my own. I cried when I watched Drew take the field, his dimple on full display along with his big smile. He looked so happy, and I'd never been more proud. I'd had this pain in my chest watching, wishing I could have been there in the stands like back in high school, but I knew that was the dull ache speaking. He'd had a hell of a first game both defensively and at bat. I remember turning off the game and thinking, *He's done it, his dream has come true.*

I'd gotten lucky, and Arizona had already played games with the LA teams I cover before he was called up. I wasn't sure how we'd interact if I were the one assigned to get interviews, but I know that I need to think about it, because if his career and mine keep on their current paths, we are bound to have them cross at some point; it'd be inevitable. I guess that would be another plus of this new position—my interactions with most of the teams in the Texas and Missouri markets would have limited games with Arizona. If I got this job, I wouldn't be covering the visitors and would only be with the home team, so we'd be in the same ballpark but not on the same sideline. It would limit any on-air awkwardness; we could wave, and life would return to normal.

The only negative of thinking about making this career adjustment was the ending of my relationship with Dax. He had potential; he is in production on one of the other network shows in LA. When I'd told him about the news I'd received from a 'source' about the jobs in Texas, Arizona, and Missouri, he'd expressed zero interest in joining me on the adventure to move to another market. He'd said that LA was his market: he let me know he liked me, and the sex was good, but not enough to change his career path. I've since chalked it up to my relationship wasteland, which, if I'm being honest, all added up to careers trumping love every time. Drew was the start, maybe the most painful example, but I've always attributed that to the price of first love.

In fact, before his loss from my life, I thought that if you loved someone, it meant forever. I'd done a little casual dating in college before meeting Peter my sophomore year. Peter was studying journalism too, and it seemed like we could be headed towards real feelings, and I'd been surprised that I was starting to feel them. I'd been on the edge of telling Peter my feelings, but before I could, he'd gotten a position in Denver to cover the pro football team. He'd dumped me so quick that I'd almost gotten whiplash. I'd only dated casually again until Dax here in LA. I'd met him working on one of my 'extra' assignments, and we'd hit it off. We'd both been understanding about limited date nights and had been more focused on the sex when we had time together.

I liked him but hadn't gotten to know him well enough to ask myself if deeper feelings were possible. So, it seemed fitting that this relationship would end because I was choosing my career. Maybe it was poetic justice that I finally decided to follow my dream. I'd told my best friend Meg over video call that if I got one of these jobs, I might just need to stay away from men. She'd laughed and said that maybe I needed to avoid relationships and get a few boy toys instead.

Chapter 2: Friendsgiving

-Annie-

November

God, it is good to be home in Oklahoma, I think. I've missed getting to see my family and friends. I've been focused these first days at home on spending time with my parents and Miles. Soon my friends will be home from their respective places around the country. Meg's been off in Dallas living her best life with her roommate James Arthur. Luke has been in law school in Texas conquering the pressure of his chosen profession. Craig is in Arizona living his best life possible.

On my first night home, Miles somehow got me to agree to talk to the high school newspaper and visual news teams about my college and professional experience. Since he graduated, my brother has been teaching English at the high school. He fits the part with his shaggy blonde hair and five o'clock shadow that never seems to grow out. Along with the news teams, Miles has been working as the QB coach for the football team. He takes his coaching and teaching seriously; those kids are like his babies, and he wants to give them the best. I think it's funny that he supports the newsgroup with Dad at The Reporter, and me making good in sportscasting on TV. Miles now has his own stamp on journalism. Dad laughed when I'd agreed, telling me, "He is using all his connections for those kids. I've already visited them earlier in the fall." I'd laughed too, because it is so like Miles to want to serve others; he is a teacher through and through.

***

It should feel weird to be back in my old high school surrounded by teenagers who make you think, *When did I get old?* I'm here now, walking the halls with my brother and wondering, 'Did we look this young?' and 'Where did the time go?' He walks me by the Wall of Fame, covered with the faces of the school's most famous graduates. I can't say I remember this from my days in these hallways, but it was probably here the whole time because I see photos with pictures of mostly men dressed in athletic jerseys from the '70s and '80's.

Then I get to the end, and there we are. They have added a photo of me with my professional headshot from the network with a little tag "Annie Campbell: Network Sports Reporter" with my class year. Next to my picture is a headshot photo of Drew in his Arizona uniform with a little tag "Drew Davis: Shortstop for Arizona" and our class year.

My brother breaks into my thoughts, "It's crazy to see you on the wall, right? I remember when you were a baby," he mocks, sounding like Mom or Dad when they reminisce, "Ha ha, you're only like a year older than me, you don't remember me as a baby. But yeah, it is crazy, I don't know if what I've done is Wall of Fame worthy," I say, being honest. I don't feel all that famous, but it's cool that someone thinks I'm famous enough to be on the wall. "Well to the kids, it's enough. Enjoy your fame," Miles says, giving me a nudge before starting to walk again. I follow Miles to the newspaper club classroom, and even though it has been six years and the computers and equipment have been upgraded, the room still feels the same.

***

Miles introduces me to the students, then surprises me when he asks one of them to turn down the lights as he turns on the computer projection on the wall. "I'll let Annie speak for herself; it is her job, after all." My brother gives me a slight elbow nudge and hits the play button on the video. I watch clips of myself reporting during high school at football games and baseball games. I watch small clips of myself interviewing Daniel and Miles after a game, then my post-state interview with Drew and the guys. The video clips show me in Norman, on the field at a football game, and my viral interview when the baseball team won the college division championship. The last few clips are of me interviewing players and coaches in LA.

When it ends, the kids give a round of applause, and I blush a little—it's still hard for me to be the center of attention. I can be on the sidelines and have no problem not blushing, but now I'm focused on their recognition and can't control the blush. Miles jumps in after he turns on the light. "So, any questions?" A few students raise their hands. I pick the girl in the back. "Was it weird interviewing guys you go to school with?" "Great question. No, it wasn't: it did result in me getting to know them better. It helps that they know talking to me would get them on the school TV each week." I pick a boy in the middle of the room. "Do you think you got advantages because you're hot?" Before I can answer, Miles cuts in, "Dillion, I thought we talked about being professional with our questions—calling my little sister hot isn't what I'd call professional." There is my protective big brother, I cut in to soften the blow for the kid. "I think what he probably meant was attractive," I cover. He nods yes in agreement. "Well, I don't think it hurts that people think I'm attractive, but I don't focus on trying to be attractive; I focus on being the most prepared person in the room. I want to get the best interview or coverage for my network and the viewers."

Miles gives me a nod of well done, and I take a few more questions before the bell rings, dismissing the students. Miles has football next, so he walks me out to my car on the way to the locker room. "Thanks again, Annie. I think it's good for the kids to see what they put in now can translate into a career. That it isn't just all make-believe." "Thanks, Miles. It was fun to talk to them and answer their questions, even the awkward ones." Miles laughs at my comment and asks, "What are you doing now?" I roll my eyes before answering. "I have to go home and get the house ready for Friendsgiving, which you promised to attend this year," I tell him. He laughs, holding up his hands. "I remember, I have a reminder to get rolls from the store on my way to Mom and Dad's house after practice." I hug him, and we say goodbye. Now, off to the hard stuff: cooking a meal that people can eat. *Thank God for Mom's*, I think as I drive towards my parents' house.

*✳✳

Friendsgiving started our first year in college, after we'd all missed having our lunch group gatherings over food. We'd started having Friendsgiving a few days before our actual Thanksgiving at Meg's suggestion. The only person who had never attended from our group was Drew. I'd agreed the first year, expecting him to be here, only to learn that the Davises were taking a family vacation for the holiday. As our Friendsgiving had become tradition, so had the Davises' vacations at this time of year. I thought I'd been the reason Drew didn't attend the first year, but as time has gone on, I've taken it less personally. Now, it's a fun little event I look forward to each year without the guilt or hope that revolved around Drew's absence or appearance.

I am hosting at my parents' house, as history has established, since my parents love seeing us "kids" get together. I am in the kitchen helping my mom cook. I may be hosting, but cooking isn't my strongest skill. In LA, I have lived off pre-made meals and craft services at the baseball games. The mashed potatoes, gravy, and pumpkin pie I have volunteered to make have mainly been cooked by Mom, but I'd at least peeled and sliced what I could. The doorbell sounds, and I can hear Dad talking to someone. I ensure Mom is good, covering the last items on the stovetop before I head into the living room.

Before I can fully enter the room, I'm wrapped up in strong arms. "Annie Campbell, it's nice to see you in person," Craig says against my hair and releases me. "You, too. We didn't make anything healthy in that kitchen, forgive me," I joke because Craig is a personal trainer now, focused on keeping himself and his client at their top performance. I'm not sure why I say his *client* in my head when I know who his famous client is—Drew. I should just think Drew, but my brain always edits it to client, like that will soften the blow or make the little pinch in my heart go away faster. Craig cuts into my internal thoughts with "Annie, come on, Friendsgiving doesn't count, you know that. The more butter, the better." Craig heads into the kitchen, and I hear him say hello to my mom.

The doorbell rings again, and I tell Dad I'll get it. I open the door to Meg and Luke, our little Texas transplants. "Annie, are you ready to marry me already and activate our marriage pact?" Luke says as he hugs me. "I thought we had until thirty before the pact terms kicked in," I laugh as I release him. "I guess I'll have to look into the legal language," he laughs. "Yeah, put that law degree to good use, why don't you?" I reply before he says, "Almost law degree. Meg cuts in and I wrap her in a side hug. "Missed you, BFF". I release her before grabbing the items she has in her hands. "Miss you more, Annie Marie," she tells me, willingly handing over the dishes. She turns to head back to her car as she says, "I'll be right back with the turkey." I am in the kitchen with Mom and the guys when Meg opens the door for Miles, with his hands full of both the rolls and turkey.

"He insisted on carrying everything," Meg says as she rolls her eyes. "Well, it seemed like the nice thing to do, *Megan*," Miles addresses her with a glance before setting the food on the table. "Oh, he just called her MEGAN, she must be in TROUBLE," jokes Luke. Meg gives Luke a look and turns her attention back to Miles's comment, "Is that right, Professor?" Meg quips as she moves his long, shaggy hair out of his eyes. "Oh, is it Professor now?" Miles gives her a smirk. "I think he looks like the male teacher all the girls are getting their first older man crush for," pipes in Luke. "Gross," I say, because he is my brother. Everyone else just laughs in agreement with Luke.

I trade with Mom, finishing the items that still need to be stirred. She gets hugs from everyone before heading down the hall, "You kids have fun," she says before she tells Dad she is ready to leave. My parents are invited but want to leave us all to catch up. "I'll make sure that Miles does all the dishes," I shout, and can hear my parents laugh as they close the door.

We set the table as a group, and while putting out plates and food, Meg asked me, "So when do you start your interviews?" "What interviews?" asks Craig as he sets out forks and knives. "I am trying for a position closer to home and doing some interviews with the Texas and Missouri divisions," I reply. "I'm voting for Texas—then my Annie Marie can come be my roommate," says Meg, doing her little toe bounce thing. It's her tell that she is excited about the possibility of us being in the same city again after all these years. "Which one are you hoping for, Annie?" asks Luke as he enters the room. "If I get the Dallas coverage, it would be great to live with Meg, but I'd like Kansas City as my backup. You all know they've always been my team," I reply. Luke nods in agreement, because the Griffons have always been my team, even when they had no chance at a playoff run. "Interesting," is all Craig's gets to reply before he is interrupted by Meg's "Dinner is served."

***

11

We spend the meal eating too much food and catching up on how life has been since the last time we've all been in the same room. Meg is over-stressed at work and says she is following my example. She is going to start looking for her next opportunity when she returns to Dallas. Miles gives her a look of concern, but it's gone before I can ask him about it. Luke tells us that he's been busy trying to finish law school and that he is the most boring. He makes sure to point out that he hasn't even had sex in months. We all can't help the laughter that follows his confession, because he makes such a dramatic emphasis on the word *months*.

Miles is the next to speak "Nothing can be as dull as returning to your old high school. Going from starting QB to English teacher isn't the stuff of dreams". Luke pipes "You heard the part about no sex for MONTHS, right?" Miles raises him one with the word "Years." This only causes us to all laugh harder. I do make a comment that we need to stop this conversation before I hear any more about my brother's sex life.

Craig loves his life in Arizona and lets us know he isn't having the same problems as the other guys in the sex department. At that, Meg pops off about the fact that she's gotten laid plenty. Then she pulls me into the conversation by asking me about my sex life. I joke about being happy on my own and that I'm all stocked up on batteries for the future. Miles makes a gagging noise and repeats my comments from earlier about not needing to hear about my sex life with or without people. We eventually move on to safer topics. We finish the meal with pumpkin pie and a toast to another year of Friendsgiving.

Chapter 3: Negotiations Have Failed

-Drew, Age: 25-

Six years later—November

It is nice to have some time off with my family after the end of my rookie year in the big leagues. The baseball season had been long and exhausting, but it was the best year of my career. Having it capped off with the win for Rookie of the Year for the division was just icing on the cake. I owe my success last season to my team: I have a great agent in Dominic Stone, who has helped me climb the ranks from the minors to the big league. He is always looking for ways to increase my visibility and continues to tell me to do things I hadn't even thought possible, like getting me to be a spokesperson for a health drink brand. He keeps telling me he is working to get an athletic clothing brand deal, but his primary focus is on the contract extension with Arizona.

My trainer happens to be my best friend, Craig Mitchell. The timing of him finishing his baseball career at Norman and graduating with his athletic training degree with a license to do personal training couldn't have worked out better. I'd asked him if he wanted to work with me in the offseason, which turned into him following me when I got called up last season. Our hard work had paid off; it was clear with the way I played all season. We'd both agreed that he'd stay on as my trainer for the upcoming season. We also decided that I would eat whatever I wanted for this break. I am enjoying not being in season and the Thanksgiving holiday before we get back to Arizona to start training for the new season. Spring Training doesn't begin until the end of February, so I have time to rest and indulge before kicking it into high gear with my diet and exercise.

So, here I am, enjoying a drink at the beach next to my parents on another family vacation for Thanksgiving. Thanksgiving has never been a big holiday in the Davis house. Mom never enjoyed trying to get all the food to come out hot simultaneously, so we'd found a new tradition for the family. I admit that my reason for starting this little tradition six years ago was to not have to be in Oklahoma at the same time as Annie. Having her just next door and just out of reach had seemed like the worst kind of torture.

I'd known that first year she'd be home, I'd been a part of the same friends group text chain. I'd seen Meg's suggestion to start a Friendsgiving when everyone was home. I'd seen everyone's excited "I'm in" comments, including Annie's. I'd sat in my room, typed "I'm in" and had almost sent it because I'd wanted to see her, to see if I could convince her to get back together, but I'd known that would be selfish.

So, the Davis Thanksgiving Vacation was formed, and I never replied to the invitation in the chat on the topic. This year, the only Davis not in attendance is Daniel. He is currently on active duty in an undisclosed location. He'd turned his life around after his college accident and worked hard to prove he had changed. He'd entered the military two years ago and never looked back. He is still cocky, but he is the best version of my brother I've known. We do video chats, and he emails me occasionally to give me updates or to ask me to make sure to include his name on presents to our parents when he's away. He'd video-called us all from his undisclosed location to wish us the best for yesterday's holiday, just in case he wasn't available again this week.

He told us that he should be back in the states in the new year, and he would make stops in Oklahoma, where my parents still live, and in Arizona to visit me when the season started. Mom and Dad told him that he better make it home safe, and he promised them to do his best. I'd told him I'd have a bed ready in Arizona and a VIP game seat waiting for him, too. He'd laughed and said the VIP treatment sounded like a plan and well deserved for all his years dealing with the smart-ass shortstop. I couldn't help laughing at his too-true description of me, and I told him to stay safe before we disconnected the call. Since our call with Daniel, we'd all spent a lot of time just sitting in the loungers at the beach, listening to the waves rush in and out.

***

It had been nice to soak in the sun, eating and drinking what I wanted, but I'm back to reality. December in Arizona doesn't feel like December. It's probably weird, but I kinda miss being cold. Arizona is the place I've been living the most over the last few years. After getting promoted to the main lineup, it is my home again. I needed to think about getting started on baby steps to training again. I'd enjoyed my break and my body needed it, but it is time now to start making small efforts to make Spring Training in less than three months easier.

I want to come into training like I'd left the season, at the top of my game. I'm working out in the apartment complex gym when my phone rings, flashing "Dominic Stone" across the screen. I swipe and hear Dominic's voice cut off my workout music in my headphones. "Drew, got a second to chat?" His voice isn't as easygoing as it was on the last call about the prospect of a new brand deal. "Yeah, Dom, I'm just working out. What's up, man?" I reply. "Drew, I think we are going to have to force Arizona's hand, open up to the market as a free agent," he says in that same serious tone. Before I can answer, he continues, "It's not unheard of in the league, and it's a common move to get a club to sign a longer-term contract with a better guaranteed payout."

I wasn't planning on leaving Arizona; I'd grown up in their system, knew the expectations, and had a great season last year. Free agency wasn't even on my radar. I re-rack the weights and reply, "Ok, so what's the next move if I go free agent? When would I find out where I'm going to land with that approach?" "The best-case scenario is that it will make Arizona put up the money we are asking for to keep you. Worst case, I know of a few programs looking to strengthen their line-ups. If I have your approval, I'll start doing some digging." "Permission granted," I reply. He tells me a few more details, and we end the call. I guess I'm a free agent now.

Chapter 4: Quiet Free Agent

-*Drew*-

Mid-December

Dominic has been working on getting a new contract signed, and true to his word, he's done some digging about other teams looking for a shortstop with my skill set. I don't want to feed any rumors that I am unhappy in Arizona, so we've been keeping the fact that I am going about negotiations as a free agent behind closed doors. So far, the only ripple has been a few networks reporting that I've not signed an extension on my rookie contract as expected.

Dominic has gotten some interest behind the scenes from a few ball clubs. I am still talking with Arizona regularly, and the coach has called, asking me to stay. I appreciated him calling and trying to make it work, but I want to see what else was out there, too. I've started to have a few conversations with the interested teams, Kansas City and Atlanta. I feel like I am betraying Arizona and all the efforts they put into me, bringing me up their club ranks.

Craig has been a great sounding board during our training sessions. He reminds me they still have to give me the best offer, my body will only last for so many seasons, and I need to make the most out of the years I have left. We both joke that it is a weird conversation at twenty-five, but it's the reality for professional athletes. Bodies can only take the strain for so long; my time on the field wouldn't take me to traditional retirement at age sixty.

Atlanta's been an interesting club to talk to because I haven't kept up with them much. The general manager seems like a nice guy, and he is trying to sell me hard on his vision for the club. He seems like he is trying to build a good team, but it's just that they are rebuilding, and I'm not sure about it. In the best-case scenario, a rebuild can surprise and make a big run, or in the worst-case scenario, they don't work well together, and it's a very ugly season.

The final team is Kansas City, the Griffons, Annie's favorite pro team. When Dominic had given them as one of the interested teams, I couldn't help thinking about her. I'd been guilty of doing an internet search with her name and going down the rabbit hole of watching her top interviews. Craig had walked into the kitchen, and I'd slammed my computer shut so hard, I was surprised I didn't break the screen. He'd made some off-hand comment to save the kitchen porn for when he was out of town.

***

The GM at Kansas City is trying to lock in a few missing pieces the organization felt could have helped them win the Series last year. They want to see if they can capitalize on last year's near-championship win. He's been selling me hard on the caliber of the coaching staff, the family feeling of the team, and the fact that there are no greater fans than the ones in KC. The last statement makes me look at my living room wall at the painting of the biggest KC fan I've ever known. What would Annie think if I joined the Griffons? Are they still even her favorite team? I return my attention to my phone call, thanked him for his time, and tell him we'll talk again soon. After disconnecting, I'm interested, but will I always think of her when I hear the team name? She's already the girl I can't seem to replace. Will she be the ghost haunting me every day I step on the field there? I am trying to figure it out, reminding myself she isn't really a factor in this decision.

"So, how are the negotiations going?" Craig asks when he comes into the apartment carrying bags of groceries. "I think I'll tell Dominic to rule out Atlanta. It doesn't seem like a great fit right now," I reply as I joined him in the kitchen. "So, it's Arizona or Kansas City. You have a strong feeling about either of them?" he asks while preparing our lunch from the items in the bag. "They are both good clubs, but if I leave Arizona, it would be fun to be at an organization primed to make another deep run into the playoffs." I mean it; playing in the Series, The Championship, would be amazing and more than I thought was possible. I've dreamed of getting to play baseball professionally and winning the Series like all kids do, but to think it could be possible still feels like a kid's dream, not a real thing. "I personally think we should head to KC. I think it's time to leave the desert," Craig says with a smile before turning to place things in the pan.

***

Five days after Christmas, I verbally agree to sign with the Griffons for a ten-year average salary of $22 million a year over the contract terms. I will get a signing bonus of $5 million. It's all crazy numbers, and I don't know how my agent pulled off the deal. Dominic calls and happily announces, "Kansas City, here he comes," and tells me I had better start moving. I've been taking calls all day from the Griffons GM to their ownership team, each offering congratulations and welcoming me to the team. We've agreed to keep it quiet until I am in KC in three weeks to sign my contract formally. Then we can kick off the media storm of my moving to their club.

"I think I found an apartment downtown—someone I know is recommending it." Craig has been on his phone frequently, looking at all things KC. I've even seen him looking at apartments in KC before I'd verbally accepted the offer. I realized I wasn't the only one interested in the opportunity, and I think it helped me make the decision, not that I'd tell him that. He already has a big head and enjoys telling me to do another round of the most challenging exercises as my trainer. He doesn't need to know that he influenced my choice to leave the desert. "Seems like it has an open penthouse unit, a lot of the other athletes lease or rent space in the building, so it's got a great security presence, too," Craig says as he offers me his phone to look at the photos. "Yeah, let's get in contact with the building management and lease it," I say, having looked over the information he showed me. I hand his phone back to him.

"Well... What if I told you I've already done that?" He doesn't look guilty at all for already kicking off this process for me—well, us. Craig is my roommate in Arizona, and I don't see why he wouldn't be my roommate in KC. "Send me the information, and I'll get it to Dominic and his team to coordinate payment, contract, etcetera." My friend looks a little bashful now. "Would you be mad if I sent it to Dominic, and he's already starting all of that?" Craig gives me a little smirk when he finishes his statement. I chuckle before telling him, "Nope, please tell me you've called the movers to pack all of this," I say, pointing around the current condo. "I haven't, but I will once I get Dominic and his team to get us a move-in date," he says, looking happy with himself.

"On another subject," he holds up his hands, "don't kill me for asking, but please tell me that you ended it with Mandy." "Well, I mean not officially, I'm not sure I have anything to end," I say honestly. Mandy and I have been hooking up off and on during the season. I asked her to go with me to a few events, but it wasn't more than that. The funniest part is that Craig has hated her from her first sleepover. She'd commented on Mom's painting in the living room, something like, "Who's the average-looking girl?" Craig had looked at the painting and back at me before saying, "There is nothing average about her."

If I hadn't known he loved her like a sister, I'd have felt weird about him talking about Annie like that, but Mandy didn't know that. She'd said, "Sounds like you have a hard-on for Drew's sloppy seconds." It was the wrong thing to say. "She's the only one to make him happy and not just on her back." He'd said what he needed to say and refused to be in the apartment when she was over. I should have told her to leave, but I wasn't looking to get into it with her. At the time, I was focused on sex, and it had been good with her, even if, to Craig's point, she'd only made me happy in bed. Annie's only place in my life was on that wall, in that painting, in a moment we shared something magical.

I'd let Mandy's comments go, not wanting to interrupt the good sex for the girl I didn't have. We'd text here or there, hook up when I was around, and go weeks before our next interaction. "Give me your phone, and I'll handle that too," he holds out his hand like I'm going to hand him my phone. "She can get the realty check she deserves." "I think I'll handle this one for all our sakes," I say.

Craig shrugs before saying, "Moving to KC is going to give you a much-needed improvement in the woman department." I laugh before I give him something to think about. "If you say so, man, or maybe you'll let a woman get her hook in you". I go to my room and call Mandy to let her know I'm moving out of Arizona. True to the nature of our arrangement, she tells me 'good luck,' and we get off the call within ten minutes. Now all I have to do is figure out how to get all my stuff across the country. It will be nice to return to the Midwest, and I can't help the feeling in my chest that it feels like I'm headed home.

Chapter 5: An Offer of a Lifetime

-Annie-

December

I jump from Oklahoma to Texas, back to Oklahoma, then to Kansas City, then back to Oklahoma, all in three weeks. I've gone through multiple rounds of screen tests with each market's production team and feel like my chances are pretty good with them both. The screen test in Kansas City felt different; it was so much easier. The producers asked me why I wanted to be the on-field talent in KC, and I'd word vomited my love for the club, even going into details about my favorite Griffon players growing up. The producers had seemed impressed when I'd been able to name players across multiple years and positions. On my way home to Oklahoma, I see I've gotten messages from both Meg and Craig. I start with Meg and open our chat.

Meg Patterson

So how did it go?

Annie

I think it went great.

> It may have even gone better than Texas

> I know you don't want to hear that

Meg Patterson

> That is good for you, but sucks for Me!

> You do LOVE the Griffons, do you still have that old red Griffons hat?

Annie

> Do not throw shade at vintage gear

Meg Patterson

> Well VINTAGE shouldn't mean   holes Annie

Annie

> Well it's been well loved

Meg Patterson

> Ha, ha. Let me know when you get the offer

Annie

> I'm not even sure I'll get an offer

Meg Patterson

> Trust your BFF, you're getting an offer

Then I go to the message from Craig to see that he is just as impatient as Meg.

Craig Mitchell

> I need updates, Texas or Kansas City?

I don't know yet Mr. Impatient

Tell the Network I told them to hurry it up I have plans to make

Oh ok, I'll get right on that

I'll just tell the president of the network that my buddy Craig has plans to make

So please let me know where I'll be working next season.

Thank you

Smart ass

I'll take that as a compliment, but I'd rather hear nice ass for future reference

Yuck, gross. I am not going to say that

Have you seen my ass lately, I do a lot of squats

I'll take your word for it.

Craig Mitchell

Let me know when you know

I'm proud of you no matter what

Annie

Thanks Craig, I don't know what I'd do without you

Craig Mitchell

Ditto, Annie

***

Four days before Christmas, I get a call for an official offer to join the Kansas City network division. It takes everything in me not to shout "yes" into the phone and interrupt them. I instead find myself doing Meg's little toe bounce happy dance while the producers gave me the breakdown of my offer. I would be signing a three-year deal to be the exclusive on-field talent supporting the Griffons club on the network. I'll also be the one to do player spotlight interviews before the games to be used as part of the pregame packages. The salary is more than it was in LA, so it's a no-brainer to say yes. They are even going to give me a moving allowance to get out of my lease in LA, move all my stuff, and help me get into an apartment in KC—they go so far as to send over some recommended apartment complexes for me to look at to help me start the process as soon as possible, since I need to be in KC by mid-January.

I accept verbally on the call and quickly review the paperwork before sending it to my legal expert and long-time friend, Luke. He'd been the one to help me with my contract last time, and I want to make sure he doesn't have any concerns with the new one. I want to tell someone so bad, but my parents are already in bed, and I don't want to scare them by waking them up. So, I'd started a group call with my friends Meg, Craig, and Luke.

"Annie, everything ok?" Craig answers. "Yeah, Annie, everything ok?" Meg repeats. "Did you just send me an e-mail?" Luke says as he joins the call. "I got the KC job," I half scream into my phone. My friends whistle and whoop in celebration on the line. I get statements like, "Always believed in you" to "They'd have been fucking stupid not to hire the best woman for the job." When the celebration settles, Meg asks to hear the details, and I spend the next fifteen minutes reading over the contract with them. Luke tells me he will review the agreement after we get off the call, so I won't have to wait to sign. Meg says to let her know when I move into my apartment, and she'll take a flight to KC to help me set up my apartment and unpack boxes. Craig jokes that everything seemed covered before asking me to send over the recommended apartments. He says he could save me some time researching the different locations and send me his recommendation on which ones look the best. I thank them all, because they are a girl's best friends.

***

Everything goes so quickly after I get the offer. The next day, true to his word, Luke sends me back the contract with a few suggestions, and I forward those suggestions to the network. They accept them, and I sign a three-year deal two days before Christmas. On Christmas Eve, Craig sends me his top two suggestions for apartments for lease in KC:

Craig Mitchell

I like the Plaza or Power & Light apartments. Both seem to be in good areas in the city

Annie

Let me pull those up

Where would you live?

Craig Mitchell

I think I love the Power & Light if it was me

Annie

The rate seems reasonable

Craig Mitchell

Yeah, better then LA that is for sure

Annie

Thank you, I'll call them tomorrow

Craig Mitchell

Let me know if I can help with anything else

But not moving, use the networks money

Annie

I thought you had big strong muscles

Craig Mitchell

Muscles yes, interest in moving no

Annie

LOL, I'll update you when I hear back

***

Two days after Christmas, I complete the lease agreement for a one-bedroom apartment in downtown KC's Power & Light district. It is the best option for me being single; it has a lot of things to do and places to eat nearby, and the ballpark is only fifteen to twenty minutes away. I text Craig a picture of the Welcome packet I'd gotten, and he replies that he can't wait to visit. Then I book my flight to LA, because I have an apartment to pack up and move. Kansas City, here I come!

Chapter 6: My New Home

-*Drew* -

End of January

I get to Kansas City, and it's freezing. I may not be the best judge of temperature, having just played in Arizona for the last six years off and on, but it seems too cold to play baseball right now. I mentally remind myself that I missed this, having seasons, and that I'll get adjusted after a few years. I know we have months until the season starts playing home games here, but I think Craig and I may have to train outside so my body understands what winter and early spring mean in the Midwest again. My driver pulls up to the apartment complex, and the area seems to have a lot of options, from restaurants to grocery stores to bars and clubs, and it is all within walking distance. I don't plan to live here for the whole ten years of my contract, but it seems like a great place to be right now to get to know the city that will be my new home.

The security team at the front desk is nice, and they help me get my keys and understand where all the different amenities are located. I take the elevator to the penthouse level and enter the apartment with my new key. Craig came into town two days ago and helped coordinate all the movers, and the only thing he didn't unpack was my bedroom boxes.

The place is nice, and I like that his room is on one side and mine is on the other, giving us a little more privacy. In the last place, we shared a wall, and I had to purchase the best noise-cancelling headphones for whenever Craig had woman over. I'm glad we will not have to repeat the process here. "You made it," Craig says, giving me a quick handshake and a hug. "Yeah, it looks great, you've been busy," I tell him, because there isn't a box in the kitchen or living room. "I didn't touch your boxes." He says with sarcasm. "The only thing I've touched of yours is the painting, and I've had them come and install it on the wall there." Craig points, and on the back wall is the painting of me and Annie.

I keep hanging it up because it's one of Mom's best paintings, and I like remembering what it felt like to be that happy. Maybe when I meet the right girl, I'll stop putting it up, but it still feels right to have it hanging up as a centerpiece of my world. "Man, you did well. It all looks good. I'm sure Mom will approve when she visits." Craig beams at my words. I go to my room and start to tackle the boxes. I am glad the moving company built the bed frame and set up the m attress.

***

The next day, I get a private tour of the facility and the ballpark. It's an impressive setup. I can't wait to step out of the dugout onto the field on opening day and hear the fans cheer. I go to my spot in the infield and look out at all the seats. I have the best view of the ballpark, and I can imagine it full of fans cheering. I rejoin the staff member who was walking me around the club. We visit the locker room even though my name isn't on the locker. The number 17 locker is waiting for me to sign the deal officially. My guide takes me through the on-site history of the club, and it's fun to think that I could be an image in this area one day soon if I do well here. We end up back in the offices, and I meet with the coach's and a few of the owners. We discuss the plan for when I'll sign and the following press release.

Chapter 7: First Interviews

-*Annie*-

End of January

Meg helped me move in over the weekend, and we worked hard and unpacked my stuff. She'd even helped me hang the painting. It felt too special not to hang an original Jennifer Davis. Meg had looked at it after we'd gotten it straight and said, "It's always crazy to me that you two didn't make it." *Yeah*, I thought, still holding on to that question of if I'd done the right thing with Drew for the billionth time before she continued. "I get why you'd broken up with him, but in that moment, I thought, there is no reality that the two of you didn't go off and have little baseball-loving kids." She looked at me a little sadly before saying, "But then I thought I'd marry Tom, and we both know how that worked out. So, maybe I wasn't so great at calling long-term love, right?" She looked so sad when she finished her little speech, so not her usual confident self.

I wrapped her up in a hug and say, looking at the painting, "The painting reminds me that love is like baseball: time stops, yet everything around you moves fast, and before you know it, you're out or you've made it home." Then I asked her a question that her sadness had triggered. "Do you still miss him?" She'd pinched her brows before answering in only the way Meg could. "Tom, no. Being loved, yes." We both agreed that we needed to get out and break the mood. We'd walked to the taco place around the corner and had too many margaritas, laughing and chatting. On the way back to the apartment, I could have sworn I saw someone who looked just like Craig, but Meg said she didn't think so, and I let the thought go. It felt strange; it seemed like him.

***

Meg went home on the first flight out of Kansas City this morning, and I am off to my first day with the Kansas City network team. The club has given us room to conduct the interviews for a few free agents signing with the Griffons today. I will be doing some small interview questions, like, *Why KC? What are your hopes for the upcoming season?* and so on. When I get to the ballpark, I get to the office where I'm given my official VIP Press pass that will get me through security on days like today and on game days. I text it to my parents, who give me 'likes' on the photo. At some point, I will see if I can get Dad and Miles tickets to a home game, but that is a problem for when the season starts.

I recognize Emma Truman, my new producer. She looks like she did during my interview. She has a sleek shoulder-length brunette bob that is perfectly styled, and you'd miss that she was wearing makeup because she did it so well. She is dressed casually in her black jeans and sweater, but she still looks professional. She can't be more than 5'2", making her shorter than everyone in the room filled with the rest of the team. She still stands out as soon as we enter the room; her presence grabs attention. It almost makes me laugh to see these big camera crew guys turn when we enter the room, take notice of Emma, and jump to attention.

"Everyone, let's welcome our new sideline reporter from LA, Annie Campbell," she says to the room at large. I spend the first hour saying hello to all the lighting, sound, and camera crew. Eventually, Emma takes me to the back of the room to a table and chairs that she is using as her workspace. She has her stuff thrown across the table from her bag and phone to her tablet and notes for today. After I sit down, she starts, "Thanks for showing up camera-ready. We have four players lined up today and are coordinating more interviews for later in the week."

She looks up at me. I nod, before she continues. "Any questions on the players in your prep email?" I shake my head no. "I think I am good—we've got Alex Christopher, George Smith, Carlos Ramirez, and Justin Simmons, in that order, right?" I say, recalling the email I'd received yesterday and studied until my eyes crossed to remember all the information I needed for today. I was going to have to memorize the player line-up and be able to share facts and stats about them all. I would have a producer in my ear to help, but the more I came prepared for these conversations, the better. Emma gives me some tips and tricks that help get the guys to be more relaxed in the formal setting, and around 1 p.m., we start interviewing our first player.

The first guy is going to be a female fan favorite. Alex Christopher is an attractive man with brown hair, hazel eyes, a smile that hints at a sense of humor, and, as a bonus, he is a flirt. He flirts with me while getting his mic pack placed and tested. We do the interview, and he's got an easy charm, but he can also believably express his gratitude. He was a strong first baseman for his last team, and we talk about how he wants to take his experience all the way to the Series with the Griffons. I shake his hand after the interview, and he holds it too long and tells me he'd love to see me again. I don't fight the laugh that escapes me before informing him he'll be seeing me all season on the sidelines. With a smirk, he says he looks forward to our future conversations and let's go of my hand, following the team rep out of the room.

Emma joins me when the door closes behind them. "That one is a flirt. You watch out for guys like that. I've been there, done that in my twenties. Also, this is maybe a good time to tell you the network doesn't have a policy or rule against us dating the players, but I'll tell you from my experience it can get weird when you have to work with them after." I thank Emma for her advice, and I'm intrigued to learn more about her with that little nugget of information. I also have my own baggage with baseball players, but I don't tell her that. I just say, "I'm taking a break from men," and she laughs and says, "Aren't we all?"

My interviews with George Smith and Carlos Rivera go pretty well; they are both outfielders who will split the rotation with the vets. Both guys are much less flirty than Alex and more direct in their responses. Carlos is my favorite. He's from Puerto Rico, and he is just so excited to get to play baseball. I know I feed off his energy, leaving the interview with a bigger smile than when I started. I know that I'm going to enjoy getting to talk to him more throughout the season.

My workday is flying by with these interviews, and before I know it, we are on the last one for the day. Justin Simmons. He's the big name of the day; he's one of the new pitchers for the bullpen that the team has worked hard to get. He has a history as a great closer and an even better reputation as a family man. The interview feels more like a conversation, which is probably why I get lost in it and don't sense the tension in the room.

Chapter 8: Breaking News

-Drew-

End of January

I have two days until I go back to the facility to sign my contract. I've been working with the team to ensure I'm ready to answer questions about the move. I want to make sure that I don't misspeak or give someone a clip that can be taken out of context and make it seem like I don't appreciate my time at Arizona. My team drafted a statement, which is ready to post on my socials, thanking the Arizona club and fans, then a second statement to show how excited I am for my future here in Kansas City.

Out of nowhere, all our well-laid plans go out the window because Dominic gets a heads-up that Arizona will announce my departure today due to a leak at one of the major networks. Dominic asks me if I can get to the facility today, as the owners were signing with other free agents. We could head off the story so that it won't seem so unbelievable if I sign today. If Arizona announces first, that will be okay, because we'd follow up with the Kansas City deal signing, making it look like it was all organized to take place today. It will look like it was planned and not the fucking mess of a day it has turning into.

Craig is out, and I text him that I am signing today but that we should go out and celebrate tonight when I get back. He replies with a thumb-up. I rush to get in my suit and find a crimson tie as close to the team colors as possible. I arrive at the facility about forty minutes later, ready to sign a deal. Dominic has luckily been in town for the agreement to be signed in two days, so he's waiting for me at the front office.

"So, we will sign, and the team will post all your pre-approved statements. I've coordinated with the media team to get you in with the network reporter assigned to the team to get the exclusive first take on your move to Kansas City. We're lucky that she's finishing up with Simmons now, so that the timing will be almost perfect. Any questions?" He asks me, knowing he has covered all the bases in this situation. Being the smartass I am, I say, "Yeah, did you bring a pen?" He laughs and says he's sure he can find one, and we follow the secretary into the conference room. I sign my biggest deal, locking my future in Kansas City for the next ten years. I shake hands and do the press pictures in record time; if someone didn't know it, you'd think it was the plan all day long and not worked out less than an hour ago.

My phone goes wild as we walk to the interview room for the exclusive interview with the Griffons network reporter. "So, I'm working on the new girl's name, but she will be the sideline reporter exclusive to the Griffons. She just got hired, so she may be a little green. I'll stay in the room just in case she asks something that we don't want you to answer," Dominic says, looking at his phone as we walk. I hope that he doesn't jump in. If this girl is new, I want her to feel comfortable. I always think of Annie in these moments and want to treat the interviewer like I'd want someone to treat Annie.

I wonder if Annie has seen that I've joined her favorite team. This is just one of a million moments over the last six years that I wish we'd stayed friends. The only message I've gotten from her in six years was the night of my first start in Arizona, and it simply read, "Congratulations, Drew. I knew you'd make it: great debut." I should have replied, but I'd read it when I was tipsy, and all I wanted to send her was shit like "You should be here," or "I've got a new girl on my arm," or "I miss you, can we try now?" The first was the truth, and the second was partly true, as a new girl was with me at the time, but even I knew that if Annie appeared in front of me, I'd have left the new girl and done everything in my power to be with Annie. The third was true, but overkill. So, I'd never replied, only letting the message show it had been read.

We get to the media room, and the producer lets me and Dominic know it will be a minute because they hadn't expected me. She has given everyone a much-needed fifteen-minute break. It's not a problem. I sit down in the interview chair and pulled out my phone. I have so many messages, but I skipped to Craig's. Maybe he has figured out the plans for tonight.

Craig Mitchell

LOOK AT THIS MESSAGE NOW

I MEAN IT MAN ITS A 911 TYPE MESSAGE

I FUCKED UP, ANNIE IS THE REPORTER

SHE DIDN'T KNOW ABOUT YOU SIGNING

SHE IS CHEWING ME OUT RIGHT NOW FROM THE BATHROOM!

SHE HUNG UP ON ME

ANSWER YOUR FUCKING PHONE

Drew

Message received

Payback will be violent

Like by thinking about her, I've manifested her the girl of my past is about to be in front of me for the first time in six fucking years. The kicker, our first conversation will be in front of a room of people and in front of a camera. I take deep breaths, and as I do, I hear the door open and close. I know it's her without turning around; the room's energy changes. I'm going to turn, and I'm going to see my Annie for the first time since she walked away from me.

This day has taken a seriously crazy turn in only two hours. When our eyes connect, I can't look anywhere else; my eyes are glued to her. What's that saying about a man not knowing he's starving until you offer him food, and then he loses his mind? That is how it feels to look at her, like I've been starved, and now I feel like I'll never get enough of just looking at her.

Chapter 9: Exclusive Interview

-Annie-

End of January

I finish the interview with Justin Simmons and wait for the 'all clear' before we get up from the chairs. I thank Justin for his time and wish him luck on the upcoming season. After he leaves the interview space, the room breaks into chaos. Emma comes over to me in a panic. "We have a change of plans. It looks like the club has some breaking news, and the network wants you to get the exclusive with the new guy. He should be here any minute." I roll with it to prove they hired the right person. "Sure, what do you have for me on the new guy? Position on the field, last program, anything would help. I don't know all the players in the league, but I can ask some questions about why KC, etcetera," I tell her, trying to help in any way I can. She scrolls on her phone and says, "What do you know about Drew Davis out of Arizona?"

"Wait, what, why?" I ask in succession to quickly to be casual. Why would anything about Drew in Arizona be so important here in Kansas City? What is going on? She passes me her phone, and the trending sports story headline reads

"Arizona loses out on resigning star breakout rookie Drew Davis to the Kansas City Griffons on a $220 million, ten-year contract." *WHAT THE ACTUAL FUCK*, my brain screams, but my mouth says, "So, the guy headed to this room is Drew Davis?"

I hand Emma back her phone. "Yes, he should be here in ten minutes max. He is already in the building to sign his contract. Do you know anything about him? If not, I'm trying to get some intel right now, and I can feed you a few questions." Emma isn't looking at me as she is talking; she is searching for all things Drew on her phone. I can see his picture on her screen, "Oh, gosh, he's good looking," she says, quickly flashing me her phone before continuing to scroll.

"I know Drew, or rather I knew Drew—we went to the same high school," I say quickly. Emma looks up at me, and then a smile breaks out on her face, "Oh, this is going to be a great exclusive. The hometown boy is getting his first interview at this new club from the girl next door." If only Emma understood how truly spot on her statement just was. "Can I run to the bathroom and freshen up before the interview?" I ask and grab my bag. "Yeah, if he gets here before you're back, we will get him mic'd," she replies and heads toward some camera guys.

I truck it down the hall and to the bathroom. I look in the mirror, because I really need to freshen up my makeup, but that is not why I asked for a quick break. I pull out my phone and called the one person who would have known that Drew Davis was signing with Kansas City. He didn't tell me, and I'm so fucking pissed at him. I swear he is going to get an earful of what I have to say. Craig Mitchell's name appears on the screen as the phone starts ringing, and I switch the phone to speaker. "Annie, how are you? How's the apartment?" He answers like he doesn't have a care in the world.

"Craig Michael Mitchell, why the hell didn't you warn me?" I say, almost yelling, and I have to remember I'm in a bathroom only a hallway from the team. "Annie, why didn't I tell you what?" Craig sounds confused, but I hear his tone change before saying, "Well, shit. Annie, I couldn't tell anyone until he signed. I was going to tell you, I swear, as soon as I got the text he'd finished signing." He does sound remorseful, but I'm not letting him off the hook. "Craig, ask me what I'm doing today for the network. No, no let me tell you what I'm doing today for the network: I'm interviewing the guys who are signing as free agents. I'm getting their exclusive first interviews for the club," I finish and take a deep breath.

"Oh, shit, Annie, I didn't think you'd cross paths this quickly. I was going to ease us all into this, I swear I had a whole plan," Craig is sounding a little panicked now. "Does he know I'm here?" I ask Craig, because maybe he's given Drew the heads-up I didn't have. "Well, about that, I've also kept your new job quiet. Again, let me refer back to the previously mentioned plan," Craig is sounding increasingly worried. "I interview him in five minutes, Craig. Call him, message him, send a freakin' carrier pigeon, I don't care, but don't have me ambush him."

I can feel myself calming down as I finish the sentence and add quickly, "We will talk later, bye." I end the call, freshen my makeup, and take one more look in the mirror. I don't look half bad for being in interviews for the last few hours. I always thought I'd see him again on the field with crowds, an open sky over our heads and a baseball field under our feet. I never imagined an intimate interview in a conference room. I chant in my head to *breathe* before heading back in the direction of the interview room.

When I open the door, I know he's already here. It's like high school all over again, like my brain is hard-wired to his frequency. His back is to me in the chair where we are doing the interviews, and I see him reading his phone. His head jerks up and he looks at his agent in front of him. Then he slowly turns, our eyes connecting, and I'm frozen. God, he looks better than he did in high school. I mean, Drew has always been hot, but in high school, he still had that innocent guy next door thing. Grown-up Drew is more the stuff of dark romance fantasies. From his slightly overgrown brown hair, to the five o'clock shadow along his jaw, to his dark blue eyes locked on me. My brain does a happy dance seeing my fantasy man in front of me.

I finally register the look of shock on his face. This is probably what my face looked like when Emma said his name. What was that, less than fifteen minutes ago? Speaking of Emma, she appears out of thin air, breaking the staring contest between us. "Annie, are you ready? You look great. Let's get this done. The network wants to air the interview on the main sportscast tonight," she says quickly, then to emphasize her point, she checks her watch. She grabs my bag and heads back behind the cameras to her table of chaos. I take a deep breath, look back at Drew, and walk in his direction. *Here goes nothing*, I think, and I remind myself to breathe.

Drew stands up, and for a second, I'm not sure if I should offer him my hand to shake. It's what I've done all day. It doesn't feel right, so I go for the hug. Luckily, he does too and wraps his arm around my back. "Craig didn't tell me," I whisper against his ear as we share this hug that lasts longer than I'd expected. Before he releases me, he says, "At least I wasn't the only one." When he releases me, he smiles, and I learn that grown-up Drew's dimple is just as powerful at impacting my heart rate as high school Drew's had been. We both sit and let the camera and lighting people do another check. "My producer found out we know each other, and she is going to want me to start this interview like we are old friends." I say trying to give Drew a fair warning. "We are old friends, Annie. It's fine, you do great interviews. I'll follow your lead." His reply is kind and I vow to make this interview as easy as possible; for us both.

"Ready when you are, Annie," I hear in my earpiece. I nod and get the count in and kick off the interview. "I'm lucky enough to be here with the baseball player making major headlines across the baseball world tonight. His surprise signing will have major impacts on both the organization he leaves behind and the one he's joining. If you've been living under a rock today, I'm talking about the surprise signing of last year's division Rookie of the Year, standout shortstop Drew Davis, to the Kansas City Griffons." I turn from the camera to Drew and feel that dull ache. He looks relaxed with a casual smile, ready to start this interview. *Here we go*, I think, and remind myself again to breathe.

Annie:

"Drew, thanks for joining me for this interview."

Drew:

"It's a pleasure to be here, Annie. I have always enjoyed talking baseball with you."

Annie:

"Yeah, it's been a few years, but it's great to see you here in Kansas City."

Drew:

"Did I surprise you, Annie?"

Annie:

"Yeah, me and the entire baseball community."

Drew:

"I've always enjoyed surprising people."

Annie:

"Why Kansas City?

Drew:

"I like what the club is doing here: they came so close last season to winning the Series, and I want to see if I can be part of that magic and help the team make

another run.

It also doesn't hurt that it's a team I've been a true fan of since high school."

Annie:

"What's made you a fan for all these years?"

Drew:

"It may sound lame, but a girl I knew back then loved the Griffons. She'd convinced me then to follow the team. She was very adamant they'd win the Series and that I should join the fandom before I looked like a bandwagoner."

Annie:

"She sounds like a smart girl."

Drew:

"She is a very smart woman, I would agree."

Annie:

"Why leave Arizona?"

Drew:

"I enjoyed Arizona, but I feel like I could be a key player here with the Griffons. I see Kansas City as my future."

Annie:

"Do you have anything you want to share with your fans?"

Drew:

"I look forward to a great season—let's go Griffons."

The word "Cut" is shouted, and the red light is turned off on the camera. I lean forward in my seat. "Give them a few seconds: your interview surprised the whole team, I think they are making sure I got what they need to air tonight." He leans forward, too. "Can I talk to you off camera, when we are done here?" I lean forward a little more. "Yeah, sure, that won't be a problem." Emma interrupts our moment, walks over and gives me a few questions that we need to cover. I go over them with Drew and cover the next few questions on camera. I can't help but breathe in and out deeply when we get the final "Cut." I stand up and hug Drew, "Thanks for making that so easy." "Not a problem, Ang—Annie," I hear him correct himself, almost calling me Angel like his old nickname. It's weird how hard my heart is pounding.

Is it possible to have a heart attack being confronted by first love? I'm unsure, but I don't want to be the case study. The crew helps me and Drew, remove our mic's. "Do you all mind if I steal Annie for a second?" Drew addresses the room. "No problem, you were her last interview," Emma replies from behind the monitor. Drew takes my hand, and I swear butterflies spring to life in my stomach at the contact. He leads me out and across the hall into an empty room. I have no idea what is happening, but I like the feel of his hand in mine.

Chapter 10: My Best Friend Manipulated Me

-*Drew*-

End of January

The interview is a fucking blur: I know I say words and that she smiles her fake smile at me, but it feels like I have the sunshine on me after living in darkness. I must not say anything too crazy because Dominic never steps in to ask to have a question rephrased. I feel like I'm in the Twilight Zone; the only girl I've ever said 'I love you' to and haven't seen in person since she ripped out my heart is sitting in front of me, asking me questions about baseball, like it's normal to be here. In that first awkward hug, she warned me that Craig hadn't told her either. That fact from her made this feeling in my chest a little less tight. We were on the same playing field. We were both going to kill Craig. Looking at her reviewing the questions with her producer, I get my first honest look at her without her watc hing me.

She's still drop-dead gorgeous, in a professional dress, nothing overly revealing, but it still hugs her body. She has her long blonde hair curled in waves and, in my personal opinion, a touch too much makeup. I want to reach out and smudge it to see if she still has freckles across her nose. I need to talk to her after the interview. I need a moment alone with her. Her producer goes back behind the camera, and we resume the interview.

After the final 'cut,' Annie stands up and gives me a less awkward hug than the first, and I return the hug as she says, "Thanks for making that so easy." She releases me, and I reply, "Not a problem, Ang—Annie." I almost say Angel; it's so easy to think of her that way, with her standing right in front of me and feeling her in my arms. The sound guys remove my mic, I clear my throat, and ask the room, "Do you all mind if I steal Annie for a second?" Her producer says, "it's no problem" and Annie isn't protesting. I don't know why I do it but I reach out, taking Annie's hand. She's surprised by the move, but she doesn't pull away, instead grips my hand. I lead us out of the room and across the hall into an empty conference room.

The door closes behind us, and all I want to do is push Annie against it and see if her lips feel the same because her hand in mine feels completely right. Instead, I let go of her hand and move to the other side of the table. It feels wrong, but I need to put distance between us. "How long has Craig known you'd be working here?" I ask her. "I got the job right before Christmas," she answers without hesitating. I think back on my conversations with Craig, and I see it now, all these little moments when he'd suggested that KC was the place to end up. "I think our friend has been playing me," I say before continuing, "He told me it was time to leave Arizona, that KC was my future. He even had an apartment building already picked out when I agreed to the deal here."

I'm rambling until Annie breaks through my word dump. "What apartment building?" I look at her, but she doesn't let me answer. "Let me guess, the one-off Power & Light?" She looks as annoyed as I feel. "Yes, I got one of the penthouses," I answer, and she laughs but her words have a tension to them. "I am going to kill him, because Drew, I may not be in the penthouse, but I'm one of your neighbors." I can't help but laugh out loud because of course she is. What was Craig thinking? I know he's always enjoyed being a mastermind of my love life, or rather of ours— hers and mine. I am really curious how he saw this is going?

"I think we owe our friend a visit," I say to Annie. She nods her head in agreement, when she speaks this time she sounds more in control. "I have to go check in with the network team, but I can meet you back at the apartment building lobby in like thirty minutes." I offer her a smile, "See you in thirty minutes."

When we leave the room, Dominic is waiting for me, and he doesn't say anything until she disappears back into the room with the production team. "I could be wrong but isn't that reporter your ex-girlfriend?" He says as we walk towards the parking lot, "Yes, it is in fact her," I reply. "She's grown up," he says, and I cut him off. "Do not say the next thoughts in your head." He laughs but drops the topic moving on to business. On the drive back to the apartment, I want to call and give Craig a hard time, but I know it will be better to confront the little mastermind with Annie. I'm sure she'll have a better plan for Craig than anything I could think of.

***

Annie arrives like she has run from the parking lot. "Drew, I'm sorry they kept me back to make sure I liked our interview—it's going to go live in like forty-five minutes on The Baseball Show," she says, breathing heavily. "Did you run from your car?" I ask, because I have to know why she is so winded. "Yes, if you must know, I felt bad that I made you wait and I would have texted, but I figured you changed your number." She smiles but I know it's not a real one before she joins me on the sofa in the lobby. "I have the same number, feel free to text me, I promise I'll answer this time." I make eye contact with her to make sure she understands I mean it. I get why she thinks I changed my phone number; she's sent a few messages over the last six years. I've never responded. She changes the subject, "How much are we going to torture Craig?" she asks. "A lot," I reply, and she smiles and this one is real. "I have a ruthless plan, but it is probably going too far." She continues, "Do you know if he is in the apartment?" "Yeah, I know he's there because I texted him to be home thirty minutes ago so we could talk," I tell her.

"What if we fight, like yelling and screaming fight," she says. I can't help it, I respond without thinking "He would be shocked, we never fought." A sad expression passes over her face, but it fades quickly. "That's kinda the point, right? We are playing up that his plan backfired. But we don't have to, if you think it's too much." She sounds like she is trying to cover or plan something else, and I say before she can introduce a new idea, "Annie, I'm game to make him feel a little uncomfortable, but I'd like one dinner or lunch. I'd like to have a conversation before we have to talk in front of the whole baseball community again." She looks at me, her emotions playing out all over her gorgeous face before she answers, "Sure, a lunch or dinner, but don't hold back in front of Craig. I can take it." "Ok," is all I get out before Annie is up and moving towards the elevator.

Chapter 11: Is This Pretending?

-Annie-

End of January

The elevator ride is slow, and I'm trying to figure out how to start this fight with him. It's weird, because he was right: we never fought. I mean, we had disagreements, but they'd been mostly sports-related, and I guess you have to count our break up but it wasn't a fight really. I have to call on fights from my other relationships as inspiration for this little performance. Drew cuts into my thoughts, "I think I'm going to have to be the angriest to make him believe it. You did dump me, after all." "Drew," I start, and he holds up his hand. "Annie, we can get into the real stuff at that lunch or dinner. Let's just focus on making this awful for Craig." "Ok, you're right, you have to sell the anger or he will know we are faking it," I reply knowing he's right.

The elevator doors open, Drew gives me one more smile, and then it's game on. His face changes and he's left looking serious, "Annie, did you follow me here?" He steps off the elevator. I respond, "Don't think so highly of yourself, Drew. I told you I had no idea you were signing with the Griffons." He's quick with his next comment as he places his key in the lock, "Annie, isn't it your job to know what's going on in the baseball world?" I think *good one* because yes, actually, I should have known—my only saving grace is no one knew until the story broke. "Fuck you, Drew. I was just a little busy talking to other players, you know, the ones who made their decision to move to Kansas City public knowledge."

Drew swings the door open, so I can't see his face when he delivers the next jab. It throws me as I step into the apartment. "You left me, Angel. You left and didn't look back, and now, during the second most important moment of my career, you just appear. Do you think that I need you to hold my hand this time, because I don't, I don't need you." *Oh, shit,* that little jab felt very real. I have to catch my breath and remember we are playing it up for Craig. I slam the door, Drew turns, and I see the shadow of someone in the living space, but I focus on Drew, "Yeah, I left Drew, I had to. Don't think I hadn't heard your coach that day: I was distracting you, and I was only there TWO DAYS. I saw the writing on the wall, so you should be THANKING ME" I play up the thanking me with my tone, and he turns.

I step back into the closed door, and he steps into my space. I'm having a hard time remembering we are pretending, because Drew looks angry and devastated all at the same time before he says in a deep tone, "I'm not going to thank you, Angel, for breaking my heart, or 'setting me free,' but if you need some fucking thank you's, then I'll thank you for the opportunity to play the field—there were so many. Do you want me to name them so you can earn all your credit? I think it started with Ashley, then Sarah, I think next was—" I cut him off with my hand on his chest. I don't know why I touch him, but I do and he cuts off. I don't want to hear about the girls after me; my heart feels like it is going to beat out of my chest, and I can't help the tears that escape my eyes. When I find my voice, it sounds broken and sad, but I cut into his little speech, "Stop it, Drew. Just stop, you're being cruel. I know, I knew that there would be others, but you don't have to rub it in my face. Do I need to name my others to let you know I've moved on too?"

My tone changes back to something resembling my real voice, and I try to push him back, but he doesn't budge, which makes me a little angry. I make eye contact with him, his dark blue eyes are full of storms. I let myself feel whatever this is now and launch into my own little jab. "Fine, Drew, if you want a play-by-play, fine, well, there was." I panic, because there were really only two guys I've been with since Drew, and neither seems all that important while looking at him. Still, I started it, so I wing it. "Peter and Dax. And you know what, because I'm so lucky in love, they both chose their careers over me too, just like you did." I punctuate the words 'just like you did' by tapping them into his chest. Drew closes the space between us, pinning me hard against the door and it happens so fast my only reaction is to place both of my hands on his chest, "I didn't get a choice, Annie—you left me, you broke it, and you don't get to blame me, I didn't choose any of it."

Drew is breathing hard, I can feel it under my hands and against my body, and I forget that this is for show because it feels real now, so I say the next real thing. "Drew, you let me leave. You knew it wasn't possible to have both, so you let me be the fall guy. Does it help you sleep at night getting to tell yourself that I broke us, that it was all my fault?" I let the question hang in the air, and then say in a voice I don't recognize as my own, "You let me go, and you moved on. Don't think I didn't see the photos, Drew. Do you think I just left Arizona and moved on? Because I didn't, but you did, so don't act like it was so hard." When I finish, my voice has returned to that broken sound again. I've given voice to how it had felt to see some girl on his arm in some clip online, just a few weeks into freshman year and only two months after we'd broken up. Drew goes to speak "An—" but he's cut off by another voice. "Guys, please stop, I think that is enough."

Drew is still pinning my body between his and the door, and he looks at me before he takes a few steps back. He runs his hands through his longer hair, messing up his perfectly styled locks. "Guys, this is my fault. I should have warned you both—don't take it out on each other," Craig steps into the little area looking guilty. I don't get any satisfaction from seeing him looking upset. "Craig, why didn't you tell me?" I say, still standing against the door, and I realize that I have tears on my face. I wipe them away with the back of my hand. Craig looks distraught as he looks between us. "I should have. I see that now. I thought we might be able to talk over a meal or something before Drew signed, but he wasn't supposed to sign today. I thought I had more time to set something up." Craig pauses before continuing, "I am sorry I didn't tell either of you."

Drew cuts in, "We can talk about this later, I need to get some space." He leaves the room without looking at me. Craig makes to hug me, and I hold out my hand. "You know I love you, and you're one of my best friends, but hear me now, Craig Michael: do not keep these kinds of secrets from me again." Craig looks so disappointed as he responds, "I promise Annie, I've learned my lesson." Craig hugs me and I let him. "I'm worn out, I'm going home," I reply into his chest. "Can I walk you home?" Craig says against my hair. "Sure," I say, and move away from the door. I get an open view of the living room and can't help the small glimpse I see, including the painting of Drew and me. At least I'm not alone in still hanging the old artwork. I know why mine is on my wall, so I can't help but wonder what his reason is. I follow Craig to the elevator and wish I'd never thought of this stupid plan.

Chapter 12: Too Far

-*Drew*-

End of January

I leave Craig and Annie in the entryway and head to my room. My body is tense, and my mind is spinning. What had started as little jabs had turned into real ones. At some point, gone from pretending to really fighting. We both had some things to say to each other about the breakup. I know I was more heated and crueler in my delivery than I meant to be. I hadn't meant for any of what I'd said to come out of my mouth, but looking at her and hearing her say that I should "thank her" had turned off any rational thoughts. I'd unleashed all the pain and hurt from six years ago.

When I saw her cry, it felt like a kick to the gut, but then she got angry, calling out my cruelty. She'd gotten in her next heart-stabbing jab, telling me I was like everyone else, that I'd chosen my career over her. I couldn't help my body's all-out rage at the comment. I'd closed the tiny space between us needing her to only look at me. Needing in some way to convey I'd have given it all up for her. My mouth unleashed, my thoughts, true and cruel: they all felt raw to my system. Her reply had rocked me to my core. She'd started angry, but her voice changed by the end. She'd looked and sounded devastated.

There were so many thoughts in my head, but the one front and center one was that she hadn't moved on or lost hope of us getting back together that first few months. That is until she'd watched me do it first. I'd lost track of why we had been fighting or pretending to fight. I was about to respond to her confession when Craig had interrupted me. It took all my focus to step back from her, to lose the feel of her body against mine, and I'd hightailed it out of there.

I can hear them talking in the entryway now, and I know I'm listening harder trying to catch what she is saying. Eventually, I hear the sound of the door. I take another deep breath and pull out my phone. We really do need to talk, so I go to my message app, type in her name, and open the old conversation history.

Drew

Lunch or dinner?

I'm pretty open until the start of Spring Training, let me know.

And Annie, for what it's worth, I should have waited

I see the word at the bottom of my messages saying 'Sent' and then fall back into my bed. *What a fucking disaster*, I think. I shouldn't feel like my whole world just ended again. I don't know why I sent the last message, but I couldn't leave it alone—my brain spirals. I think about all the possibilities; If I'd waited and shown up at the first Friendsgiving, maybe we'd have figured it out, maybe she wouldn't be the one that got away, maybe she'd have been the one at my side today holding my hand in front of the photographers. But the biggest *maybe* running through my head is we could have had a future together. All the maybes spinning and swirling in my brain will not let me go. I see the future I wished for and all the ways I ruined it. She's not the only one to blame. Hearing the front door open and close is the only thing that breaks the cycle. I can hear his footsteps, then moments later, a knock on my door.

"Drew, man, can I come in?" Craig's muffled voice comes through the door. "Yeah," I say, hearing the door open. "Man, I'm sorry, I didn't see that coming." He looks toward the entryway, as if he still hears us fighting. "I don't think I've ever heard you two fight like that, like at each other," he says before tacking on, "I've heard you argue with plenty of other people, just never Annie." My heart does a weird beat at her name. I'm going to have to get used to hearing it. *I'm going to see her at every game all season long, get over it, heart*, I tell myself.

"Yeah, well, we had some unfinished business, it seems," I reply. "Maybe it wouldn't have come out like that if, you know, we'd both known that the other person was taking a job in the same fucking city," I tell him, trying to keep the anger from bubbling up again. "That is on me; I thought it was going to go over so much better. That maybe six years was enough time for the two of you to think about being friends again at least," he says defensively. "Why didn't you tell me she took the job before I signed?" I question. "I didn't want you to change your mind. Yes, Annie was interviewing in KC, but she was also still interviewing in Texas."

He takes a breath before continuing, "You settled on KC, I didn't want you to second-guess it because you found out Annie was going to be here, too. Plus, if I'm being honest, I thought it would be fun to live in the same city as my best friends." Craig gives a little shrug when he finishes. "You still should have told me. But I get it, she's your friend," I say, and before I get in anything else, Craig cuts me off, "You know she was your friend too before you started dating." Yes, she'd been my friend, but in all honesty, looking back, there had always been an undercurrent of wanting more with her. I had always been drawn to her, wanted her, even when I thought it would never happen. When we finally got together, I'd been so sure of my feelings, it hadn't taken any time to know that I loved her. Who knew those feelings would hurt so bad all these years later?

"Can we talk about something else?" I ask Craig. "Yeah, man, do you still want to go out?" He asks but I don't get the impression he wants to go out either. "I think I've had all the excitement I can handle for the day. Why don't we order in to celebrate the contract?" I suggest. Craig nods and volunteers to order and pay for dinner as he leaves my room. I change into my joggers and a T-shirt before entering the living room. Craig is watching the sports network, and they are going over the day's news, upcoming hockey games, basketball games, and teams to watch at the collegiate level. I head to the open kitchen to grab a drink.

I have barely shut the door to the fridge when her voice cuts into the room over the speakers. "I'm lucky enough to be here on site at the Griffons' facility with the baseball player..." I turn and stand behind the couch, watching us talk on camera. We have easy banter, and if I weren't the one on screen, it would look like we are both on the edge of flirting. The interview clip ends and cuts back to the guys in the studio to hear their thoughts. Craig looks over his shoulder at me, "That is more like what I thought it would be like." He turns to the TV to hear the commentators comment on my signing. My phone buzzes in my pocket, and I pull it out, hoping it will be a reply from Annie, but it's a message from Dom inic.

Dominic Stone

> Interview is playing well on socials

> KC fans are excited for you to take the field

Drew

> There is some positive news

Dominic Stone

> Also looks like your girl is getting positive   reviews

Drew

> She isn't mine anymore

Dominic Stone

Could have fooled me and all of social media

Drew

Funny Dom

Really funny

Dominic Stone

I'm funny

Congrats again on signing

Drew

Congrats on the payday to you too!

Chapter 13: Making a Plan

-*Annie*-

February

It's been weeks since the events at Drew's apartment. After Craig walked me home, I video-called Meg. I'd given her all the details, letting myself fully cry. Once I got myself together, I told her that Drew had sent me a text message, letting me know that he wanted to set up that lunch or dinner. In true Meg fashion, she told me she thought there was still a lot left to say. She's said something like 'Annie, don't regret not clearing the air, especially knowing you will work near each other all season.' I'd known she was right. I'd pictured all the times I was going to have to interview him and act like he wasn't the guy that had wreck my love life. I'd gotten off the phone with her and let myself have a glass of wine for surviving the day. I promised myself I'd message him back tomorrow, when I had a clear head.

Tomorrow had turned into over a week. I didn't mean to have it go this long, but I've gotten busy. I've had more interviews with guys joining the team over the week. I'd focused on each player, ensuring I gave them my time. Over the weekend, I explored my new city, getting various snacks and treats in the marketplace and riding the streetcar around the city on a big loop. I found so many places to visit on the loop, like the local library that looks like actual books.

I've even met Craig at one of the restaurants near the apartments. He'd apologized again and insisted on paying for my dinner to apologize. I let him know I forgave him, but no more masterminding. It wasn't his specialty, and I'd joked that he should stick to his day job. He'd offered me sessions at the local gym if I ever wanted to meet him for a workout, and I'd told him I'd think about it. We'd moved on to safer topics, and it was nice to have him in the same city again.

Then that tomorrow turned into two weeks. It wasn't on purpose, work was busy, I have been in a lot of working sessions getting ready for the season. I've spent my time jumping from corporate, to division, to local networking calls about Spring Training. Each group wanted a mix of things for coverage. I've been taking notes, and after each call, Emma would recap how we would handle the coverage.

On the local call, we are introduced to the sports reporter for Kansas City, Nick Jackson. He seems really nice, and when I bring up being new to the city, he offers to show me a few hidden gems around the city. I thank him, telling him I'll think about it. I even make a joke about waiting until it is warmer, since my year in LA broke my ability to adapt to the swings in temperature that the Midwest offers. He laughs and agrees that KC really shines in the spring weather. He puts his cell phone number in the chat box for the call, telling me to reach out anytime. I put the number in my phone and text him back so he could save my number. He replies quickly, 'Thanks.' I return to my main message screen. I see Drew's name a few messages down and remember I've never replied. I shouldn't put it off any longer. Spring Training is in a matter of weeks, and we should have this conversation before we both return to Arizona. I open the message and type.

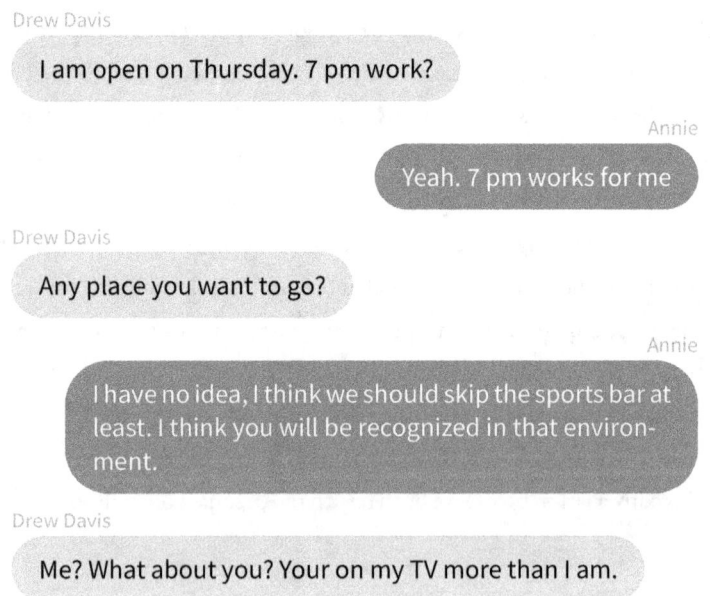

> I got caught up with work. I'm so sorry

> If you are open, I could do dinner on Thursday. Let me know what works for you

I go back to my prep work, studying the roster of the team. A large part of my job is getting to know these guys. What's their story? Single, married, kids? Has baseball been their life, or did they find it later? Did they go straight into the minors like Drew, or did they work their way through college to get here? Do they have a funny hobby or interest? It all helps to add to the story I'll be trying to tell on the sidelines, makes our conversations feel more natural. I'm about to change to the next player profile when my phone buzzes. I pick it up and can't fight the rush I get at seeing his name on the screen.

Drew Davis

> I am open on Thursday. 7 pm work?

Annie

> Yeah. 7 pm works for me

Drew Davis

> Any place you want to go?

Annie

> I have no idea, I think we should skip the sports bar at least. I think you will be recognized in that environment.

Drew Davis

> Me? What about you? Your on my TV more than I am.

> What about the taco place?

> Craig said it was pretty good and he wouldn't make me do extra reps for breaking our routine

> That almost makes me want to go somewhere else. LOL

> But really the taco place sounds good to me

Drew Davis

> Want to meet downstairs and walk over?

Annie

> Sure

I put my phone down, taking a deep breath before returning to work. After I finish the next player profile, I sit down with my dinner and call Meg. "What does a girl wear to a dinner with her ex-boyfriend?" I ask as soon as she appears on the screen. "Hello to you too Annie." Meg smiles before asking. "Depends on what you want. Do you want him to be overcome with lust, or do you want him to focus on your words?" I roll my eyes at her. "What if I'm confused about what I want? I do need him to listen to my words but I also secretly want him to think I'm distracting. This is so weird." I say, putting my hands over my face. Meg leans into the camera. "Uncover that face Annie, you are amazing. I think I'm going to have to see options to get this just right."

***

Thursday arrives before I know it. I'm dressed in Meg's suggested outfit of skintight jeans, a form fitting sweater and casual sneakers. It's a nice casual outfit; it doesn't scream sexual but does show my body to advantage. I'm both comfortable and confident. I'm sure this dinner will have some uncomfortable moments, at least my outfit feels like a sort of armor. I grab my coat, heading to the elevator five minutes before our planned 7 p.m. time. I look down at my phone, typing a message to Meg for a last boost of support.

When the doors open, I don't look up right away, a throat clears, making me look up. "Sorry," I begin, but my eyes connect with Drew's, which startles me. I thought I had five more minutes to prepare to see him. The surprise at seeing him send stupid butterflies fluttering inside of me. "You getting in, Annie?" He laughs, and I realize I'm standing just outside the open elevator, staring at him. "Yeah, you surprised me, that's all," I say as I join him in the elevator. My phone buzzes, and I look at the new message from Meg.

Meg Patterson

Good luck tonight

You're fucking hot! Remember to tell me how he reacts to the outfit.

And you're a reporting badass, it's ok to remind Drew if he forgets any of that! I love you!

"You can tell her I didn't forget," he replies in a deep voice. Hell, if it doesn't startle me again. *Damn it, get ahold of yourself*, I think. "Did you read my message?" I ask because he obviously did. I look at him and catch the humor cross his face. "I mean you are holding your phone all the way out here, Annie," he says, doing a dramatic example of holding his phone out in front of him, very much in front of me so I can read a message on his screen. "I wasn't that bad," I laugh despite my nerves. "But I'll tell her." I make sure to move my phone closer to my body when I type my reply, which causes Drew to laugh.

I put my phone in my bag as we leave the elevator. We make some small talk on the short walk to the restaurant. Drew gives his name to the hostess, asking if we can have a booth in the back or the most secluded area of the restaurant. The girl says, "Sure," smiling at Drew and giving me all kinds of side eyes before walking us to our table. No one is immune when it comes to this man. At the table I take off my coat and hang it up on the hook at the end of the booth. When I turn around, Drew snaps his head up from what I assume was him checking out my as s. *Thank you, Meg for the suggestion of these jeans,* I think before scooting into my side of the booth. She hands me my menu but lingers next to Drew, telling him about the specials for the night.

I get the appeal; his brown hair is flopped over to the side, and he's got that sexy five o'clock shadow that men get. He is giving her his attention, and I know what it feels like to be on her side of the attention. I get to look at him, and I do my own checking out. He's in a long sleeve shirt that hugs his shoulders. He's gotten more muscle since he was nineteen. I can see the difference as well as I felt the difference that night he pushed us into the door. I can't help trying to remember the feel of him against me.

I must have been daydreaming because Drew clears his throat from across the table. I look up, saying, "Sorry, I got distracted. What did you say?" He smiles and damn it, the five o'clock doesn't hide his dimple. I focus on what he's saying, "I was asking if you thought that shared platter sounded good. Seems like a good sample of tacos," he says totally unaware of the turmoil in my mind looking at him. I look over the options and agree that it works. I get water because I don't need alcohol mixed with this conversation, or with how I'm already feeling distracted looking at him.

"So, about that fight," I start right as he says, "I'm sorry." We both laugh. He nods, and I go again, "That fight went too far, and I'm sorry for my part in it." He nods and repeats, "I'm sorry too. I got caught up and took it to another place with my reference to other people, Annie. For what it is worth, and I know that it probably isn't worth very much, I hated hurting you. I hadn't meant to make you cry," he says, running his hand through his hair. "How do we do this, Drew?" I say, shaking my hand between us, "How do we exist in the same place, in our jobs that will cross paths a lot, I'm sure? You already seem like a fan favorite, and you haven't even hit the field yet in Griffon Crimson."

"I think we talk like this, we find a way to be around each other." He shrugs, "Maybe we can even try to be friends again," he says, and I feel how genuine he is about the possibility that we could get back to friends with some time. I can't fight the little voice in my head saying, *I don't normally get turned on by my friends.* "I like that idea. You've always been my favorite person to talk about sports with." I offer the confession as a peace offering. It's safer than my internal thoughts. He takes my olive branch and offers me one in return, saying, "I missed our conversations, too. I watched the interview. I could see our old banter come back a little, and it was nice to see that we didn't lose that part of us."

I take a deep breath and launch into the elephant in the room, "The other night, we both said things, and I think we should try to answer a few of the top questions that we need answered. So maybe we can move past, well, the past." I look at him. He isn't giving me a lot to go on; his expression is so stone-faced, but his jaw feathers. I almost try to take back my words, and then he says quietly, "Why was loving me not enough?" *Well, don't take it easy on me,* I think before I answer.

Chapter 14: Dinner Plans

-Drew-

February

It takes Annie over two weeks to reply to me. I honestly thought she wasn't going to and the first time I'd see her again would be Spring Training. Then, out of the blue, two days ago she texted me asking if I could do dinner tonight, and I agreed. We need to talk, and I need to apologize to her for how I acted the other night. I was surprised about the built-up anger I'd shown in our pretend fight. I guess I never got it out of my system in all these years. I've burned out the anger in my system now, so maybe we can talk like adults.

After the gym, Craig and I come back to the apartment. "What are you thinking for dinner?" Craig asks and I swear this has become our nightly roommate conversation topic. "I can't do dinner tonight; I'm going out with Annie." I try to sound like it's no big deal, but Craig has been my friend for too long. He gives me a smirk. It's almost like he thinks we are going on a date. My brain goes into triage mode. I quickly corrected his assumption, "It's not a date. It's a meal to try to talk and not do what we did the other night." He'd put up his hands before saying, "Never said it was a date. I'm just happy that you guys are trying to talk." I leave him in the living room so I can shower and head to my not-date w ith Annie.

I wear jeans and a long-sleeved shirt, trying not to overthink my choices. I did spend way to much time picking this basic outfit. I mean, she's seen me naked and dressed up for prom. I'm not going to be surprising her with my outfit choice. I decide it would be better to be casual; this isn't a date. It is just two people meeting for dinner to talk. At six minutes before seven, I head to the elevator. I am thinking about what I want from this dinner with Annie. Thoughts like: find closure, understand how to work together, and maybe stop dreaming about her pass through my thoughts. I'm not sure that last one is even possible. Six years didn't make it stop and I imagine her being around will only make them more frequent.

The elevator opens on the tenth floor, and she is looking at her phone. I take her in and she's beautiful. She's not wearing much makeup, and I can see that she does, in fact, have those freckles on her nose. This is the Annie I needed to see. The woman that connects me to the one I met and loved. I hit the hold button, clearing my throat to get her attention. She looks up, apologizing before she realizes it's me. I know the moment she connects those dark blue eyes with mine because it feels like a shock to my system. I hold the button, looking at her before I check my brain, "You getting in, Annie?" She comes to stand beside me, and I release the button. Her phone buzzes, and she holds it out. I don't mean to, but I see Meg's name and the message on her phone.

I clear my throat. I shouldn't comment, but before I can help myself, I comment, "You can tell her I didn't forget." Annie looks shocked that I could read her message. I give a dramatized reenactment, holding my phone in front of her face. My actions make her laugh, breaking the tension between us. When she goes back to her phone, she holds it a little closer and at an angle, and I can't help but l augh.

The walk isn't so bad: again, another benefit of living downtown. We talk about easy topics like the weather or the shops around us. We get seated at a table in the back. I want us to have a little privacy having this conversation, just in case we get overly animated with this round of talking. I think she catches me checking her out, but I play it off and listen to the waitress. I couldn't help myself, she'd taken off her jacket, and the jeans and sweater hug her body to perfection. I do think that I get a little redemption when she's staring at me after the waitress leaves. It reminds me of how she looked at me in the past. Shit if it doesn't make me feel good that she's at least a little impacted by me too. She agrees to split a taco platter that the hostess pointed out. After we give our orders, Annie starts the conversation, and we both jump in to apologize for the fight.

The conversation changes when she asks me, "How do we do this, Drew?" I tell her my truth, that we can talk and that maybe we can be friends again. She doesn't flinch or tell me *hell no*, and I take it as a good sign when she tells me that I'm her favorite person to talk sports with. I push down my additional thoughts that I used to be her favorite person, period. I have to remind myself that it was a long time ago. I tell her that I miss us too. Like a professional, Annie directs our conversation into that red area we've been nearing but haven't crossed. "The other night, we both said things, and I think we should try to answer a few of the top ones we need answered." Well, here we go. It's time to pull out those hard-hitting questions. Can I plead the fifth if I don't want to answer? Can she?

What have I always wanted to know? What is the thing that has bothered me the most over the years? I think back to the day she walked away. I'd sat in my room, devastated for hours. I'd sat there wondering how love wasn't enough. How could it not be enough? So, I ask, "Why was loving me not enough?" She looks sad when she answers, "Drew, loving you... loving you was not the problem, and it was enough. But at the time, I'd been so worried about compromising your dream of going pro. I didn't want the love we had for each other to turn to hate. I was just so sure, you loving me would compromise your chance, and you'd end up hating me for costing you your dream of the big league. I felt like it was better to break our hearts then versus the alternative of watching us break, for that love to turn into something ugly."

She takes a deep breath and then takes a sip of her water. I sit in her answer. It does help to understand a little about her why. I still don't think she would have compromised me getting to the big leagues. I can't fault her for her feelings and her reasons. She's right in the fact our relationship only brings me good memories, minus the moment she broke my heart. She sets down the water a little too hard and the water sloshes over the edge. "Can I ask one now?" I look at her and see the hint of anger and hurt reflected at me. "Yeah, of course," I reply bracing for the question. "How easy was it to move on?" She asks, taking a long drink of water after, she's gotten the question out. "Not as easy as it was to fake it." I think back on that time, and I think I know what she's talking about. "If you are referencing those pictures from the club in Arizona, I'd gone out with the guys at the end of the season to celebrate our rookie year, and those girls had been hanging around all night. When someone asked for a picture, I'd agreed, and the girl sat on my lap. I'd gone with it."

I take a drink of my own water before continuing. "When the pictures made the internet, Craig asked me what the hell I was doing. I told him I was moving on. After all I was single, so I'd played it up because I didn't want it to get back to you that I was still moping around. In reality, Annie I can't say I ever moved on. I've only had superficial relationships after us. I went out and got photographed but I've never wanted a woman to be part of my life like I did with you." I want to elaborate and tell her she's still the only woman I've loved, but I think I've said enough to get her to understand it wasn't easy. I watch her reaction, and I see some of the tension leave her body and it makes me relax too.

We get interrupted by the food delivery and we eat in comfortable silence, only commenting on which tacos we like more. Once the tacos disappear, Annie asks me another real question. "Why haven't you come home during the holidays, like Friendsgiving or Christmas?" This question is much easier to answer. "The easy answer is I was avoiding you. That first holiday season, I'd been trying to think of ways to get you back. To convince you that we could make it work, and

I realized that is all I was ever going to do if I came home. I'd look next door, and I wouldn't be able to stop myself from walking across the yard and begging you to change your mind, and that felt pathetic.

So, I'd asked my parents to go on vacation instead with the excuse that Mom hates cooking and I needed a break from baseball and training. I made sure to come back to Oklahoma when I knew you were at school." "I'm sorry," she says, sounding so remorseful before continuing, "They are your friends, too, and I made that harder." "Annie, they are still my friends. I mean, Craig is my roommate and trainer, you didn't ruin my friendships." Then I ask my question, "Do you still have my mom's painting?" She smiles and I feel it in my chest. "Yeah, it's in my living room in my apartment." It feels good to know that she's kept it, and it isn't shoved into some box of things from her high school b oyfriend.

We spent the next hour talking, each round of questions getting easier. As we walk back to the apartments, I ask her a question that I've wanted to talk about with her all night. "Annie, who do you think is going to win the Series this year?" She smiles and she looks like the Annie I dream about, my Angel. I shake my head and focus on her answer, "You know, I hear the Griffons just got this hotshot shortstop, and you know they are my favorite team. So yeah, I'm betting on them to take it in four." We reach the tenth floor, and she leaves the elevator, waving goodbye. When the doors close, I see my smile reflected at me, and I thin k, *when was the last time I had this fun on a not-date.*

Chapter 15: He's Funny

-Annie-

March

I've been in sunny Arizona since the end of February, covering all things Griffon baseball. I've gotten to meet the guys on the team in small chunks over the last few weeks, from the new guys to the vets. I've been watching a few of the vets for years as a fan. It feels pretty cool to talk to them both in front of the camera and off camera. An additional benefit of being on location is getting to know Emma. We've gone out a lot on this little trip, and our favorite spot has the best margaritas. We may have consumed a few too many on more than one occasion, but it has been worth it because we both opened up about our pasts with baseball players. I confess all the sordid details of my relationship with Drew. She thinks that nineteen-year-old Annie made the right decision, but also tells me that grown-up Drew is fucking hot. She makes little quotation marks with her hands when saying, "fucking hot." "He and I are just going to be friends," I tell her. Emma had winked at me, saying, "Friends with benefits can be a fun arrangement"

Emma talks like she's just so much older than me, but I've discovered she is only thirty-one. She fills me in on a relationship gone bad with Camden Wilder a few years ago. He's a hotshot pitcher who plays out of New York. As I've seen over the years, the poster boy of asshole baseball players. His face has been on several tabloids the last two years as he's been dating an actress, and he may or may not have been cheating on her the whole time, if you believe what you read in tabloids. Emma tells me that she'd met him on her first big break for the network, she'd been in charge of home game production. Their paths had crossed and he'd flirted with her and had shown interest in her work. They spent months dating and hooking up, he'd even asked her to go to events with him. She thought she was in love with him and was even considering following him to his next team. He told her he was going to be traded, and he wanted her to go with him. Her world came crashing down when she'd surprised him after an away game. She had found him making out with a girl in the lobby of the team's hotel. He tried to make excuses, but she had discovered that he was never really in love with her. Heartbroken, she'd broken it off with him and decided that her career was more important than any man could be. Emma tries to sound tough through her confession, but I see the hurt in her eyes. I understand that pain and it makes me like her even more.

***

The next time I see Drew, I can't get Emma's little quotation-marked statements out of my head. He is fucking hot, I notice, confessing only to myself and the butterflies in my stomach. I have to focus on something other than the fact that he still affects me. I focus on the fact that it's nice to have a friend here with me until my traitorous brain thinks about what it would be like to have benefits with Drew.

The fans are all abuzz about him, and the male and female fans love him for different reasons. I've gotten a few interviews with him over the Spring Training season. The network team has commented that we have great repour. They tell me that every time the social media team posts one of our videos, it gets major attention. I know I shouldn't, but I look at the comments on the videos. A lot of people are enjoying Drew's sexy guy-next-door thing, and I can't miss the comments about me along the same line. There are more than a few comments that suggest we need to hook up already because we have 'major chemistry.' It makes me laugh, because those people have no idea that we have, in fact, hooked up many, many times. I have to stop myself from thinking about those times a lot more now with him around all the time. I also get the news that I am getting great feedback from the market research team. I'm well-received by the male demographic, and the female demographic likes that I'm not only relying on my good looks and that I know baseball.

***

Today, I will sit in on the KC local coverage to talk all things Griffons baseball. I'm excited to join the conversation, which feels like a sports show versus my interview coverage. I get to talk about what I think about the team and how I feel Spring Training is going. Over the week, while prepping for the show, I texted and video chatted with Nick a lot. He's been great about sharing the live show format with me, giving me little anecdotes about his peer, Martin. I've searched online and found clips of them last season. They make me laugh: Martin is this gruff older gentleman who thinks he is top billing and the authority in all thing's baseball, and Nick is the down-to-earth nice guy who never takes his co-anchor too seriously. It makes for some back-and-forth conversations with the ir guests.

They also have a 'get to know you' rapid-fire questions segment that they do with anyone they bring on as a guest. It's funny how on-the-spot questions can throw off the visitors. I told Nick that this was probably the only part of being on their show that made me nervous. He said he'd give me the inside scoop and sent me a list of over a hundred questions that could be a part of the segment. He added that if any of the questions were a problem, I could let him know. I looked over the questions, and they all seemed pretty straightforward. Questions like *what's your favorite animal*, or *if you could talk with a past athlete, who would it be*, even some as easy as *who is your favorite team or favorite player*. Nick told me they do a random five to ten questions, depending on when the episode airs, which makes sense to me, as some segments go longer if you're in a good conversation.

Yesterday, on our regular check-in call, I told Meg about the upcoming segment and how Nick had been so helpful. She'd looked him up online before I could ask her about her job search. In only the way Meg could, she'd told me he would make for really good boy toy material with his tan skin, black hair, and green eyes. I reminded her I wasn't looking for one, and she'd let me know that I'm a lucky girl because he found me anyway. It was my sign to have some fun off the baseball field and maybe hit some bases behind closed doors.

***

I arrive up at the show's location in my Griffons jersey and jeans. I've done my hair and makeup before showing up. The show had offered me hair and makeup, but I didn't mind showing up camera-ready. It is easier knowing how I look, and it helps me feel better on camera anyway, so it isn't a big deal. I have a backup top just in case the jersey is too casual. From my research, I see that Martin and Nick have a pretty laid-back approach to their appearances. I've noticed that Nick has sported a Griffons ball cap and T-shirt on more than one occasion. So, I think I'll be fine, but it never hurts to be prepared. I'm talking to one of the producers about the general flow when Nick shows up in the ball cap and T-shirt and gives me a once-over before saying, "I like the vintage Griffons jersey, Campbell." "I aim to please, Jackson, plus I needed to fit in," I reply and reach and tap the brim of his ball cap, which earns me a laugh from Nick. Martin joins our little group, and we go over the details again with the producer.

We get mic'd up, and I'm led to the guest chair next to Nick, and he gives me a reassuring smile as the show is counted in. Martin does the standard show lead-in and summary of what is on the lineup for today's show. Nick starts my introduction, "We are lucky enough to have, joining us today, Annie Campbell, sideline exclusive reporter for the Griffons. For all of you not paying attention, Annie has been climbing the ranks in the sports broadcasting world with her interview questions on the sidelines in LA last season and her quick thinking in capturing the moment with Colt Strong after the walk-off to win the college championship a few years ago. Welcome to the show, Annie."

It's a nice introduction, and I smile and respond, "Thank you for the intro-duction, Nick. It's weird to be on this side—I'm used to setting up the guest." My comment gets both Nick and Martin to laugh. Then we get into all things Griffons baseball, from the returning players I'm most excited to see back, to the expanded power of the bullpen, to the new guys joining the team. I don't avoid talking about Drew, but I don't get into his stats like I could. We get into a lively debate about how Carlos Ramirez and his potential to cover ground in the outfield will be important this season. Martin wraps up the segment, and Nick turns to me before saying, "As it is tradition, are you ready, Annie, to play Rapid Fire?" I give an over-exaggerated expression of nerves and answer, "I'm as ready as I can get, let's go." I know that Martin and Nick will go back and forth, asking me around ten questions.

Martin:

"Favorite season?"

Me:

"Does baseball season count?"

Nick:

"Guilty pleasure?"

Me:

"Still wearing my dad's vintage cap from the last Griffon Series win: it has holes, and I've been told from more than one person it has to go, but I refuse to give it up."

Martin:

"Early bird or night owl?"

Me:

"Night owl, I am not a morning person."

Nick:

"What superpower would you have?"

Me:

"Mmmm, the ability to read minds."

Martin:

"Favorite baseball position?"

Me:

"Shortstop."

Nick:

"First love?"

Me:

"Drew Davis."

I cover my mouth after saying Drew's name, and I can feel my skin go red. Nick saves me by saying, "You and all of the female fans of the Griffons." I laugh, and before I can add anything, Martin cuts in and with his gruff expression, asking the next question.

Martin:

"Text or call?"

Me:

"Text for scheduling, calls for family and friends to catch up."

Nick:

"Favorite sports memory?"

Me:

"Mmm... that's hard. Either going on ballpark trips with my dad and brother or watching my friends win the state championship back in high school."

Martin:

"Favorite food?"

Me:

"Tacos."

Nick:

"Ice cream or cake?"

Me:

"Cake."

They both thank me and then make the closing statements for the show. "Cut" is yelled from behind the cameras, and Nick turns to me. "Annie, that was great. Thanks again for coming." "Thank you for having me. I had a lot of fun, even considering that mistake in the middle of rapid fire," I say. I almost want to ask him if we can cut the question from the segment where I answered Drew's name, but I know that his response and my reaction are kind of the point of the segment. Asking him to cut it would be rude and unprofessional.

"So, you like cake and tacos, I'll keep those in mind for that tour," Nick cuts into my thoughts. "Please do, I always need more places in KC for good food. I can always add to my restaurant and bakery list." We laugh and talk as we get our mics removed. I'm about to leave when he leans in and hugs me goodbye. I get a flutter of butterflies before we separate. "Thanks again, Annie. Text me when you're back in KC, and we can meet for that tour of the city." "Sounds great, can't wait to see the segment when it's ready," I say and start to walk back to my car. Nick raises his voice to reach me as I walk away. "I'll send it to you as soon as we have a copy ready for air."

Chapter 16: Back in Arizona
-Drew-

March

It's weird to be in Arizona but not staying in my apartment. The hotel is nice, so I have nothing to complain about; it's just different. We started team workouts, and there are already some guys I can see myself being friends with... even if I'm not entirely comfortable with how much they flirt with Annie during their interviews. An image of Alex Christopher comes to mind. That guy flirts with her excessively. It pissed me off until I watched him for a few games and found out that he flirts with everybody who is female. He flirts with the owner's wife, the athletic trainers, and the middle-aged fans; it doesn't matter to Alex. I still didn't like him flirting with Annie, but the fact that it isn't wholly unique makes me feel better. I find myself enjoying our in-game chats in the dugouts. He may be a flirt, but he's a hell of a ball player at first base. We have already shown our ability to make the double play, and it's only Spring Training.

I've had some moments with Annie on the sidelines and maybe flirted with her too. If Alex could, I figured it was fair game to enjoy her company. I always made sure to be respectful of her serious questions. I just happen to tell her she looks beautiful in Griffon colors in the first interview, and then in the second one, she'd had a bug land in her hair. I noticed, so I reach over and run my fingers through her hair to help remove it. I may or may not have let my fingers linger in her hair after the bug disappeared.

It felt normal to touch her and fix it; she'd thanked me, but couldn't hide, either time, the blush that broke out on her cheeks. She only seems to blush with me, and I enjoy that I still get her to blush. Dominic and the team are loving the banter and interactions. They tell me the fans are eating it up. Dominic told me a national news station used the clip in their 'good-looking guys doing nice things' segment. I laughed because I didn't even know that was a thing. How many years has it been since I laughed and smiled this much? Six years. I know the day that I started smiling less: July 18th: the day that my world turned dark. I brush the thought away, returning to the present and how good things are going.

***

I'm enjoying my rest day with my parents at their hotel pool. They'd flown into town this morning. They don't want to be at the same hotel as the team, but don't want to be at the same one as all the visiting baseball fans. So, they decided to stay at a hotel farther from the training facility. I'm lucky that they want to support me and come into town to see a few games. It helps that my mom loves to go to Arizona. That was her only regret about my move to the Griffons. I consoled her by telling her the Griffons have Spring Training in Arizona. Hence, she is present here now, enjoying the Arizona heat. We haven't done anything all that special, but it's been nice to see them. I let them know that I got them and Daniel some great seats for opening day. I wanted to treat them to a suite, but they were already booked this year.

It will be my first official opening day in the majors, and they'd all wanted to come. We are hanging out by the pool, catching up, when my phone starts

81

buzzing and buzzing and buzzing. I should have left it in my parents' hotel room, but Dominic is working on a contract for an endorsement deal. I didn't want to hold up his efforts if he'd gotten an offer today. When I look at my phone, I have messages from Dominic Stone, Craig Mitchell, and Annie Campbell. I should open Dominic's first, he's the reason I have my phone on me, but I don't. Annie and I have been doing well on camera, but she hasn't texted me since our dinner, and I'm curious what has spurred a text now.

Annie Campbell

I had an interview a few days ago

FYI your name came up, so I just figured I'd give you a heads up it's airing today

Drew

Thanks, details?

Annie Campbell

...

Nope, I've done what I came here to do

Drew

And what was that Annie?

Annie Campbell

Tell you it's not bad for you, just forget I texted

Enjoy the rest of your day.

Drew

Now I have to find this interview

Annie doesn't type anything else after a few minutes of waiting I move over to the message from Dominic.

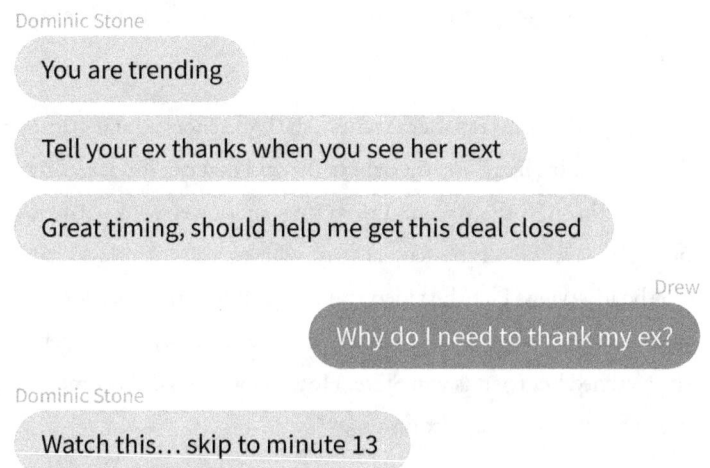

Dominic sent me a link that directs me to one of the local news stations in Kansas City. The cover image is of a smiling Annie joined by two other guys. I'll go back to watch the beginning; for now, I will take Dominic's advice. I skip to minute thirteen in the video to see why I need to 'thank' Annie. The younger guy looks over at Annie. He's all smiles, and he says, "As it is tradition, are you ready, Annie, to play Rapid Fire?" Annie looks nervous and I sit-up straighter watching her. "I'm as ready as I can get, let's go." The guys start trading off questions, and I see why they call the segment 'rapid fire.'

Nothing too crazy is being asked. Annie is giving great, quick responses. I laugh when she brings up her hat, because it had holes six years ago. I can only imagine what it looks like now. I log her answers and see if they've changed since the girl I knew at nineteen. I'm doing pretty well, and it makes me feel good to think she's still Annie. Then I get to the part Dominic is so excited for, as she says her favorite baseball position is shortstop. *Well, that was uneventful,* I think. I'm unsure why it's trending but before my thought finishes, I hear the following question and answer. What did she just say? I have to pause my phone and scroll back. *I must have heard it wrong,* I think, before hitting play again and hearing the younger guy ask, "First love?" and Annie's rapid-fire answer of "Drew Davis."

I don't pause the video. I watch her reaction: she looks shocked at her answer and covers her mouth. It's like she can't believe she said that out loud, and the blush is visible even through the screen. The younger reporter winks at her, giving some quip about so do all the female fans, which causes Annie to laugh and return to the interview. I let the video run to the end of the question segment. I am smiling already when she says that one of her favorite sports memories is when she watched her friends win State. How many times did I come up in the interview? I play it back again, counting.

Mom interrupts my thoughts as she walks over from the pool. "That sounded like Annie on your phone. I didn't realize you all were talking again. She always did make you smile like that," my mom says, pointing at my face. "Well, it's a video of Annie doing an interview," I tell Mom. She looks disappointed, so I add, "But she's covering the Griffons this year, so we've been talking and texting some." Mom smiles at me before saying, "I always enjoyed how she'd fumble around trying to call me Jennifer but always defaulted back to Mrs. Davis. It always made me laugh." "Yeah, Annie likes to be polite," I say. I sit and chat briefly before I say I need to make a call. I head back to my parents' room to watch the whole interview. Watching the interview, I notice how much attention the younger reporter gives Annie. I don't like it, and I especially don't like it when they are talking about me. I have to take a deep breath and remind myself that she isn't mine. She hasn't been for six years, and these feelings of jealousy are ridiculous. I open up my phone and text Dominic back.

I'm not sure why this is going viral?

She just made you lovable, plus that video has already gotten 250K+ views, it's only been up for like 30 minutes

Ok well cool, go market my lovability

I jump over to Craig's message, and he is asking about my name trending. I should give him hell that he knows I'm 'trending.'

Do you know why your name is trending?

Oh, never mind, figured it out

I heard I'm lovable

Yeah, people are doing all this research on you and Annie in the comments. I've started to see pictures from our yearbook. I thought it was clear you all know each other from the first interview.

Well I hope it's the good ones

Yeah I thought we already covered this

Let me see, I've seen the homecoming photos, Prom photos

I'm ruined, those are so going to kill my image

Oh shit someone just posted the photo of us shirtless at the soccer game

I gotta tell Luke someone beat him to the wild stories he was holding as blackmail

He will hate that he didn't get to do it

This thread is wild… Someone just posted your Draft day video

Damn, people are nosy

How are you going to deal with this?

I don't know I guess talk to Annie

I leave the messages with Craig and go to the message with Annie. She either doesn't know that we are trending or is avoiding me.

So I'm guessing your warning about that interview was before it because the #1 sports trending topic

Annie Campbell

I stopped looking, Emma is determining how to play this at tomorrow's game

Drew

I say you interview me after I get another home run

Annie Campbell

I'll let her know your plan to have a home run then maybe we can interview you

Drew

Write my name in ink for that interview

Annie Campbell

Right on that

Drew

Are you ok?

Annie Campbell

Yeah, I've never been ashamed of dating you

Just wish I'd said unicorns or dolls

Drew

Good to know that unicorns and dolls came before me and also that you aren't embarrassed by me

Annie Campbell

Yeah, I'd trashed them to hide the evidence before the hot guys moved in next door

You ok?

Drew

Yeah, Dom says you made me lovable

so I'll owe you when I sign my next endorsement deal

Annie Campbell

I'll take a pizza

Drew

I thought tacos are your favorite now?

Annie Campbell

I was stuck on one topic, I still love pizza

Drew

Pizza it is

What does 'stuck on one topic' mean? I have no idea at first, until I think back on her interview. I'd come up a lot in that conversation, and we'd had tacos at dinner. I shouldn't, but I feel excited to be taking so much of Annie's attention, if the interview is a guide on the subject. Annie doesn't reply again, so I move to the new name in the text messaging mix.

Luke Harrison

I got scooped

This is hilarious, did people really not know about you and Annie?

Drew

Yeah, looks like it is surprising a lot of fans

Luke Harrison

I mean you do flirt with her a lot in all the interviews

Drew

No more than Alex

Luke Harrison

Yeah, but she doesn't flirt back with him

Drew

Interesting

Luke Harrison

Like you haven't noticed, come on man

Drew

I plead the fifth

Luke Harrison

Ha ha using legal jargon on me

Drew

whatever works

Luke Harrison

I can't wait to visit this summer I need a break

Drew

> Yeah, it will be good to have you out here. Maybe you can get Craig to go out and not focus on my drink count

Luke Harrison

It will be my goal

Let you get drunk & distract Craig

After I finish my messages with Luke, I leave my phone behind in the room. I make my way back to hang out with my parents for a few more hours before I have to head back to my hotel.

***

The game goes well, and I get a home run, just like I'd told Annie I would. We win by two runs, closing out the Spring Training season with a good showing as a team. We could have a strong season if we stay healthy and continue to play well. Making it back to the Series is the goal we all are striving for. On the way out of the dugout, Coach tells me I'm getting the interview with the reporter. There is no fighting the grin that comes to my face. I shake hands with the guys from the other team and then make my way over to Annie. "Told you," I say, and she laughs and says, "You did, I should never doubt Drew Davis and his ability to read baseball." Her expression turns serious. "They want me to address our past. I thought I'd make a joke in my intro, are you ok with that?" "I don't have a problem, unless you don't want to," I answer honestly because, like she'd said yesterday during our text conversation, I'm not ashamed about our past. We both face the camera, and the guy counts us in.

Annie:

"Annie Campbell, here in Arizona, with my ex-boyfriend, I mean, shortstop for the

Griffons, Drew Davis. Drew, thanks for joining me after the last Spring Training game."

Drew:

"Thanks Angel, I mean Annie."

"It's great to be here with you, talking about our history, I mean baseball."

Annie:

"Yeah, you're welcome for helping you trend yesterday."

Drew:

"Thanks for that." It's interesting what people can find on the internet."

"Did you know we went to prom together?"

Annie:

"Oh, that was you..."

"I mean, it surprised me most that I was at the draft."

Drew:

"Yeah, I blacked out that day. Glad I can now identify the woman I kissed after my name was announced."

Annie:

"We are both so lucky the Internet helped us remember all those moments. Now that we've had some fun: yes, Drew and I dated back in high school, and yes, we are friends now."

Drew:

"Yes, we are in fact friends, so all you haters can calm down, just enjoy the show."

Annie:

"On the subject of baseball. How are you feeling about opening day?"

Drew:

"I am really excited about opening day in Kansas City. It will be my first official day in the big leagues, so come out KC, and make sure to get your number 17 jerseys ready!"

Annie thanks me, and the camera guy says, "Cut." I reach out and tuck a strand of Annie's hair behind her ear. It had broken loose from the others, and it felt natural to just tuck it for her. "Well played, Angel," I tell her, looking into her blue eyes. She takes a deep breath before saying, "Yeah, you too, Dimples." I smile and fight the need to kiss her. If I get to kiss her again, I'm not doing it with an audience. "See you back in Kansas City," I say. I walk towards the dugout, and the whole time, I resist the urge to turn around and look at her one more time.

Chapter 17: Opening Day

-*Drew*-

End of March

"So, that's the apartment tour, or the penthouse tour if you will," I say to my parents and brother as we return to the open living room, making a dramatic show of my arms. Mom gives a clap and I bow. "How long do you think you'll lease the place?" Dad asks me as he sits with Mom on the couch. "At least this year and next year. I want to get a feel for where more of the vets live and what part of the city I want to settle down in," I answer. "It's got a view," says Daniel as he looks out the floor-length windows that leads to the balcony. "Yeah, it's going to be hard to beat the city view for sure," I agree with my brother.

"How's it going for you, being back stateside?" I ask Daniel. He returned from his last tour a few months ago but has been reserved this time around. Mom let me know she's worried on more than one call. Watching him lost in thought, I can see why she's been worried. Daniel looks way from the window, "It's been different. I'm getting adjusted, and as I'm sure Mom has told you, I've been attending those group sessions." He's turned to face Mom and gives her a look, and she shrugs, "I'm your mother, Daniel, I'm going to worry about you whether you like it or not." We continue chatting before I notice the time, realizing we should start heading to the restaurant or we will miss our re servation.

We are all in the elevator talking as we head to the lobby. The elevator slows and stops on the tenth floor, and I can't help the hope that springs to life. The doors open, and the woman I can't get out of my head appears. She is dressed in jeans and a light jacket and looks fantastic. She is looking at her phone again, and I laugh, "You gotta stop looking at your phone when you're waiting for the elevator." I see the smile cross her face as she looks up from her phone, but whatever she's about to say gets lost when she sees my whole family in the el evator.

"Oh, sorry." She steps into the elevator, "Hello, Mr. and Mrs. Davis, Daniel. Are y'all in town to see Drew's big start tomorrow?" Daniel is the first to respond, "Yeah, it seems we've gotten the old neighborhood gang back together to celebrate this guy's game day tomorrow." Daniel jabs me in the ribs, giving me a hard time like brothers do. "With that train of thought, y'all will love who's meeting me downstairs. Annie waits a beat, "It's my dad and brother." Mom cuts in before Daniel can say whatever he was about to say. "Where are you all going for dinner?" Annie shrugs, "I'm not sure. Dad loves steak, so I think we will head to the restaurant down the block, but we could also end up at the sports bar. I didn't make a reservation, so we are winging it." Mom turns to me with her most mischievous smile. "Drew, Hunny, aren't we going to that steak restaurant? Do you think you can add three more people to our reservation?" Annie and I both start to talk at the same time. Annie says, "Oh no, we can't impose," as I say, "Sure, I'll call from the lobby." I make a mental note to thank my mom later for this opportunity to have a meal with her, even if it's with the rest of them. I can't help thinking how right it feels to be together before my fir st opening day.

In the lobby, we are joined by Mr. Campbell and Miles, who look surprised to see the whole Davis family with Annie. Mom and Dad talk to Mr. Campbell, and I pull my phone out to call the restaurant. "You don't have to include us,"

Annie says quietly, standing beside me. "It isn't a problem; we are still neighbors. And, Annie," I lean closer before I speak, "I'll never turn down an opportunity to spend time with you." The blush is there on her cheeks, and then her brother interrupts the moment. "What's the plan, Annie?" She turns her attention away from me and to her brother.

"The Davises invited us to join them at the steak restaurant that Dad wanted to go to; they already have a reservation." I step out of the group and call to change the reservation. The woman on the phone is nice and adjusts the reservation. When I rejoin the group, Miles is talking about how weird it is to be a coach now. Daniel calls him a "Do-Gooder" and follows up with that he's probably a great coach. I announce to the group, "Reservation changed. Are you all ready to head out?" We walk out of the apartment building towards the restaurant. Daniel and Miles are chatting like old friends. I laugh, I swear it feels like yesterday that the two could barely be on the same field at state together. I guess that is what time does, makes old wounds fade.

I end up walking over with Annie and her dad. "So, Davis, you ready for tomorrow?" He asks as we walk down the block to the restaurant. "I'm ready. I can't wait to prove I'm the right guy for this team," I say, and then Annie cuts in, "Dad you know that Drew had a great showing at Spring Training. As Griffons fans, we are in great hands." She gives me a small smile and turns her attention back to her dad. He glances from her to me, then says, "Annie, you've always been a good judge of the team's potential. What do you think? What are the odds that we will return to the Series? Do we win it all this year?" Annie's face lights up and I have to remember to breathe. "Dad, there is no doubt that we are making to the Series. I'm already trying to figure out what I'll be wearing on the sidelines. I don't think the network is going to let me wear my Griffons hat." Annie's answer makes me smile. What would it be like to be in the Series? It's more than I'd even dreamed possible. What would it be like to get there, knowing she's a part of another one of my life highlights? We reach the restaurant before I can get too far into that thought. I go to the front to let them know the name and the updated count.

Dinner is full of stories, laughter, and good food. I've forgotten how well our families get along. To anyone watching, we look like one family and not two. The only difference from six years ago is that I don't have Annie by my side. She's sitting between her dad and brother across the table. I get to watch her all night, and it's nice to see the smile that seems like a permanent fixture on her face. She's already fumbled over calling Mom Jennifer a few times tonight. Mom smiles at me each time it happens. I'm not talking, as I'm observing the group and the flow of conversation. I gave my card upfront, so when I asked if we are ready to leave and Annie replied, "What about the check?" I tell her it is taken care of. She looks like she is about to fight me on this, and I hold up my hands. "I got that deal for my lovability, call it payback for the favor." "This is more than pizza, Drew," is her reply. I give her my biggest smile. "Yes, so?" She looks like she wants to fight me, but she lets it go, and we all move towards the exit to walk back.

On the way back, I notice Daniel walking with Annie at the back of our group. I can't hear what they are saying, but she turns and hugs him. He returns it, and the look on his face is relief. My heart races because I don't like seeing her in his arms, that old feeling of jealousy fills my chest. Its short lived because I notice my brothers face and know he's finding closure on his past with her. I still try to focus on the words she says next and overhear, "Thank you for that, even if it was so long ago." If I had to guess, Daniel must have apologized for his actions in high school. Daniel keeps working to be a better guy. I'm proud he is my brother, which isn't something I'd have admitted a handful of years ago.

Outside of the building, the group breaks apart. All our visitors get into their cars to head to their hotels, leaving Annie and I, to walk into the building alone. "Thanks again for dinner," Annie says next to me as we walk to the elevator. "It really wasn't a problem. It was nice to see everyone getting along and having a good dinner," I tell her honestly. "It was a relaxing night. It's what I needed before tomorrow's opener." The elevator reaches the tenth floor too quickly. She makes to leave but holds the door and looks at me, "You are going to be amazing tomorrow, I know it." She releases the door and disappears into the hallway. When I get back to the apartment, Craig is watching TV and throws out a question about dinner. I fill him in on the family dinner and how the Campbell's joined us. I say something I may regret later, but I confess to Craig, "I miss her." Being the friend that he is, he doesn't make me clarify who the 'her" in my statement is; he just says, "I know." We go back to watching the gam e on the TV.

***

The energy in the stadium is something I can feel before I even walk out on the field. I feel the adrenaline and the electricity of Opening Day. The fans cheer when we enter the field for warmups. I see my parents and brother by the fence and wave. I see Annie too and this time I know it's her and my heart hurts looking at her. Coach pulls my attention calling us into the dugout. He gives us a pep talk about playing hard and reminds us to find enjoy in the game. We head out onto the field, and the crowd goes wild. We line up for the national anthem, and I take it all in and I'm grateful. I place my hand over my heart and take a deep breath to steady my heart rate as it plays. I hear the umpire's "play ball" and take my position on the field. I take in one big review of the stadium before the first pitch. Seeing a crowd this big and all of these fans in crimson is amazing, then I make my brain shut it out and I focus on baseball.

The first few innings go as expected, and it's 0-0 in the seventh when I step up to bat. My walk-up song, "Lose Yourself" by Eminem, excites the fans. I've had a mixed night, but I've been watching for the right moment. I like the tells on these pitchers, and I think it's time. I have that feeling I get before a big at-bat. I step into the box, preparing for the pitch, which comes in wide. "BALL" is yelled from the umpire, and I step out of the box. We have two runners on first base and third base. I step back in the box, knowing this is when I swing for the fences. When the ball cracks against my bat, I know it's going into the fountains behind the fence. The crowd knows it too because they get loud and the announcer says, "HOOOMMMMEEE RUUNNNN, DREW DAVIS" and the fans let out a collective "DAVVVIIISSS" as I round third base to home. It's a fantastic feeling, home runs always are, but this is my first one here in KC. I try and fail to not look in Annie's direction and she's cheering with the crowd. I high-five my teammates once I'm back in the dugout. With a score of 3-0, we win our opening game, leaving the team and the fans with hope that we will make it back to the Series. Like the last Spring Training game, Coach tells me I'll be interviewing with the reporter. It's the perfect end of my home opener that I get to talk with my Annie .

Annie is already talking to Simmons, as he pitched his first game for the team tonight. He did a great job with throwing a no-hitter. I step forward next to Annie's opposite of Simmons. She turns and gives me a little bump of her elbow. "Way to knock it out of the park, Dimples—that was amazing." I'm not sure she meant to call me Dimples again, but I'll take it and her excitement. "Yeah, it's one heck of a good feeling to get the HR in my first game in KC," I say to her and the camera. At the camera guys, "Cut." She puts the mic down and gives me her attention. "I have to remember not to call you Dimples: I'm so sorry about that. You just have that big smile, and that dimple still gets my attention, I guess." She shrugs. "Annie, you call me Dimples anytime you want." I give her a little bump of my elbow, "I'm glad you haven't become completely immune to my dimple, Angel." I smile, showing off said dimple, loving that she is still impacted by it and maybe by me.

Chapter 18: Tour of the City

-Annie-

April

"Meg, I don't know how to make it stop," I whine into my phone during our regular video call. "Why are you so worried about what strangers think about your past relationship?" Meg asks with a perplexed look on her face. "Meg, I have to stop reading these comments; they're making me crazy. Can I be honest with you?" I look at Meg, and she looks at me, "Annie, you know the answer to that question is always, yes." "I've been having very vivid dreams about Drew. Last night, the dream was so intense that I woke up having an orgasm. I'm worried," Meg laughs at my confession. "Annie Marie, what was Drew doing that resulted in the big-O?" Meg's smirk tells me that she doesn't think this is as dire as I do. "Focus Meg. I am having very detailed sex dreams about the guy I broke up with six years ago. My brain is broken and a filthy, dirty place," I say dramatically before following up with a pathetic sounding, "How do I make it stop?" Meg gives me a questioning look. "Why make it stop? Sounds like they are satisfying." Meg isn't helping. "Because it's all in my head. We aren't getting back together. We are trying to be friends." I know my voice is rising, but I can't help it. I need her to understand we are not going back there; we ended in the past. *Right,* I tell myself, *but if Drew made a move, would I stop him?* I answer my own question with a resounding *NO*. I'd accept his move and show him the way into my bedroom. Hell, I'd probably tell him not to wait to get to the bedroom.

"Annie, are you listening to me?" Meg's voice cuts into my internal thoughts. "No, I'm sorry, I got distracted, please repeat your advice." Meg starts over, "Before you started daydreaming again about your ex, I said that you should try to find a spark with someone else. Like, oh, I don't know, that reporter Nick." Meg makes a good point; maybe I should finally take Nick up on that offer to go explore the city. I should investigate that little flutter that happened at Spring Training. "Ok, I'm game. When we get off this call, I'll text him to set up that tour he offered." My best friend smiles on the other side of the video.

"Enough about me, have you gotten any interviews? What jobs have you been applying for?" I ask, changing the subject away from the sad state of my love life. Meg smiles before answering. "I have a few applications I'm excited about. One here in the DFW area and then one somewhere else." I clap my hands, "Tell me it's KC, please. I could use my best friend in the same city." I tell her, meaning it completely. "I'm not going to jinx it. When I know more, you'll be the first one I tell." I know that look on Meg's face: it means she will not tell me this secret. "Fine, I'd better be the first one you tell." "Deal," she says, and then we talk about other interesting but less essential topics until we both realize the time and end the call. I hold to my word and go to my messages app.

Annie

Hi, sorry it's taken me so long to reach out.

But is that private tour of KC still an option?

Nick Jackson

No problem, I know your schedule is all Griffons

Yes, the tour is available whenever you are

Annie

I am free on Monday all day

Or I could make a half day work before an evening game

Nick Jackson

I'll take the Monday.

Weather actually looks good too

Annie

Where do you want to meet?

Nick Jackson

I can pick you up, if you text me your address.

I text Nick the address to the apartment building before I change my mind. We set the time for the tour to start at 11 a.m. His only requirement for the day is that I wear shoes made for walking. I tell him that it isn't a problem. I feel good about the progress of events. I'm looking forward to seeing Nick and seeing the c ity.

***

Monday morning arrives before I know it, and I'm a little nervous. As I head down to the lobby to wait for Nick to pick me up, I take a deep breath to steady myself. I don't know where we are going, but I'm excited to see some sights. Sitting in the lobby, it surprises me to hear my name. "Annie, what are you doing down here?" I look behind me to see Craig and Drew coming from the elevator. "I'm waiting for my ride," I tell them, being honest. I'm not sure why I don't say 'Nick' or 'my date,' but it's what leaves my mouth. So, I go with it, trying my best to hide being flustered. "What are you up to on this rare day off?" Drew asks.

I side-step his question, "It doesn't look like you are taking the day off," because they are dressed in workout gear. "Nope, this guy needs to do a recovery workout today to keep all his joints and muscles ready to hit more home runs," Craig says before pointing out the window. "Annie, is that your ride? The guy is waving at us." I look up and see Nick in his car; true to Craig's comment, he is waving to get my attention. "Oh, yeah, that's him. You guys have a great day," I wave to them both as I exit and join Nick at his car. "Annie, glad we are making this work," Nick says as I enter his car. "Yeah, me too," I tell him and take one look back at Craig and Drew through the glass windows. I notice Drew's pinched eyebrows. I want to know what it means but then again maybe I don't. I return my attention back to Nick.

"I was thinking, you probably know a lot of what's in this area around your apartment, right?" Nick asks. "Yeah, a little, I've taken the streetcar and visited the market, but that's about all the exploring I've done, " I tell him. "Have you visited Union Station or the WWI Memorial yet?" He questions. "I saw them on the streetcar, but I didn't go inside either," I respond. "I think we start there. When we get hungry, we can drive to the BBQ place at the gas station. And before you knock it, it's the best place in town, you wait." Nick grins as he describes the plan for the day. "I'm game," I say, matching his excitement. We walk around the historic Union Station. It has all these free exhibits. I enjoy looking at the arched ceiling and hearing Nick talk about its history. He gives me facts about the style of the building or about what the rooms would have looked like when the station was the primary source of travel. He gets really excited walking me around the free mini-train exhibit. He's cute and I enjoying s pending time with him.

When we finish walking around the station, we cross the road. The nice part of his plan is that our next stop is right across the street. Heading up the hill to the WWI Memorial, I notice the breathtaking view of the city. The museum is interesting, and its examples of warfare and artifacts are heartbreaking. I have to get my parents here when they visit in the off-season. There is so much to see; I don't feel we have enough time to cover even half of what the museum offers. Before we leave, we go up the tower and get a beautiful view of the city. "You were right, this view is amazing." Nick smiles at me saying, "It sure is." I feel a blush on my cheeks because he's looking at me, not the city. I think he's about to kiss me, but the moment is broken by the sound of my stomach growling. Nick laughs before taking my hand, leading us back downstairs. It's nice holding his hand; he only releases it when we return to his car.

We have a comfortable conversation the whole drive to the BBQ place. True to Nick's word, the brisket and burnt ends he suggests are amazing. About halfway through the meal, Nick asks me, "So, how are you dealing with the season?" I can understand why he asks; the baseball season is long. I'm committed to all the same games as the players on the field. I answer honestly. "I'm adjusting to the schedule and flights. I am lucky that I like the whole team and I'm a die-hard Griffons fan. I get front row seats to every game, so there is that extra perk." Nick smiles and its nice but I can't help the fact that I look for a dimple and it's not there. "Yeah, getting front row seats every game has to be a perk for sure," Nick replies.

I focus on Nick and his green eyes that feel like I'm in a forest. "I still can't believe our interview went viral like it did, can you?" Nick asks me, pulling me back into the conversation. "I was surprised for sure. I never imagined that people would be interested in Drew's love life." Nick grins, "Who's to say there aren't just as many guys interested in the love life of Annie Campbell? The hot sideline reporter," Nicks replies, and I try and fail to fight the blush that appears on my face. "Its flattering people care at all, but there isn't a lot to say. This is the closest I've been to a date in months."

I don't catch my statement until Nick smiles, "I'm counting this as a date, Annie. Just so you know, and if you're open, I'd like to have another one." I look at him, really look at him. I like that he was direct about this being a date, and the fact that he wants another one. Nick is a handsome man, and I enjoyed today. It was fun walking around the city. I answer before I second guess it, "Yeah, I'd like to go out again." But I have this nagging feeling after I get the words out. My heart tells me that he isn't Drew, but no one will be Drew. He was my first everything big when it comes to relationships: first love, first time, first heartbreak, all of it. The whole point of going out today was to remind myself that Drew is in my past and he isn't my future. I focus on the man in front of me, getting lost in our conversation in the present.

When Nick pulls up at my building, it's already dark. We spent a whole day together. My face hurts from all the laughing and smiling I've done today. I go to get out of the car, and Nick says, "Hold on." He jumps out of his side of the car, walking around to get my door. He offers his hand to help me out of the car, and I take it. I join him on the sidewalk, and he shuts the passenger door. He wraps his arm around my waist, asking me for silent permission. I lean in as he does, and our lips meet in a soft kiss. It's sweet and gentle, but I feel no rush to deepen it. No burn to ask him to stay. I smile when we break the kiss knowing not all chemistry is instant.

"Thanks for the tour of the city," I tell Nick before stepping out of his arms and walking towards the front doors. I look over my shoulder at him, "Until next time." He shouts, "I look forward to sharing more time with you." He waves before he weaves his car into traffic. I stand there, watching his car disappear.

I'm left wondering why a nice guy and a good kiss didn't leave me feeling more. I enter the building lost in thought, so confused, and I know that a call with my best friend is in order. I need her to help me sort out all these conflicting thoughts and emotions.

Chapter 19: Coaching Charity Baseball

-Drew-

June

Baseball has been my primary focus through April and May. It's the excuse I give myself for not going out, for not going to bars or clubs like Alex Christopher. For not flirting when I've been approached. I tell myself that I'm not looking to date for a million reasons and none of them are because of the blonde sideline reporter at each game: the one I search for when I take the field, or who visits my dreams regularly. I may or may not have started looking at my collection of Annie photos on my phone again. Those specific pictures of her have been the only thing helping me to relieve my off-field tension. I should have deleted them years ago, but I've never been good at letting her go.

The problem now is that it makes me notice her more... makes me fantasize about her and the way it felt to be with her. I wonder what it would be like to see her body now. How does she look in a bikini? Does she still have that lingerie set? These questions come to me often. I fight them back again and again, trying to remember that we are friends now and that is all. After my confession to Craig in April, I've avoided bringing up Annie again. I'm sure as hell not going to bring up to my friend, that no amount of porn is distracting me: that the only thing I can jerk off to is old pictures of her on my phone. There is a limit to what I'm willing to share, and this is one of those things.

I should go out and see if someone can get me out of my Annie Campbell rut. It wouldn't feel so lame if I thought she was having the same Drew Davis problem. She isn't. I've seen that male reporter more than once in the apartment building. Craig has also been so helpful in bringing it up every time he has seen them out. The most recent time was when he joined a few guys on the team out in P&L. He'd come back to the apartment telling me all about seeing Annie out with a group of people, including her producer, Emma, and Nick.

I try to play it off with Craig, but I know he sees right through my frustration when I head to bed early. The kicker comes when Dominic reaches out in late May to see if I'll do the local sports talk show with Nick Jackson and Martin Smith. I have to physically hold back my frustration at my agent for even asking. Dominic has no idea that I'm fighting this need for Annie. He doesn't know that Nick Jackson is the guy with her now. I don't tell him "no," but don't say "yes" either. I tell him that I'm focused on baseball right now. I ask him to push it to the end of the season. He tries to remind me that waiting means it will be near the playoffs. He tries and fails to convince me to do the interview now. I practically yell at him after he tries again to get me to reconsider, "Not right now," and he drops it. I feel like an asshole, but I know that now isn't the time. I know if I did that show now, I'm likely to say something unprofessional to one of the anchors. Something like, "She's mine," "Back the fuck off," or something worse like, "I still want her." Annie isn't mine, and I need to get myself under control before I talk to her new boyfriend.

***

I'm at the ballpark earlier than usual to do my film study for the upcoming series. It's good to see the possible pitchers and their styles. It helps me to determine when to take risks and when to play it safe. I'm walking through the offices when I hear my name from an open office door. I stop and turn around to see who called my name. I see it's the General Manager, but this isn't his office. I check the name on the door as I enter: Meera Johnson. "Drew Davis, just the man we are looking for," he tells me and the woman behind the desk, who I assume is Meera.

"That's me, but I'm not sure what I did," I reply, earning a laugh from them both. "I'm Meera Johnson. It's nice to meet you," says the woman. She stands up and reaches out her hand, and I shake it. "Please have a seat, Drew. We have been in discussions regarding the charity game. We are looking for good team captains from the roster for the upcoming game," Meera says from behind her desk, looking like I just got an opportunity of a lifetime. The GM speaks up when I don't immediately reply. "We would love for you to be involved. You're making a big name here in KC already, and we want to bring the fans into the ballpark early to see the game, support the charity." "Who plays in the charity game?" I ask. Meera answers, "It's a combination of big-name Hollywood Stars from the area. They come into town to participate with their famous friends to help us get the community involved and excited.

We also include local media personalities and members of the other pro-sports teams in the area. We think you'd be a great addition as a coach this year." I think the event sounds like a great thing for the city. "I'm down to coach one of the teams. Think you can do me a favor? Try to get Annie Campbell in this game. It would be fun to see her trade sides with us guys. I believe the fans and the team would get a kick out of seeing her on the field. It could also be another element you could use on social media to gain interest." Meera looks impressed with my suggestion and gives the GM a nod of her agreement. "We will see what we can do," Meera says. I get the impression that this conversation is over, and I thank them both for their time and go about my original business.

I leave the office with my spirits lifted. I'm impressed with myself for the quick thinking in throwing out Annie's name. I must be getting used to talking with Dominic, because I just spun that to my advantage. I text Dominic to let him know that I've volunteered to do the coaching for the charity event. I let him know that the game is in three weeks. We should make sure to help the organization with hyping the event. I want to make sure I'm using my social media team to get the fans to donate to the charity or pack the stands for the game. Dominic asks if I'm telling him how to do his job before joking with me that he's going to start telling me how to catch a baseball.

***

Two days later, I'm minding my own business, getting ready for an evening game, when I get a text from Annie.

Annie Campbell:

> I was just asked by the GM of the Griffons to join the charity baseball game, he said and I quote, "Drew Davis said you'd be a great addition"

Drew

> Your name may or may not have come up as part of a list of people that would be a good fit

> Are you going to do it?

Annie Campbell

> It's for kids, so yes, I'm going to do it

> I reached out to Craig to help me

Drew

> Why Craig?

> You know a baseball player that can help you

Annie Campbell

Aren't you the coach?

They said I'd get assigned to a team, I can't have you know my secrets if you're the other team's coach

Drew

> I'll be your coach Angel

Annie Campbell

What insider knowledge do you have?

Drew

> I'm your coach, so trust me

Annie Campbell

Sure, I'll believe it when I see it

After our little exchange, I return to Meera Johnson's office and knock on her door. "Come on in," I hear her say before I open the door. "Got a minute to talk to one of your coaches?" She gives me a nod and points to the open seat in front of her. "What can I help you with, Drew?" I cut to the reason I'm here, "Do I get a voice in who is on my team?" It seems like a simple question, and she raises her eyebrows. "I bet I can guess who you want on your roster." She gives me a smile, and I bet she will get it right in one try. "Annie Campbell."

"I'm that obvious?" I ask her with my most innocent look. "Drew, she's already been assigned to your team. We couldn't break up the trending pair of exes after all." She seems amused that I'd even question if Annie would be on my team. "Meera, I appreciate your time," I tell her, starting to get up and go back to my pre-game rituals. "Before you go, anyone on this list that you don't want?" She slides over the list, and I'm impressed with the names on the paper. "I think you could move Nick Jackson to the other team. The rest look like a fun mix of individuals." She makes a note on the paper before waving me to be on my way. I'm not sure why I feel like I just won, but I do. I have a good feeling about tonight's game and the upcoming charity game in a few weeks. When I return to my locker, I pull out my phone and text Craig.

Drew

You already agree to train Annie?

Craig Mitchell

Yes, but I know you already know this!

So, why are you asking?

Drew

Let's include her in our training sessions over the next few weeks

Don't tell her I'm going to be there but don't not tell her if she asks

Craig Mitchell

You have it bad!

Drew

I have no idea what you mean

Craig Mitchell

I can't wipe the smile from my face all day. I'm going to spend more time with the woman I can't stop thinking about. One of my teammates commented that I must have gotten lucky. I shrug it off, telling them I'm just in a good mood. They don't believe me and keep trying to guess the woman's name, even in the dugout during the game. Alex is the most persistent. He doesn't seem to fathom that my good mood could be from anything other than getting pussy. Each time I'm trapped with him in the dugout, I'm getting peppered with questions. "What's her name?" "Blonde, brunette, or redhead? "Where did you meet her?"

I've kept silent or answer with "Wouldn't you like to know" responses. He keeps giving me a hard time about it until the end of the game. After the game, I see Annie on the sideline, and I know I will get caught staring, but I'm not sure I care. She is interviewing a few of the guys who had big plays tonight. I must be zoned in watching her because it startles me when Alex throws his arm around my shoulder. He looks from me to her and, just loud enough for me to hear, asks. "She's sexy as sin. Did she look like that when you all fucked?" I elbow him in the ribs hard. He grunts in response but smiles. "She's always been the sexiest woman in the room," I tell him before heading towards the locker room. I can hear Alex's laughter following me as I leave before he offers up another comment. "I think I know what the woman looks like now."

Chapter 20: Training Session

-Annie-

June

The adventure day with Nick made me realize I spend all my time at home or at the ballpark. I haven't done enough exploring or getting to know people in my new city. My life has been all things Griffons, and I think I need to get out more. I tell my only friends, Craig and Emma, that I need to leave my apartment. I need to make friends outside of those related to baseball. Craig agrees that he also needs to get out more. We've gotten together a few times before games. We grab lunch or wander around our new city, trying to find the best places. We drove to this cute bookstore five minutes from our apartment. Craig humored me and helped me find a handful of new book boyfriends. He picked up a cover of a shirtless guy and held it next to himself. Maybe this is my next career move. My chest should be on display like this. I laugh and ruffle his hair. "Ask Drew's agent if he can get you in contact." He'd laughed and set the book down.

We even start a fun ratings system based on our old game back in high school. This time, instead of ranking the potential of dating a person, it's Yes, No, or Maybe related to restaurants, bars and entertainment. We joke and laugh, and at the end of one of our meals, we give it our rating. It's nice to have Craig live close again. We'd spent all of our time together in Norman before he moved to Arizona. I didn't realize how much I'd missed his ability to make me laugh or not to take myself so seriously. I guess it's what comes from knowing someone almost our whole life. He can level set me with one quick quip about my ugly duckling stage. I can jab back and remind him when his voice was changing and he would squeak or crack, going up or down two octaves.

The biggest surprise was when I talked to Emma about needing friends. She hadn't even hesitated before inviting me to her girls' night out. After a few weeks, I am finding my place in the little group of women aged twenty-five to thirty-three. I've even invited Nick to a group gathering that includes spouses and significant others. Emma is the only one in the group who didn't bring anyone. She's told me on more than one occasion that she is happily in her single woman decade. During that exact outing with the larger group, we'd run into Craig. I'd started joking with him, and before either of us realized it, he was getting a seat brought over by the waitress, and he'd informally joined our dinner.

I've been going on dates with Nick. We've gone back to his apartment on more than one occasion to make out. For some reason, I've made an excuse each time to leave before we start removing clothing. I've told him I want to get to know him better before we take it to the next stage. Each time he smiles, telling me he understands and doesn't want to rush me. I like him, he's a nice guy, and I know that we would have already had sex if I didn't keep finding a reason to leave. I don't know why I keep putting up a blocker with him. I want sex; I want to feel something other than my vibrator between my legs. I don't know why I hesitate to move to the next stage with him.

In May, I finally got my best friend involved with my hesitation. I told her I liked him, but I didn't get the flutter in my stomach when he touched me. There was no rush or deep burning desire that flooded my system. Meg told me to give it a little more time. If I liked everything else, sometimes sparks happen with the most random people after knowing each other longer. She'd looked all distant when she'd made the statement.

It made me wonder if she was thinking about Tom or the one who came after him towards the end of her senior year. She'd been vague about the guy over time. I always thought it was more than that, but she'd said it wasn't meant to be more, even if she'd started to believe she was falling for him. He was going home, and she was going to stay in Texas. Since then, she'd only done the casual dating and hookup thing. We needed a subject change. I asked for details about her new job, and her look of distance turned to sunshine.

I learned in May that her secret job interview was actually back in our hometown. She'd been so excited about the opportunity, surprising me. I'd always thought Meg would stay in Dallas. She's in charge of the school district's involvement in all future development projects, starting with the high school's athletic center updates. She had a whirlwind of a move and started the new job right after the Memorial Holiday. She sounded different when discussing the job, as if she's finally looking forward to the future. I expressed my happiness and surprise at the announcement. I wish I had been able to help her move, but baseball was in full swing. Meg understood and told me I could make it up to her by visiting often in the off-season. We are only a few short hours from each other now. She promised to visit in August or September before the season ended. Nothing can help you figure out your problems like your best friend. I vowed to give Nick and me more time to see if we spark.

***

After our dinner date, we head back to Nick's apartment. We are making out, and it's nice, but that is the only description I can still give. He runs his hands over my body, which isn't sparking anything deeper. His fingers brush under the hem of my shirt, and I let him keep his hand moving. Maybe I need him to touch me to feel his skin on my skin to feel that extra spark. He cups my breast, and there is nothing. No spark, no need, just his hand on my skin. I think it feels weird, and then I realize that his kiss feels weird, too. Not the gross, yuck kind of weird, but rather the kind that feels like you're kissing your friend.

I break the kiss and move away from him on the bed. "Annie, is there something wrong?" He sounds worried, making me feel worse, but I know it's time. I have to call it: Nick isn't my guy, and we aren't going to be anything more than this. "It isn't working for me. I like you, but it isn't more than as a friend." I tell him the truth because he deserves it. "Oh" is his only response at first. "I thought it was going well" is his follow-up. I fumble for what to say, "It was, I just don't feel anything deeper. I'm sorry, Nick." He pulls me in and gives me a sad smile. "Thanks for being honest with me, Annie. Let me walk you out." It's awkward, but I get it—it's time to leave, and I schedule a car to pick me up. "I'll see you around," I tell him. "Yeah, see you at the Griffons' games, Annie. Give me a few weeks to get over this, but I think you're right that we could be friends." Nick is a nice guy, and I appreciate him trying to make it less weird. After my car picks me up, I let myself breathe. I wonder if I'll ever find someone who makes me feel something real. I can't help the next thought, 'like I felt with Drew?'

***

"I broke up with Nick last night," I confess to Emma the next day, while we have lunch before today's game. "Why, I thought you looked cute together?" she asks. "I never got that feeling of need that I thought I would," I tell her. She shakes her head saying, "Yeah, if it never comes, it never will. You can't force chemistry." She's right, chemistry is not something that you can fake. A couple either has it or they don't, and Nick and I didn't have it. "I think it's good that you called it. Now I'm not the only single woman in our little group," She laughs. She isn't being cruel with her comment, more trying to ease me into my single status again and making me feel less bad about it. "Oh, yes, we can be the spinsters of the group," I add. We both get a good laugh out of it. We finish our lunch before returning to the broadcast booth to discuss the upcoming game with the visiting reporter.

We cross paths with the Griffons' General Manager. The fact that we cross paths isn't unusual. He's usually around the ballpark before games. He's a friendly guy, and he's stopped to talk to us before about a player he'd like to be interviewed. What catches me off guard is how direct he is in wanting to speak to me today. "Annie Campbell, you are just the woman I was looking for," he says so matter-of-factly that I'm concerned about what comes next. He usually addresses Emma and me collectively, not calling either of us out. "I hear that you can swing a bat. Can I count you in on the Charity game to support the kids in KC?" *Well, this isn't the direction I saw this conversation going*, I think before answering.

"Oh, I haven't swung a bat in years." I go to make an excuse, but before I can fully deliver it, Emma elbows me. She interrupts my answer with one of her own. "She'd love to support the kids." The GM looks over at me excitedly. "Yeah, it's for a great cause," I add. He seems satisfied that I've agreed. "Drew Davis said you'd be a great addition." He gives us the rundown on the format of the game. I learn that the game will be before a home game at the end of June, before the two-week break for the derby and pro game.

He lets me know that Alex Christopher and Drew Davis have volunteered to be the team coaches. No teams have been formalized yet as they are still trying to figure out who is participating. He lets me know that as soon as they coordinate all the "celebrities," the Griffons' team will be in touch to let me know who my captain will be. He lets me know that Meera Johnson will give me the details, and he'll pass it along that I've agreed to play in the game. He is gone soon after, heading in the direction of the team's offices. "That was interesting," Emma says as we continue on our way back to the booth. I can't help but mentally agree with her. "Yeah, I think I have a few messages to send."

Annie

Can you spare me a few workouts?

Like you said you would earlier this year?

Craig Mitchell

Yeah, anything you want to focus on?

Annie

How to not embarrass myself at this charity game at the end of the month

Craig Mitchell

Interesting.

I'll make sure you look good swinging a bat and running the bases without dying.

Annie

Yeah, I haven't worked on arm strength unless you count Pilates

Craig Mitchell

It counts but we can add some weights to help give you a little more power in your swing

Do a little cardio.

I got you!

Annie

Thank you

I message Drew after my conversation with Craig. He is the reason, after all, that the GM stopped me. He'd recommended me for this little event, and I have to give him a hard time. As our conversation goes on, he seems offended that I asked Craig to help get me into baseball shape. Craig is a personal trainer who happens to be his trainer. It was the perfect choice.

His response makes me wonder if I should have asked him. As I sit thinking about working out with him, I imagine him shirtless, helping me perfect a move in the gym. I feel my face flush just thinking about it. There is no way I'd be able to focus. I highlight the fact that he's a coach, possibly the other team's coach. He seems pretty sure that I'll be on his team. I do and don't want him to be my coach. I'm confusing myself with my feelings about Drew. The conversation ends, and I return to the booth to get ready with my team for tonight's game.

***

I have two and a half short weeks to remind myself what it feels like to swing a bat. Then, I'll have to do it in front of a crowd of Griffons fans and celebrities. Can't forget that some big names are coming into town, and I really don't want to embarrass myself. I breathe, reminding myself that Craig will get me into baseball-hitting shape. He will not let me embarrass myself in front of such a large crowd. I turn off my alarm, feeling ready to start this training session.

It's probably why I am in the lobby ten minutes early, waiting for Craig to appear. He will be shocked that I beat him down here, since I'm not a morning person. He told me we will focus on arm strength training and cardio to give him a starting point for my sessions. I dressed in what I usually wear to Pilates: a pair of leggings, a sports bra, and a mesh tank. I've got my hair braided back into a ponytail and not a stick of makeup on. I'm not going to the gym to get a date; I'm going to burn calories. I know Craig will be a tough trainer, and he knows me so well that he will not let me get away with an easy workout.

I'm mentally preparing to be sore when a voice I'm not expecting breaks past my headphones. "Annie, are you ready?" It's not Craig's voice, but Drew's. *Well, there goes all my mental prep for this workout.* Why does hearing his voice make me regret not having a touch of gloss on my lips? I am ridiculous. I turn to see both Craig and Drew heading my way, both dressed to go to the gym. "This guy asked to tag along," Craig says, motioning towards Drew. "That's not a problem," I tell them both.

A new mental prep starts to take hold in my brain. *Do not stare at Drew,* I tell myself. We all chat as we walk around the block to the larger chain gym. I follow the guys to the weight section of the gym. Craig starts right away when we get into the room. "Drew, you know the basics. Do your warm-up reps, and I'll get Annie started. We can do your more advanced combos together after I get her started." Drew gives him a little "Yes, sir," and he heads off to start his own thing in the free weight section.

Craig works with me, showing me a few machines, he wants me to focus on. He tells me the count and reps he wants me to do on each machine. "Do you want me to stay and help count reps?" I fight the argue to hit him. "No, Craig, I think I can count." He laughs and tells me to find him when I'm done. I turn on my music, blasting my pop mix playlist. I can get lost in Taylor, Sabrina, and Ariana. I force myself to hit all the reps that Craig listed. I do lose count a few times watching Drew. The man takes his shirt off and I can't look away because the machine I'm on looks right at the free weights section. He is all long chiseled muscles, and my brain goes straight to what it would feel like to trace those musc les.

He is doing some bench presses at one point, and it's a fucking distraction. His muscles are straining, and I can't help but wish I was watching them strain for a whole different reason. I realize I'm just sitting on the machine and watching him. I look around, and it seems like no one has noticed. I close my eyes and move my arms again, trying to focus on my music and not the tempting man in front of me. I try to focus on my reps, but when I open my eyes again, I have to concentrate on not watching the ripples of Drew's abs. When I rejoin the guys, my arms are jelly. I lost count so much that I'm sure I did way more reps than Craig had given me originally. Now Craig has lost his shirt, too; it's not that hot. "You all are ridiculous going topless." I think, but then when Craig and Drew look at me, I realize I've said it out loud. "If you must know, it's more comfortable; you should try it," Craig says. "Oh really, you think I should go topless in here?" I look around the gym at the other people working out. It's a mixture of other men and women in various exercise outfits.

Drew clears his throat after my comment. I can see him checking out my chest. "Fine, let's do this," I say, and I pull off the tank top and throw it at Craig. Now I'm just in my sports bra and leggings. Still plenty covered, but I'm showing off my stomach now, and more of my cleavage is on display without the tank top. Craig laughs before saying, "Now you are ready to do some curls." He hands me some weights and tells me how many sets and reps to do. My arms protest from the machine work, but I don't say anything and take the weights. I watch my reflection, but before I realize it, I'm watching Drew in the mirror. He's doing some move that raises his shoulders.

Craig cuts in on my thoughts. "Annie, that is probably good on the curls. You can do your traps like Drew if you want." I feel the warmth on my face because I was caught checking out Drew. I do the same move and then ask if I should do cardio. Craig agrees, and I excuse myself to run. I put my headphones back in and try to run off the feelings— of lust and need that washed over my body—but it never fades. Running doesn't burn it off. Watching Drew's body ignited my own body, and I can't burn off this lust until I'm safely back at my apartment with my vibrator in hand. I may find my release with his name on my lips.

Chapter 21: Batting Practice

-Drew -

June

Working out with Annie is a practice in patience. It's both amazing and painful to see her body like this. Every time we've met over the last week and a half, her outfits have shrunk more and more. Like, she is trying to retaliate for the fact that we go shirtless. That first day, she'd already been in those leggings that fit like a second skin, and her tank top was fitted, showing off all her curves. Then she'd taken Craig's little comment and ripped off her tank top. Yes, she wore a sports bra, but it gave me a better look at her body and more skin to admire. I wanted to grab her up and take her to any room with a door and rip off the bra and leggings. I want to give into my desire for her.

Each workout has resulted in more distracting displays of skin being exposed. In the second session, she'd stripped as soon as we got into the weight room. This time her bra looked more like a bikini top than a sports bra. I noticed all the guys in the weight room admiring the view. I don't blame them, but I also want to pick up her shirt and put it over her head to cover up all that glorious cleavage. She wore a similar top to the last training session but today is going to be when I lose my shit. She's not only in this little top but has paired it with skin-tight shorts. Her legs are on full display, and Craig is playing into it having

her do fucking squats. I've stopped trying to keep track of my reps as I watch h
er.

"You can't seem to stay focused," Craig says next to me at the weight rack after Annie heads to the treadmills in another gym section. "No fucking idea why that would be. Do you?" I say with all the sarcasm I intend. Craig just laughs at me. "Man, this was your idea to work out with her." "I'm not the one who got her stripping at the gym, then showing up like that," I tell him, giving him a scowl. He continues laughing, "A lot of women dress like that. It's never been a problem before."

What do I say to that? I mean, he is right—plenty of women dress just like Annie is, and I'm able to focus. "Drew, just tell her already," Craig says, standing closer and speaking a little quieter. I go to make some excuse, but before I can, he holds up his hand to cut me off. "Man, come on. I know you, and I know her. Just tell her you're ready to give it a second try. *Is it that obvious?* I mean, I'm not hiding it, and I've noticed Annie watching me and Craig working out. Does she feel this pull, this need, this wanting for me? Like I do for her? "I'll think about it, maybe after the charity game is over," I tell him, and he pats me on the back before adding, "If you don't, I'm going to throw you both in a locked room, and you don't get to come out until you all figure this out." He gives me a wink as he walks to find Annie in the other room.

***

I got back late yesterday from our away series against LA. When I got home, I was already sore and tired. I wake up feeling well-rested but still sore. It must have been that slide into home base. I check my phone, realizing I've missed our last scheduled workout in the gym with Annie. We only have one more session, a planned batting practice, tomorrow. To give us both time after to get ready for the night game.

I've already talked to the equipment team, and they don't have a problem with us using the cage. Players always bring their kids in to enjoy the team facilities' privacy. I use the excuse that I want to help out someone in the charity event. I notice a few notifications from miss calls to messages. I open the app and see that I have missed messages from both Craig Mitchell and Annie Campbell. I jump to Annie's first; it's my brain's default setting.

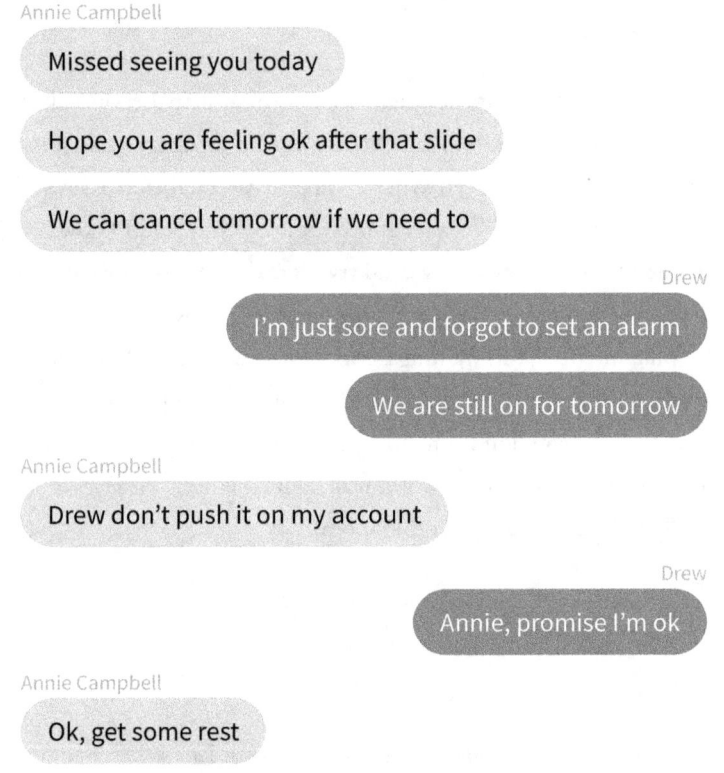

Annie Campbell

> Missed seeing you today

> Hope you are feeling ok after that slide

> We can cancel tomorrow if we need to

Drew

> I'm just sore and forgot to set an alarm

> We are still on for tomorrow

Annie Campbell

> Drew don't push it on my account

Drew

> Annie, promise I'm ok

Annie Campbell

> Ok, get some rest

I jump to the text with Craig, and I'm hit with a photo of Annie. She's in shorts and her bikini-style top again, but they are both in a matching fire truck red.

I totally understand why she favors the color; it looks good on her body, but maybe not as good as that red lingerie from all those years ago. I text Craig back that he is a cruel man before I get up and head into the kitchen. And lo and behold, there is the man himself. "I had to practically fight the guys off her today in that red outfit." Craig says by way of greeting. "I bet you did, she looked fucking fantastic in it," I say, trying not to think about her and failing. "She looked disappointed that it was just me this morning, FYI," he says before drinking his water. "I get it, man, I need to say something," I say, grabbing water and taking a swig. "You know her birthday is the day after the charity game, right?" Craig says like I don't know. "Yes, I know when her birthday is. I'll never think of the number twenty-eight and not think of June or her."

I give Craig a look of *Come on, man*. "What do you think about us surprising her by getting the gang back together? I've already talked to Meg and Luke. They can both come into town for the charity game and her birthday. Meg does have to leave pretty quickly after. She can't take off many days, but Luke can be here for a few weeks. If you're cool with him taking the couch?" Craig asks it like I'd say no. "Let's do it, it's been too long since we all got together. We have a birthday girl to surprise. Oh, and Craig, can you get us a reservation at that Argentine place in a private room or something?" I ask, and Craig grins, knowing his plan has now spurred on my own. "Anything else, *boss*?" I laugh at his exaggerated 'boss' and tell him. "No, I think I'll work on the rest alone."

***

While waiting in the lobby, I wonder if Annie forgot to set the alarm today. I check my phone, and it's right at our agreed time when I see her exit the elevator. She has that old hat over her hair, and a Griffons jersey from all those years ago over a pair of leggings. "You look the part of a slugger," I tell her, and she laughs. "I look like something... I may or may not have hit snooze on my first alarm. It took me a few extra minutes to remember why I'd set the dang thing in the first place." She laughs at herself.

My brain thinks about her in bed, and I wish we had different plans for the day. I give my head a little shake to refocus. "Do we need to drive separately or are you coming back here before the game?" she asks and I change all my previous plans. "I'll drive us and come home before the game." I lead the way to my blacked-out Corvette, opening the door for her. "Nice upgrade." Annie says mocking my flashy car. "Stop judging me. I splurged on my dream car when I got the new contract."

She smiles after my statement. We carry on an easy conversation on the drive to the stadium. I open my window to say hi to Tim, asking him for an update on his kids. He's one of the security guards for the players' parking lot. After we are parked Annie looks over at me, "It's so like you to know everybody". I look back at her, "These people make it easier for me to do my job on the field. It's the least I can do to know their names and a little about them." I shrug as I answer, and I feel her touch my arm and it's like a electric spark to my system. I have to focus on her words, "Drew, I meant it as a compliment. It's nice to know the humble guy I knew is still the man before me." It's nice to know she still sees me.

The moment is broken when we exit the car. I feel the loss of her skin on mine with more awareness than I should have. I get out and lead the way to the batting cages. I'm in the middle of explaining to Annie that I'll feed the machine on the other end, when Steve appears. Steve is the head of the equipment team and I'm surprised to see him. "Davis, I'm happy to run the machine if you want to help the young lady." We share a look before I thank him, and he heads back to the machine.

I make a mental note to learn a few of Steve's favorites to get him as a thank you. I turn my attention back to Annie. "Change of plans, Steve is going to start the machine, I'll be right here so I can help you make adjustments." She lines up in the box, her bat sitting off her shoulder at the ready. She doesn't look bad, so I move out of the way and yell to Steve that we are good to go. The first pitch comes in, and she takes a big swing and whiff of the ball. I hear Steve shout, "Let me fix the speed."

Annie steps out of the box, moving towards me, "How fast was that? The speed of light?" I laugh. It was fast, but maybe not as dramatic as she felt. "I think somewhere in the '60s or '70s." She looks at me with big eyes. "Don't you hit pitches in the 90s and above?" I like that she looks impressed with me, "Yes, but I strike out at those speeds, too." I try to soften the blow. She still looks concerned so I offer, "If it helps, the game will only be like slow-pitch speed."

Steve shouts, "Ready?" Annie doesn't look so sure. I walk around the netting, place my hand on her hip, and guide her back into the box. I should have touched her, but my hands feel good on her body. It feels like they belong here. I have to focus on reassuring her. "You got this, Angel." She gives me her *of course I do* look, and I remove my hands and feel the loss of her. I distract myself by shouting to Steve again that we are ready. This time, the pitch is slower, and she makes contact with the ball with a satisfying crack. She looks at me with a huge, radiant smile. *Well, fuck me*, I think, *how do I not act on that?*

After about twenty minutes of stop-and-go pitches, we call it. "Told you that you would be great," I say as she joins me on the other side of the cage. "You got a few in the tank, or do you need to save it for the game later?" She holds out the bat to me. "Angel, I think I can show off a little." I tap her hat on the brim before taking the offered bat. I go into the box and rocket two or three balls. "How are you doing that, so easily? I get an idea. I shout to Steve "Can you hold the pitches?" He nods his ok, and I wave Annie into the cage. "Come here, Angel." She gives me a skeptical look but joins me in the cage. "It's all about using your body and not just your arms. Getting your body in the right position, results in a home run."

"Dimples, you still talking baseball?" Her comments make me think about what I said. I can't fight the smile that I'm wearing as I think about her question. Is Annie thinking about non-baseball positions? She's got me thinking about her body in a lot of positions, none of them related to baseball. "Angel, you trying to distract me?" She blushes, and I almost pull her into my arms, but I remember we aren't alone. "Come here and hold the bat again."

I stand behind her and run my hand down her front leg. "Less weight here." I say softly and I slide my other hand down her back leg. "More weight here." She exhales a heavy breath, and I wonder if she feels as turned on as I do. "When you see the ball coming shift your weight to the front leg." I emphasize my point by running my hand over her front thigh again. She lets out a little sound. I need to step back before I do something stupid. I shout as I go behind the netting to Steve that Annie is ready. I know I could have just told her what to do, but it was my excuse to touch her. *I needed to touch her*, I tell myself. She connects hard on the next five pitches pulling me back to the reason we are here. When we are done, Steve waves and leaves at the other end of the cages. I know we both need to get back, but I also want more time with her.

"Hey, you wanna go on the field and see what it feels like out there, catch a ball on the field?" She looks excited. "Yeah, that sounds like a fun." I disappear into the locker room to get my gloves before leading her out of the dugout and onto the grass. We play a little game of catch, and she does well. I shout to her, "You wanna be the shortstop in the charity game?" She shouts back, "I'm not sure I'm shortstop material." I shout back, "I think you are. I'm the expert, remember?" She laughs, missing the ball bouncing off the end of the glove. "I'm already making mistakes; Coach I think you need to rethink your strategy." Annie shou ts back.

She looks at the empty stadium seats. ""I know I work here, but the park feels so much bigger from field." I'm over shouting so I walk towards her as I reply, "Yeah, as you said all those years ago, I have the best view in the place." I'm not looking at the stadium, I'm watching her. I really need to talk to her about us, because I want her. I'm not sure I ever stopped wanting her. I need her to know and I'm about to confess everything I'm feeling when she looks at her watch. "Oh, we should get back. It's getting late and I can't show up like this for TV." I have to bite my tongue not to tell her that I prefer this version with all her freckles showing. I let her change the subject and take the glove she offers me. "Be right back," I tell her before slipping into the locker room. I put the glove she'd been using in the front of my locker. I have the feeling that I'm going to be lucky with that glove for the rest of the season.

Chapter 22: Home Run Feelings

-*Annie*-

June

June 27th got here so much faster than I thought it would. The calendar event in my phone of "Charity Game" is highlighted as my next event. I review everything for the millionth time and figure I'm as prepared for today as I can be. Emma cleared it with the network to have me in the Griffons jersey for the TV coverage tonight to spotlight the event and the charity opportunity. It feels weird to be dressed in a fitted white tank and a pair of black leggings with a crimson stripe down the side instead of my sideline reporter standard outfit of a dress or suit.

I get to the game early, parking in my normal media area versus the celebrity parking I was offered. Double checking the gate that is open for the players to enter when I hear, "Annie, wait up." I turn to see Nick jogging to catch up to me. We exchange greetings standing in front of the ballpark and it doesn't feel awkward, which is a relief. "Are you looking forward to the game?" I ask. "Yeah, is it time to confess that I stopped playing baseball in middle school? Nick says laughing. "I'm also trying not to act star struck with all these A-list celebrities on my team." I pat his arm, "Just remember that a line drive will scare them as much as it does you and you'll be fine." He laughs.

We start walking only to be stopped with a loud. "What do I have here—a traitor already, Jackson?" Alex Christopher jogs to join us. He throws his arm over Nick's shoulder before continuing. "I mean, I'd turn traitor for Annie, too." Alex throws me a flirty smile. I roll my eyes and reply to Alex, "No one is turning traitor. We are talking. It's what adults do, Alex," I say, slowing down my words like I'm talking to a child. It makes Nick laugh, and Alex gives me a wink. "Annie, I'm sure there are far more fun adult things to do". He nudges Nick, "Right?" Nick laughs but looks away from me. I have no idea if Alex knows we have history but that just made it awkward.

As if he can't tell his joke turned awkward Alex continues, "Y'all enjoy talking." He releases Nick, and we all walk into the ballpark. Nick and I get a security team member escort to the box reserved for the "celebrities." The box has an assortment of snacks and drinks already set up. Off to the side is a table with all our jerseys, and I say goodbye to Nick and make my way over to the woman at the table. I give her my name to see what number I was assigned. I'd requested number 28 in the email two weeks ago, but the reply I received informed me that one of the event organizers had already selected that number. So, I'd just replied to give me any open number.

Looking at the jersey, she hands me, I don't think my number was selected randomly. The number '17 Campbell' jersey I'm handed doesn't feel like I got any random number. I want to text Drew and see if he had assisted with this, but I hold back. I'm overthinking it. It could be random, 17 is just a number, it doesn't mean the same thing to me as it does to others. So, I slip the jersey on over my tank top and rejoin the people in the room. It's a fun little pre-party. I get to meet all the famous faces in the room, and I am a little in awe. I haven't laughed this hard in years, the room is full of funny people, and I forget to be nervous about what comes next. That is, until they announce we can meet our coaches on the field.

A representative escorts us out of the home team dugout. The announcers over the loudspeakers announce the start of the Charity Game. The crowd cheers for each person as we go onto the field. I'm surprised I get a loud cheer when I'm announced. As I take my place in the line with my teammates for the event, I see the stands. While it's not full, there are already more people here than I expected. I think to myself, *'Please hit the ball at least once.'* Before I can get too far down my mental rabbit hole, I'm interrupted by the chants of "Annie, Annie, Annie" coming from behind the dugout.

I turn to see which fans are chanting specifically for me. I'm greeted by familiar faces. Craig, Meg, and Luke are all dressed in number 17 jerseys, chanting "Annie, Annie, Annie." I can feel the big smile on my face as I wave to them. "I hope you don't have plans for your birthday tomorrow," Drew says from behind me. I turn and look at him, and I have to fight myself to not wrap my arms around him. "I have to work the day game, but after that I was planning to relax." He is still wearing a smile as he steps closer for only me to hear. "Change of plans, Angel. After the game tomorrow, we are getting the friends group back together to celebrate our Annie," Drew says, his grin turning into that full, dimpled smile that makes butterflies appear in my stomach. My heart races as he walks away: not because of the crowd, but because he'd call me 'our Annie,' like he still has a claim on me.

I don't have time to think too much about how I'm feeling. The teams do some warm-ups and photo-ops on the field. Then the umpire explains the rules of our charity game before announcing, "PLAY BALL." We are considered the home team, so we take the field first after Drew leads us in a pep talk. He reminds us that this is for fun and charity, but that he can't lose to Alex Christopher, so we need to win. We have fun during the game as much as we play ball. I make a catch at shortstop and results in an out. I can't fight the urge to look at Drew. Our eyes meet and I don't want to look away from him but I do and try to focus on anything but my sexy coach.

The game is all tied up, and the umpire announces the last inning. My team is up to bat, and I'm the second one up this lineup. I watch the person before me hit a solid grounder and make it too first. I am about to head to the plate, when Drew steps in front of me. His hands end up on my shoulders, and I feel the heat through my jersey. He says for only my ears again. "You've got this, Angel." He has been encouraging us all, but I feel special each time he does it for me. He releases me and steps out of my way, and I take my place in the batter's box. It's like the pitch comes in slow motion. I see the bat hit the ball, and then the crack of the action registers. I drop the bat, taking off for first. I lose track of the ball as I run. I am about to stop when I hear Drew's shouts of "RUN, ANNIE."

I take off towards second, and I see the other team stumbling in the outfield. Out of the corner of my eye, I see my teammate rounding third to head towards home. I know that when they hit home, we will win the game, but I don't slow down; I want to make it home, too. I blame it on all my years playing competitive soccer, but I want to get a point on the board. I find a gear from all those years ago, fueled by adrenaline, and hightail it towards third. My foot hits the bag, and I can hear the crowd cheering as I round the corner and sprint towards home plate. My whole team is waiting at the plate, but I don't focus on them. I only focus on Drew's smiling face, yelling at me "Home, Annie, make it home".

My foot hits home base, and I don't think: I do. I have no idea why I do it, but I launch myself into Drew's arms. He catches me as if we'd planned it. We are beaming at each other before the team crowds in around us, cheering. I lay my head on Drew's shoulder. I hear all of the noise from my team and the fans, but I focus on him saying "I'm proud of you" next to my ear as he pulls me into a deeper hug. Eventually, everyone calms down. Drew pulls back, and my feet are back on the ground. We stand looking at each other, his arms around my back and mine around his neck. The moment feels like slow motion again. I want him to kiss me. I don't care that we are in front of a crowd, but he doesn't.

The moment is broken, and time resumes, a photographer is asking for a team photo. The charity game is over, and all the 'celebrities' are taken off the field. I head over to my regular sideline spot. Before the Griffons game starts, I get a small break, and my friends join me at the net. "Annie Campbell, look at you pulling off an infield home run to win the game," Luke beams at me. "I'd say I'd spring for drinks, but I'm the only sucker still looking for a job." That draws a laugh out of us all. "I do have connections to a baseball player who promised me endless bottle service." Craig elbows Luke in the ribs. "Didn't you already use that excuse a few years ago in Arizona?" Luke looks at him with a serious expression "I amended my terms when he signed his new contract. You heard the work 'endless' right?"

Luke winks at Craig. Craig rolls his eyes, mocking Luke. "I think our girl is a badass," Meg pipes in. "I like the jersey," I can't help but comment. Meg isn't one for sports jerseys in her regular wardrobe. Her exception is her football spirit collection, which she swears brings good luck to her team on Saturdays or Sundays. "You all have fun watching the Griffons, tonight's game should be a good one." I tell them. Luke wraps up Meg in a side hug, "Can we please go eat on Drew's tab now?" She hugs him back, "Only if you can get muscles over here to eat all the junk food." Craig rolls his eyes. "I eat a balanced diet, we all get a cheat day. Do any of you understand my job at all?" Meg wraps him into their hug. I love seeing my friends together. My camera guy gives me the signal that its show time. "I gotta go work—see you all later." They give me a wave and he ad up the stairs.

The Griffons' play a great game. They easily control the game to get the win. Drew has a top-notch performance, hitting a home run and making some great double plays. When I see him walking towards me, I can't help the rush I get at getting his attention again. "Annie," I hear Emma in my earpiece pulling me out of checking out Drew. "They want you to talk about the charity game first so they can play your hit and win next to you on camera. Then get into the Griffons game." I nod into the camera and give her a thumbs up. When Drew arrives at my side, I give him a little summary. "How will I know when to stop talking?" He asks and I offer him a head set so he can hear Emma's cues. He looks sexy as he slides it on. I reach up and slide one side off his ear that isn't going to be seen. When I speak my voice is husky, "So you can hear me too." His dark blue eyes are big, and I want to play into what they are telling me. I'm saved by the camera guy giving me the cue to start.

"Annie Campbell, here with Drew Davis, Griffons Shortstop. Before getting into the Griffons game, we'd like to spotlight the charity game Drew coached and I played today. It supports several children's charities in the Kansas City Metro. You can follow the link on the team's website to make your donations today to support the kids." I give a moment for the logos to appear on screen. Emma's "ready" lets me know I can go to the next part. "We also have two wins to celebrate today," I look over at Drew, and he is beaming in my direction, "as our team came away with the trophy at the charity game today. How did that fee l, Coach?"

Drew looks at me, and the look in those dark blue depths feels charged again. He smiles and turns towards the camera. "What Annie here isn't telling you all is that she hit the infield home run that won the game. It was amazing." "Hold," I hear from Emma in my ear, and Drew pauses and looks at me and I feel butterflies again. I'm lost just looking at his face, "OK, ready" feels like it is blasted into my ear when Emma speaks. I have no idea what they show on air, but I'll have to check it out later. I feel a slight blush rise to my cheeks at his on-air praise. Drew speaks before I can. "Told you she was amazing." Our eyes connect and I hear myself talking, "Thank you, Dimples." I don't care that I've called him by his nickname on TV again. I spent the rest of the interview distracted by him and wishing he'd call me Angel.

Chapter 23: Getting the Friends Group Back Together

-*Drew*-

June

It's good having Luke in town for a few weeks. It's only been about twenty-four hours, but having the group together feels right. I haven't been around them all since high school and I didn't realize how much I missed us. Luke seemed to need a break from all things law school and studying for the bar. The guy looks like he hasn't seen the sun all spring, and the dude is Native American, so it's alarming. Over the next few weeks, I plan to infuse him with time away from classrooms and libraries. He already has a nice pink sunburn from being out at the stadium all day yesterday. He already seems lighter too. I got everyone game day tickets for today's early afternoon game. After the game we can all relax at my apartment before Annie's Birthday dinner.

Craig insisted that we don't change my game day routine, so we have our traditional chat up over smoothies. Craig, Luke, and I are at the kitchen bar, talking and chatting it up about life, when Luke changes the topic from baseball to the girl we are celebrating today. "Are you two back together? I meant to ask Meg, she always knows what's going on, but I got distracted yesterday between her news, beer and the games." We all laugh before I answer. "No, we aren't." I want to add 'Yet' to the end of my sentence, but I don't know if that is what

Annie wants. I need to get us alone and figure it out. "She literally launched herself into your arms in front of everyone." Luke says looking confused. "I've never had a woman launch herself at me looking like all she wanted me to do was kiss her." He shoves Craig's arm. "Have you?" Craig shrugs. "No woman launching themselves at me either. Seems IMPORTANT". Craig gives me a look *of told you.*

"Luke, man, did I tell you about the two of them at the gym? You should have seen them." Craig starts making exaggerated looking me up and down movements. Luke laughs, and Craig continues his actions. "I already told him if he doesn't tell her that he forgives her, I'm locking them in a tiny room." I hold up my hands in surrender, "Ha ha, you're so funny," I mock him back. "And, like I told you, I'll talk to her after the charity game. But not today—it's her birthday. I'm not bring this up today?" I give him a look, and he holds up his hands in his own surrender. "Fine, we all spoil Annie today, but after today," Craig gives me a serious look. "Yes, after today, I'll figure it out," I say with my hand over my heart.

"Do you think it's just the fact that you want to fuck her again, or do you still love her?" Luke asks in the silence and shakes his head like he didn't mean to say it. "Gross, I should not say the words *want to fuck* in reference to Annie ever again, it's just... yuck." He takes a drink of his water and sloshes it around like he is trying to clean out his mouth. We all laugh, and his initial question is lost in the moment. My mind holds on to it even when the guys drop it. I know without a doubt that it's not just about fucking her. Fucking her would be a bonus. This is more than wanting her body; it's about missing her in my life and by my side. I want the chance to see if we could get back to what we had before. Loving her was the easiest thing I've ever done, and my life hasn't felt the same without her. Thinking about it, even just a little, has my heart racing.

The game is hot, the sun is blazing, and Kansas City is humid today. Despite all of that, we are playing a solid baseball game. In the bottom of the seventh, I get a good read on the pitcher. He sends a fastball up the middle, and I rocket it over the fence. Home run bases are the best; the crowd comes alive. I get to look around and take everything in. Today, my everything is looking over at Annie. I run the bases, and I don't think I do. As I round the bases and before I hit home plate, I make a heart shape in her direction. It's our old code, and I want her to know that on her twenty-sixth birthday, I'm dedicating the run to her.

Other guys make big defensive plays towards the end of the game to secure the win. They are the ones selected to talk to Annie after the game. I'm jealous, but it helps that I get to see her later at dinner. I'm at the edge of the dugout, watching her interview Carlos and James, when an arm goes over my shoulder. "I hear that it's Blondie's birthday today," Alex says next to me and gives me a nod. "When they get near the end, a few of us guys are going to join them and sing her "Happy Birthday." I assume you'll join us," he says, and I give him my elbow reply, and he laughs. "You have a weird love language, man, but I'll take that as a yes." He never breaks the smile or the laughter on his face.

Carlos looks over his shoulder at the end of the interview. I guess it's the signal, because Alex starts to walk towards the group with a few of our other team-mates. I am for sure going to be a part of this song and dance. I don't think I can help myself where this woman is involved. We break into a bad version of "Happy Birthday." The remaining crowd by the dugout even joins in on the song. Annie blushes red at being the center of our attention. She tells us all thank you and gives the fans a wave and a clap. The camera guy says "Cut" shortly after we finish our song. Annie gets hugs from all my teammates.

I wait to get mine until the end. I am not disappointed when she turns to me, radiating her joy. "Did you tell the team?" she asks, never once losing her big smile. "Nope, Alex found out. I'm not even sure how," I reply with a smile and a shrug. I step up and give her a bear hug. I wrap her in my arms, and she returns my hug, but it isn't like the others she shared with the guys. We both linger a little longer her head on my shoulder. I feel every place our bodies touch, her curves molding against me.

"Thank you for the flowers," she says against my neck. "What makes you think it was me?" I say against her hair. "Oh, I don't know. The fact that they are almost exactly like the flowers that you sent me seven years ago." I can feel her smile as she mocks me with her response. "I confess nothing, but it's nice to see you today, Angel," I say, still holding her against me. I feel her pull back, and I want to wrap her up tighter, but I release my hold, and she is looking at me, lost in thought.

"Oh, gosh, you're right—we've never spent my birthday together." It doesn't feel true, yet it is. Why does that seem so weird? Our eyes meet as she finishes her thought. God, I want to kiss her. I wonder how mad she'd be if I leaned down and captured her lips with my own. I want to know how she tastes and not just try to remember it. Fuck it, I think, and I'm about to move my hand from around her back to her face when a chant of "ANNIE, ANNIE, ANNIE" breaks out from the netting behind me. We both look over and see our friends. I know I give them a scowl, and I'm sure the only one who gets it is Luke, because he gives me a wink. The moment broken, I release Annie from my arms. She heads in the direction of our friends, and I tip my cap and make my way in the direction of the locker room frustrated at their well-meaning interruption.

***

"Party planner, extraordinaire!" Luke shouts through the apartment a few hours later. "You can tack on 'best looking of the group,' and I'll answer you," Craig shouts back at him from his room. "That would be a lie. I'm almost an attorney, so I can't outright lie. I bend the truth." He laughs at his own joke before continuing. "So, I could say something like 'party planner extraordinaire and relatively attractive,' something like that." I hear Luke's huff before his laughter continues. I come out of my room to a full-on wrestling match. Craig has him in a headlock.

"Ok, children, let's not break anything before we go out," I say, laughing. "Does anyone know if the girls are ready for dinner?" I ask my two friends still wrestling in my living room. "Don't look at me. I'm not the party planner extraordinaire," Luke says as Craig releases him from the headlock. "Yeah, I got a message from Meg about thirty minutes ago asking me to call when you were ready," Craig says, pulling his phone out of his pocket, opening it to a message, and typing. He looks up before hitting the send button. "I assume coming out here means you are ready to leave." "He looks dressed to me," Luke says from the couch. "Hilarious, man, hilarious," Craig replies to Luke before looking at me. He must agree because he hits a button and heads toward the door. "Just agreed to meet them downstairs in five minutes." "Oh, shit, I thought I had time to pee." Luke gets up from the couch running in the direction of Craigs room.

We beat the girl's downstairs, true to his party planner extraordinaire title. Craig goes to the minibus he organized to let the driver know we are almost ready to leave. I'm talking to Luke, facing the party bus, when he looks over my shoulder and cuts me off. "If it isn't the two most beautiful women I've ever seen. Tell me your single." "You always know how to make a girl feel good." I hear Meg's reply before I see her. "Hey, I thought you couldn't lie," pipes in Craig, coming back into the lobby. "I'm clearly just stating facts, look at them." Luke shrugs at Craig with a smirk on his face. I can make out Annie's and Meg's reflections in the window.

I already know I'm going to be distracted all night. I take one last deep breath and turn around to face them. I swear inside my head, and then, for good measure, do it again out loud: "Fuck." She's breathtaking in that little black dress. I'm not capable of understanding how those little straps are holding up her boobs, but somehow, they do. I don't care that I'm gawking at her. I scan her body, taking in everything about her. The dress is shorter, showing off her long legs, with the little black heels on her feet.

I clear my throat, trying to remember how to make sounds that resemble words. I take a step, trying to adjust myself in my pants without anyone noticing. She's got me hard already; all she did was walk across the lobby. My friends are talking about something, but I have no idea what to say because I've been lost in studying her body. "Let's get to our birthday celebration," Craig announces, and I feel myself nod in agreement. I motion for the women to go ahead of me. I have to fight my urge to take her hand, or pull her into me, or kiss her until she looks all dazed. Instead, I enjoy the view of her ass in that dress as I follow her into the party bus.

The drive to the restaurant isn't long, but that doesn't stop Luke. He takes the champagne from the ice bucket before popping the top and pouring us all a glass. "To our Annie! Here's to another year of good friends and making big memories." Luke clinks his glass against Annie's, and then we all repeat the move of clinking glasses before tipping back the bubbles. It's not my usual drink, but I'm not about to break tradition. "Thank you, guys. This is amazing. I'm so excited to celebrate with all of you—it means the world to me." Annie gives Meg a little bump on the elbow in the seat next to her and gives us guys a nod. Craig continues in his party planner mode, "I got with your friend, the producer. She helped me invite a few more people. They are going to meet us at the restaurant. I hope that is ok," Craig says from his place on the bus. She beams with joy at Craig. "Craig Michael, who knew that me destroying you at dodgeball would give me one of my best friends." She leaves her seat, slides next to him, and hugs him. He looks slightly surprised but accepts the hug and returns it in kind.

"Annie, it was me destroying you, please keep the story straight." She pulls back from the hug, laughing. Turning to the group next to Craig, she announces, "You guys are going to love Emma and her friends are amazing too" When we get to the restaurant, I recognize Emma standing with a group of couples. She looks over our group as we get off the bus, giving a little extra attention to

Craig. When Annie gets off the bus, she walks in our direction and wraps herself up in a friendly hug. Her action blends the groups, and 'happy birthday' and introductions begin. Craig gives me an elbow. "I'm going to go check in." "I'll go with you," I offer, and we head in the direction of the hostess stand.

The hostess takes a moment to review her system before saying, "We have your group in our private room for tonight. Are you ready to be seated?" "I'll go get the rest of the group from outside," Craig offers and disappears back through the restaurant. "Can I give my card over to cover the table?" The hostess takes my card. "Oh, let me ask the manager. I'm newer, but I think I've heard we can do that." She walks off before quickly returning with an older man. "Mr. Davis, we'd be happy to take the card now if you prefer. We will return it and the bill at the end of the meal." I agree as the rest of the group arrives behind me, and he shows us to our table.

Conversations flow easily between our mismatched group of high school friends and Annie's new friends here in KC. It feels both old and new. I realize too easily that this is what life could be like with her. I'm sitting across from Annie again, which is both nice and torture. I wish I was the man at her side, getting to hold her hand or run my hands across her skin on her exposed shoulder. If I can't be right next to her, then across is the second-best option, because I get to look at her all night without it being overly obvious that I can't take my eyes off her. She seems really happy sitting between Meg and Emma. I like seeing her so happy. I'm glad to know I've been able to give her this birthday dinner. It feels like I'm making up for my absence all these years. The restaurant does a fantastic job of bringing out appetizers, drinks, and our meals. I owe Craig a bonus for helping organize all of this, because the night has been precisely what I'd pictured. He's been a great person on this adventure, keeping me level-headed and pushing me to be my best. I make a mental note to thank my friend again for all his planning.

After dinner, the staff brings out a cake with a two and a six candle. We all sing 'Happy Birthday' to Annie. As she goes to blow out the candles, she looks at me before closing her eyes to make her wish. When she opens them again, her eyes are glued to mine. I swear they sparkle from more than the flicker of the candles before her. She doesn't look away as she leans down and blows out the candles—the group cheers in excitement. Looking at me so directly, I can't help wondering what she wishes for. I also can't forget the last time we did birthday candles of a different kind together. Cake is passed around, and I look at Craig and raise my spoon to my lips in satisfaction. He'll probably make me do extra work for this, but it's worth it. The waiter brings me the bill to sign, and I thank him. Annie's eyes go wide watching me sign the check. Did she think I was going to let anyone else treat her on her birthday? Well, she'd better get used to it: I have every intention of treating her like the most important person in my world, if I get my way.

Our group breaks up outside the restaurant with hugs and handshakes all around. The husband of one of Annie's new friends gives me a handshake with a comment on how I'm really down to earth, and it's not an act for the press. It catches me a little off guard, but I tell him thanks. The five of us get back on the bus and wave to the rest of the group as they head to their cars. I'm one of the first on the bus, and slowly I'm joined by the rest of the group, with Annie the last of the group to get on the bus.

She surprises me by sitting next to me and not Meg. She wraps her arm around mine, her hand resting on my forearm. It sends a rush through my system, and I feel like a teenager again. I can't even remember the last time a woman touching my arm got me flustered. She ups the touch by leaning her head on my shoulder before saying, "Thank you, for the best day." "It was my pleasure, Angel. Gonna tell me what you wished for?" I can't help myself from asking after the looks we shared. "No—then it won't come true, and I really want this one to come true," she says so quietly beside me that I almost don't hear her. We don't speak again for the rest of the ride back to the apartment building, but we don't move our bodies from being right next to each other, either.

Chapter 24: Girls' Night Out

-Annie-

July

The morning after my birthday party, Meg and I are eating breakfast in my apartment chatting up. Her phone screen lights up with my brother's name on the notification. Meg looks up from her phone, "Miles is my contact for that athletic facility project. He's the coach representative. He is making sure my designs capture all the needs of the student athletes, as well as the needs of the staff supporting them." Miles would be great at that having been on both sides of the experience. "That has to be nice that you already have a relationship with my brother," I say, and Meg chokes on her coffee. "Oh, Meg, are you ok?" I jump up in concern before she clears her throat a few times before saying, "Yeah, yeah, I'm fine, went down the wrong pipe." She takes another slower sip of her drink before saying, "Enough about me. What about that little snuggle fest on the way home with Drew?"

I feel the blush on my cheeks, thinking about the bus ride back to the apartment. It had felt natural to be close with Drew. "It was nothing. It was just what it looked like," I say and smile at her, trying to downplay my feelings. I should know better. My best friend isn't going to let this go. "When are you going to tell him that you want another chance?" Meg says to me, giving me a raised eyebrow in the process. I don't try to play off this question, "I'm not sure he will forgive me. I hurt him, Meg; I walked away from him, let him go, let us go." The ache I feel in my chest at my words is painful; it hurts to breathe. Meg reaches over the table and takes my hand. "People can forgive, Annie. It is obvious he wants you. Maybe that means he's already forgiven you. The last few days have been more than enough to convince me." I try to take in all of Meg's feedback and to process it.

Drew and I have been flirting for months, both in front of and behind the camera. I've enjoyed the glimpses I've gotten of adult Drew. He hasn't changed in the ways that count he's still the same guy as he was at nineteen. The money and fame didn't change him. He's still so focused on being the best he can be, I saw his focus on the field and in the gym when we trained at the gym. I'd learned, too, that Drew's body is something that makes me burn. It's the kind you see in movies and on romance novel covers. I'm not even sure someone could adequately describe just how tempting his body is to me. I dare someone to try. "What do I do?" I finally break the silence, and Meg smiles before saying, "We plan a new seduction."

***

The week after my birthday, we finally reach mid-season, which means I get two long weeks to relax and not focus on baseball. It also means that I have seven days to put my plan to seduce Drew into action. He is part of the derby and pro-game, so I know he will be off in New York for the second week of our break. After the girls' night out tonight, I will make my move. The plan Meg and I devised seems like a good combo of our best skills. I will ask Drew for that pizza, and then I will find any reason for us to get to one of our apartments. I even wrote down a list of excuses; privacy, another drink, see how the rich people live. They aren't all the best excuse but better than nothing.

From there, I'll have to let the moment play out. It will either end with us naked or firmly in the friend zone. I'll have an answer either way, and I need an answer. I have been abusing my vibrator boyfriend with images of Drew's naked chest and the feel of his body against mine. The images fuel my body into liquid heat, but my vibrator boyfriend is only curbing the feeling, because I'm still horny as he ll.

This feeling is why I'm wear my sexy red dress that hugs my body and matching red heels for tonight's girls' night. I curl my hair in waves and do my makeup with a smoky eye. I'm dressing up for me and no one else. I want to feel sexy and wild. Looking at myself in the mirror I can't help from wondering what Drew would think about me like this. Would he make a move? Would he wrap his hands in my curls and pull me in for a kiss? Would he put his hands on my body in this tight dress? It would feel amazing; I just know it. I have to physically restrain myself from going to my nightstand. I want to pull out my battery-powered friend to take the edge off this need. I don't have time, as I look at the clock. I agreed to meet the girls at the restaurant in fifteen minutes. I give myself one more look before grabbing my bag and making my way out of my apartment.

I meet the girls, and we have a few drinks and chat about the latest spicy romance we have all agreed to read. We joke that the only men who can get away with saying "good girl" are the ones in books. We joke about how it would sound ridiculous in real life, but it has potential if said at just the right moment. We are having a great girls' night and haven't even started dancing. We are leaving the restaurant when my phone buzzes on the table with a message from Craig Mitchell.

Craig Mitchell

> **What are you doing tonight?**

Annie

Out with Emma and the girls

Why?

Craig Mitchell

Wanted to see if you wanted to go out with us for Luke's last night in town

Annie

Wish I could

Brunch tomorrow?

Craig Mitchell

Yeah, I'll text you tomorrow on a time

You all going anywhere specific?

Annie

We want to dance but haven't settled on a specific spot

Want me to text when we get somewhere?

Craig Mitchell

Let me figure out the plan and I'll text you

I think we are mostly going to bars

Annie

Sounds like a plan

We make it to a dance club in P&L, and we are lucky enough to snag a booth. We sit and chat, laughing over the music for a while and drinking our margaritas. Eventually, the first songs plays, and we get up to dance. Emma tells me to go, saying she'll be fine at the booth. I join the group and get lost in the music. We mostly dance with each other, but guys come and go. We stick together, and if any of the guys get too handsy, we move and shift him away. It is the ultimate female power move at the club: helping out your friends but not having to ruin the fun of dancing.

At one point, I look up and see a familiar face. Dancing with a redhead, I spot Alex Christopher. He makes eye contact with me over her head. He smiles and gives me a once over and a wink before he focuses on grinding with the red-headed woman. I shake my head, because even on my night of freedom, I'm still surrounded by baseball. I hadn't expected to see one of the baseball guys out. I assumed they'd all get out of the area to relax but Alex is known for going out. I can't help wishing that I could make the Griffons player I fantasize about appear. As I dance, I think about him, and I decide to hell with it. I'm going to text him about that pizza date when I go back to the table—I'm over waiting.

Chapter 25: It Was Supposed to be a Night Out With The Guys

-Drew-

July

I'm not sure how we've gotten to mid-July, but the season has been fun. It helps that we are fighting for the top spot in our division. Nothing is as fun as when you're on a winning streak. We get two weeks off, but I only really get one, as I'm going to the Home Run Derby the week of my birthday. Tonight, a few of the guys from the team are joining Craig, Luke, and I to go out in KC. I'd made the mistake of asking Carlos in the dugout to hangout tonight, I thought I was going to give Alex a heart attack. Alex had insisted he knew the best places and he's somehow gotten included in the plans on hitting bars with us. Craig looked into a few spots that have VIP areas so that we can go out and have a good time and have a little space from the fans. The fans in KC are great, so it's more of a precaution than a requirement for the night.

Even though he has been on vacation, Luke has spent a lot of time at my apartment looking over his bar exam study aids. The man has put in it a lot of work and he only has one test separating him from his future. Getting him to come out to Kansas City for the last few weeks and away from only studying is another reason to celebrate. We walk over to the bars in P&L and meet Alex, Carlos, and a few other guys from the team. We have fun joking, drinking, and laughing at each other. Craig and Luke have no problem fitting in with my teammates. They both played baseball, even if they don't now, so they understand what it feels like to play. Luke was an outfielder in high school, and he and Carlos are trading their war stories.

Craig and Alex are debating something about the next place to visit. I hear Alex, "Dude, the club next door gets the best woman. Have you noticed them walking by all night? I've been there a ton it will be fine." Craig shrugs, "Fine, but I'm not responsible if you get photographed." "If they are female fans, I'll take as many photos as they want," Alex laughs and pats Craig on the back.

We make our way to the bar with the pulsing music, and the bouncer nods. He tells us as he holds the door open to keep up with the great season. Luke must feel good because he says, "You got it, man," as he walks in, making Craig and I laugh. We get directed to a table off to the side, outside the main bar and dance floor. I guess this is the perk of playing well; even the clubs around here know us and let us enjoy our well-earned drinks. Alex chugs a drink before announcing "I'll be back" in his best Terminator impression. He heads in the direction of the dance floor and disappears. He must have scoped out the dance floor as we enter ed.

I should be looking too, but I can't get the feel of Annie's body off my mind. We didn't even kiss after she'd launched into my arms at that charity game, but I can't get over the feeling of her arms wrapped around my neck and mine around her back. My mind has been hyper-focused on the moment she'd pulled away, and I should have kissed her. I think about the ride back from her birthday party and the feel of her beside me. The fact that I should have kissed her then, too. I look around this club at all the women dancing and find them all less than compared to her. As I watch the crowd moving and shifting, I see the back of a blonde in a skin-tight red dress. I'm actually surprised I notice her at all with the direction of my thoughts, and then I lose her in the crowd again. I turn my attention back to my friends. We drink and throw around all sorts of crazy sto ries.

Eventually, Alex make it backs to the table with a red-headed woman in tow. He sits down next to me, and she takes a seat on his lap. He leans into her, whispers something, and she laughs. Then he turns back to the group, "Guess who I saw on the dance floor?" A few guys shout out the names of a few of Alex's previous hook-ups, and he puts up his hands to stop the comments. "No, ok, enough." He makes a dramatic pause before announcing to us all. "I saw that sexy as sin reporter." I was only half paying attention to him until that statement. *Wait*, my brain thinks, *who is he talking about?* "Who?" I question. "Oh, I guess I could have said your ex. That would be easier to identify her. I'll remember that for next time." He laughs at himself. My brain tries to catch up. I haven't drank that much, but did he just say that Annie was here? Then an image flashes across my brain of the blonde in the red dress from earlier. No wonder I noticed her—I fucking should have known it was Annie.

I try to sit for a few minutes after Alex's comment, but it's no use. I know Annie is here, and my brain and body refuse to sit here any longer. I stand up, and Luke smirks at me. "Where are you going?" Before I can make up an excuse, Craig cuts in. "One guess." Luke says way too loudly, "He's going to go find Annie, isn't he?" Craig shouts back just as loud, "Ding ding ding, we have a winner." I walk away and flip them the bird. I can make out their laughter over the pounding of the music. Or is that the pounding of my own heart? I'm not even sure. I walk to the dance floor, and a few women try to get my attention, but I don't stop for any of them. There is only one woman that I need to find. I'm worrying that she's left or gone to another place when I see red.

Her back is to me again, but I know it's her. This close, I can't believe I didn't figure it out earlier. She's in her favorite color. The dress looks like it's painted on her body; it's so tight, it hugs her ass to perfection. I'm moving before I think about it. I slide my body against her backside, and she freezes before turning to look at me. I see her smile and mouth move, but I can't hear her over the music.

So, I bend my ear to her lips. "What took you so long?" I lean back and look at her smiling face. I lean down and say next to her ear, "I finally decided to come after what I wanted."

We don't speak again for a few songs; we just grind our bodies against each other. I get this weird feeling like I've been here before. I realize it's because this reminds me of prom. We're just older and not together. This time, Annie doesn't have a plan to seduce me at the end of the night. I think maybe it's my turn to seduce her, to get her back, because I don't want to keep playing this game. I don't want to learn she's gone out with that reporter again. It should be us; we are the story, the headline, the trending topic, and I'm determined to give us our happy ending. I lean down and say into her ear. "You ready to get out of here, Angel?" She turns in my arms and wraps her arms around my neck. She pulls me into an earth-shattering kiss, and I go willingly like a man being led to water. I'm not sure how long we make out in the middle of the dance floor. I'm only focused on the feel of her lips against mine and our intertwined tongues.

Eventually, we break apart, and I tuck a piece of hair behind her ear. "Let me grab my bag." She makes to leave, and I wrap my hand in hers, and nothing in the last year has felt more right. She pulls me along to get her bag and waves goodbye to her friends. I only recognize her producer as I'm led away as quickly as we arrived. She continues leading me out the door and into the night. I remember this feeling from all those years ago: I'd follow this woman anywhere.

Chapter 26: About Time

-Annie-

July

I am dancing with one of Emma's friends, Cassie, when I feel a strong body against my back. I don't know how I know, but I know that it's not just any guy making a move, that this body belongs to him; to Drew. He startled me, and my body stopped moving to the music. I have to confirm my thoughts, and I look over my shoulder. "I knew it was you," I say into the loud club, but he shakes his head like he can't hear me. He bends his head down to place his ear closer to my mouth. I want to kiss that spot where his ear and jaw meet, but I hold back the urge. "What took you so long?" He leans back and looks at me. His gaze turns heated before he bends down and, with his lips against my ear, says, "I finally decided to come after what I want." It sends a shiver down my spine. I like that he wants me.

I turn my face away, knowing my skin is heated and not just from the dancing. I'm turned on by his words, because I want him, too. I try to shut off my brain again and enjoy dancing. Enjoy the feel of his body moving against mine. It's intoxicating, my brain is going a million wonderful directions, and I've never been more glad that I've only had one drink. I'm clear-headed enough to know that this is all Drew. It's an intoxicating combination of lust, want, of need, of right, of butterflies that don't just flicker inside me, they soar. He's the only boy—correction, only *man* to affect me like this. It's like my body is hardwired to respond to his. I'm not sure how long we've been dancing when I feel him move and his mouth is against my ear, "You ready to get out of here, Angel?" *Yes, I'm ready to get out of here with him*, I think. I spin to face him, but facing him now, I don't find words because all I want to do is kiss this man. It's been building inside of me for months. I want to know if this is all in my head or if we still have that spark.

I wrap my arms around his neck, pulling him into an all-consuming kiss. I feel his strong arms wrap around me and fuse us even tighter together, leaving no gaps between us. I suck on his bottom lip before changing the angle, and then he does the same, but gives my bottom lip a little scrape with his teeth before releasing it. I can feel how turned on I am, and if we don't leave this club soon, I'm going to be having sex in the bathroom. I'd much rather go two blocks down the street and have the opportunity to get naked completely with this man. I want to see Drew naked and under me or over me. I don't care what position, I just want him naked. So, as hard as it is, I slow down the kiss and pull back from him. Even in the dark strobe lights of the club, I can see my lust reflected at me. Before I can move, he reaches out and gently tucks my hair behind my ear. *It's time to go*, I think, then shout, "Let me grab my bag." I step out of his arms, grab his hand, and head in the direction of the booth. We weave our way to the table, and I grab my bag and wave goodbye to Emma and the rest of the girls. Emma gives me a smirk and a wink as she waves me goodbye.

The July night isn't exactly cool against my skin, but it's not as hot as the club has been. It feels refreshing to be outside. Our hands are still wrapped together as we walk towards our apartment building. At the red light, we have to wait to cross. Drew pulls out his phone and is typing a message. I'm trying not to be nosy, but who the hell is he texting right now? All I can think about is the fact that I want this hot as hell guy next to me naked. I want him very, very naked. He looks up from the phone and holds it up. "Sorry, I figured I should let the guys know I left." I shake my head in agreement: yeah, that makes sense. He had come with the guys, and they would probably wonder where he had disappeared. "I told them I'm not coming home tonight," he says as the light changes, and we start to cross the street. I guess that answers the question of 'his place or mine.' I can see the front doors of our apartment building in the distance. "It's good that I live within walking distance," I say sarcastically, causing him to laugh.

A thought crosses my mind; I don't think I have condoms at my place. I was so determined to be man-free, I hadn't purchased any since moving to KC. "Drew, the only problem with my place is that I don't have condoms." He doesn't overreact. "Good thing we can run up to my apartment first." Before I think too hard about it, I say what I'm thinking. "I'm on the pill. I haven't been with anyone since LA. I've been tested since then with no concerns." I feel the blush run over my body. I'm not even sure why I said it. I've always made a guy use a condom even after I went on birth control, but I don't want to have to wait or get interrupted if we go back to his place. I want him, and I want him now.

Before I realize what is happening, I feel the brick against my back and Drew's body pressing into my front. He has both hands on the side of my face, and he's all I can see. "Annie Marie Campbell, are you telling me we don't have to use a condom? Because I haven't been with anyone since Arizona. I got a clean bill of health when I did my physical back at Spring Training." I nod yes, and he says, "Words, Angel." "Yes, Drew, we don't need a condom. I just want you now." As the words leave my lips, his lips fuse with mine. He presses against me—I can feel his hard length against my stomach, and I know he's turned on.

He breaks the kiss and looks down at my shoes. "Can you run in those shoes, or do I need to carry you?" "Don't you dare carry me into that building, Drew Joseph." He laughs, and before I can react, I'm being lifted over Drew's strong shoulder. "Someone is going to see up my dress," I say, and I feel him chuckle

155

before I feel his arm wrap around the place where the skirt meets my legs. Drew starts to walk, almost jog, the rest of the way to the apartment building. He sets me back on my feet at the doors, before I'm even fully stable, he takes my hand and pulls me along as he opens the doors to the building. He waves to the security guy as we approach the elevator, and he presses the up arrow.

The elevator opens quickly, and he is already hitting ten before I can say my floor number. I must look confused because he breaks the silence as the doors start to close. "I remember from when we had tacos that first time." I'm impressed with him remembering. He smiles and moves me until my back is against the elevator wall. "Angel, when it comes to you, I remember everything." He is about to close the distance between us when the elevator stops. The display on the elevator reads ten, and I have no idea how the elevator got here so quickly.

He steps back from pinning me against the side of the elevator. I grab his hand, pulling him towards my apartment. I get us to my unit and have to dig in my bag for the keys. Drew is kissing the side of my neck, and I forget what I'm doing. I feel his breath as he says, "Angel, I think you have to turn the key to unlock the door." He returns his attention to my exposed skin. I don't answer. I try to focus on making my brain move my hands. I feel the lock click, and I open the door. I spin in Drew's arms and pull his mouth back to my own as I take backwards steps into my apartment, pulling him along with me.

I hear my door shut, but I'm too focused on the feel of Drew's mouth and his hands running over me. I run one hand over his ripped body but it's not enough. I'm dropping my keys and purse on the floor, it's too far away to the table or kitchen counter, and I need my hands on this man. My hands find his shirt's hem, and I know what I want. I break the kiss to pull it up his body, and he helps me remove it. I throw it in the direction of my living room. I get the quickest glimpse of Drew's chest before his hands are on my cheeks, pulling me back into a kiss. My lips are going to be so bruised after this night. I suck on his full bottom lip, and he groans. I only get a moment to relish getting him groaning, as I feel myself being lifted, and I wrap my legs around his waist while my body hits the back of my door.

His lips leave mine, and I can't help the whimper of frustration that leaves my lips or the moan that follows when he kisses down my jaw. His kisses continue down my neck to that spot that drives me crazy. "I need you, Annie," he says against my skin, and I hear my husky voice reply, "Then take me." I feel his hands on my ass move to the hem of my dress and push up the material. I hear the sound of ripping fabric, and I don't even care as I feel the thong fall from my body. I only care that I want him this bad and I need him too. My mind and body want more, need more; I need Drew inside me. I hear the sound of a zipper only a moment before I feel the skin of his dick against my clit. He drags his dick down me. I stop breathing; every ounce of my body is focused on this moment, the feel of him stretching my body as he enters me with a hard thrust. I moan loudly at the overwhelming sensation.

He's bigger than I remember, and he fills me completely. It must be feeling good for him, too, because he says loudly, "Fuck, Annie, you're so fucking wet." I should blush, but I don't have it in me to focus on anything but him. He pumps in and out of me a little harder each time. I can hear the sound of my body slamming against the door, of our heavy breathing, of our moans. The sounds turn my blood hotter, and I want more. I wish my breasts weren't pinned in this dress. I want to feel his skin against mine, but I know we have more time.

This is just the first time, and this time will be fast, hard, and quick because it's been building, and we both need to find release. I wrap my fingers around the back of Drew's longer hair before pulling his mouth to mine. The kiss is hard and bruising, and our tongues mirror what our bodies are doing, sliding in and out of each other in hard, quick passes. Before I know it, my body is tensing, and the pulses of pleasure build to a breaking point. I know I'm on the brink of a n orgasm.

Drew must feel it too, because he thrusts harder, faster, deeper until I scream, and I can hear the sounds echo in my apartment. Drew keeps thrusting and says in a dazed groan, "Annie." I know he is warning me that he's about to cum. I can read it on his face and the haze of pure lust that drives him. I hold him tighter and say, "Don't stop." He doesn't stop: he thrusts harder until he growls my name again, and I feel him release inside me. He pins me more to the door as he climaxes. I don't feel claustrophobic or smushed. I feel consumed, and I only want him to give me more.

Chapter 27: Finally

-Drew-

July

From the moment Annie said we didn't have to use a condom and that she wanted me, I've been a man on a very specific mission. Our apartment building seems too far away, but I know I can't fuck her against the side of the building. I look down at her shoes as I break the kiss and ask her if she can run in them. My mind makes the decision for me, as I hear her say, "Don't you dare carry me into that building, Drew Joseph." I love that she knows me so well, and I laugh as I pick her up and throw her over my shoulder. Annie doesn't fight me but says with laugher, "Someone is going to see up my dress." I make sure to have my arm right at the edge of her very nice ass and the bottom of her skin-tight red dress.

As I jog us the last block to the building, I imagine I will get to peel this dress from her skin. I have to take a deep breath to help myself calm down; my dick is already rock hard. I don't need to cum in my pants thinking about a naked Annie and all the things I'm going to do with her. I set her down at the front of the building, and all I want to do is feel her body against me, but I know we need to get upstairs, inside her apartment door, before we can get undressed. I take her hand and race through the lobby to the elevator. I hit the number ten button on the elevator door and look over at her. I can't stop looking at this sexy w oman.

She has a confused look though, and I realize I hit her floor number without asking for it. "I remember from when we had tacos that first time." It's my way of telling her, "Yes, I've wanted you this bad since you stepped back into my life." She smiles. "Color me impressed, Dimples." I smile back at her and continue my confession. "Angel, when it comes to you, I remember everything." She looks shocked by my honesty, and I look forward to continuing to shock her. I will remind us both that we know each other and that it may have been six long years, but nothing has changed. I know her, and she knows me, and this fire is j ust reigniting.

I want to kiss her because I need to taste her again, but the elevator dings and the doors open to the tenth floor. Annie grabs my hand and pulls me into the hallway. We walk quickly to a door that must be hers. Annie is digging in her bag, and the column of her neck calls to me. I lean down to kiss my way down her skin. I've missed her skin. I plan to kiss and touch every inch of her body. At some point, I realize that Annie's stopped working on her door. She is leaning her body into mine, enjoying my lips on her neck. I hover just over her skin. "Angel, I think you have to turn the key to unlock the door." My lips are back on her neck, licking over her warm skin. I hear the lock click, and then Annie spins in my arms. Her mouth is on mine, and her hands are gripping my shirt and pulling me into her apartment. I kick the bottom of her door to shut it, which makes a loud bang behind us.

I feel Annie's hands find the hem of my shirt. Her fingers scrape along my abs as she moves the material up my chest. I break the kiss, helping her get it over my head before the shirt disappears in a blur behind us. I grab her face and pull her back into a hard kiss. I can't get enough of her and want to make it to a bed, but there doesn't seem to be enough time to figure out where her bedroom is. I make a subconscious decision and lift her with my hands under her thighs and ass. I spin us and pin her hard against the door. Annie must agree with my move because she wraps her long, tan legs around me and moans into our kiss. I need her now, and I can't wait. I break my lips away from her body. "I need you, Annie." Her reply is the sexiest thing I've ever heard. *Oh, Angel, I'm going to take you so many ways before this night is over,* I think.

I slide my hands up and under the material of her dress, over her bare ass, and I find the side of her thong. I pull it until I feel the material break free from her body. I use one hand to undo my pants, slide the zipper down, and pull my boxers and pants down enough for my dick to spring free. When the head of my dick is against her clit, I moan. I slide it down her pussy, and she's so fucking wet already. I know I won't be able to take it slow or be gentle. When the head of my dick finds her pussy, I don't ease in; I thrust hard into her, and we both groan at the movement.

I don't slow my pace, and she doesn't ask me to. If anything, her body is egging me on, meeting each of my thrusts, by arching into me. The words escape me: "Fuck, Annie, you're so fucking wet." She must like them because she moans, "Dreeewww." She wraps her fingers in my hair and pulls it to bring our mouths back together. I can feel her body start to tremble around my dick and in my arms. I feel how close she is, and I move faster and harder. I push her over the edge as she lets out a half-moan, half-scream. Her once tense body relaxes, but she still clings to me as I pound into her. I'm on the edge of my own climax. I groan her name, and she tells me, "Don't stop." I don't stop, pounding harder into her until I cum inside her, and it's the best fucking feeling I've ever experienced.

I must be squishing her, I realize as I come back into my body. I've pinned her against the door with my whole body weight. I pull back, and she unwraps her legs from around me. Her heels hit the floor, and her legs shake as she leans against the door. We look at each other, both wearing big smiles. "You have a very sturdy door." Annie laughs at my observation. "It appears to pass the test;

I am curious about how sturdy my bed is?" Annie smirks at me to gauge my reaction. I give her a gentle kiss and step back from her. "Lead the way, Angel." She turns, giving me her back but stops.

"Unzip my dress first, Dimples." I like this confident Annie, "Yes, ma'am" I kiss her neck. I do as she requested and unzip her sexy red dress. She slips the material down her body. The material is on the floor, and she kicks it away before turning. She is completely naked, minus her heels. Her nipples are peaked and asking me to suck on them. Before I can touch her, she walks through her living room, going down a hallway. I hear her say across the dark apartment. "Lock the door and come join me." I do as I'm told, and I hit the lock on the door. I'm out of my shoes, pants, and boxers in lightning speed. I'm walking naked down the hallway to find where Annie disappeared. My dick is already hard again, ready for round two.

I enter her bedroom, and she isn't there. Where the hell did, she disappear to? I listen and hear the water in the bathroom. Understandably, she may need a minute. I mean, I did just cum inside her. I sit down on her bed, leaning against the headboard. She opens the door, and the room's light makes her silhouette more striking. Looking at her like this, I realize again that I haven't tasted her nipples or even held her boobs. I need to feel them in my hands. She walks over to me with her bare feet. I can admit the heels had been sexy, but this is my Annie now. Sexy without even trying. She straddles my hips, pinning my dick against her pussy. I try to move, and she stops me. "I want to see how you've changed." S he whispers between us.

Her hands slide up my stomach, tracking each muscle before running, over my chest. Her hands travel across my collarbones, shoulders, and biceps to my forearms. She guides my hands to her hips just above her ass. I make to move, but she shakes her head. She leans into my chest, and her lips touch my shoulder. She traces her tongue across my shoulder to my neck, then crosses my jaw to repeat the pattern on the other side of my body. She is making my blood boil with need. I feel my dick twitch against her pussy. I grip my fingers into her hips. She continues her review of my body, tracing her lips and tongue up my neck and then down my chest. She starts to slide her body down my chest and moves her pussy off my dick. I can read her thoughts; she is headed to taste my dick, and I want it, but that can wait. I stop her because I haven't gotten to explore her body either, and it's my turn. "Later, Angel. I want my turn to see what's changed."

Chapter 28: What's Changed

-Annie-

July

Walking naked back to my room, I realize that I need to clean up from our sex against the door. I head into the bathroom and freshen myself up. When I'm done, I look into the mirror, getting the weirdest feeling of déjà vu, like I've been here before. It's like during the last six years apart, my body hasn't known this level of satisfaction. Being honest with myself, sex with Drew is so much more than it had been with either of my exes. I hear a noise on the other side of the door, pulling me from my train of thought. I give myself one more glance in the mirror before opening the door.

I don't make it far, because there is a very naked Drew in my bed, and his body is glorious. This version of Drew is larger, each muscle defined and toned. As I walk towards him, I mentally thank Craig for all his efforts in training Drew. Drew is all ripped muscles, from his toned torso to his muscled thighs stretched over my bed. If I hadn't already touched him, I'd think he was an image from my fantasies.

I waste no time before I straddle his hips, feeling his dick settle between my legs. As much as I want to feel him inside me again, I know that I want to explore him. When he makes to move, I hear my words in the silent room. I don't wait for his agreement; I start touching him. His hands are on my thighs as I relearn his body. I run my hands up his stomach over the ridges of each of his abs before moving up his chest and over his shoulders. I let my hands travel back down his strong arms to his forearms. I move his hands to my hips. He makes to move, and I stop him with a shake of my head. I lean in and kiss his shoulder before I follow the line of his collarbone and traps. I enjoy running my tongue over it now, but I love hearing Drew's groans and having his hands tighten on my hips. I continue my path, crossing his neck and jaw.

I skip over his lips—as tempting as they are, they will distract me. I repeat my actions until I've reached his other shoulder. I make my way back to his neck and kiss my way down his sternum. I start to slide my body down so I can taste my way to his dick, but Drew stops me by holding my hips in place. I look up at him, and he gives me that dimple and, in a gravelly voice, takes control. "Later, Angel. I want my turn to see what's changed." I smile as I egg him on, "I'm going to hold you to that."

His hands have more calluses than I remember as they touch me. They are rough against my skin, and I like the feel of them on my skin. He runs them up my stomach but skips my breast. I moan in frustration, but he doesn't change course. He continues to trail his hands over my collarbone, across my shoulders, and down my arms, he grazes my skin with his hands back up the same path, but this time down my sternum, back to my stomach: yet again avoiding the place where I want to feel him. I let out a little frustrated "Drew." It makes him chuckle, and in that deep voice, he says against my neck, "Angel, is there somewhere I need to explore?"

He doesn't wait for my answer; his hands move up my breast and finally touch my nipples. I let out a satisfied moan at the contact. He wraps his rough hands around them, giving them both a squeeze, sending arousal straight to my clit. In the half light, I watch as his mouth descends on my nipple. I grab his forearm in response, not sure if I'm trying to push him away or fuse him to my breast. The pleasure is too much and yet perfect. He breaks the hold on my nipple with a loud pop before moving to the other side, repeating the sweet torture. I'm grinding my hips against his dick, and I get the most fantastic idea. I grind myself up until the head is at my core. I change the angle of my hips, causing his dick to slide into my body. My groan is overwhelmed by the sound of Drew's groan against my nipple. "Well fucking played, Angel."

I grind myself up and down his hard dick. He stopped sucking on my nipple to watch me ride him. His hands are back on my hips, helping me grind down harder on him. "Annie, I could watch my dick disappear into you for the rest of my life." The confession falls from his lips as I slide back down him. It causes the burning need inside me to be interrupted by the little butterflies soaring through my body. His words drive me to an earth-shattering rhythm as I grind on top of him. Drew moves his hand from my left hip, dragging it down to rub my clit, and it's too much. I arch into his touch, moaning.

My body is trembling with the building orgasm I'm chasing. As if Drew can read my mind, he wraps his arms around me, holding me flush against his chest. He takes over, driving his hips into me in quick, fast, hard strokes. His new pace is everything I needed, and I break apart in his arms. I can still hear the fading sound of his name from my lips. He barely slows down his thrusts before flipping me to my back. He wears his heart-breaking smile, that dimple etched into his strong face. I pull him down into a kiss, wrap my legs around his back. Our lips turn to soft kisses before he pulls back and speaks against my lips. "I've missed watching you orgasm. Nothing compares to it, absolutely nothing, Angel."

Chapter 29: All Night

-Drew-

July

Watching Annie ride my dick is fucking hot. She is so fucking beautiful; watching the lust play over her face is something that will never get old. At one point, I actually say my thoughts out loud but I'm not entirely sure. I'm trying to focus on not coming again as she sets an amazing pace. Her bounces up and down my cock feels so good. I move my hand from her hip to her clit, rubbing the little nub, earning me a moan from her lips and an arch of her body. She is everything. Watching her ride me, I realize there is no way I will let her go again. She's mine, and I'm hers. No other man will get the chance to see her like this again.

I notice her leg is trembling as she moves, and I know she is close to another orgasm. I wrap my arms around her and take over the movement. I drive my hips and dick hard and fast into her pussy. She lets me take over, and I know the moment her orgasm overcomes her. "DRRREEEWWW" is screamed into the room. I don't slow my thrusts, but I do flip us over so I can watch her reaction. She pulls me into a kiss that starts hard but turns gentle. This kiss speaks unspoken words, of feelings we once shared, that maybe wouldn't be so hard to find again. As the kiss ends, I say part of what I'm thinking against her lips.

During our kiss, I'd slowed down my thrusts. I watch her face, enjoying her expression as my dick slides in and out of her tight pussy. I can see her pleasure building again slowly. She runs her fingers through my hair and says, almost too quietly to hear, "I've missed you." I feel the same, and I know that she doesn't mean the sex: she means me, she means us. "Let's not miss each other anymore," I tell her and mean it. I push harder and faster into her body. I feel my balls tighten; my climax is so close. Annie is arching into each thrust, meeting every st roke.

I want to hold out to give her another orgasm, so I try. I rub my fingers over her clit, causing her to moan. She is getting close, but I am on the edge. I groan her name, and her words are the thing that cause me to fall. "Cum, Drew, please finish it." I pound into her body with a hard, deep thrust. I cum so hard as I feel her pussy squeeze and tighten around me. I feel pretty confident that I was able to get one more orgasm for my Annie. I don't pull out of her right way enjoying the feeling of her pussy spasming around my dick feels too good. I do roll us to have her back on top of me. "I know I need to clean up, but I'm not sure my legs will work." She sounds good post-sex, her voice sexy and satisfied. I help her slide off my dick and my body, and when she moves to the bathroom, I follow her. I turn the sink to warm water, and she hands me a washcloth. I take it, but I pick her up and place her on the counter before she can turn away. "Let me." She doesn't say anything, but when I open her legs, she doesn't fight me when I use the warm cloth to clean up her pussy.

I clean myself after and then head back into the bedroom first to give her a few minutes. When she comes back into the room, I lift the covers. She slides against my side with her head on my chest. We are both tired, and I feel her yawn against my chest. "Sleep, Annie. I'll be here in the morning." She replies in her sleepy voice, "Promise?" "Promise, Angel." She falls asleep quickly against me, and I kiss the top of her head. I take longer to fall asleep, trying to figure out how to turn this moment back into an *us*, back to those three little words.

***

The light from the window wakes me up. My first thought is, *where are the blackout curtains?* Then I remember I am not in my room, but in Annie's. I move, but I'm not met with warm skin, just empty cold sheets. I open my eyes, looking around Annie's room. She's kept it simple: the bed, one nightstand, and a dresser on the wall. I can't believe she's up before me. In all of our teenage sleepovers, I'd always wake up first. I notice the shower running from her bathroom. I think, *I could use a shower.* I make my way to the closed door, trying to open it quietly. I'm greeted with Annie's wet body in her glass shower. She's in profile, and it's mesmerizing, watching the water cascade down her beautiful body. She has her eyes closed, washing her hair.

I only have seconds to get to that shower before she notices me. I walk as quietly as I can for my size. She opens her eyes as I open the shower door. Her shocked expression transforms into a smile. It makes my heart race; seeing her smile directly at me like this; giving me hope. My plans from last night could happen... Maybe there could be an us again. "Good morning, Angel. It was no fun waking up to an empty bed." Her eyes widen at my words. "Drew, you looked so peaceful. I thought I'd get in a shower after all of our activities last night." She looks worried about my response. I want to reassure her that I'm in this, she's going to have to tell me she doesn't want me to get me to leave. "Angel, I'm totally ok with morning shower sex, you don't have to convince me." Annie looks down at my dick with a look of satisfaction crossing her face. I can't help the slight flex of that muscle. "Why are you still on that side of the shower, then, Dimples?" Annie asks and I can tell I've shifted the mood. *Why indeed*, I think before I step into the warm water and against her wet skin.

Chapter 30: The Morning After

-Annie-

July

I wake up next to a warm body, and not just any warm body. Drew's warm, very naked body. All of last night flashes through my mind. I don't regret a single second or sore muscle today. My body has that pleasant ache of being well-used. What's crazy is that I still want more of him. Why did I try so hard to prevent this from happening, to avoid the chemistry we have? I'd tried to distract myself with Nick, which made me feel guilty for not feeling a spark with him. This is why: Drew was why. Now, in the light of morning, I wonder what will happen next. Is there more, or is this it—some very, very good, mind-blowing sex? Being honest with myself, I want more than just sex with Drew. I want a second, grown-up ch ance with him.

The real question is, does he? Will he want more, or was last night all he needed? I'm not going back to sleep with these thoughts and feelings swirling. I make small movements to get my body off of Drew's without waking him. I tiptoe to the bathroom, then quietly open and shut the door. I look at myself in the mirror. I have the look of a woman who has been well loved. My lips are swollen, my hair is messy, and I look 100% happy. I move to the shower, turning on the

water to the temp I like before stepping in, and it feels good against my sensitive sk
in.

I am washing my hair and rinsing out the shampoo when I hear the door on the
shower squeak. I open my eyes and see Drew's dark blue eyes taking me in. He
brings up waking up alone. I hadn't thought of that when I came to shower. I
explain my reason for leaving him alone in my bed. My answer brings a smile
to his face. That dimple is present, and it drives me crazy as always. He makes
a wicked gleam to his eye as he brings up shower sex. I can't help thinking 'yes,
please' as I look over his body, my gaze resting on this hard dick, and it twitches.
I can't help asking why he's still on the wrong side of the shower.

Drew's body is against mine in seconds, his lips and mine joining in a kiss that is
a mix of hard, desperate ones and gentle ones that hint at the fact that we don't
need to rush. My hands start on his chest, sliding down his now-wet body, across
his slick abs. *I'm never going to get over these abs,* I think. I move my hand down
to that sexy V cut into his skin until my fingers wrap around him. He groans
against my temple, which drives my actions. I move my hand up and down his
shaft. "Angel" is groaned from Drew's lips, and I know I want to make him do
it again.

I make my next move, pushing him until his back is against the wall of my
shower. I get on my knees before slipping his dick into my mouth. I've surprised
Drew, because he lets out a loud, "Fuck, Annie." His hands are in my hair,
directing me to what he wants. He doesn't take it easy on me, and I don't want
him to. He thrusts into my mouth, and I gag, but I don't stop him. "Good girl.
Your mouth looks so good around my dick, Angel." His words turn me on more.
I'll have to share with the girls that I experience a moment with the 'good girl'
comment, and it does, in fact, turn me on more to hear him say it. I use my hands
to slide around the base of his shaft. I pump them up and down as he thrusts
in my mouth. I am enjoying sucking on his dick, but he surprises me by pulling
out of my mouth. "Enough of that, Angel, my turn."

He moves so quickly, I can't register the change. He grabs my arms, pulling me up and spinning me until I'm the one with my back against the shower wall. My right leg is lifted over his shoulder before I can blink. He sucks my clit into his mouth, and I moan loudly into the bathroom: "DDRREWW." It echoes in the small room. This feels beyond amazing: I get lost in the slide of his tongue, the sucking of my clit. I feel a building climax, and I want more, more, more. He's about to use his fingers, and I hear my voice, "No." He looks up from between my legs, and it's a fucking hot thing to see. "I don't want your fingers, I want you." I watch the smile appear across his handsome face. "I think that can be arranged, Angel." He sets my leg down and stands up. I think he is going to lift me, but I'm spun around, and my breasts are pressed against the shower wall. He slides his dick down the seam of my butt to my core and then slides into to me to the hilt.

"FUUUUCKK" comes out of my mouth, it's so good. I can hear the sound of our slapping wet skin as Drew drives into me. The sound is an added element to drive my passion hotter, and my climax is breaking over me. I scream his name into the bathroom. "I'm making it my goal to make you scream my name like that daily." He drives harder into me for a few more strokes before my name leaves his mouth and he pins me against the wall. Against my ear, I hear him say so quietly, "Annie, my Annie." I mentally agree. *Yes, I'm all yours.*

We begin an actual shower, washing each other with the soap. Drew wraps me in my towel from the rack, and I get him one from under my sink. Drew's stomach growls, and I break our post-sex silence. "It sounds like you are hungry, but I think we should talk about last night before seeing if the guys still want to do brunch." Drew looks at me, confused. "What brunch?" "Craig was going to get with you all about brunch before Luke heads back to Texas." Drew shrugs, "I don't think we got to that conversation before I disappeared to find you on the dance floor. Do you have a granola bar?" he asks. I have no idea if I have a granola bar, but I at least point him the direction of the kitchen.

"I am not sure, but I think I may have some protein bars. Help yourself to whatever you want." He kisses me before walking naked in the direction of the kitchen. I get dressed in a pair of leggings and a T-shirt before joining him. My living room looks like a disaster with all our discarded clothes, but I'm quickly distracted by Drew. He is only dressed in his boxers when I enter the open space, and it's something I could get used to seeing. He is eating a protein bar. He offers me a bite, and I take it because I'm starving. He nods over at the wall that has his mom's painting. "I want to try for that. Do you think it's possible?" The butterflies come to life in my stomach, and I think to myself, *God, I hope so.*

Chapter 31: Conversations

-Drew-

July

Our shower sex was confirmation that last night wasn't a one-time thing for either of us. I'll have to send Alex a thank-you card for getting us to that dance club and telling me she was there. Never thought I'd be thankful for his man-whore ways until now. I leave Annie to get dressed, trying to find food before my body starts eating itself. I have been working out very hard with Annie. I plan to refuel before returning to our new workout session. I may have to tell Craig I've found an alternative to the gym for the next few weeks... or years. I slip on my boxers before opening the pantry door. I see all sorts of snacks and unhealthy treats that Craig will lose his mind if I grab.

I settle on the box of chocolate peanut butter protein bars. I am eating my first bite when Annie appears in leggings and a Norman shirt. Her damp hair is pulled over her shoulder, and her face is makeup-free. She looks even hotter to me like this, with her freckles on full display, than she did last night, all dolled up. I hold out the open bar, and she leans in, taking a big bite. We are standing in the open living room and kitchen when I notice the painting on the wall. I don't mean to say it out loud; I'd been looking at us and thinking: *I'd like her to look at me like there couldn't be anybody else.* I feel my lips moving and the words leaving my mouth. "I want to try for that. Do you think it's possible?"

She looks at the painting of us on the wall. She doesn't speak immediately, but I'm not concerned, because I'm looking at her now. I feel the moment she lets herself think about us, about what it felt like to love each other, about the possibility of having it again. Eventually, she turns and looks at me. "I hope so. I want to try to get back to that. If I'm being honest, I don't think it will take me long to feel about you like I did then." She takes a deep breath before continuing. "I know that I'm going to have to earn your trust. After all, I'm the one who left. Do you think you can get over that?" She looks concerned about my answer to her question.

I have to fight my desire to kiss her because we need to talk right now. We need these words to get to a real second chance. "Annie, I forgave you a long time ago. All my remaining resentment was burned off when we had that pretend, not-so-pretend fight. I've spent months wanting my Annie back. I have only one thing I need." Annie doesn't hesitate, "Name it, Drew." I cup my hand on her cheek before laying out my cards. "Promise me that if I have a bad game, series or season, you aren't going to leave. Promise you won't start to blame our relationship for my bad play. I'm human, I will have off games." She doesn't make me wait; she places her hand on my chest over my heart. "I promise not to run or to leave you because of our careers. I promise, Drew." She leans up on her tiptoes and kisses me. I pull her closer, knowing she's all in with me and it's all I need.

I'm unsure how long we make out, but I place my forehead on hers when we break apart. "So, what now? I would love to take you back to bed, but I think the mature answer is that I should get dressed. We give our friend a send-off brunch before he heads out. But after brunch, Annie, plan on being naked for hours. I think we have years of make-up sex to catch up on." She doesn't look upset by my statement or idea. "Mmm, I hear that make-up sex is the best. I think I have a *lottt* of making up to do." She jokes and I can't help laughing. We separate to

175

get ready to leave her apartment. Annie grabs her purse and sneakers. I find all my discarded clothes and get dressed. I reach out my hand to her, and she slips her fingers between mine as we leave the apartment.

The lights are still off when we enter my apartment. I turn on the kitchen light to give the space some light. "FUCK" comes from the couch in the living room. I switch them off quickly as Annie chuckles. "Sorry, Luke." He sits up on his bed on the couch. "Luke, rough night?" Annie laughs from my side. Luke looks between us. "Mom and Dad are back together. Does this mean we can be a family again?" Luke quips from the couch. "I see the hangover hasn't broken your ability to be sarcastic," I laugh. "What am I if not my humor?" Luke asks as he stretches himself awake. "I am going to miss having to avoid you two, and all the make-up sex, but I'm ready to have my bed back." He laughs as he stands up

"You should have taken my room." I tell him, I had text him I wasn't coming home. "I really should have. Maybe you should get a house with a guest room. Then, when I visit, I'll have a Luke suite," he says before heading in the direction of Craig's room. "Rise and shine, buttercup." He bangs on the door until grumbles are heard from Craig's room. "Why are you so loud?" Craig's voice comes from the door as Luke heads in. I can hear them bickering. "I swear, you can't take them anywhere," I say to Annie as I pull her toward my room.

"Where are we going?" she says from behind me. "My room—you should get adjusted to the space. We will be spending a lot of time locked behind this door." I give her a smile over my shoulder. "Sounds like a plan as long as clothing is optional." Annie sounds so cute as she makes her amazing suggestion. "Oh, Angel, clothing is very, very optional. Unless you want to pull out that sexy red lingerie from all those years ago, then that is mandatory." She looks surprised that I brought up the lingerie, but how could I forget. "Oh, you remember that outfit?" she asks, blushing. "Oh, Angel, I'll never forget it. I have the photographic proof to help me remember all the details." I need to stop talking about a lingerie-clad Annie. I feel myself getting hard, and if I keep thinking about her in lingerie, we will not make brunch. "I can't believe you still have that picture." She sounds shocked.

I start to undress, and her eyes go all big and lusty, watching me. "Angel, stop looking at me like that. I can't be held accountable if you don't stop." I walk into my closet. "You have been like my personal pinup girl. The photo is part of my Annie Collection." She walks to the door frame and leans against it. "This should feel creepy, but I'm flattered that you still have them." Annie has a smile on her face, so I take it she's not mad, yet I feel like I owe her an explanation on why I never deleted the photo. "Annie, I kept the picture because I just couldn't delete it, I never wanted anyone like I've always wanted you. Even though we ended, it was my way of never being without you. I-" Annie interrupts me by launching herself at me. I catch her and we hug; this moment isn't about lust or passion, its more. Annie whispers, "thank you for not letting me go." I kiss her temple because I think if I try to speak now I'll tell her I love her and its too much.

Eventually, we release each other and I throw on a T-shirt and joggers as she goes back to watching me dress. Fully dressed, I walk over to her, placing my hands on either side of her face. "So, what's part of this so-called collection?" Annie asks me the spark of mischief in her eyes. "Angel, it's a collection of all my time with you. I have the original sexy picture of you in a bikini, you in my jersey in high school, you in nothing but my Arizona jersey, and my favorite, you as my birthday present. It also has photos of us together from homecoming to prom to the draft. I couldn't delete any of the moments with you." She smiles. "How about we add to those pictures and make new memories?" Annie asks looking both happy and concerned. "I'm going to hold you to that, Angel. I want my Annie Collection to be all my phone has." She puts her hand on my chest. "Deal, but I need some pictures of you with these abs, I thought you were toned in high school. I had no idea these were even possible." Why is her talking about my abs making me want to kiss her? Honestly, it's the look on her face as she talks about my abs that has me distracted. I lean in and kiss her and my Angel kisses me back gripping my shirt in the process. I'm about to take it to the next level when the d oor swings open.

"OOOOHHH, GRRRROOOSSSS. Daddy is kissing MOMMMMMYYYY." Luke dramatically covers his eyes. Craig leans in and smacks him in the head. "VOLUME CONTROL, asshole. Some of us have a hangover." Annie interjects "I love you guys," with a smile on her face. My heart races hearing her say those three little words. I know she means us as a group of friends, but I can't help hoping I'll hear those words directed at me.

Chapter 32: Brunch

-*Annie*-

July

Standing in Drew's bedroom feels so normal. What doesn't feel normal is Drew's little confession about my pictures. I'm Drew's pinup girl, which is a phrase I'd never expected to hear about myself, much less be thinking about. It's nice to know that I've made an appearance in his fantasies, because I know he's been a main participant in mine. It makes me want to look in my drawers to find that little set and see if it still fits. I've held on to it but never worn it again because it had felt wrong to show it to someone else. My body has filled in since nineteen, and I'm not sure it will fit, but it could be worth it to find out. It also makes me want to go shopping for something new and fresh. I make a mental note to ask Meg for her recommendations. I know that she loves good lingerie. She'll let me know where to look online and where not to waste my time.

I'm going to have to let her know I never got to our seduction plan, but that I'm having the sex of my life anyway. Drew says something about a collection; I have to know what he means. He gives me a detailed, picture-by-picture run-down of the collection of photos he's kept of us. I deleted all our photos from my phone finding them to painful, but I do have them in my cloud, so I get why he has kept them. He places his hands on my face, pulling me into a kiss. He sucks my bottom lip into his mouth, and I want to lock us in this room and never come out. Then I hear, "OOOOHHH, GRRRROOOSSSS. Daddy is kissing MOMMMMMYYYY." I look over my shoulder at the now open door to see Luke being dramatic and covering his eyes. Craig appears next to him and smacks him in the head. "VOLUME CONTROL, asshole. Some of us have a hangover." I love these guys, and I tell them so.

Luke puts his hands over his heart. "Oh, Annie, I love you too. However, I am starving. Can you two love birds save the dirty stuff for after I leave, or do you all need a quickie?" He laughs and heads back out into the living space with Craig not waiting for either of our reply. I feel my cheeks flush because I'm thinking about a quickie and if that would be possible. I mentally tell myself to cool down. Drew looks amused by my flushed skin. "Dimples, I think the children are hungry. We'll have to take a rain check on that quickie." He laughs at my statement. "Angel, I have no intention to do anything quick with you especially naked." He grabs my hand we head into the living room.

***

Ten minutes later, we are at a booth in my favorite brunch spot. If we'd come at rush hour, the hostess would still have done anything to please our group. She can't be more than seventeen. She's sporting a blush of deep red, as she looks over our little group. I can't blame her; none of them are bad to look at. Craig has all those muscles and his red-blond curls. Luke's bronzed skin and easy smile have always given him a natural charm. Then there is my Drew, with far too many things to point out about him that would make her blush. As we pass their booths, a few older gentlemen wave and shout to Drew. "Good game," or "Keep it up, we have half a season to go." He gives them all a wave and a nod. "Thank you," or "I'm looking forward to the back half." He gives them all a moment of his time. I squeeze his fingers in mine. He squeezes them back even as he gives someone else his focus.

"So, in all seriousness, you two are back together, right?" Luke wastes no time asking after we all get our coffees. Drew looks at me before looking at the guys. "I mean, we didn't give it a label, we aren't in high school, Luke." I don't know why it bothers me, but it does a little. If I'm ever asked why I say the next thing out of my mouth, I will have no answer. "I'm going to call him my boyfriend, even if I'm twenty-six." I go to move my hand out of his but feel him tighten his fingers around mine. Drew lets out a deep breath, and I feel his other hand tipping my chin to make me look at him, not the guys.

"Annie, be my girlfriend. I don't need one, two, or five months to know I only want you." It mirrors all those years ago when he'd asked me to be his girlfriend in my backyard. "You sure? I don't want to be so high school about it," I say mockingly, looking into his dark blue eyes. "I've never been more sure," he says, moving his hand to my cheek, pulling me into a kiss and I go willingly. "Glad we got that cleared up while I could be a witness," Luke laughs from across the booth. "Thanks for your services. Send me your bill," Drew cracks back at Luke.

Craig has been quieter, which could be the hangover, but I notice how off he is. "Craig, you, ok?" He looks up from his coffee at me. "Yeah, just distracted." Before he can say more, Luke cuts in. "Our Craig was kissing a woman last night at the club." Luke elbows Craig's side. In return, Craig gives him an elbow to the side, but it looks less playful than Luke's and like it was meant to shut him up, but it doesn't. "She was hot, I still don't know why you didn't bring her back to the apartment." Luke continues unphased. "Yes, we kissed and it was good but who said I was going to ask her to come back to the apartment? Also you are the reason she bolted." Craig is looking at me, and I don't understand until he speaks again why. "I know she's your producer and friend."

My brain takes a moment to connect the dots. "Wait, YOU kissed Emma?" I say it too loudly, and a few people look over at us. "Annie, I don't think the people outside heard," Craig points towards the windows, looking out on the street. "Sorry, I wasn't expecting that." I say in a much more appropriate volume. He explains that he was looking for Drew and found Emma alone in the booth. He'd gone to say hi, and she'd filled him in on our quick escape hand in hand. They'd ended up drinking, talking, and then she'd said something about a couple on the dance floor making out.

She said something about it being so long since she'd done it that she'd probably forgotten how, in all his drinking wisdom, he'd taken it as an invitation. He'd leaned into her space and kissed her. She'd kissed him back, and in his words, clearly remembered how to kiss. Luke cuts in to Craig's story telling us how he found Emma in Craig's lap, his hands on her ass. Emma had scrambled off Craig's lap, grabbed her bag, and left the bar in a frenzy, according to Luke, it had been impressive. "So, what now, Craig?" I ask him to try to gauge if my friend is interested or if it was a one-time thing. "You tell me, Annie, that kiss from my side was worth exploring." I believe Craig, he's never said he was interested when he wasn't, he's not one who is dishonest about who he's into. Luke lets out a whistle but is interrupted by our food arriving. I guess I will have to contact my friend Emma to see what her thoughts are about their kisses.

Chapter 33: Time Alone

-Drew-

July

I am impressed that I don't have to wait to ask Annie to be exclusive. I'll be calling her my girlfriend at every opportunity. It is more than I thought I'd get this soon, yet it still doesn't feel like enough. I have to tell myself that we had sex for the first time in almost seven years. *Maybe it's because we have been spending so much time together the last few months,* I tell myself, *that it feels so big.* Why does it feel so easy and natural to be with her? We finish brunch with Craig and Luke, primarily focused on Craig's surprising make-out.

The conversation shifts to Luke and his life in Texas. Craig skillfully directs the conversation away from his adventures. "Are you still in that study group?" Annie asks Luke. "Yes, I keep getting text messages that I'm behind. Alexis will not drop it," Luke responds, looking annoyed. "Who is Alexis?" Annie asks with a smile on her face. "A pain in my ass." Luke says seeming frustrated and I can't quite label, Luke continues. "Figure of speech, get your head out of the gutter." Luke is looking right a Craig, who laughs next to him before asking, "When do you think you'll be back to visit?" In true Luke fashion, he answers with an extravagant reply. "I am trying to pass the B-A-R. Give me a freakin' break on planning any more vacations, until I tell you if I passed or failed it."

The time goes by quickly with us all talking, joking and laughing. The brunch spot is almost empty when Luke finally looks at his phone. "I need to head to the airport soon." I flag down the waitress to ask for the bill, but before I can take it, Annie hands her a credit card, and the waitress walks away without a backwards glance. "What the hell do you think you're doing?" I say, only half joking. I don't want her to pay for me. We both know that when it comes to money, I'm good. I appreciate that she doesn't expect me to pay, but she will have to get over it. "What does it look like, Dimples? I'm paying for your brunch," she punctuates the statement with a kiss. "Drew, Annie has that TV money," laughs Luke from his side of the booth. I lean in next to her ear and whisper, "Mmmm, I can think of a lot of ways to repay you." She shivers and smirks at me. Yeah, we are both thinking about ways I can repay her that involve us being naked.

Craig offers to take Luke to the airport when we return to the apartment. As soon as the door shuts behind them, I take Annie's hand, pulling her into my room. As we walk, Annie asks me, "How has it only been twenty-four hours since we kissed for the first time in years? Does it feel crazy to you how easy this all feels?" I look at her, taking in all the details of her face before I answer. "I am glad it feels easy for you, too. It feels the opposite of crazy and the most logical thing to be here with you. Like the last six years without you were a bad dream, like I just woke up in the reality I wished for on my nineteenth birthday." She takes a deep breath. "Drew, what did you wish for on your birthday exactly?" I shake my head, "Nope, I've already said too much as it is. It hasn't come completely true yet, but when it does, I'll tell you. I promise, Angel." Annie eyes me with curiosity, "What now, Dimples?" I pull her tighter into my body and say against her lips, "I make love to my girlfriend."

The kiss starts slow, like we are both learning the lines and textures of each other again. It starts to build when Annie sucks my lower lip into her mouth. The move is something that makes me think about her sucking my dick. I can't help how hard I am at the thought of her lips on me. Annie removes her hands from around my neck, running them down my chest, before reaching them under the hem of my shirt, and pulls it up. I don't make her ask, I pull back and bend over to help her pull the shirt off. "I don't understand how you got so much bigger since nineteen. I just can't." I can't fight the smile her confession brings to my face.

I reach for her shirt, helping her remove it. "Lots of hours at the gym. Glad you appreciate all my hard work." I eventually say and she only "Mmm's" in reply. I reach around her back and unclasp her bra and kiss along her neck. "On the bed, Angel," I say against her soft skin as I kiss her neck. She says nothing, but walks over to my bed, and positions herself in the middle of the king-size bed. I follow her and when I reach her, I hook my fingers into the waistband of her leggings, peeling them and her underwear from her body. I'm the one in awe at her perfect body. It almost feels like I'm in a dream, being with her like this again. I never thought I'd see her looking back at me this way. My mind can't understand how many things had to work out to get us here, to have this moment with her now to have this second chance.

I remove my joggers and boxers before covering her with my body. We are skin to skin from our chests to our toes. We both start to touch, gliding our fingers along each other's skin, building this moment into an inferno. My dick is resting against her clit, and slowly I push it harder into the little nub before moving it down her core. I drag my dick back up to push again against her clit. Her eyes start to grow heavy, and she lets out a little moan.

On the next pass down, she lifts her hips just enough to slide the head of my dick into her. I'm never going to get over how good it feels without a condom. Having my dick inside her feels like home. I take the hint, pushing into her until I'm completely inside her. She wraps her legs around my hips, holding me here while she looks at me in awe. It's like she feels like I do, that nothing has ever felt more right.

She drags her hands over my body to wrap around my neck. "Drew, make love to me." Her words are whispered between us. I can't deny her anything, so I slowly make love to my Annie. I take my time and savor each moan and gasp. We change positions, flipping so she's on top of me at some point. She takes her time riding my dick and rolling her hips, in no rush to reach the end of this building passion between us.

I suck on her perfect boobs while she pours herself into sliding our bodies together and apart. I can tell the moment that we are at the edge of her building orgasm. She starts to have less control, and her rhythm starts to change, like she can't keep up the slow torture any longer. I reach between us, rubbing my fingers over her clit as she guides my dick. She opens her eyes, looking at me with an open mouth, no sound escaping, until she does it again. She moans, "DREW." I know she is close. I push us over the edge by holding her hips, helping her rise and fall faster, harder. It only takes a few strokes until her pussy pulses around me, causing me to cum inside her.

I think I pass out from how intense my climax was from lovemaking. All I register is Annie's arms around my neck, hugging me, and mine wrapped around her bare back. I'm still inside her, as she's still in my lap. We are just clinging to each other. I feel wetness on my shoulder and realize that Annie is crying. I go to pull back because I need to see her face, but she holds her arms tighter around my neck. "Annie, why are you crying? Talk to me, Angel." I hear the concern in my own voice. She takes a deep breath in my arms before answering.

"I'm so unbelievably, completely, overwhelmingly happy. I refuse to let you go again. I forgot what it felt like to be cherished, what it felt like to cherish someone else, too." She pulls back, looking into my eyes. "I want to say three words to you right now, but we should wait to say them, Drew. Let's make each other earn them again. Let's learn about everything that happened over the last six years. Let's make them last forever when we say them this time." I want to hear them. God, I want to hear her say *I love you*. I almost tell her I love her, too, but she's right. We have things we need to talk about. Gaps to fill, things to make clear before those words can be said and mean forever. I reach up and brush away a tear, "Ok, Angel, we'll wait to say those three words again until we've had time to cover the time apart. But after we do you can't stop me from saying them for the rest of my life."

Chapter 34: Covering the Past

-Annie-

July

I feel ridiculous crying after we make love, but I still can't stop the tears that fall. How did I forget how good it feels to be cared for? How did I forget how perfect it feels to be in his arms? How did I forget what it feels like to look into his eyes and know nothing else matters? Maybe my brain has been trying to save me from additional heartache, because none of my relationships could live up to him. I cling to him, knowing I never want anything to keep me from his man. I'll never want anyone else like I want him. I should have known before the events of the last twenty-four hours, but maybe I needed to feel his arms around me again for it all to come into focus. To see him look at me with wonder, for the dots to connect. I love Drew Davis, and I'm not sure I ever really stopped.

Drew breaks into my thoughts. When he asks me what's wrong and he sounds concerned. What do I tell him? How do I start to describe the feelings swirling through my muddled brain? I take a deep breath before saying how I feel. I tell him how happy I am, how I forgot what this feels like. I have to look at him, so I unwrap my arms from around his neck and place my hands over his pounding heart. I make my confession as honestly as I can. "I want to say three words to you right now, but we should wait to say them, Drew." The look on his face is many things, but they all speak to the fact that I'm not alone in my feelings. Before he interrupts me, I continue.

"Let's make each other earn them again. Let's learn about everything that happened over the last six years. Let's make them last forever when we say them this time." His face is like a movie. So many emotions play across his tanned skin and tense jaw. I see his frustration at being asked to wait, and his understanding. "Ok, Angel, we'll wait to say those three words again until we've had time to cover the time apart. But after we do you can't stop me from saying them for the rest of my life." I feel my heart pounding with his confession, and it matches the racing heart under my hands. I wrap my arms around his neck again, pulling him into a long, binding kiss to seal our deal. At some point, he grows hard in my body again. We continue to make love until we are spent and our bodies curl around each other in exhaustion.

***

I wake up in the warm cocoon of Drew's body the next morning to the sound of knocking at the door. "Go away, Craig," I feel and hear Drew say. "Man, I know you're off, but it's already 11 a.m. We discussed that you still need to move your body." Craig sounds amused with himself. "I moved my body all night, go away." I flush red at Drew's words, but Craig is determined. "Drew, get up. You pay me to make you get up." Craig sounds less amused this time. "I haven't eaten yet; the gym can wait until later." Drew grumbles back not seeming to want to get out of bed. "Annie, tell him that you like his muscles. Tell him he needs to get up and go to the gym to keep them." Craig says trying to get me to convince Drew to get up.

"Craig Michael Mitchell, do not use me," I shout, but I'm laughing. "Annie

Marie Campbell, you get that man out of bed and dressed. I'll even let you come and wear one of those ridiculous workout outfits. You two can make googly eyes at each other in the mirror as foreplay." Craig is laughing out loud now. "Fine, fine asshole, I'm getting up, but only if Annie agrees to wear that little red one I missed out on." Drew kisses my shoulder when he finishes his reply. I can feel his smile against my skin. "Ok, I'll go home and get changed." I announce and Craig claps from outside the door.

"I'll make you both a smoothie." I hear him say before he pads away from the door. "Good morning, Angel." Drew sounds good in the morning, and I think I could get use to waking up to him each day. "Good morning, Dimples." I turn around and kiss him. "Craig is such a buzzkill. I was looking forward to morning sex." Drew gives my neck a kiss making me think about how good that sounds. "Here's to you staying at my place next time so we can be uninterrupted." I say and then pull the covers off of us and get out of bed. *Oh, I'm sore,* I think as I stand up and stretch. It will probably be good to do some light exercise today. Drew is still in bed watching me. "You getting up, Dimples?" I grab my discarded clothing. "I was just enjoying the view this morning," he smiles, flashing that dimple before he pulls himself out of bed. After I am dressed, I give Drew a kiss as I go to leave, "Text me when you boys are ready. I'm going to go to my apartment and change." He slips his hand into my hair at the base of my neck and pulls me into a another distractingly good kiss. "See you soon, Angel." He releases me and heads in the direction of his bathroom.

Craig is pouring a smoothie into two to-go cups when I enter the open living room. "Here you go, Annie." He picks one up and hands it over. I take a big drink, and it's tastes good, I get hints of vanilla and strawberry. "You make a killer smoothie." Craig smiles at my compliment, then he rushes me out the door to get dressed. I go to my apartment and quickly find the red workout set Drew requested. I brush my teeth and fix my hair before returning to my room to cha nge.

Maybe its all the sex we've had in the last 2 days but I get the urge to look for that red ribbon lingerie set. I've never been prouder of myself for not throwing it away or wearing it for anyone else. I try on the lingerie first. It's a little tight but still looks good on my body. My breasts look even better as they are fuller now, and they barely fit when I tie the little red bow over them. I almost take a picture to send to Drew, but I stop myself. I should wait and let him get the whole image in person. His birthday is only a few days away. I already know I'll be regifting myself as his present. I hear a knock at my door and quickly hide the set in my drawer and change into the workout outfit. "Coming," I shout from the bedroom. "This is awkward, don't let me interrupt," Craig shouts from the other side of my apartment door. I swing open the door.

"The vibrator just isn't the same now." My joke gets a chuckle from Drew but a "GROSS" from Craig. "Serves you right for making the sex joke first." I follow the guys to the elevator. Drew slides his arm around my waist and leans down to whisper next to my ear. "Your ass looks amazing in those shorts. It's going to distract me the whole workout." I laugh and turn to Craig, asking. "Today is a leg day for me, right?" Craig smirks, "Sure, Annie, it can be leg day." Craig's agreement earns a groan from Drew.

Drew removes his arm from around my waist and smacks my ass. "You are going to be the death of me, Angel," he says loud enough for Craig to hear. "I am going to start charging you more if I have to deal with this," Craig says, pointing at us in the elevator. "In that case, I guess I can do this." Drew pulls me against him and gives me a bruising kiss. "I don't make enough to deal with this," Craig laughs from the other side of the elevator. We head to the gym joking and trying to push Craig's buttons. I do plenty of squats with a pair of dark blue eyes following my every move the whole time.

***

Drew has to take a few calls with his agent about some photo shoots he has to do while he is off next week. I tell him to meet me at the pool if he has time. I haven't spent enough time there myself and the weather is perfect for a day at the pool. I wear my bikini and head to the pool to soak in the beautiful summer weather. I enjoy dips into the water and warming my skin in the sunshine to dry off. As I'm sitting here, I recall that Drew brought up still having that picture of me from the cruise. I sit up, make sure my breasts and body look good, and then I smile and take a selfie. I check the phone, liking how I look without makeup. I pull up my text messages, select Drew Davis from the list, and send the picture with a message from our past.

Annie

Suns out, girls out!

What do you think now?

I know that Drew is on a conference call. I don't expect an answer anytime soon. I hit the video call button next to Meg's name. She picks up after the second ring. She is still at work. "Oh gosh, I'm sorry, I forgot to check the time. My brain is in full vacation mode." She laughs at me, "No problem, Annie. I just finished a meeting. Looks like vacation mode looks good on you!" Meg smiles on the screen. "I have news." I can't fight my excitement. "Spill, did you lock Drew in his bedroom yet?" She jokes, not knowing that I have done that and more since the last time we talked. "Well," I say and blush. "Annie Marie, tell me everything." Meg leans back in her chair ready to hear my news.

I tell her all the details from the last couple of days, from the rush of the first time together, to the slow lovemaking, to our confessions. When I finish, she looks so happy for me. "Annie Marie, this is the best news. I told you he still wanted you." Meg wears a smug smile. "You did," I confirm. "I'm jealous that you've had such good sex. I need some bone-crushing, blood-rushing, orgasm-inducing sex

192

myself." I go to answer, but I'm interrupted by someone clearing their throat. I can't see the guy with the camera angle pointed at Meg but I hear him crystal clear. "Well, Megan, that could be arranged," is all I get before Meg disconnects the call. That was interesting. I find it curious that she disconnected the call. I also wonder why that guy's voice sounded familiar. I'm trying to place the voice when a large shadow covers my body, distracting me.

I look up at a shirtless and swim-trunk-wearing Drew with his dimple on display. "I thought it was about time to see you in a bikini in person." He sets his towel down on the chair next to me and leans down to kiss me. "Ooh, you're right, we've never spent a summer together." It's weird to think that even though we were inseparable all those years ago, summer is the one season we never got together. "Let's make up for all those missed moments." He says as he wraps his arms around me before throwing me over his shoulder like I weigh nothing. He marches over to the pool and throws me in. I go under, and before I can even reach the surface, I see Drew's body in the water next to me. When we surface, we are both laughing, and he pulls me against him. I wrap myself around him, kissing him, not caring who could be watching. I slip out of his arms moments later to his surprise. "Catch me if you want any more of those." I shout as I swim a way.

We spend an hour laughing, swimming, and kissing in the pool. Eventually, we leave and lie on the towels in the warm sunshine. "Do you have sunscreen for that chest?" His arms and face are a darker tan than his chest and shoulders. His paler skin is already turning pink from the sun. "I don't," he says, and I pull the lotion from my bag. He pulls me to straddle his hips. "Drew, people can see us, you know." "What, my girlfriend is just applying sunscreen. It's none of their business if it's easier for her to reach all my crevices from my lap." He flashes me his smile and shrugs like *Who cares?* "Mmm, ok then," I say as I open and apply the lotion to his body. His body is so toned. I'm getting turned on running my hands over his body, I need a distraction. "So, where do you think we should start on this plan to cover our time apart?"

"Maybe we take it one question at a time." I like his suggestion. I make to go back to my chair, and he holds me where I am. "If we are going to have conversations about other people. I, for one, think that I need your skin and body to remind me that you're with me now." I agree to stay, but I tell him, "Scoot over," so I'm not straddling his lap. He does, and I lay against his body, laying my head on his shoulder. "Where do we start?" I ask. "Maybe with the hardest part." He replies like its obvious. "Which is what, Dimples?" I ask trying to see where this is going. "Our numbers?" It takes me a minute to think about what he means. My brain clicks, and I make the connection that he is talking about how many relationships or people we've been with since we broke up.

This one seems easier for me since I've already told him. "You already have mine. Two. There are more if we are talking dates, but they didn't end with more than a kiss." Drew is quiet for a while under me. "God, I feel like an asshole." His voice is full of emotion. "My number is more than two, unfortunately, a lot more than two." He sounds frustrated with himself. I want to make this easier for him. "If it helps, I kinda assumed with all the internet alerts I've gotten over the years with images of you and all the brunettes." I blush, scrambling to cover what I said. "I turned on an alert for your name on my internet browser when you got drafted. I didn't want to miss an article or reference. After we broke up, I didn't turn it off. I still wanted to know how you were doing. It was my way of not losing you completely. I didn't realize it would also alert me to pictures until the first ones started to appear. I should have turned it off then, but I didn't. I'd get the alert and see the new girl, and I'd compare myself to them each time."

Only the sounds of the city playing out around us after my confession. I feel Drew's hand on my face, and he pulls my face to an angle where we look at each other. "Twenty-two is my number. It isn't something I'm proud of, but you should know that you're still the only person I've given those three words. That none of them have been more than a need to distract myself, to fill a moment, and none of them have had me the way you did, the way you do." I push up and give him a small kiss before returning my head to his shoulder. "I've never said those words to anyone else either." I confess.

Chapter 35: Past Regrets

-Drew-

July

I hate myself already for saying that we should discuss our numbers. I don't really want to hear about all the guys that Annie has been with, but we should talk about it, the people between us. I feel Annie go still on top of me. She hasn't pulled off my body at the question, but her body is now tense in a way it wasn't before I spoke. I move my hand at the small of her back and trace the edge of her bikini bottoms. Should I say mine first? Should I wait to hear hers? How do I make sure not to get pissed when I hear it? All these questions pass through my mind in seconds, while she is quiet against me. In a calm but firm voice, she states. "You already have mine." *Wait, how do I know hers?* I think before she continues with her number. "Two." I know she says more but I'm stuck on the number two. Her number is two more than I want it to be. I still wish I were the only man to have been with her, but two is so much lower than mine. Twenty lower than mine in fact, if we are only using the definition of sex, and I feel like a man-whore. Why didn't I keep my fucking dick in my pants? I am pissed at myself but then I remember that I never thought I'd get to be with Annie again. I stopped looking for anything serious after we broke up. I'd only been scratching an itch; I'd only been focused on sex as a relationship status.

I've taken too long to respond; I know it but hell this sucks to say out loud. I take a deep breath and confess my feelings. Her hand is tracing the lines of my abs as she confesses to having an internet alert on me. *Hell,* she's seen some of the women I've been with. She has actual images in her head of me with other women. I've avoided looking at Annie's social media accounts, so I didn't have to see her relationships and the guys lucky enough to be with my girl. I followed her career, having seen all her interviews from college to when she went to LA. I've also gone down the rabbit hole several times over the years and gone through all our old photos from the start to the end of our relationship, which is how the collection of photos still exists on my phone.

I have to look at her face when I say this; I need to confirm that she isn't disgusted by me when it comes out of my mouth. I tilt her face to look at me. "Twenty-two is my number. It isn't something I'm proud of, but you should know that you're still the only person I've given those three words to. That none of them have been more than a need to distract myself, to fill a moment, and none of them have had me the way you did, the way you do." I look into the eyes of the only girl, the only woman, I've ever loved, and I try to read her mind. She isn't wearing a look of disgust like I expect, but she is serious then before my eyes it's gone. She pushes up and kisses me. "I've never told anyone else either." She says against my lips. My soul gets a validation that I didn't even know I needed. In this, we are still each other's first and only, and in this, we can hold true that real love finds a way to come back. Annie lays her head back on my chest, tracing my abs, and I return to tracing the edge of her bikini. I'm relieved that particular question is co vered and done with.

"What is your type now, Drew?" *Well, shit, maybe we can't both check this box off that easily.* I have to remember that Annie has pictures running through her mind. "You." It's the truth, but I know she will be asking me more questions. If you look up pictures of 'Drew Davis' or 'Drew Davis girlfriend' in an internet search, it will bring up pictures of me with women, and none of them look like

Annie. There is a reason none of them look like her. I was trying to erase her image from my mind, the pictures I had of us, of my future with her. "How is that true? They all looked more like Meg than me." Annie says and I feel the hurt in her question.

I need her to understand. "That was the whole point, Angel. I didn't want anyone who looked like the girl I couldn't have. Every blonde reminded me too much of you. I will confess something I haven't told anyone, even Craig because I need you to understand why I avoided anyone that reminded me of you. At my first start in Arizona, I thought I saw you, just for a second, I thought *she's here*. But when I blinked, it was obvious it wasn't you. I'd gotten pissed at myself for wanting you there, for still looking for you. I got my first home run shortly after because I needed to hit something hard. I was pissed at you for not being there and at myself still wanting you there. It didn't work. When I rounded third, I had to fight myself not to make that stupid heart shape at the camera because I still wanted you to know I wasn't over us."

She is looking at me with tears running down her cheeks. I hadn't told the story to make her cry. I wipe them away, feeling like an asshole again. Her voice cracks as she says, "I hate that I wasn't there for that moment. I recorded it and watched it after reporting on my game in LA. I was so proud of you for living your dream. It made all my heartbreak a little less sharp because it was worth it to see you so happy." She is crying harder now, and it is killing me. "Angel, I'm right here. I'm not going anywhere, and I'm not letting you go without a fight this time." I take both of my hands and pull her into a gentle kiss. I can taste the salt from her tears. She pulls back and looks directly into my soul. "Drew, I promise to fight for us, too." My heart beats in a crazy rhythm and I can't fight it, and I don't want too, I love this woman in front of me, and I don't know how I got so lucky to get her in my arms again. I hear myself whisper back, "Then Angel, it sounds like we can't lose." We spend a little more time in the sun before we call it a day and head back inside, agreeing that we need to spend time together dressed. We decide to get ready separately, so we won't distract each other before we go on a second first date.

Chapter 36: First Date Round Two

-Annie-

July

Our time at the pool was both fun and stressful. Getting past the most challenging part of our time apart was required. It broke my heart to hear that he looked for me at his first pro game last year. I secretly vow to myself that I will be at every big moment from now on. I will be the woman he finds in the crowd, giving him back that heart shape after a home run. We agree that we should get ready in our own apartments, or we will never leave the apartment complex. Drew suggested that we go on round two of our first date, and I think it sounded like a great idea. I check my phone and find that I'd missed a call and a few text messages from Meg while we had our conversation at the pool. I open the text messages and read them first before returning her video call.

Meg Patterson

So sorry about hanging up

I'm home. Call me back, I feel awful

Meg answers quickly and jumps in with, "Annie, I'm so sorry about hanging up." I laugh because she is so worried, and it's so unlike Meg to be so focused on this little detail. "Just tell me if the guy is hot already?" Meg's cheeks go pink. Like pink-pink, like I've never seen before. Well, that's not true, she'd blushed about that guy in college; his name started with a C, I think. He was the fling she'd had after Tom. "Oh, Meg, he must be hot—you're blushing, I can tell through the screen." She covers her face and answers me through her fingers. "Ok, I'll admit it, he is hot, and I want him. I really want him, but Annie I need to tell you--- I hear the knock on her side of the call. She looks a little confused as she says over the video, "Someone is at my door. Can we talk later?" We say our goodbyes, and I head to the shower to prepare for my first date with my new boyfriend.

I stare at my closet in my underwear, unsure what to wear on this grown-up date with Drew. He told me to be comfortable, that the date isn't going to be fancy. I don't think he will show up in sweatpants and a T-shirt, so I guess I need something better than a pair of leggings, but not as dressed up as my sideline reporting suits. I pull out a black skirt that will go with my blacked-out sneakers. I struggle with the top until I see a sleeveless black and white striped top. I look comfortable but also stylish in a laid-back way. I grab a small cross-body bag and call it complete. In the mirror, I add a little eye shadow and mascara to complete my look. I head into my living room, trying to be patient and wait for Drew to text or call me. I try to call Miles, but it goes to voicemail. I leave him a *call me back tomorrow* message. Then I call Mom to chat with her about what's going on back home. About ten minutes into the call my phone vibrates and I switch from my video call with Mom to my messages.

Drew Davis

You ready?

> I have tried to give you plenty of time but I need to see my girlfriend!

> I was ready 30 minutes ago

> I was waiting on you to be ready

> OMG

> I'm on my way

"Who's the fella?" Mom asks from the video chat. "What makes you think it is a guy?" I give her a sarcastic smile through the camera. "Annie, you are beaming." I guess she has a point, I am beaming. "Any guesses?" Mom is quiet and trying to figure out who I'm talking about. I hear a knock on the door. I take her with me as I open the door. Drew doesn't register the phone at first. "Hell, Annie, those legs will have me turned on all night." Mom cheers on the phone, and I hear her calling for Dad. Drew is blushing as I take his arm and pull him into my apartment.

"Hello, Mrs. Campbell," he says into the phone. "Oh, Drew, you don't have to call me Mrs. Campbell, call me Kim." I almost call out Mom, because she's the one beaming now. She yells for Dad again. Drew gives me a look, and I give him one back. Now he can feel my pain when his mom asks me to call her Jennifer. Dad enters the kitchen, looking like he ran from the game room. "What's going on?" Mom points the phone in his direction, obviously showing me and Drew on her phone together. "What is so important about Annie and Drew?" Drew laughs, and I can hear Mom saying, "THEY ARE BACK TOGETHER" from off-camera. Dad still looks confused. "I thought they WERE TOGETHER months ago," he says, looking off camera at my mother and then back at us.

I can't fight the laugh that escapes me. Drew leans in and says, "Don't worry about it, Mr. Campbell, we should have been together months ago: we're just making it official now." Dad makes a look off camera again. "I told you when I came back from the opening day that I thought they got back together." Dad is talking to Mom again clearly. "And I told you Annie was still seeing that reporter guy at that time," Mom spouts off at Dad. I try to change the subject before they continue talking about another guy in front of Drew. "Ok, well, glad that we can clear up the confusion for everyone about our relationship status." I interject before they start discussing the details of my life, like I'm not even here.

Drew takes the phone from my hand, and I can see Dad's perplexed expression, which matches my own. "Mr. Campbell, have you seen a pro game from the suites?" I can't see Dad, but I hear him over the speaker, "No, why are you asking, Davis?" Drew smiles and I don't look away, he's mine and I can soak in his smiles and that dimple as much as I want to now. "I can get some tickets in the next couple of weeks for you and some friends if you're interested," Drew tells Dad, and I hear Dad's reply, "Yeah, that sounds great, Davis, thanks." Drew's expression changes to serious, "Oh, and Mr. Campbell. Let's grab a drink or dinner, just us, when you're in town. I'd like to talk about that advice you shared with me before the draft." Drew looks at me and then turns his attention back to my dad. "Sure, Drew. Let's have that talk in a few weeks." Dad sounds different and I wonder what that was about. "Thanks, Mr. Campbell. Have a good night." Drew hands me back the phone to say goodbye to my parents. "What was that about?" I ask Drew after I hit the end call button. Drew shrugs, "He gave me some advice about what to do with my future after I made the majors. I'd like to discuss it now that I'm here and it's not a hypothetical anymore." He kisses me on the forehead. "You ready for this date?" Drew changes the subject and I let him. "Yeah, where are we going?" I ask, since I still don't know. "You'll just have to wait and see." Drew says playfully as he takes my hand.

Drew opens the door for me before climbing behind the wheel. "I know one thing that will be different from our first date, Dimples." He looks over at me as he starts the car. "What is that, Angel?" He says as he takes my hand and kisses the back of it. "We will not be making out or getting naked in the backseat this time around." I laugh, looking to the non-existent backseat of the sports car. Drew laughs from next to me, looking at the backseat, too. "Yes, we don't have to sneak around anymore. We can go back to either of our apartments. We can use every surface in one and then switch to the other." He has a wicked glim in his eyes. The thought of having sex in new spots in my apartment does turns me on. "I like the sounds of that." Trying to distract myself from how warm I am, I ask, "Do I get any hints about the date?"

He drives the car out of the parking garage with a smile. "Nope, it is a surprise. Any interest in playing a game while we head to the destination?" Drew is a master at changing topics, and I let him again. "I'm game to play." I reply and it already feels a little like our first date and the rounds of questions we played then. "Ideal vacation?" He asks me. "A beach, I don't care where," I say, then ask him a question. "What about your ideal vacation?" "I've enjoyed the Bahamas, or Turks and Caicos, which was beautiful." "Is that where you have been spending Thanksgiving?" He looks over at me as he answers. "Yeah, places like that. We also liked Hawaii a lot." We are heading north out of the city now, crossing the river. I wonder where we are headed. I've only explored a little in this direction, and it's mostly been what I can reach by the streetcar.

"What's left on your life bucket list?" he asks me as he changes lanes and takes an exit to another highway. "Not a lot, actually. After I got this job, there are only a few things left: get married, have kids, and get a tattoo. What about you? Any dreams left to reach for?" I ask him, watching his face as he thinks. "I think I have those same ones left: get married, have kids, buy my first house, get a tattoo. We could check one off the list tonight if you are interested." My brain jumps straight to being his wife. "A guy on the team has a tattoo guy. Let me know, and

I can make a call." He says and I can't help that I'm slightly disappointed that he brought up tattoos, but it makes the most sense, as we just got back together. We drive into a small town set into the hills overlooking the river. He focuses on the map directions until he finds a parking spot just off Main Street.

"Last chance, Annie. Any last guesses?" I look around and see a park and restaurants. "A picnic?" "Nope. You are going to kick yourself when we get there." He gets out of the car and walks around, opening mine. He takes my hand, and we walk along the street before turning up a row of stairs. There at the top is a sign for "Mini Golf." I smile, stopping him on the stairs. I take a few more steps so we are now eye level, and I kiss him. "So, it's a rematch. What are we betting this time around?" I ask with happiness. "Oh, are we betting this time? I do recall winning last time, Angel." I reach out and touch his dimple as he smiles. "I get to pick your tattoo if I win, Dimples." "Well, if I win, I get to pick yours, then, Angel." He seals the deal with a kiss. We continue up the stairs and enter the little shop to get the clubs and golf balls.

I forgot how competitive we are as we go back and forth on the little scorecard. We are about to start the seventeenth hole when a little boy notices Drew. I hear him trying to get his dad's attention. "Daddy, Daddy, Daddy, it's number 17. Daddy, that's him, right?" The boy is pointing, and the Dad tries to make him stop. "Pointing is rude, Collin," I hear the Dad say before looking in our direction. I see when he realizes, *Yes, in fact, number 17 is in front of me.* "Daddy, can I tell him, please, please?" Collin says, pulling on his dad's arm. "What do you think he needs to tell me?" Drew whispers next to my ear, making me jump.

I look over at him, and he is wearing my favorite smile. "Let me go find out." I hand Drew my club and ball before walking over to the father and son. "I couldn't help but overhear that we have a Davis fan," I say as I lean down and look Collin in the eyes. "Do you all want a picture?" Collin looks over, overcome with pure joy. "Daddy, Daddy, it's the pretty lady that asks the Griffons questions. Daddy, remember you told Uncle she could come over any time.

Remember, Daddy?" Collin looks so proud at placing me. His dad seems a little embarrassed. "Isn't that nice?" I stand up and wave Drew over. Drew bends down and holds out his hand. "Nice to meet you, Collin." Collin is positively bubbling over with excitement as he reaches over and shakes Drew's hand. Collin starts talking, giving Drew all his joy at meeting him. "I wanna be a shortstop just like you. You're my favorite Griffon player. I asked for your jersey for my birthday. I got to see you play in June, and you hit a home run. It was so cool." Collin is talking so fast, trying to make the most of his time in front of Drew. "Thank you, Collin. I love meeting other shortstops. Got any tips for me?"

Collin's eyes go all big at Drew's question. "Daddy, what do I tell him?" He looks at his dad, worried that he doesn't have anything to tell Drew. Collin's Dad looks down at his son before offering him a suggestion. "Why don't you tell him to hit more home runs, buddy?" "Yeah, what my dad said. Hit more home runs will be a good plan," Collin says, shaking his head up and down while he talks. "Do you have a phone so I can take a picture?" I ask Collin's Dad. He pulls out his phone before bending down like Drew so I can take a photo of three of them. I get one with just Drew and Collin before going to hand the phone back. Collin's dad clears his throat. "Can we get one with you, too?" I am surprised but flattered, "Oh sure, yeah." Drew laughs before taking the phone from my hands. I replace him next to Collin. Collin screams "Cheese," causing me to offer my genuine smile versus the one I give in my professional photos. Drew hands the phone back to Collin's dad. He also gives him a number. I wave before heading back to the starting point for hole seventeen.

"What number were you giving him?" I ask when Drew joins me at the starting point. "Oh, just the number to call my team. I can get a jersey signed for the kid." If I didn't already love him, it would be hard not to after seeing him interact with that family. "Angel, what's going on in that brain of yours?" Drew is smiling at me. "Thinking about that kitten tattoo you're going to get on your butt when I win." He laughs, pulling me into his arms, kissing me. I can hear Collin asking his dad in his not so quiet voice. "Is the pretty lady his girlfriend, Daddy? Is she?" and then his dad's reply of "Looks like it, buddy."

They turn the corner, and their voices are lost to the sounds around us. Drew refocuses me as he places his ball to start the round. "Angel, I can't wait to win this bet and pick your first tattoo." I do my best to distract him, but he is laser-focused. He gets a hole-in-one on seventeen, and I completely choke on eighteen. Drew does a little celebration when I declare him the official winner. He pulls out his phone, typing out a message, which is quickly followed by a buzz. "Looks like he is open in two hours. We can go try that pizza place across the street to burn time." I can't help reminding him, "Drew, please remember that I have to be back on TV in less than two weeks." He takes my hand. "Angel, I'm not going to pick anything crazy, promise. We'll keep them small." It looks like I will be making good on a bet tonight and checking off another first with Drew Davis by my side.

Chapter 37: Permanent Marks

-*Drew*-

July

I don't know why I'm so excited to get a tattoo. I've thought about getting one but never found the right thing to permanently mark on my body. Now I am so pumped to get one because it's with Annie. This idea may be new, but the facts are that it's been true for seven years, and I don't see it changing. A few guys have talked about the artist we are going to see as the man in town. He does all the athletes' tattoos, from the baseball team to the pro soccer and football players. I figure if I'm going to trust anyone with Annie's beautiful skin, I will go with someone that comes highly recommended.

As we drive to the shop, Annie is quiet. "I can cancel." I tell her because I don't want her to feel pressured. She looks over at me before shaking her head. "No, I am good. A little nervous about not knowing what you have in mind, but I trust you." I like that she trusts me, and I trust her. I don't want to give too much away until we are there. I play up the what-ifs of what I could be thinking. "How much do you like the number 17, Angel"? She gives me a little side eye. "Drew Joseph, are you going to etch your number into my skin?"

"What about 'hashtag: reserved for Drew Joseph Davis' on your hip bone?" I laugh. "I see the direction of your ideas." Annie says on a laugh. I reach out my hand, and she takes it. The map shows that we are less than five minutes from the shop. "Angel, if you don't want to do this, you don't have to, seriously." I squeeze her hand gently to emphasize my point. "I am fine, promise." She repeats the squeeze of my fingers in her hand. "So, I have a simple idea. Can we talk about it before we get there?" I'm not sure she realizes it, but she exhales loudly. "That is probably smart. I'm all ears, Dimples." I know I've done the right thing, because she's really smiling. "I know we said we would wait to say those three words until a future date, but you never said we couldn't write them down. Right?" She looks at me, glowing. "I never said we couldn't write them down , true."

We arrive at the tattoo studio to meet the recommended artist, Sam. The guy is covered in tattoos and looks like he'd be an ass, but I guess I shouldn't judge a book by its tattooed cover. The guy is actually really down-to-earth. He doesn't waste time asking what we want or if we need to look at a few samples. I look directly into Annie's eyes when I say my idea for the tattoos. "I want her handwritten 'I love you.'" I point to my left inner forearm. "Right here."

Looking at her again, her dark blue-gray eyes are shining. "Where do you want mine?" I ask her and she smiles, and I swear that my chest can't take how beautiful she is when she smiles like that at me. "I'll put it in the same spot." She points at her left inner forearm. Sam takes us back to a glass countertop and hands us both a notebook to write, "I love you" a few times. He asks us to look over the versions and pick our favorite one. The size of each tattoo is going to be a little bigger than the line on the notebook paper.

He tells us to give him a few minutes, and he will return to get us. I take Annie's hand. "Last chance to back out." She laughs, not looking nervous at all. "Dimples, you should already know that I don't back out of my dares, or in this case, bets. I like the idea, it's better than I would have picked." Now she has me curious what she would have picked. "What would I have been getting if I'd lost?" She looks at me and then looks down. "Well, I was thinking a huge 'ANNIE' right over your dick, but then I thought that wasn't very tasteful," she grins. "But in all seriousness, I was thinking about a small 'A' on you and a small 'D' somewhere discreet on me. Your idea is better—I'm glad that you won." She punctuates her point by stepping onto her tiptoes and giving me a chase kiss. Sam reappears in the lobby, which breaks the moment. He asks if we have gotten tattoos before, and we both say "No" simultaneously.

"Okay then," he announces before he walks us through getting a tattoo and the aftercare. He makes a point to explain that I need to take care of it, or that all my time in the sun will ruin it. I make sure to tell him that I'll follow his instructions to the letter. He asks, "Who's first?" and points at the chair. I squeeze Annie's fingers. "I'm going first." Annie looks like she is going to try to fight me. I joke, "Nope, called it, no take backs," which earns me a smile. Sam gets set up and does the transfer image on my arm, asking me if I like the placement on my left inner arm. I agree with him that I do, and less than twenty minutes later, he wipes down my arm.

I have Annie's 'I love you' permanently etched into my body. During the process, Annie held my right hand. I focus on the feel of her next to me and around me. The process didn't feel great, but it wasn't all that bad either. He repeats the process for Annie, and I hold her hand like she did mine. "Oh, ouch, you didn't even flinch. You made it look too easy." She squeezes my fingers as the needle moves across her other arm. The process takes about the same amount of time, and then she is wearing my 'I love you' on her skin.

Sam asks if we want a picture, and we take one together and then one with him. "Can I add it to my celebrity wall?" he says, pointing at the wall of himself with other famous people from the city. "Sure, I don't have a problem unless Drew does." Annie looks at me from the side. "Works for me, man." I shake his hand before we leave. We leave the shop hand in hand, our love written permanently on our bodies. I feel good about checking off one of our shared bucket list items to night.

Now I have to be patient and check off the other three with her by my side in time. I wonder how long is long enough before I can start forever with her as I drive us back to the apartment. I already put the ball in motion with her dad, making the suggestion earlier that we should continue that talk from seven years ago. I make a mental note to talk to the front office about when I can schedule a handful of seats for her dad in one of the suites. Is August too soon or perfect to start working on forever?

***

Craig is watching a movie on the couch when we return to the apartment. "Hi, guys." He looks over at us, then double-takes at our wrapped arms. "What did you all get into tonight?" "We got tattoos, of course. I would show you, but Sam told me to leave this on for a while longer." Annie says it so matter-of-factly, like that is what you do on a first date. Craig looks between us like we are crazy, and maybe we are. I don't feel crazy. I feel like my life is finally making sense.

"Did Sam also remind you about having a photo shoot in two days?" Craig is talking to me. "It's amazing what they can do with Photoshop. Plus, it's a nice tattoo; they will probably leave it in the shot." I don't tell him that I'm going to insist they don't cover it up. "Oh, that reminds me, you both are going to come with me to the derby and game, right? We can celebrate my birthday the next day in New York." I look between them. "I already have a ticket, so yes, I'm going." Craig is all sarcastic. "What about you, Angel? Come celebrate with me." She doesn't make me wait. "Yes, I'll come to the derby and celebrate your twenty-sixth birthday, Drew." She pulls me into her arms and gives me a deep, passionate kiss.

"You two are interrupting my movie," Craig announces from the couch. "How far are you into it?" Annie asks Craig after breaking our kiss. "I don't know, like ten minutes or something." "Start it over. Let's have a movie night like we used to." Annie is looking at Craig, being all serious. Not waiting for his answer, she continues. "Tell me you have popcorn and real butter in this apartment, or I'll go down to mine to get supplies, Craig Michael." Craig rolls his eyes at Annie, "Annie, why do you think I hate butter? I love butter, butter is the best." Craig gets up and heads to the kitchen. Annie follows him, and they move around the space like it's normal to all be here together.

We all sit on the large couch, Craig on one end and me on the other, with Annie snuggling up to my side between us. We start the movie over, watching the action-packed film while passing the buttered popcorn back and forth. At some point, Annie falls asleep next to me. I wrap my arm around her, enjoying that she is comfortable enough to be so relaxed. The credits roll, and Craig looks over at her. He is quiet when he speaks. "Told you that KC was the right decision." "Yeah, it looks like you were right," I tell him while looking down at her.

"I thought I fucked up after that fight in January. Glad I didn't completely read it wrong." He looks guilty on the other end of the couch. "That was supposed to be fake. We had a whole plan to make you feel bad about the setup. The fight turned real, but it needed to happen. We both needed to burn out the anger and hurt we carried all these years." I look down at her again. My life feels complete now in a way it never did without her. "Please give me a sixty-day eviction notice before you two set up house."

I look up at Craig. He doesn't look disgusted or pissed that our living situation could change with Annie back in the picture. He seems happy for me, for us. It makes sense because he worked so hard to get us here. I owe Craig a huge favor for his part in all of this. I have no idea how to express to him that I'm so grateful for his meddling ways. "Man, I'll sign over the penthouse to you in a heartbeat when she agrees to live together. Tell me where you want to live, and I'll buy you a house."

Craig chuckles at my statement. "You are both my best friends. I'm just glad we can get back to normal. But I had better be your best man over Luke; he didn't do anything to assist with this." He is pointing at Annie and me on the couch. "Deal. You can be my best man." We wrap up our conversation as I lift Annie off the couch, and she snuggles into my arms. I wake her up long enough to help her remove her shoes and change out of her outfit. I offer her one of my shirts, and she takes it and slips it on before climbing into my bed. She wraps herself in the covers like it's her own. I remove my own clothing, minus my boxers, and climb in behind her. I turn towards her, moving until I'm spooning her. I don't remember falling asleep; I only know she's in my arms.

Chapter 38: Travel Plans and Photo Shoots

-Annie-

July

I wake up snuggled into a very warm chest. I could spend all day in bed like this with him. Drew is still asleep under my body—I can tell because he snores a little when he breathes out. I can see the bandage on his arm covering his new tattoo. Last night had been a whirlwind in all the best ways. I can't believe we both got tattoos. It will shock everyone we know, just like it did Craig. I'm not known for being spontaneous; most decisions come with careful consideration, but last night, I couldn't explain it. I just had this gut feeling that this would be ok. I'll look at his words on my arm in the future and remember getting this second chance at loving him with zero regrets. We still have to get to know each other again as adults and not the teenagers we were in Oklahoma but I'm confident by the conversations we've had that we will. I've already learned so much about this version of Drew since the season started. I don't want to sit here getting all worked up about how many days we've been back together. I want to focus on each day as it comes and savor these moments before the season starts again.

Drew flies out today to go to New York for a few photo shoots before the pro games. He'd filled me in about them while we made popcorn last night. One is for a men's magazine and the other for an athletic brand he'd signed with at the beginning of the season. He is getting a lot of great press, which is giving him these career opportunities. I hope Drew doesn't get into trouble for his new tattoo. I've seen his "Guy Next Door" moniker in the media. I think the statement still holds even with the nature of his sweet choice for a tattoo.

I move carefully as I exit the bed, quietly making my way to the bathroom. I try to brush my hair with my fingers and tuck it behind my ears. I hadn't planned for a sleepover, so I don't have anything to lessen my walk of shame this morning. Drew's T-shirt covers my body completely, but I slip on my skirt and underwear before heading into the kitchen just in case Craig is already awake.

I quietly open the fridge to see what the guys have to eat. I'm impressed with all the options. I look around, grabbing a few things to make an omelet. I scream when I see a shadow behind me. I drop everything on the island, almost breaking the eggs in the process. "Craig Michael, what the hell?" I place my hand on my heart, trying to calm down from his surprise appearance. He laughs, acting like he didn't just scare me half to death. "What ya doing, Annie?" He jokes like nothing of importance has taken place. "What does it look like I'm doing, Craig?" I pop back at him with a scowl on my face. "Please tell me you aren't attempting to cook." He joins me on the same side of the island before grabbing a pan from the cabinet. "I can cook. Omelets aren't that hard." I stick my tongue o ut at him.

Craig sticks his tongue out at me in return, "Annie, until you live here, how about you leave the cooking to me? You can sit right here and keep me company." As Craig is talking, he walks me around to the other side of the island and points me to the open barstool. He pats the chair with extra emphasis, "Right here." I take the hint and sit in the open chair. I watch him review the items I've pulled from the fridge. "You have a good idea with the omelet," he says, cleaning veggies and chopping them before putting them into a bowl. "So, is Sleeping Beauty still in bed?" I laugh at Craig calling Drew a princess. "Yeah, he looked too peaceful to wake up, but I couldn't go back to sleep. I figured it was time to get up. How are you doing with all this?" I ask him, as I point from me to Drew's bedroom.

"God, you two really are alike. He was all worried about me last night, too. You remember that I helped coordinate getting him to pick KC, right? Which I did because you were going to be here, too. Do you recall that detail?" He gives me a look, like *come on Annie*. "Ok, ok, I remember that you have been a mastermind in my sex life." He cuts me off before I can say anything else. "Oh no, no, no, that sounds gross. There was only one time for that, and we haven't reached our terms to talk about that time yet. I orchestrated your 'LOVE' life. That sounds much better." He is laughing and smiling clearly proud of himself, which also makes me do the same. "Fine, my LOVE life then. Is that better?" He nods his agreement, "Yes, that is an acceptable definition. So, I have to know, what are the tattoos of anyway?" I turn my left arm and show him through the transparent film. I'd removed the outer wrap when I went to the bathroom. You can read 'I Love You' in Drew's handwriting. "Is his the same?" Craig asks. "Yeah, just in my handwriting." Craig smirks as he says, "See, I was right: LOVE life is the right way to put it."

"What should we do for Drew's birthday?" Craig changes the subject. We spent the next few minutes brainstorming ideas for a birthday celebration for Drew. Craig told me he'd reach out to Dom to see if he could help us get into a fancy restaurant or something in New York. He also told me to send him a picture of my driver's license, and he could work with it to book my travel. I try to tell him I can pay for my flights, but he makes a point to remind me that Drew will have a conniption if I pay for a ticket when he invited me to go. He's probably right, so I agree that I'll get him what he needs to help me out after breakfast.

"Go wake up Sleeping Beauty and tell him his breakfast is ready." I walk back to the room, quietly opening the door, and sneaking back into bed. He pulls me into his body. "Why do I keep waking up with an empty spot next to me when I swear, I fell asleep next to you, Angel?" His groggy voice sounds good. "Mmm, that has to do with the fact that you again looked so peaceful. Also, you have to look pretty over the next few days, so I figured you needed your beauty sleep." I tip his chin down so I can kiss him good morning. "Breakfast is ready. Time to get up." He doesn't release me at my little command.

"When do I get to have morning sex, Angel?" he asks, looking sexy as sin in only his boxers. If I didn't know breakfast was ready, I'd peel down those boxers and have my way with him. Breakfast is prepared, and I saw the effort that Craig put into it, so sex will have to wait. "Up, Sleeping Beauty. You'll get morning sex eventually, we don't have to rush everything." He laughs as he pulls me into a deep kiss before releasing me to roll out of bed. He is sporting impressive morning wood. I really will have to figure out a good morning to give in to his interest in morning sex. Maybe something to add to my plans for his birthday, but I don't think I'm sharing this one with Craig.

We have a nice breakfast with Craig, and his omelet is excellent. Drew scrolls on his phone through his schedule for the coming days. "Looks like I have to leave for the airport in forty-five minutes. Dom has me scheduled to meet with a few of the reps for the athletic brand over dinner. Tomorrow is the magazine photo shoot, followed by the athletic brand photo shoot. I'll be free after dinner with my best friend and girlfriend." He smiles over at me after saying *girlfriend*. "The day after is the derby, then the day after is the pro-game. On the seventeenth, I have a party the whole day." He finishes his list, and I'm exhausted just listening to it. I guess it's back to work for him. I am strictly in vacation mode until we are back to regular-season games.

"What does the girlfriend of a hot shortstop wear to these events?" I want to make sure I fit in with the other people attending. "Clothing would be a good start." Craig pipes up from his spot in the kitchen. "I could make clothing optional under the right circumstances." Drew looks over at me with sparkling eyes. "Boys, be serious. I don't have Meg here to help me. How fancy do I need to get? I wear my dress suits or dresses for games, but those feel more like work mode and not girlfriend mode." Drew shakes his head in agreement, "As much as I like work Annie, I want girlfriend Annie at my events. What size jersey did the team give you for the charity game?" Curious about his question I answer, "A small." He looks down at this phone typing, "I will see if the team can add a few in your size to my gear. Maybe a few hats too. You look sexy in a hat." He types out something on his phone as he talks. "I already have a Griffons hat." I argue playfully. He pauses his actions and looks up at me, "Angel, let's not wear the good luck vintage hat. Let's leave that one for home use only." His reference to my old hat makes Craig laugh. "My hat is amazing and well worn-in," I say defensively, and he pulls me into his arms. "I love that you love that hat, but my girl can get an upgrade for the pro-games."

We all head in our separate directions after breakfast. I follow Drew into his room and watch him pack a carry-on and a backpack. "Remember that lotion for the tattoo and take off the bandage tomorrow." I call to him in his closet. "Thanks, I'll grab that now." He comes out with the items before putting them in his bag. "I wish you could go with me today," he says, sitting down next to me on the bed. "Me too, but we are going to have conflicts in our schedules. We have to learn how to deal with that." I reach out and take his hand. "Yeah, well, maybe it won't feel like a big deal to be without you for a day in a few years. Today, I feel like I just got you back, and I don't like having to leaving you." He leans down, kissing my neck. "Mmm," is my response before I push him away. "No more of that, you have to go. I have to go home to start going through my own closet. I will probably need to go shopping." He pulls me into his lap. "Don't stress. Annie, you're beautiful. Anything you wear will be remarkable." How does he always calm my nerves so easily? Its my turn to kiss him before he really does have to go.

***

Back in my apartment, I send Craig my ID photo before trying to find something that looks impressive. About an hour later, I get a full itinerary for the trip. My schedule isn't as packed as Drew's, but it's full. I get distracted from trying to pick out outfits. I'll fly into New York early with Craig. From there, a car service will pick us up, taking us to the magazine shoot, or we can head to the hotel. After the first photo shoot, the sports brand photo shoot will take place. Dom pulled some strings and got us into a private members-only club. I only know this because I looked up the restaurant, and the first thing that pulled up was pictures of amazing-looking food. The following day is Derby Day, with the scheduled car service times, followed by Pro-Game Day, with the scheduled car service times. On July 17th, it is open all morning like Drew requested before our scheduled tour of New York City, followed by a fancy dinner at a top-rated Italian restaurant. On July 18th, it shows the return flight information.

Ugh, I usually hate the 18th of July. It's the day I broke up with Drew. I wonder if he feels the same about the day. I usually watch all the movies that make me cry, where the couples don't get their happy-ever-after. It's my cover for the fact that I spend that day crying, missing him, if asked I could blame it on the movies. I'm sure none of my friends believed me but they played along. I also would indulge in a large amount of junk food, feeling sorry for myself. Then the calendar would flip to July 19th, and my life would return to my non-Drew-filled existence. I'm so glad I will not need that marathon this year.

I look back at my closet, determining that I need to go shopping. All I have in my pack pile is the ribbon lingerie, some leggings and a pair of jeans. I make It to my car and click the call button beside Meg's name before pulling out of the garage. She takes a few rings to answer, and I hear her pick up. "Stop that, I'm on my phone." I hear a male chuckle in the background. "Megan Patterson, did you answer your phone when you still have a man over?" I laugh in my car as I merge onto the highway. "Well, yes, but I'm at his place now." Meg is flustered, and I need more details about this guy. "Ok, I had a quick question to see if you have a recommendation on which one I should buy. I texted you pictures."

I hear Meg put me on speaker phone. "Oh wow, these are nice sets. This little black one is very sexy." I hear a muffled "Agreed" in that male voice that sounds so familiar. "ANNIE, I think you should get the black and red sets. The white one isn't sexy enough." I hear what sounds like someone choking on the other end of the phone. "Everything ok?" I say, turning into the shopping center with the cute lingerie boutique. "Yeah, yeah, he's just choked on his water, he is fine," Meg says, and I can hear her rolling her eyes. "Ok, well, tell your new lover I can't wait to judge him later by his photos," Meg chuckles before disconnecting the phone. Something is going on with my best friend. I'll have to get to the bottom of this, but I won't get to the bottom of it now if she's still at his place.

I spend the day walking around the shops and stores. I grab a few things, I think will be nice to wear in New York. I get these cute jean shorts that have little Griffon patches on the butt pockets— plus the black and red lingerie sets. I grab two dresses, a sexy little red dress that has a high neck with a peak-a-boo cut out that shows off my breasts, and the back only has one strap leaving my back mostly exposed, as well as a black dress that has these sexy little cut-outs and a high-high slit in the full skirt. I also get a striped white and black fitted T-shirt dress at another shop. I feel like I now have a wardrobe befitting my new title as Drew's girlfriend. I head to my car. When I get back to my car, I check my phone and have missed text messages from Drew.

Drew Davis

What you up to Angel?

I just finished the interview I think I'll be adding to our trending narrative. I may have talked about my girlfriend a few times

Get to New York already I miss you

About to go to dinner call you later

Annie

Sorry I missed you I was shopping

I now feel ready to head to New York to visit my famous boyfriend

Enjoy dinner Dimples. Miss you too!

Drew Davis

I can't wait to see what you got

Annie

I may have purchased you a present

Drew Davis

Please tell me it's in line with my last birthday present from you. I've been a really good man and it was my favorite present EVER!

Annie

You'll just have to wait Dimples

Now go enjoy your dinner

Drew Davis

Fine but I don't have to like it

I drive home and pack my suitcases, feeling ready to get to New York. I get into bed early so I can get some beauty rest. As I'm winding down, Drew video calls me and we chat before we both agree that we have early mornings. He hesitates before he says goodbye and I do too because I almost say, 'I love you'.

***

Craig and I have an easy travel day. The driver is nice and asks where we want to go. He drops me off at the photo shoot, while Craig goes to the hotel with the bags. The location is a big warehouse-looking place on the outside. I'm concerned that we have the wrong location when I get out. "This location is closed due to a private photo shoot," says a security officer in front of the door. "Yeah, I'm meeting someone inside," I tell her. I'm about to give my name when I hear Dominic's voice. "If it isn't Annie Campbell, all grown up." Dominic doesn't look like he's aged in the slightest. He reminds me of an Italian version of The Rock from that sports agent show. Dominic Stone stands behind the security guard who stopped me. He waves me through the checkpoint and gives me a big hug.

"The tattoo is a nice touch on him. Makes him look a little rougher for the shoots today." I blush at Dominic's words; I have no idea why. "Yeah, it's a nice—" I don't finish my sentence because we walk into the photo shoot. Drew is in front of the camera. He doesn't have a shirt on, and they have him in a pair of shorts that hang low on his hips, showing off his muscled chest and abs. He is curling weights, and the muscles in his arms are popping with each move. I see his new tattoo each time he curls his left arm down. I will have to buy a ton of magazines when this photo shoot is published. He looks up, and our eyes connect. He smiles, and the woman behind the camera yells, "Yes, more of that smile, that smile is great." When I finally pull my eyes from Drew, Dominic is watching me. "I haven't seen him this happy in years." I shrug with a smile of my own, "I have no idea what you are implying." Dominic laughs. "Let me know if you need anything Annie, the team and I are here." I thank him and go back to w

222

atching the shoot.

As soon as the photographer says, "That's a wrap," Drew sets down the weights, telling her, "Thank you." He makes a direct line to me and slips his hands into my hair, kissing me until I can't remember we are in front of a room full of people. I put my hands on his chest and feel the oil under my hands. I pull back, "Oh, wow! That is a lot of oil." Drew laughs and grabs a towel from the chair, rubbing it down his chest to remove it. "Yeah, I guess it helps the light find all the crevices," Drew continues to laugh as he rubs all the oil from his muscles. "We need to head to the other photo shoot in about ten minutes," Dominic says as he walks back the way we came in.

"I can't wait to see the other photos if that was the last look," I tell Drew, looking over his body. "I'll give you the sneak peek." He sits down, pulling me into his now mostly oil-free body. I have my legs hanging over the armrest, his arms around my middle, and my arms around his neck. "I feel like it's been forever since I saw you last, Dimples." He smiles and I love him and it. I hear a click and look up at the photographer. "Oh, sorry, I just couldn't help myself. You all looked so perfect in the moment. I'll make sure to include it in the photos for your agent." She doesn't sound that sorry. "Well, I'm glad I wore my cute travel outfit now." I rush out and Drew looks me over and then whispers in my ear, "It's going to be my favorite photo of the day, because you're in it."

At the next photo shoot, Drew is mostly dressed in the brand's clothing from his hat to stylish sneakers. They have him pretend to bat, and the guy behind the camera asks him for his signature move after hitting a home run. Drew does his swing, pretending to hit a home run. Then point towards the imaginary wall before making a heart shape into the camera, making me smile. They have him hold the bat behind his neck. He looks in my direction and gets that dimple smile that I love. He takes a few with a glove and a ball, throwing it to some guy out of the picture. The photographer says something similar to the first, and Drew shakes his hand before coming over to my chair. "I didn't know I was dating a model." I joke with him. "Yeah, I've added it to my resume and list of talents for when I age out of baseball." He laughs. Dominic appears out of thin air. "Looks like you are officially done for the day. See you at dinner." Then he disappears again just as quickly.

Chapter 39: Dinner Plans and Derby Days

-Drew-

July

I am so tired, even though all I did all day was get dressed and undressed before taking photos. I did lift some weights during the men's magazine shoot, but not enough to be this tired. "Is it crazy that I want a nap?" We exit the elevator, and I lead her toward our suite. "Nope, I think dinner is pretty late tonight. Let's nap, and then we can scrub all those crevices clean." God, I love this woman, and it is taking everything in my power to not tell her.

She laughs when she says 'crevices' and it makes me smile. "Did I catch a 'we' in that scrubbing scenario?" I am giving her a hard time, and I know it, but it's too fun to push her buttons. "Maybe. Or, you know, I can just supervise you scrubbing those little spots all by yourself," she smarts off from behind me. "Oh, Angel, there isn't anything 'little' about me, and you know it." My statement earns a laugh from Annie. "Mr. Full of Himself. Be a good boy. Go get your nap." She makes like she isn't joining me. I grab her around her middle, lifting her over my shoulder. She squeals and laughs on my shoulder. "Angel, I'm not sure where you thought you were going, but I need my snuggle bear to sleep." She smacks my ass as I walk us to the bedroom, laughing the whole way.

After a few hours snuggled next to her, I wake up feeling much better. She stretches next to me. "What time is it?" I check my phone and tell her it's 5 o'clock. We have plenty of time until our reservation at 7:30 p.m. "Black or red?" She says as she gets out of bed. "Do I get any context for this choice?" I ask, knowing that she isn't going to tell me. "Nope. Black or red, Dimples?" she asks again, going to the closet. "Black, I'll save red for my birthday." She goes to the closet where her items are hanging, pulling out a long black dress that sparkles a little in the light.

Annie starts to undress, throwing her travel outfit into the open chair. I watch her like she was my private striptease. She looks over her shoulder at me on the bed, giving me a wink before walking in the opposite direction towards the bathroom. What the hell? I hear the shower turn on, and I'm out of bed in a flash. I strip out of my boxers, throwing them toward the chair without looking. Annie is already in the shower, and I watch the water drip down her body and then I join her in the shower, spinning her around so we face each other.

My lips taste her under the warm water as I push her back against the wall. "Wrap your arms around me, Angel." She does it without question. "Good girl." I bend down, wrapping my hands right under her ass, and lift her. She wraps her long legs around me, and my dick is wedged right where I want it. I push her back against the shower wall now with my weight as I thrust into her body. "YESSS" leaves Annie's lips next to my ear. I re-adjust my arms under her thighs to help the angle of my thrust into her body. I'm able to bounce her body up and down my shaft, harder and faster. "Drew, harder." She is begging, and I'll give her harder if she wants harder. I can hear the sound of slapping bodies as I pound into her in a relentless, unforgiving thrusts. "Your—body—is—fuck-ing—sexy—" I punctuate each word with a hard thrust of my dick into her body. "Yes, please. More. Please more." Annie whimpers against my neck.

I don't stop, pouring everything into giving her exactly what she is begging for. I feel the moment my hard work pays off as the walls of her pussy clamp down around my dick and she moans "DREWWW" so loud into the bathroom, it echoes. "That was fucking hot, Angel." I continue pounding into her, and she whimpers against me. I cum so hard inside of her that I have to drop her legs and brace my arms on the wall of the shower to not smash her against the wall. "I think I have a new favorite shower experience," Annie says in that sexy post-orgasm voice. I agree, but I can't make words. "Mmm" is the only sound I can form.

My body is still trying to remember how to function. "Mmm, indeed." She places kisses against my chest. Eventually, I unpin her from the shower wall. She takes her time cleaning my chest down to my semi-hard dick. I take my time cleaning her body with my hands. We leave the shower clean and yet I am still wanting more, I wish I could lead us to the bed. If we didn't have that dinner, I'd call it off and take her to bed again. Instead, I force myself to leave her in the bathroom to get dressed and let her get ready.

When she comes out about forty minutes later in nothing, I have to remind myself that we have plans. I chant it in my head, 'we have plans, we have plans' until she slips on a thong and takes the dress out of the bag. She looks over her shoulder. "Can you tie me in?" Did she mean to make that sound so sexy? "Sure," I hear myself say. I get up from the bed, walk over to her and tie the black material around her neck, then secure the bra-like clasp in the middle section. This dress is all cut-outs, and the peeks of her skin are everywhere. When she turns around, I'm not sure we will leave this hotel suite. The top cuts down into a V on her chest to the band right under her boobs, and then under that band is a cutout that shows off her toned abs before it meets the long skirt. She takes a step, and her leg peeks out from a slit that goes up to her mid-thigh. "Fuck, Annie," I groan into the room. "Are you trying to kill me? Because that dress is going to be my death." She laughs at my dramatics. "I'm glad that got the desired effect." She looks impressed with herself, and I can't blame her, I'm beyond impressed.

***

When we reach the lobby, Craig looks at her once. "Really, Annie Marie, did you have to wear something that shows so much skin?" He waves at her but refuses to look at her. "They are called breasts, Craig. I've had them for a while, figured you'd be used to them by now." She laughs at our friend. "Annie, I do not acknowledge that you have tits. The Annie in my mind is formless with absolutely no parts that I'd compared to my conquests." Craig spouts his poetics, facing away from her. "Just wait until you see the red one." Annie teases him and makes me look forward to the red dress even more.

Annie and I take the backseat, and Craig takes the seat by the door of the large SUV. "So, are you ready to hit some home runs tomorrow?" Craig asks me without looking in my direction. I can't help laughing. He really doesn't want to look at Annie and all that beautiful skin on display. "Yeah, ready as I'll ever be. I have field passes for you both back in the room. Please remind me so I can show you where they are when we get back. Oh, that reminds me. I have jerseys for you, Angel. The white one is the one I'm wearing tomorrow, but you have the red one as an option, too." She puts her hand on my thigh. "I'll wear the white one to match my man. I think it will go with my new shorts." She runs her hand over my thigh, which shouldn't be sexy, but it is. "Please, for the love of God, tell me the shorts at least cover your ass." Craig sounds like he is in physical pain in the seat in front of us. "Yes, Dad, they cover my ass." Annie mocks him. "Thank God." Craig's body relaxes in front of me.

The drive isn't bad, as our location is relatively close. When we get out, I block anyone from seeing Annie until she is entirely out of the car, because damn, it's a lot of skin. I want to make sure that all the best parts stay hidden, just in case. When she is out of the car, we get the celebrity treatment, which feels bizarre because this doesn't happen in KC. There are shouts of "Over here, Drew,"

"Who's the woman?" "Pretty dress, look over here at me, Honey." I hold her hand throughout the comments and share my own back "She's my girlfriend."

We took a few pictures standing outside the restaurant before heading in. There is a loud whistle. "Annie, you look amazing in that dress." Dominic doesn't have the same problem looking at Annie as Craig, because I watch him take her in from head to high-heeled toes. "Dominic" is all I growl, and I think he gets the hint because he smiles and pats me on the back. "Drew, give a man a break. She's gorgeous and you know it." Damn, do I ever, but I still pull her into me a little tighter. She wraps her left arm around me, and I notice the tattoo on her inner arm, and it makes me smile, seeing my 'I Love You' on her skin. We are led to the table, and the restaurant is impressive. We have a fantastic meal filled with laughs and a few rounds of drinks for the rest of the group. Since I have the derby tomorrow, I'm enjoying my water and the company until Dominic looks at his watch. "Let's get Mr. Home Run back to his hotel to get some rest before the bi g show tomorrow."

***

Back in our room, I help peel Annie out of her black dress, and I enjoy touching all the additional exposed skin. She takes her time taking off my shirt and slacks, one slow layer at a time, until we stand naked at the end of the bed. "Angel, you know, I was thinking." She smirks, "Oh, were you, Dimples?" I continue unphased, "I never got any dessert tonight. I need to taste something sweet before I go to sleep." I back her up and gently push her down on the bed. She makes to scoot back, but I grab her legs before she can move.

I get down on my knees as I pull her ass to the edge of the bed. Her pretty pink pussy is calling my name. I look away only to look into her eyes, and she looks horny. "Do you think I should get dessert?" I watch as she connects the dots. A sexy smile breaks out over her face. "Dimples, I think you've earned a taste." I take that as all the permission I need before bending down to eat my dessert. I take my tongue and slide it from her clit to her already wet pussy. She tastes so good. I slide my tongue up and down her until I randomly suck her clit into my mouth. At some point, her hands end up in my hair. She grinds her pussy into my face and uses her hands to guide me to where she wants me. I pull back, still looking at her swollen pussy. "Angel, you are the best dessert I've ever tasted. Think I can have it again on my birthday?" Annie's voice is husky when she answers, "Drew Joseph, you can taste it whenever you want but stop talking and finish your dessert, like a good boy." I love it when my girl is bossy, and I dip down and suck her clit hard into my mouth.

"YESSSS" falls from her lips, and I continue my efforts until I feel her body go tense and she moans my name. She pulls me hard against her clit as she orgasms. Eventually, she releases her grip, and I half stand before joining her on the bed, pulling her body next to me. She looks dazed, and it's a look that I want to give her for the rest of our lives. She leans up after a few more minutes, kissing me. "Make love to me, Dimples." I make good on her request until we both fall asleep, exhausted, wrapped in each other's arms.

***

The next day is full of a million different tasks in preparation for the derby. I head to the ballpark before the rest of the group. I meet the other guys selected to be part of the derby, and it's crazy to see some of these familiar faces and to think I'm in the same league with them. Life is good, and I will enjoy it while I can. I know that I can't play baseball my whole life. If I'm lucky, my body will age me out sometime in my thirties, so I take in every aspect of this day like the privilege that it is. They give us the bracket and the rules for how each round will go. I'll get two minutes to hit thirty pitches and try to get the most home runs against the guy I'm directly matched up against. We get our big introductions, and the fans go wild when I come out in my Griffons gear and take my place with the other guys.

I'm the fourth guy up, so I get the benefit of knowing the number of runs I'll need before I make my attempt. I go to the little waiting area until it's my turn. There, sitting and watching, are Annie, Craig, Alex, and Carlos. Alex and Carlos are also in the pro-game tomorrow and are here to support me. I fight the urge to go directly to Annie instead of Alex and Carlos. We share a handshake and a few words, both of them telling me not to embarrass them by going out in the first round. I laugh and tell them I'll do my best.

I give Craig a pat on the back and then make my way to my girl. She is dressed in a matching number 17 jersey, jean shorts, and a Griffons baseball cap. She was hot in that cut-out black dress last night, but this version is my favorite. She looks like the girl I fell in love with at eighteen. I scoot next to her and give her a big kiss. "Angel, I don't think seeing you in my jersey will ever get old."

She smiles that beautiful, full smile. "I think I can handle getting to sport number 17 for the rest of my life." *God, that sounds good*, I think to myself. I like hearing her think in those terms. "Did I miss something? I swear that Davis kissed our sexy reporter." I hear Alex asking Carlos. Carlos looks over at us. "He did see her first man, doesn't that give him dibs?" Alex shrugs, "When you say it like that, I guess. There goes Blondie from my wish list." Alex comments can't go ignored. "Damn straight it does," I hear myself say and pull Annie against my side in a half hug. "Guys are so weird" is her only reply before she pulls me into another quick kiss.

We watch the first two guys go before I go to the warm-up area with my pitcher. I feel good when "Drew Davis from the Kansas City Griffons" is announced, and the fans go wild, but none of them are as crazy as my group in the family area. I feel the energy as I step into the box. I spend the next two minutes rocking balls into the outfield and over the fence. When my time is up, I give a little heart in Annie's direction and wave to the crowd behind home plate. I have a solid twenty-one home runs hit, which gets me into the day's second round. I do pretty well on the next round, but lose out, hitting one less than my competition.

We sit in the family area watching the other guys go when Annie's phone on the table buzzes. She looks over at it and hits the ignore button. No sooner has she settled back against me than it starts buzzing again. This time, I can't help but read the name 'Dax Preston.' I'm wondering why I know the name 'Dax' when Craig cuts in, "Annie, why is your ex blowing up your phone? Isn't that like his fifth call?"

Now I remember the name 'Dax' from our little fight. Thinking more about it, isn't he one of the two guys she's been with? I have to fight the sudden urge to pick up her phone and tell him to lose her fucking number. She hits the button again to decline the call. No sooner has she done it than a message appears, and she swipes on the message, and I can just read it over her shoulder.

Dax Preston

Call me back

This is work related, Annie

She looks at me, annoyed. "He works for the network. I'd better call him back."

Chapter 40: I'm Here as His Girlfriend

-Annie-

July

I have been enjoying the derby with Drew. Even if he didn't make it out of the second round, he has been impressive. The fans went wild for him, and I heard a few catcalls of 'Dimples' from the fans when he smiled and waved at the crowd. My little nickname has gotten some ground with the female fans from our sideline interviews, but hearing other people call him that still feels weird.

During Drew's last batting round, I started to get calls from 'Dax Preston,' and I let them ring to voicemail. I have no idea why he would be calling now; it's been months. I set my phone on the table when Drew returns, and we watch the guy get one more run. I lean into him quietly, saying against his ear, "You're still my favorite home run." He places his hand under my chin, tipping my face to look at him before kissing me. I know that there are cameras everywhere, but I don't care. I'll deal with the network when we get home; if there are questions about why I've been caught in the friends and family section kissing Drew Davis.

My phone starts buzzing again, and I lean forward and click the button to silence it again. Maybe I need to text him or something to get the calls to stop. I no sooner lean back into Drew's side than it starts again, and this time, Drew looks and doesn't seem bothered until Craig and his big mouth. "Annie, why is your ex blowing up your phone? Isn't that like his fifth call?" I want to kick his shin under the table. It's more like the sixth, but who's counting, and I'm not announcing that fact out loud. I hit the button again, more violently this time to send the call to voicemail, and then I get a text. I pick up my phone and open it, knowing that Drew can read over my shoulder. I have nothing to hide. I read Dax's message and look at Drew. "He works for the network. I'd better call him back."

I hit the call button next to his name annoyed at the interruption, and he answers after the first ring. "Annie, took you long enough to call back." Dax sounds annoyed at me, I don't go easy on him. "Dax, you said it was about work. What's going on?" I want to get to the point of his frequent calls. "Annie, the sideline reporter for the pro game has food poisoning. She doesn't think she'll be able to be on live TV tomorrow." He sounds stressed I realize as the news about the report sinks in.

"Ok, Dax, and what does that have to do with me?" I ask, not trusting my brain and the direction it's taking this news. He can't be calling me to work, Can he? "Annie, I know you're at the derby. It's all the team can discuss back in the production booth. Quoting Mac here: 'Who knew our little Annie would end up with a ball player? She always seems to focus on guys like you,' and yes, he called out that I, in fact, don't look like I've played sports in my life. So, I know you're in New York, and we need someone already affiliated with the network to cover the event. Before you ask I don't think the other sideline reporter can cover both teams. Who better than 'Annie Campbell, trending girlfriend of Drew Davis, covering his first pro-game appearance." He sounds a little bitter as he says that last line, and I want to be bitchy back, but I remember that this is a work call, and I hold it in... but barely. "I'm here as his girlfriend, Dax. I'm not here as part of the network team."

Before I can continue, Drew whispers next to my open ear. "Annie, take it." At his words, I tell Dax to hold on and hit the mute button. "Drew, I came here to be with you, to support you. I didn't come here to further my career and get a lead sideline opportunity." Drew looks at me as I give my mini speech with nothing but support in his features. When I pause, he leans in and kisses me gently before pulling back. Speaking only loud enough for me to hear, he says, "Take it, I know why you're here. You know why you're here. Who cares about the rest of it? Annie, it's too good of an opportunity to give up." I look into his dark blue eyes and see how genuine he is. "You sure?" I can't help asking him one more time. "Yes, Angel, very sure."

I go back to the phone and hit the unmute button. "Dax, I'll do it, but I don't have any of my work outfits here. I planned on wearing a summer dress and a red Griffons jersey tomorrow. Will that work for the network?" Dax lets out an audible breath. "Thanks, Annie. I'm the producer on this, so I'll tell you right now: that works." We share a few more details about the timing and where I'm staying so he can get me all my press credentials before tomorrow. I end the call feeling both excited and nervous. Craig pats my leg. "Looks like I'm the only one on vacation now." My mind spirals thinking about all the players in the pro-game lineup as I start to pull open the files Dax sent me. Lucky for me, I already know three of them pretty well. I notice one of the pitchers' names and ask the group. "Guys, what do you know about Camden Wilder?"

***

Drew is amazing. When we return to the hotel, I go into full study mode. I have my routine of organizing fun facts and little tricks that help me remember who the guys are in the lineup. I realize I've been spoiled this year, only covering the Griffons, because my brain hurts after just a few hours of trying to memorize all of the information. I check the time and realize I've completely ignored Drew, and it's now almost midnight. *Shit,* I think because I lost track of time. I put my phone on the charger and turn off the lights in the living room of the hotel suite. I quietly make my way towards the bedroom. Drew is already asleep in the king bed. I strip out of my outfit and sneak under the covers to snuggle into his warm body. He doesn't wake up but wraps his arms around me, pulling me closer. I fall asleep in his arms, listening to his breathing and his beating heart under my ear.

***

I wake up the next day, and the bed is cold and empty. I get it now: why Drew's been so annoyed at waking up alone in an empty bed. I'm about to get up when a boxer-clad Drew walks in carrying a tray of breakfast options. "I thought we should do breakfast in bed before our busy day." He announces clearly wide awake. It's the sweetest thing he could have done. "Thank you, Dimples. Tell me you didn't answer the door like that." He leans in to kiss me. "I waited until they left, but yes, I did grab the tray like this. The better question is sleeping naked something you do often, or am I just this lucky?" I laugh because sleeping naked isn't usually my thing. I'll generally throw on an oversized shirt or a cute n ightie.

"I didn't want to waste the lingerie on a sleeping man." He groans at my comment. "You don't hear me complaining, but you have piqued my interest in said lingerie." Drew wiggles his eyebrows, causing us both to laugh. "Later, I'll pull out my new favorite to see what you think. Maybe I'll even let you take it off me, too." I don't know why I enjoy teasing him so much, but I do. "I'm going to hold you to your word, Angel. For right now, let's eat before this gets cold." He settles on the bed with the tray. We eat and enjoy breakfast together, talking about the schedule for today. I thank him for supporting my job, but he gives me a look of annoyance. "Annie, I'm not sure about those other guys, but I'm not bothered by your career or the fact that you have to work today." He looks me in the eyes, his dark blue eyes all serious. "OK?" I get it, I need to let it go and understand that he will support me like I support him. Message received. "OK, fine Dimples, messages received!"

I come out of the bathroom with my hair curled and my makeup done for TV. It's more makeup than I usually wear, but it's part of that TV magic. I do it to look good on camera. I have on my striped dress under my Davis jersey, which I've half buttoned and pinned to half its length, making it look like a cute little crop top jersey. I am debating whether to wear the hat when Drew enters the room. "Is this the time to confess I prefer you without makeup?" He tips my chin up and kisses me. "Aren't you the sweetest boyfriend ever?" I step up on my tiptoes, stealing another quick kiss. "It's the truth, I love your freckles." My heart races at his words. For one, they are so close to the one written on my arm, and second, because it is nice to hear that he likes me as I am and not the version that I make myself into.

"Hat or no hat?" He looks me up and down. "Hat. It fits the whole vibe." I slip the hat on and check the full-length mirror on the back of the door. Drew walks up from behind me. "I think we should move that chair over here later." I look at his reflection in the mirror with a perplexed look. He moves from behind me, moving the hotel chair to the other side of us, then he turns me to the side. "Bend over, Angel, and look into the mirror." I do as he asks and see that we line up very nicely in the mirror.

The chair offers me support that I'd need if, say, he was thrusting into me from behind. *Mmm*, I think as he leans down over my back to say next to my ear, "I think it will be sexy as fuck getting to watch us in this position. What do you think?" I think that I wish we could make good on that image right now, because I feel how even the thought of it is turning me on. "You're killing me, Dimples," I tell him, using a similar phrase he's used with me. Drew laughs, pulling me back with him as he stands up. "See you on the field, Angel."

He kisses me one more time before heading to the bathroom to get ready. I check the time and realize I need to go downstairs to meet the car. I scramble to grab everything I need to take with me. As I rush out the door, I shout, "Love you, Dimples, see you at the game." I am on the elevator when I realize what I just said. *Was Drew in the shower already? Probably*, I think to myself. He was probably in the shower and didn't hear me. My phone buzzes with a new notification. I pull out my phone as I walk to the car, but I stop when I see the name of the sender.

Drew Davis

> You cheated Angel

> I want to be looking at you the next time you say it.

> Also, I can't wait to say it back.

Annie

> Well that clears up if you heard me

Drew Davis

> Yeah I heard you loud and clear

> Look for the man that can't stop smiling

Annie

> Will he have a sexy dimple?

> I only notice the ones with a sexy dimple!

Drew Davis

> No one is going to be able to make that dimple disappear today!

I get into the car and try to focus on work. It was so easy for those words to slip out of my mouth. I should regret saying them this early, but I'm having a hard time feeling bad about it. I pull up my work email, looking over the lineup for today's game one more time, with my own smile plastered on my face. This pro-game is throwing me for a loop and here's to hoping that this is as crazy as it gets.

Chapter 41: Hearing Those Three Little Words

-*Drew*-

July

I turned myself on in a cruel, cruel way, tipping her over the back of that chair and pointing out that I would enjoy watching us fucking in that mirror. I know she is fully dressed for work and looks perfect with her hat, curls, and my jersey. What is it about Annie in my jersey that makes me so horny? I like seeing 'Davis' across her back as she is bent over the chair. I have to remind myself that she has to go. I pull her body from the bent-over position before kissing her. I head to the bathroom to shower and prepare for the game. I can hear her rushing around the hotel suite, and then I hear it. "Love you, Dimples, see you at the game." I stand stunned looking at myself in the mirror.

I have a massive smile on my face. My Annie told me she loves me. I mean, I know that she has hinted. We physically marked the words on our bodies, but hearing her say it feels bigger. Even more so by the fact that it seemed so easy for her to yell it as she was leaving. I go back into the bedroom, grabbing my phone from the night stand. I send her a message. I know Annie; she probably realized that she had said it out loud, and now she will worry about it. I hold back from texting her those three words. I want to look into her eyes when I say them. I don't want any doubt about how much I mean them. I give her a hard time about her deliver, then return to the bathroom to get ready for the game. I wasn't kidding: my smile isn't going anywhere today.

***

That is, until I see her at the stadium talking to a guy standing way too close to her and touching her left arm. *This must be 'Dax,'* I think. Even though I'm out on the field to warm up, I tell the guys that I'll be a minute. I take off in a short jog in her direction. She isn't directly facing me, but I catch what she says to him. "Why do you care that I got a tattoo anyway?" He sounds annoyed, "It says 'I Love You.' But there is no way he means it. Annie you are smarter than this." *Well fuck you, too, man,* I think. He continues in that same annoyed tone, "I care about you, Annie. I don't want you to be hurt when he finds his next hookup." *Who the hell does this guy think he is?* He doesn't know anything about me.

I feel the need to claim her, and my brain flashes a multitude of ways to show this asshole and anyone else that she is mine. I still have enough control that I know if I do any of my bright ideas, I'll piss off Annie, or worse, hurt her career. I talk down my male brain, and when I reach them, I wrap my arm around her waist. "I wanted to see my girl before we start." She turns and smiles. "Hi, Dimples." I kiss her before she can say anything else. When we break the kiss, I make a point to look at Dax and put out my left hand, showing off my 'I Love You' tattoo.

"Drew Davis, Annie's boyfriend. You are?" I know he sees the tattoo because he looks from my arm to hers and then reaches out his hand, shaking mine. "Dax Preston, Annie's producer for the day." Annie rolls her eyes at my actions, or maybe at me showing off my tattoo. She is still smiling and isn't angry with me about my move, at least. "Nice to meet you, Dax. Annie is going to be great today." He follows my comment with one of his own. "I know. I called her for a reason. She's great at what she does." I turn and look at her one more time. "I

241

better get back to the warmups, but I need one more kiss." Annie rolls her eyes but turns and kisses me. Damn, I'm one hell of a lucky man.

***

The pro-game is a different environment. Winning and losing matter, but it doesn't impact any of us or our teams directly. It's a game that is more about bragging rights and fun. Annie interviews people throughout the game. She isn't just talking to players at change overs; I watch her interact with guys on the team in the dugout. I get annoyed when Alex flirts with her, but I know she's my girl now, so it feels different. I don't get that hot burn of jealousy or worry that she may return his interest. I have a lot of fun with my temporary teammates. I make a few plays on defense, and the crowd goes wild after a double play. I can hear the chant of 'Dimples' from the female fans. I look at the woman with her back to me, *Davis peeking out* across her back. I'll never hear that nickname and not think of her. I wish no one else knew about it: that it was still just ours. Yet, people know it because she's called me in it because she'd still had feelings for me, so I can be ok with others know it as long as I hear it from her daily.

When Camden gets the last strikeout of the inning, we head in for our last at-bat before the end of the game. Annie goes over to him, starting her interview. This guy acts like he is a gift to the world. He isn't one of my temporary teammates with whom I'm not getting along. I barely catch him responding to her. "I think you have the wrong jersey on Angel baby." I see red. It literally flashes before my eyes. *What the fuck did he just call her?* If I hear him take it one step farther, I will not be accountable for my actions. "Angel, baby, come on, let me show you what it feels like to date a real ball player." He's crossed a line, and I turn to head up the steps, but Alex is in my way. "Davis, hold up before you do something stupid."

I am about to push him out of my way when I hear Annie take control of the situation. "Camden, no thank you, I'm with the only ball player I'm interested in. From what I've heard, some of those headlines this summer are true. Interest to hear which ones? I can confirm them; I've got a credible source if you'd like to discuss them." My girl gives him a smile and turns back to the camera. *She is a badass,* I think. "Back to you all for the last inning of the pro-game coverage." The camera guy moves, but still has his camera on Annie. She goes to follow him, but Camden grabs her arm. It isn't me that leaves the dugout at his action—it's Carlos. "Get your hands off Annie." I don't think I've ever heard Carlos angry but there is no denying that is what he is now. Alex looks over at one of the guys behind me. "Keep him in here." He points at me before leaving the dugout and joining Carlos on the field.

Chapter 42: Part of the Family

-*Annie*-

July

From the moment Drew took the field, I feel him. I didn't expect Dax to pick this moment to notice the tattoo on my arm. He's been talking with me for the last hour about how I will get the coverage passed. It could be for interviews, or it could be the team asking me a question. This game is meant to give the fans that inside-the-dugout feeling, and they will be bouncing between me and the guy on the other side of the field. I don't know what triggered his interest, but one minute we are talking about work, and the next, he's changed the topic. "Annie, when did you get a tattoo?" I give my practiced answer, "Oh, a few days ago. It shouldn't be too obvious on camera." I am assuming that is why he is asking. Dax looks at it and then gives me a disappointed look. "Annie. You just met him." It looks like Dax hasn't done his homework on my history with Drew. I am annoyed that he is trying to act like he cares, when he picked his job over a relationship with me. He just doesn't like that I've moved on with someone else.

"Why do you care that I got a tattoo anyway?" I ask Dax. He looks at me with pity before loudly responding to me. "He says 'I Love You,' but there is no way he means it. I care about you. I don't want you to be hurt when he finds his next hookup." I'm about to tell him what I think about his 'care about me' comment when I feel a strong arm around my waist. I don't have to check who the arm belongs to; I know it's Drew. I look over my shoulder at him and smile before he says, looking directly at me, "I wanted to see my girl before we start." It causes me to smile. Drew leans down, giving me a quick peck of a kiss. He looks away from me, puts his left arm out, and introduces himself. "Drew Davis, Annie's boyfriend. You are?" I roll my eyes at his move, acting like he doesn't know that th is guy is Dax.

Dax takes his offered hand and introduces himself as my producer, which is accurate. They share a few moments that feels like a pissing contest. Eventually, Drew leaves to rejoin warm-ups, but not before we share one more kiss. "So, he has one too, then?" Dax says once Drew is out of hearing range. "Yeah, maybe do your research next time because this isn't new." I point from me to Drew on the field. "We have a history. We are giving it another try." Dax lets it go, and the conversation returns to the baseball game and the job.

***

I am having a blast with this game. It's not the same format as a typical game: I interact with the hosting commentary team when they are on the field, I get to host interviews in the dugouts and in-between innings. Most of the guys I don't know are nice, and I can recall a fun fact or a big play they've had this season, which helps them to interact with me. I get to interview both Alex and Carlos. They both give me a little extra attention during their interviews. Carlos is the sweetest, and when he walks up to me, he hugs me. "Our Annie, it's good to see one of the family at the pro-game." It makes me smile when he calls me family. "Miss Annie, I have to ask: why Davis's jersey though?" Why not mine or Alex's?" I don't get a chance to answer before he's making it a joke.

"It's because of his home run, isn't it? I'll start working on getting more of those for next year's game." He laughs as he says it. Usually, I try to stay super professional, but I don't fight my own laugh. "Oh, Carlos. I'd be lying if I said that was the only reason I'm in his jersey." Carlos laughs, "Don't tell me it's his personality." Carlos does air quotes when he says, 'his personality,' causing me to laugh harder. "Carlos, thank you for the laughs. I'll keep this between us." We joke a little more before he goes back into the dugout.

Drew's team does well in the top of the eighth, with a double play and Camden getting a strikeout. I hear Dax tell me to grab Camden for an interview since he will not bat. Camden gives me the once-over before we start talking. Knowing that he dated Emma makes it feel gross. Other guys have done the same thing, but I don't know their ex-girlfriends or how they treated them. I have to fight the look of disgust. We have a normal start to the interview, and then it goes sideways fast because Camden takes the jersey comments too far. "I think you have the wrong jersey on Angel baby. Let me show you what it feels like to date a real ball player." I know I look disgusted now, and I don't think—I say the first thing that comes to my mind. It isn't a threat, but I do intend for him to back off

Looking at Camden, I give him a smile and look back at the camera. "Back to you all for the last inning of the pro-game coverage." The camera guy starts moving, and I know I'm meant to walk with him as he is still recording, but I don't move. Camden grabs my arm and holds it tightly. I look at it and say, "Remove your hand." He smiles, but it isn't kind. "What the hell was that bitch?" Camden says using my arm to pull me in so he says it directly in my face. I expect it to be Drew running out of the dugout, but it isn't: it's Carlos. I can't help feeling relieved that Drew is still in the dugout but I also don't want Carlos to get in trouble either. I hear Dax in my ear, "Annie, you're still live, you're still live!" At the same time, Carlos joins us on the field. I have no idea what he wants me to do with that information, but I do feel some comfort in the fact that someone else is seeing this interaction.

"Get your hands off the lady." Camden doesn't seem to hear him or doesn't care, I'm unsure which; I just know his hand is gripping my arm harder. Camden leans down closer to me, smiling that evil smile. "You will lose your job for that comment, mark my words. You don't matter to this league like I do." I see Alex heading out of the dugout next, and he looks serious. It's not a normal look for him, which worries me and sends my adrenaline spiking. "You don't mess with family, man. Get your hands off of Annie." Alex shouts at him as he heads in our direction. I think it's about to turn ugly, so I take the moment into my own hands before the guys get into a fight. I give Camden a warning before I make my next move. "Last chance, Camden. RELEASE MY ARM NOW." I say it with all my anger directed at him. When he doesn't release me, I take one step closer and then like my brother taught me, knee him right between his jock strap, stra ight in his balls.

Dax is still in my ear, and he lets out a few comments on the situation: "Fuck, Shit, FUCK" before followed up with "Good for you, Annie. We have it all on tape; you asked him twice to release you." Camden is kneeling on the grass, having released my arm in his pain. I walk around him to join Alex and Carlos. They both pull me into a group hug. "That was amazing!" Alex says next to my ear. "Please never do that to me. I promise I don't touch women without permission. Are you OK?" He makes me laugh, and I make sure he knows I appreciate him. "You are a flirt, not a jerk. Plus, I heard we're family. And yes, I'm ok, just a little surprised he touched me."

"Damn, right we are. You mess with one of us, you get all of us." Carlos join in on the conversation. "Go back into the dugout, guys, before this gets crazier." I look down into the dugout, my eyes connecting with Drew's. He is being held back by two of the other guys on the team. He looks at them before giving them a nod, and the guys release him. Drew looks pissed, but he is looking at me. I see him take a deep breath and stay in the dugout as Carlos and Alex rejoin him.

247

I walk with the camera guy back to a waiting area where he puts the camera on a stand. "That was incredible, Annie, but are you really ok?" I know I just met him, but it is nice that he is checking on me. "Yeah, I'm ok. I hope it doesn't cost me my job." After I say it out loud, it feels possible that my decision could cost me. The camera guy looks at me with a serious expression. "I doubt it, since we got it all on camera. He touched you without your consent." I hear Dax checking in again on my headset. "Annie, are you okay with staying, or do you want to call it?" I refuse to give Camden that power over me. "I'm going back on air; he doesn't get my last interview." Dax sounds in my headset again, "Network is fine with it and is already working on an official comment with their support of your actions." I feel relief at his information, "Dax, thank you for letting me know that." I take a few calming deep breaths, look at the camera guy, "You ready to capture the last inning?" He nods before picking up his camera. I look down the lense and do my job.

Chapter 43: In Front of The World

-*Drew*-

July

I watch the guys defend Annie, and I see the moment she understands that if they swing on Camden, it will get them into trouble. I watch from my spot in the dugout as she turns to Camden and says clearly and loudly, "Last chance, Camden. RELEASE MY ARM NOW." She moves closer to him, which makes my stomach drop, before I see her drive her knee into his balls: hard. I see Camden hit the grass, before I watch Annie get wrapped up by Alex and Carlos in a hug. I don't know what they say, but I know she is ok.

I should have known she'd be able to handle Camden; this isn't the first time she's put an asshole in his place for touching her. Like the first time, I'm impressed by her ability to put a big guy in distress. Our eyes connect, and she gives me a little shrug and a look of concern. That is when I remember that I'm still being held back by the guys that Alex left in charge of keeping me in the dugout. "You can let me go. I'll stay in the dugout." The guy on my left releases my arm and comments, "She is one hell of a woman." I hear myself say, while still looking at her, "She sure is."

Alex and Carlos come back into the dugout and pat me on the back. "She's ok...

and impressive," says Carlos. "Yeah, glad that she never pulled that move on me." Alex gives me his signature smile and laughter. "Thank you, guys for going out there." I try to calm my nerves by put on my batting gear. "She's family, man. No one messes with family." Carlos is serious again, and I can't help but smile at how protective these guys are of Annie. I like that they treat her like she is part of the team and family.

It makes sense that they feel this way because she's been with us all season. I know these guys would have protected her even if she weren't my girlfriend. I've never been happier I'm in KC with these guys as my teammates. The ball game is all tied up, and one run will end the pro-game. I'm third in the rotation and watch the guys before me get on base. I'm primed from the adrenaline in my body from what took place. When I step out of the dugout, I know I'm hitting big, that feeling is in the air. I step into the box, set my stance, and when the fastball comes at me, I swing for the fences.

The ball cracks off my bat, and I know that I've hit it out of the park. I drop my bat and point at Annie as I jog towards first. I do the heart in her direction before jogging the rest of the bases. My pro teammates give high-fives and pats on the back at home plate. When I'm through the team celebration, I don't hesitate, and I head in Annie's direction. She is clearly on camera talking to someone I can't hear. I know the moment they clue her in about me being next to her. She smiles in my direction, making my heart race faster. "In true game-winning fashion everyone, here is the home run man himself, Drew Davis."

I step closer to her now, directly in front of the camera. I don't know what I'm thinking, but I reach out, pulling her in for a quick kiss. I think it could be the leftover concern from what took place or the adrenaline from the game-winning run, but I don't care as I feel her soft lips against mine. She doesn't fight me or pull back, but sinks into the kiss. "I had too, sorry," I say. "You would too," I say to the camera, to anyone watching, causing Annie to laugh. "Drew, that was an impressive kiss—I mean, home run. What motivated you to swing big on the first pitch?" She must not have meant to say the first part because she blushes a lovely pink, staining her cheeks.

"If I'm being honest, you." I continue before she asks me a deflection question. "I was pissed after what happened with Camden. The guys all did the right thing, keeping me in the dugout, and you did the right thing defending yourself, but I was pissed that I wasn't there for you. I needed to hit something, so I came out of the dugout determined to swing hard." She looks at me for a minute after I finish, as if she forgot we are on camera. Looking at me and not the camera, she whispers, "I'm ok." I look at her and I believe that she is telling me the truth but I need her to understand how amazing she is. I don't hesitate, "You are amazing. I love you, Angel. I'm so proud of you." I didn't mean to say it on camera. I've surprised myself saying that right now. I was looking at her, feeling proud of her, feeling like— hell, exactly what I said. Like I love her. It comes out of me in the moment, totally unplanned and entirely true. She gives me her genuine smile. "Love you too, Dimples." The moment is only broken by the guys dumping a very cold jug of water down my back and Annie jumping out of the path of the cold shower at the last minute.

The camera guy points the camera into the air, saying to Annie. "If this isn't the most memorable pro-game I've been a part of, I don't know what to compare it too." Annie laughs at him as she disconnects the mic and removes her earpiece. As soon as she has removed the equipment, I wrap her up in a bear hug, lifting her off the ground. "You're cold and wet!" she says playfully against my ear, but she doesn't pull away. At her ear, I tell her the truth about the moment. "I didn't mean to say it on camera, but I don't regret it. I love you, Annie." She has her arms around my neck and she says against my skin, "I have no regrets either." I take a deep breath, feeling better about my accidental 'I love you' on camera. I set her down and wrap her hand in mine. Alex and Carlos join us along with her producer, Dax. Dax is the first one to speak. "When I asked you to join the broadcast, I never thought it would be such a big night." Annie shrugs against

251

my side, "Glad I could keep it interesting for you, Dax." Annie turns serious as she continues to talk to him. "How bad is the fallout online?"

At first, I think she means from our moment on camera, but then Dax goes in a different direction. "I told you the network has already posted a statement supporting your actions. They have been very clear that it is never 'ok' to touch a person without their permission. I quote: 'We stand in full support of our reporter Annie Campbell and her actions to defend herself,' end quote." Annie takes a deep breath, turning towards the three of us. "You guys' better go finish what you have to do as part of the game. I'll see you back at the hotel." She directs to me and squeezes my hand before she lets go. She's right; we have a few events to finish before the pro-game is officially over, but as soon as I'm released, I'm going to get back to my woman.

***

After all the press events, I get back to the hotel lobby at 11:45 p.m. It's been one hell of a long day. As I wait for the elevator, I realize I have fifteen minutes before my birthday officially begins. Dominic let me know that the events of the night have gone viral. His team is keeping an eye on it, but it all seems supportive of her actions and support for us as a couple. I tell him I appreciate him and the team monitoring this for me. He had clapped me on the back, "Drew, Annie's a good person. I won't let Camden's team twist this in the press." I'd nodded and thanked him again and then quickly made my excuses to leave.

Quietly, I go into the hotel suite. All the lights are off, and I think Annie is asleep in bed. I do my best to be quiet as I strip out of my clothes until I'm left in my boxers. I walk slowly to the bed, slipping into the covers, and I feel silk covering Annie's body as I wrap my arms around her. She stirs in her sleep. "Drew, what time is it?" I tap my phone on the nightstand, and it reads "12:01 a.m.," I answer

252

her. "Happy Birthday, Dimples!" She sounds fully awake now. "Close your eyes and sit on the edge of the bed." She went from being asleep to being bossy, and I am not going to fight her. I move but don't cover my eyes; the room is already dark.

I see Annie's silhouette as she makes her way to the door. I hear the click of the switch, and the light goes on in the room. *Fuck me,* I think, because there in the doorway, in the same red ribbon lingerie from seven years ago, is my fucking girlfriend. I swear that my dick instantly hardens in my boxers. Her boobs are spilling over the ribbon that she has tied around her nipples, and I can see the outline them through the silk.

The mirror behind her gives me a perfect view of her thong-covered ass. "I thought I told you to cover your eyes," she says as she walks her sexy body in my direction. "Stop," I hear myself say, and then I think, *Shut up, brain, we want to touch that body,* but my brain has other ideas, and I like those too. "I think I need to capture my twenty-sixth birthday present with a photo. You know, to make sure I NEVER forget it." She puts her hands on her waist. "Adding to your collection, Dimples? Go ahead, but here I thought you'd want one after you opened it."

I pick up my phone and take the photo before setting the phone down next to me on the bed. "I'll take an after-opening picture, too, because you offered. I think it's time for unwrapping presents and blowing out my candles." Annie makes her way between my open thighs. Like on my nineteenth birthday, I slip the silk ribbon free, and her nipples are revealed, like any good present. I close my eyes and make the same wish I did at nineteen. *Let me keep her forever!* I really hope that I get better results this time. Before I blow out my candles, I pick up my phone and open the camera. I suck her nipple into my mouth as I click the button. I don't release her nipple from my mouth, but I set my phone down. I have no idea if the picture is any good, but I have a feeling it will make the collection anyway.

When I feel like I've sucked on this nipple long enough, I pull back, releasing it and blowing on it, earning me a moan from Annie. I lavish the same attention on the other nipple, finishing it with another blow of air. "I think that covers the birthday candle portion of the evening." I pull her into bed, but she resists my efforts. I know I look confused, because I am. I want her whole body, not just a taste. *Where does she think she's going?*

Annie steps back slowly, still with her eyes on me. "Dimples, I thought you wanted a show for your birthday?" She steps next to the chair before bending over it, offering me a beyond sexy view of her ass. The only thing blocking my view of her sweet pussy is a little red string. I am up and out of my boxers in a flash. I walk over to her bent-over body and smack her round ass cheek, and it makes a loud sound in the quiet room, but what is more deafening is the moan that escapes Annie. *Mmm*, I think, *does Annie like it a little hard, a little rough?* I'm game to explore her needs.

I lean over her back and, next to her ear, ask her, "Do you like it hard, Angel? Ask me to fuck you hard." She shivers, and then she lets out a moaned "Please." "Angel, I would like to hear you say it. Consider it another present," I smirk, waiting to see if she'll give me the words, and she doesn't make me wait long. "Please fuck me hard, Dimples." Her voice is so husky as she says it. I quickly pull the red thong from her body. It isn't hard to notice that she is already so wet. I stroke my dick in my hand and then slide it from her pussy to her clit. "Look at the mirror, Angel." I meet her eyes in the mirror as I slide my dick hard into her pussy, and she doesn't disappoint with a moan of "yes." I watch myself pound into her body; I watch her face in the mirror as I do it.

Normally, doing someone from this angle, you don't get to see their face, and I like that the first time I'm watching myself fuck a woman like this is with Annie. Getting to see her reactions to my hard thrusts is making me harder. I'm not going to last long, watching her every reaction. She is watching us in the mirror too, and I see her eyes looking, watching as my dick appears and disappears inside her body. I feel how wet it makes her to see us like this. I reach down and slide my fingers over her clit, watching her eyes roll into the back of her head. She lets out a loud, "DREWWW." "Open your eyes, Annie, watch us," I say in a commanding voice. I'm not usually the type to be commanding, but it feels right for this moment, so I go with it. Annie seems surprised but turned on by it, too, because she opens those dark blue eyes meeting mine in the mirror before going back to watching me slam in and out of her.

I up the tempo and then remove my hand from her clit. Reaching up with both hands, I pinch her nipples as I drive into her. She moans, letting me know that she likes it all. I can feel my balls tighten. I know I'm moments from finishing. I reach back down, pinching that little nub, and feel Annie tremble under my body. "Cum for me, Angel. I will catch you." I pound into her, squeezing her clit until her pussy clamps down and she screams. I release her clit, but I don't stop slamming in and out of her. I grip her hips and drive myself to my own re lease.

I feel myself slip out of her body as she slowly stands up on shaking legs. "That was incredible, Dimples." She gives me a lazy smile. "Yeah, that was... WOW." My brain isn't fully functional yet, and finding words is hard. She starts laughing as she looks at me. "Did I break you, Dimples?" "Yes—yes, I think you did!" I step into her body and hug her to me. She yawns against my chest. "Let's get you cleaned up and go to bed." She nods, and we go to the bathroom and wash up. Annie removes the bra before turning off the light and joining me in bed. I fall asleep naked and spent, already having the best birthday I've had in years, and it's only just started.

Chapter 44: Celebrating the Birthday Boy

-*Annie*-

July

I wake up to buzzing, which I realize is one of our phones going off. *Probably Drew's*, I think, *it is his birthday*. He is snuggled around my body, spooning me, and I could almost go back to sleep in his warm arms, but then the buzzing sounds go off again. I am fully awake now; there is no going back to sleep, and I know it. I should get up, but I promised myself that I'd be at his side when Drew wakes up on his birthday. I try and fail not to stretch my body. Oh yes, we had *really* good sex last night, and my body tells me so when I stretch. Then, I freeze when a kiss lands on my neck.

Oops, I think. I hadn't meant to wake him up. He continues to kiss along my neck and down to my shoulder, and I feel him growing against my back. "Good morning, birthday boy," I say quietly. "Mmmm" is the only sound he omits before he runs his hand down my leg, gently pulling it back up to my breast, and then I offer my own "Mmmm." He slowly rolls me to my back and covers me with his big body. "Mornin' Angel," he says in that quiet voice as he slowly slides into my body. "Yes, it does feel like it's going to be a good day," I agree as he offers me tender strokes.

We fucked last night, but now we are making love, and it's as powerful this morning as it was last night. We are sharing kisses and touches, none of them rushed, none of them rough. I have no idea how long we spend with our bodies connected like this. Eventually, the pressure builds to an incredible level, and I know I will explode. I tell him, and then and only then does he increase his thrusts, pushing us both over the cliff. We don't immediately separate, but Drew does change the position of our bodies, and I'm now lying with my head on his chest. "That is what morning sex should feel like, Angel." He says sounding satisfied. "I get the appeal, Dimples." Neither of us are in a rush to get up, and I enjoy drawing the lines of his abs. The phone buzzes again, and this time, Drew does pick up the phone. "Holy shit" is all that he says.

"Holy shit, what?" I sit up, worried. "Hold on." He hits the call button next to Dominic Stone, and it rings on speaker phone. "Finally, you answer. Happy Birthday, by the way." His agent is direct when he picks up. "Can you tell me what is happening?" Drew isn't tense, but he isn't at the same level of relaxed as before he looked at his phone. "It appears your girlfriend is making all the morning news stations this morning, like every single one. The story is making major news on socials, too." Before Drew can ask a question, I ask one of my own. "How bad is it?" I feel my heart racing. I am sitting here naked, thinking about the possibility of losing my job. I know the network supported me, but public opinion is hard to overcome. I realize I need to get my phone, but I'm glued to the bed beside Drew.

"None of it, if you don't count the comments. I rarely count the comments. You seem to be getting a lot of praise for staying calm in the situation and communicating clearly with him to release you. People also seem to like that you didn't rely on any of the guys to save you. People are particularly impressed by seeing Camden knocked down, as his reputation for cheating has been a rampant subject in the tabloids. Annie, let me know if your team needs any PR help on this. We are always happy to help." Dominic sounds calm the news isn't b ad.

"Thank you, Dom. I'll let you know after I talk to the network." It was nice of him to offer and I really will think about it. "Thanks, Dom. I appreciate the team keeping us updated on how this is going," Drew adds. Dom is his agent, not mine. The call ends, and I get up, throwing a robe over my naked body. I head to the suite's living room area to get my phone off the charger. I have so many messages. I have no idea where to even start. Maybe I'll start with the fact that Emma has called four times. She may be my producer, but she is also my friend, so she has a vested interest in what happened last night.

"I fucking love you!" Emma answers the call after only two rings. "Well, I love you, too!" I say, laughing back at her opening. "Seriously, Annie, that was the best, most wonderful moment of baseball. Watching the clip of you rocking him in the balls was already great, but watching it go viral was even better. It felt like karma in the best possible way. The clip making all the major news stations this morning is the exact thing Camden deserves." Emma sounds like I've just given her the best gift of her life. "How did you date a guy like that?" I can't help but ask the question after meeting him.

"I have horrible taste in men, I know I've told you this, Annie." I can't help interjecting on Craig's behalf, "I hear that may be improving." I remember that I haven't talked with her since the girls' night. "Oh, well, that... Mmm, well that wasn't planned." She is clearly a little flustered. "Craig is one of the good ones, promise. I think you should think about it." I offer, but don't push it. "I'll think about it, but we have some work to discuss now. The network has been requesting that you do some interviews or talk shows. They know you're in New York and want you to stay and do some press. What do you think?" *What do I think? I think that this is unbelievable.*

I'm going viral for kneeing a guy in the balls for grabbing me. Defending myself shouldn't be getting this much interest. "I can't do anything today, it's Drew's birthday," I tell Emma. She says "That's fine I'll tell them that you're in for press." I realize that I don't have a wardrobe, "I will need a day to get interview outfits. I don't have anything here to wear." Emma ever the problem solver replies, "I'll make a few calls and get you a stylist from the network. Annie, enjoy today with Drew. I'll email you and text you the details." I thank her and we disconnect the call, promising to talk later.

I sit quietly on the couch when Drew comes out of the bedroom. "Is now a good time to admit I was eavesdropping?" I smile, because it's so like him be honest to a fault. "I'll stay in New York a few more days after today from the sounds of it." He sits beside me, and I lay my head on his shoulder. "You doing ok with all this, Annie?" He asks. "Yeah. It seems crazy that it's getting so much attention. I kneed a guy in the balls, what's the big deal?" Drew laughs, and it vibrates through his body. "For all mankind, is now a good time to admit how bad it hurts. Like, it hurts a lot to get hit in the balls. Daniel texted me 'Happy Birthday.' He told me he can attest to the pain of being on the receiving end of Annie Campbell's defensive move." I don't fight the laughter that Drew's comments bring out in me. "Daniel also told me to tell you that he was impressed. He holds no grudges, because he had earned it, too." I calm down and let him know that I'm leaving kneeing Daniel out of my interviews. He laughs at my comment. A knock at the door makes us both turn towards it. We hear Craig's voice through the door. "WAKE UP, BIRTHDAY BOY: IT'S TIME TO SEE NEW YORK CITY!"

I slip into the bedroom to shower and get dressed in jeans and a T-shirt. Today is about celebrating Drew and spending time in NYC. I come out of the bedroom with my Griffons' hat over my fishtail braid and only mascara on my face. "You look beautiful, Angel." Drew says making Craig roll his eyes. "I only have mascara on." I laugh at his comment. "I stand by my statement." Craig interjects, "You guys make me sick with all the cute couple stuff." Craig rolls his eyes again but is also smiling at us. "Oh, do we make you sick?" laughs Drew before he pulls me into a kiss. I let him slip his tongue into my mouth before I nip at his bottom lip. "Ok, ok, point made, assholes." Craig is covering his eyes when Drew breaks the kiss. Looking between Craig and me, he asks for at least the third time, "What is the plan for today, anyway?" Craig gives me a nod of his head, asking a silent question of whether he should tell Drew. I give him a nod of 'yes,' and Craig jumps into his planning mode. He gives us the rundown of all the sites, and restaurants, we will visit on our big day around NYC. We are going full tourist mode today. None of us is trending or on TV or a pro at anyt hing.

Today, we are three mid-twenties adults from the Midwest getting to take in the Big Apple. We pay our respects at the One World Observatory, visit the Empire State Building, and look out over the city that goes on for miles. We eat bagels, and pizza and drink coffee at a Friend's pop-up shop. We see Times Square, and I have no idea where to look because there are so many screens. We are walking around Times Square when a group of women walks by and they shout, "So proud of you." I look around, trying to figure out who they are talking to. *That was weird*, I think, and I continue to walk hand in hand with Drew. A moment later, a woman with a Texas accent starts waving and talking.

"Oh, hello, excuse me." I know she spots Drew because, come on, he's so hot that he stands out in a crowd. I turn, but she isn't looking at Drew; she is looking at me. "I told my daughter that you were the reporter from the baseball game, and we just wanted to say good for you, Honey." *Oh, wow, they want to talk to me.* I wasn't expecting this at all. "Oh, thank you, I did what anyone else would do." The lady shakes her head no and follows up, "No, Honey, you did what we all should do when a man thinks he can use his power over us. You tried with words first, then you showed him with action that he had no right to touch yo u.

That's what we need more young girls to see and understand. We can't let men like that control us." I hadn't thought about it like that. I thank her again, and she turns back to her group. I feel Drew's fingers squeeze mine in comfort. "You ok, Angel?" He asks for only me to hear. "Yeah, I didn't think about it like that before. I was reacting the way my brother taught me to. I didn't think about girls or women not getting lessons or support in defending themselves. Now I understand why its gotten so much attention." Drew looks over at me with a dimple on his face.

***

Hours later, I change into my little red backless dress for dinner. I get a whistle from Drew when I walk out into the room. "Happy Birthday to me." He wraps his arms around me, pulling me into a kiss. "I've always loved you in red." He pulls back and spins me in his arms. "I've always said it is my signature color." He nods his head in agreement before giving me another kiss. When we meet, Craig looks down. He gives me an eye roll. "Annie, really?" I give him a side hug. "You look pretty, even if the dress is short." I smile against his side. "See, it's not so hard to say nice things. I'm proud of you." Drew gives his buddy a pat on the back, and we head to the car. We enjoy a relaxing, drama-free dinner with laughter and good Italian food. By the night's end, I'm worried I will bust out of my red dress from the many dishes I've sampled.

I check my phone while we wait for the car outside the restaurant. Emma has laid out everything, and each day of the three additional days has been organized with events for me to attend. "It looks like I'll be staying for three more days. They extended the room, so I don't have to change hotels. Emma has a selection of outfits being dropped off in the morning." I watch Drew for a sign of an adverse reaction, but he doesn't show one at the change to our plans. "Can you leave me a shirt of yours?" He hugs me before looking at me. "Of course, Angel." I break another piece of information, "I'm going to miss two games, but you'll get to talk to Nick on the sidelines." Drew does not look impressed with this news. "Nick is nice, give him a chance. I really think you'd like him." Drew looks less impressed at my defense of Nick. "Oh, is he really NICE?"

I look at Drew with his tone; he seems annoyed and jealous. "Are you jealous, Dimples?" He is now avoiding eye contact. I step in front of him, taking his jaw in both hands, and make him tip down to look at me. "Seriously, Drew, it wasn't anything more than a few kisses. I figured out pretty quickly there was no spark. I was hung up on my ex-boyfriend." The storm clouds in those dark eyes are still there but are softening. "I don't like thinking about you with someone else."

I appreciate his honesty, but I want him to understand. "I'm serious, Drew, I kept dreaming of you, while I tried to date him. It wasn't fair and I called if off. He knows baseball, and I think you can appreciate that." Drew mumbles "Not likely." I try to give him perspective. "Luke kissed me a few times, and you seem fine with him." Drew pulls me into his arms. "Those kisses took place before me, Angel. It's different." He wraps his arms around my hips. I don't want to end his birthday on a sour note.

I lean up to whisper in his ear, "Do you want birthday dessert or more candles?" Drew kisses my forehead "I like this subject change, Angel. I'm starving for more birthday cake, but I could use more time with my candles too." I pull back asking, "Red or black, Dimples?" I see the lust on his face as he thinks about this choice. "I'm sticking with red as the theme for this birthday." Back in the room, I change into my new red lingerie set. We celebrate the birthday boy a few more times before falling asleep, wrapped around each other.

Chapter 45: It Doesn't Feel The Same Without Her

-*Drew*-

July

It's weird leaving New York without Annie as we originally planned, but as we discussed, our careers are going to take us in different directions sometimes. We both have to find our peace with that. I want to show her that I support her career, I will back up my words with my actions. Craig and I head back to KC, and I don't waste a second to start putting my plans into motion. Because more than ever I know my future is her and I want to call her my wife. We wasted enough time, and I don't plan on wasting any more of this life without her by my side.

I call the club to request a suite for Annie's dad and guests. The team rep is amazing, and I get possible dates in minutes. I call Mr. Campbell, and we look into a weekend a few weeks from now. I also text Meg for ideas about rings, which results in her calling me and screaming in excitement. "Ring shopping!" She'd exclaimed and the berated me in the next breath with, "Drew, this has to be done in person." I know I want something special for Annie and Meg is probably right that it would be easier to design a ring in person. "Sounds like you better come visit KC if it has to be in person. Mr. Campbell is coming in August: come down at the same time." I give her the dates, and she tells me she will check with work to see if she can get a day off to make it a long weekend. I think I'll ask her since she's already on the phone. "You think Mr. Campbell will give his blessing?" Meg makes a scoffing sound on the other end of the phone, "You know he will." We say goodbye with her promise to get back to me ASAP.

***

I record all of Annie's interviews, watching them all with Craig. I feel lame that I miss her so much, and I'm glad when baseball starts back up. I get lost in the game day routine when I return to the field. The only thing that throws off my game is that I don't see my girl when I look on the sidelines. I see the guy who tried to get in my way, and I don't understand the energy that goes through my system at the thought. It's all wrong, and I know it. I know it when I miss a throw to first, and when I strike out on multiple at-bats, and again when the coach calls me into his office after the game.

He gives me the out, blaming today's performance on not being as rested as the other guys. I played in the pro-game and the derby, but I don't deserve the out. I go home in a piss-poor mood. "Someone got flowers!" Craig shouts when I open the apartment door. "What?" It is the only thing I can think of as a response. It's a weird thing to hear from Craig. "Look at the flowers, man." He is standing at the kitchen bar, pointing at flowers. A vase on the bar sits filled with red roses and a teddy bear in a red dress. I smile because it is ridiculous, and only one person would have send me this. I take the card and read, "It sucked, but I'm going to be home soon—get better before I'm back. PS: Love you, Dimples. PPS: I thought you might need a substitute snuggle buddy.

I take a picture and post it on my socials with the caption, "When your girl knows it was a shit game but loves you anyway." Craig grabs my phone and starts to scroll through the photos. "Do you have any not lame or cheesy photos in the last, say, fifteen days? I bet you that you don't have any without Annie." He continues joking. I usually wouldn't care that he is scrolling through my phone, I have nothing to hide, but I remember in a panic, that I have those photos from my birthday. I haven't moved them to my secret collection yet.

"Man, stop scrolling now." Craig thinks I'm joking as he swipes through my photos. I know when he gets to the ones I am worried about because he throws my phone at my head. "Fuck, man, what the hell!" I catch the phone, being the baseball player I am, and look down at the photo that caused his action. It's a very nice picture of my mouth on one of Annie's boobs and her exposed nipple, and the other boob is on full display. "I think I'm going to have to burn out my eyes. Why do you have a picture of her tits on your phone? No, nope, don't answer that. I know why, and as a guy, I understand. As her friend, I want to burn your phone and figure out how to take down the cloud."

Craig looks pale, and I feel a little bad. He really is her second brother, and I know he loves her that way. He runs his hands through his curls. He has let his hair grow here in KC, and his curls are everywhere. "I did try to warn you, man. The flowers are nice." He gives me a look that says *fuck you*, and then he says it. "Fuck you, man! Remind me that your phone is a bomb the next time I try to touch it." He punches me in the shoulder as he leaves the kitchen. He shouts as he heads to his room. "Tomorrow, I'm making you do all the exercises you hate as retribution." I laugh so hard as he slams the door. *That's one way to get over a bad game,* I think. I head to my room and call my girlfriend, hoping we can do a sexy video chat.

***

Today's game will be an improvement; I'm determined not to let this be round two of poor performance. I do all the right things during warm-up, focusing on baseball. I haven't looked for her once because she isn't here, and I know it. I focus on baseball and enjoy being in the zone. I don't get a home run, but I knock one into the outfield. It brings two guys home, getting me to second. I eventually score a run when Alex hits a solid grounder a few bats later. I slide into home plate. I know that all is right in my baseball mojo. I'm on fire on the defensive side of the ball, getting several assists on outs. When the game ends, Coach gives me a pat on the back, telling me good job.

Before heading out of the dugout, he tells me I need to talk to the interview guy. *Well, shit,* I didn't mean to play well enough that I have to go be on camera with Nick. I take a deep breath, put on my professional hat, and do my job. "Drew Davis, great game, man," Nick says before he offers his hand. "Nick Jackson, nice to meet you." I shake his hand and glance at the camera pointed at us. I think it's on and that we are on TV, but I have no idea. I mentally note to ask Annie if there is a way to tell.

Nick isn't glancing at the camera, and it is the tell that he isn't used to this kind of interview. "Nice to meet you, Nick. I think you have a few questions for me?" I give him a little verbal nudge to get things started. "Right, lets dive in. How did it feel to have such a big defensive game?" It isn't a bad question. "It felt good being out there and helping the team get plays going in the right direction tonight. Couldn't have gotten that last out without Carlos's efforts in the outfield, so I can't take all the credit." Nick asks me a few more questions, and the guy at the camera says, "Cut." Nick thanks me and says he hopes I can join the local show soon. I tell him I'll consider it and that I'll have my team contact the show with dates. As I walk away, I hear the camera guy asking Nick. "Who do you think they will get to replace Annie?" I want to turn around and ask him what he means, but I keep walking, thinking, *Why the hell would they replace Annie?* When I get back to my locker, I text Dominic. If anything is happening at the network, he'll be able to figure it out. I don't know who he has on his pay roll but no secret is safe from Dominic Stone.

Drew

Are they replacing Annie?

Dominic Stone

Well hello to you too Drew

I'll check around

Drew

Thanks man

Two hours later, I have my answer from Dom. I don't know how to feel about it. Dominic tells me that the network will be offering Annie a job as a panel voice on *The Baseball Show*. Dominic explains what this means for Annie's career without mincing words. He tells me he isn't surprised, that her PR had been on point with the network, and that the fans loved her. She seems to have captured baseball fans' hearts around the country, not just the Griffons fans, especially as she has taken on the news shows and talk show hosts as part of the coverage after the pro-game. I ask him the question that is running rampant in my mind. "Where do they shoot the show?" He answers quickly with LA, unless they are filming on location at the Series, and then the team travels. I thank him for the information and get off the phone.

I have been sitting here in the silence of my room, wondering, how does our future work from two difference cities. It is crazy that KC already feels a little less like home, and she hasn't even taken the offer yet. Hell, I don't know if she even knows it's coming. As if thinking about her conjures her, Annie's name appears on my phone. Annie's face appears, and she looks stressed. "Drew, the network is asking me to travel to LA before returning to KC."

She doesn't look happy, which determines how I handle this. She has no idea about the offer yet. "When do you get back from LA, Angel?" I ask in as neutral of a voice as I can muster. "I'm not 100% sure yet. As soon as I know, I'll call or text you. I can't wait to get home." She sounds and looks tired, and I wish I could make this easier for her. I make some small talk about the 'why' of it all, and I go to tell her what Dom told me when she tells me her flight is boarding, and she has to go. She smiles at the camera and says the words I can't get enough of. "I love you, Dimples. Get some sleep." I tell her I love her too and we disconnect the call, but I don't sleep. I worry all night long about what our future holds.

Chapter 46: The Offer

-Annie-

August

I am on day two of talk shows the network wants me to cover. I watch the KC game on my phone in the car between locations. Drew is off the whole game, and true to my word, I don't blame myself. Ok, no, that is a lie. I do blame myself a little for this impromptu stay in New York, but I don't think about leaving him, not even a little. I want to make him smile, so I order seventeen red roses to be dropped off at the building with a little teddy bear wearing a red dress. I put a little note together that I think will make him laugh. I spend the extra to make sure it is a rush order before I get ready for the next talk show.

The comedian host is totally amazing, as nice in person as he is on camera. He has daughters and tells me he has shown them my video. He tells me he has been practicing the move with them, but not as the test dummy. I laugh and tell him that is probably a good idea. I don't have any missed calls and realize that Drew is probably getting out of the stadium. I'll wait to see if he calls me after he gets home and sees his flowers. I go back to the empty hotel suite and undress before showering. I hear my phone from the bathroom, quickly turn off the shower, I grab the towel, and scurry to the phone in the bedroom.

Drew's face flashes on the screen. I swipe the answer button, and his face appears on the phone. "Angel, why am I looking at the ceiling and not your beautiful face?" I finish wrapping the towel around my body and pick up the phone. "I was trying to dry off; I jumped out of the shower to answer your call." A wicked smile crosses his face as he takes in my explanation. "So, you're naked," he says in that sexy voice. "I am in a towel." I correct. "I think you still owe me phone sex." He says in his sexy voice and now looking at me with his 'I want to have sex' face.

I would jump him easily with that look on his face. "Oh, do I?" I purposely unwrap the towel and lift it to the edge of my screen so that he can see it isn't wrapped around my body. Then I flip the camera view to show that it is now thrown on the back of the chair. "Fuck, Angel." I watch him rip off his shirt, exposing his upper chest's, i get a glimpse of his toned muscles. He was sitting on the bed, but he gets up, propping the phone next to something on the bed. The show really starts now as I can take in his whole exposed chest, and as I watch him slip down his joggers, exposing his hard dick.

He has a nice dick, and he is clearly turned on right now. I watch him crawl back into the bed before picking up the phone again, and I see only his shoulders and face again. "You look happy to see me, Dimples." I sound horny as I say it, and I can tell I look horny in my little window on the screen. "I'm always happy to see you, Angel, and you know it." He smiles at the phone, and that dimple turns me on more. "How do you want to do this?" I ask because we are totally having p hone sex now.

I've never had video phone sex before, and I have no idea where to start. "Use the pillows and prop up the camera. Put it lower so I can see you touch your pussy." Drew directs me and I like the idea of it as I can feel myself getting wet, and my nipples are raised. I do as he suggested with my phone. I take my position on the bed, and I realize that he is getting a full view of me from my breasts to my pussy. I put a pillow behind my head to be at the right angle to see the screen and him. I minimize my video box so that all I see is him.

He has moved his phone while I was adjusting mine, and now I get a good look at his chest, abs, and his sexy dick. "Hell, Angel, you look so hot. I think you should be touching yourself. Touch your boobs for me." I do as he directs, reaching up and touching my breast. I imagine that my hands are his hands; I pinch my nipple and make myself moan. I watch him as he strokes his hand up and down his shaft. It's making me burn hotter, watching him watching me. "Move your hand down and play with your clit, Angel," he directs me, and it's hot. If someone had previously told me being directed to touch myself was going to make me so turned on, I'd have laughed at them, but now his directions are only making me burn hotter.

I let out a moan when my fingers find my clit and give it a little squeeze. I don't wait for his directions now. I glide my fingers down to my core, dipping two of them into myself. "Yes, take what you need, Angel." He groans over the phone. I am hypnotized by his rhythm as he pumps his hands over his hard dick. I'm already so wet, which isn't normal for my solo sessions, but I guess I shouldn't be so surprised because my body has never had a problem getting wet when Drew is involved. "Watching you fuck yourself is so sexy, Angel." He groans over the phone. "I like watching you, too, Dimples." I hear myself mumble.

I don't recognize my own voice. I move my fingers in and out faster, curling them to the right spot. I know that I'm close, and I slide my second hand down to play with my clit. "Dimples, I'm going to orgasm." He pumps himself harder, faster, and I hear his groan as he finishes over his hands and stomach. His release spurs me on, and I pump my fingers into my core harder, and I cum hard. "You're so gorgeous when you orgasm, Angel." I feel myself blush, but my body is already warm from the orgasm, so I don't think Drew can tell over the phone. "You coming was so hot, Dimples. You motivated me to find my own."

We both clean up from our shared orgasm. "The flowers are nice, but I especially liked my new snuggle bear. She still isn't as good as you." He pans the phone over to the side of the bed I've been using, and there is the little bear with the red dress. "Glad you liked the flowers, Dimples. Good to know that I can't be so easily replaced." We talk for a little longer until I let out a long yawn. "Angel, it's late, you'd better get some sleep." I check the time and realize that it is past midnight. "Ok, fine, I'll sleep. I love you." "Love you too, Angel." We disconnect the call, and my last thought before falling asleep is that I can't wait to get home.

***

Two days of press turned into four. I can't say no, so I make the best of the opportunity. I do a mini media blitz. I go from news shows to talk shows to podcasters. If it's produced in the New York City area, I've talked to them. I feel exhausted, and I miss Drew. We went from seeing each other at every game as 'friends' to spending every day wrapped in each other's arms after we kissed at the club. This week has felt like torture, and I realize that I want to go home. Home isn't just KC now; it's him, he is my home. I've missed so many games, or at least it feels like a ton of games to me. That kills me too, because I miss the team; like they said at the pro-game, we are my family. I am in the car to the airport when I get a call from Emma.

"How is it going?" She sounds stressed. "I'm good, how have you been? How has Nick been doing?" She lets out a sigh before answering. "He is ok. He forgets to do the setups, and his interviews are a little awkward." Emma lets out a huff. "Well, I'll be back soon. Let the world know that if you knee a guy in the balls, you must talk to everyone about it." My comment makes her laugh. "Too bad he isn't having to make the rounds to amend for his bad behavior. At least the media loves you. Have you seen the comments from your late-night interview? Everyone loves that you are the girl next door, Annie." Emma sounds like I'm doing a good job, and I find comfort in the fact that someone I trust in the business says I'm doing all the right things.

"Ok, friend hat on now. I need to whine about missing Drew." Emma laughs again in my ear. "I wish I had your problems. Go ahead and whine to me about missing your sexy shortstop." "He looks so sad every time we video chat. I also miss the sex: it is *so* good." Emma laughs, "Annie, it's only been a week." I whine back, "But it's so good." She laughs again. She is the best at letting me whine about my life. "What about you, Emma? Any sex in the cards with a red-headed person we know?" Emma, pauses before answering, "I, well... No. No sex. I will admit, since I had to hear about you missing your shortstop, that I've enjoyed personal time with the referenced redhead in my fantasies." I let out a whistle, "Emma, I must say both good for you and gross." I laugh, and so does she. I'm about to tell her I have to go because we are almost to the airport when she i nterrupts me.

"Hold on, Annie, I'm getting a message from corporate." I sit silently, waiting for her to return to the line. "Annie, looks like you're being requested to change plans." Emma is totally in producer mode again. "What? No. I want to go home." I whine and forget that we are talking work now, not personal life. "Looks like corporate wants to talk to you in person. Let me jump off this call and get you booked to LA versus KC as soon as possible, since I know you're already at the airport." Emma disconnects the call without getting a response from me. I let the driver know that I have to wait to learn my flight information. He parks near the airport to wait for our marching orders. Emma calls me back in record time, letting me know my flight is only thirty minutes later than my originally planned flight. I update the driver, and we are off to the airport.

***

After getting through TSA, I realize I hadn't even asked Emma why corporate wanted to see me. What the hell does the network need to talk to me about in person? It can't be bad, can it? They just sent me on this crazy media campaign, but is this a setup? Did I say something wrong on one of the shows? I don't think so, but I can't be 100% certain because I can't remember all the different segments. I love my job and don't want to lose it over something like this.

I spend the next ten to twenty minutes spiraling. Could the league be pulling my credentials? Could they give me a permanent ban from baseball? What will I do for work? I'm thinking through everything the network could need to say to me in person that can't be handled with a simple video conference meeting or phone call. Eventually, I check the time and see I still have time before boarding to make a call. I pull up the name of the person I am missing most, which will help me clear the voices in my head. The phone rings a few times, and then I hear his voice, and my nerves don't disappear, but they mellow.

"Hello, Angel. Your flight says it's about to board." He sounds strange as I interject. "Drew, I have some bad news." I cut right to the chase, because he is excited for me to be home. "Corporate asked me for an in-person conversation, so I'm being asked to fly to LA." He is quiet on the line before he finally speaks. "Well, that sucks. I miss you." I let him know that I miss him too. I mean it; my heart aches from missing this man.

I word vomit all my concerns to him. He listens, not cutting me off or trying to tell me I'm crazy. When I am all word vomited out, he finally breaks his silence. "I don't think they would fly you to the other side of the country if they had bad news. Hear them out. It's probably going to be something big for you. Annie, I want you to know-" I get distracted by the notification that the plane is boarding. I want to dive into this more with him, but I have to go. "I love you, Dimples. The plane is boarding. I'll text when I land but I have to go." He quickly replies, "I love you; Annie have a safe flight." We disconnect the call, and it's not until I'm flying over the country that I realize his *I love you* sounded sad. I promise myself I will make this trip quick and get home to my man.

The trip is not quick, and I've been asked to do more press here in LA. I have no idea why I need to do more talk shows and podcasts. I have missed so much of my real job, I'm starting to get frustrated. My only saving grace is that Drew is on fire on the field again. It eases my guilt that my absence isn't affecting his performance on the field. I'm grateful, because I am exhausted and don't need anything else to add to my problems. I'm in my ride share on the way back to the hotel when I see Meg Patterson's name on my phone screen. Who better to talk to than my best friend? I swipe the phone to answer it. "Annie Marie, why am I in KC and you're not?" She sounds like she's enjoying her time in KC, and I'm jealous. "I have this last meeting and then I'll be on the next flight home." I mean it, I don't care if they want me to go to the moon, I will politely decline because I want to get home.

"I still can't believe they waited this long for their little in-person talk." Meg and I totally agree on this topic. "In less than two hours, it will be over, and in a total of five hours, give or take, I'll be back in KC." Meg laughs at the determination in my voice. "The real question is which apartment you'll be visiting first?" She is teasing me, because the answer is obvious. "Is that even a question?" I laugh back at her. "Nope. You are going to go straight to Drew and get it ON." She sounds so old with her *get it on* reference. I hear a male voice in the background, and I know exactly who it is this time. "Tell Drew I miss him?" "Miss you to Angel." He shouts before Meg cuts him off, "We are catching up, and I'm giving him the talk about his intentions with my girl." Meg sounds very serious, but she must be playing it up because I hear Drew laughing over the phone. "I told her my intentions are all dirty things."

"Ask him how dirty? I need details." I ask Meg causing her to laugh and repeat the question to Drew. I hear him from a distance giving details. "We start in missionaries—or do we start with you on top?" Before I can listen reply, I hear him get muffled, and Meg hushing him with, "Drew, her dad is right there," followed by his "Shit." I am laughing so hard in the back of this ride share that the driver is checking on me in the rear-view mirror. This is what I needed before going to talk to corporate. This is what my heart is missing.

***

The corporate offices are nice, and they have a mini sports complex in the center with tennis, pickleball, and basketball courts. No one would be surprised that our business focuses on sports. I get checked in, and a lovely woman takes me to a conference room. The meeting attendees on the calendar invite are just me. I'm really nervous about who will be waiting for me in this room. To say I'm shocked is an understatement because the main broadcasting team of ex-baseball greats from *The Baseball Show* are in the room. I shake the hands of Brett Johnson, Garret Michaels, and Vinny Romano. I feel lucky to be in the room with these guys as they sit down. Brett leads off the conversation, cutting right to the point. "Annie, any idea why three old guys are joining you today?"

I shake my head no and say, "Absolutely no idea." Vinny laughs before continuing. "We need someone just like you to put these two—" he points at the other guys "—in their place." Garret jumps in, making it clear. "What these knuckleheads are saying is that we are here to offer you a spot on the show." *Holy fucking shit*, I scream in my head. Their show is the biggest show for baseball fanatics.

It's my biggest career dream to appear on *The Baseball Show*. "The money guys will talk money, but we are here to sell the show," Vinny interrupts my inner thoughts. "I don't know what to say," I tell them honestly, because this isn't what I expected. "It's *Yes, and when do I start*?" Brett pipes in, but he smiles as he delivers the statement. "Oh, I..." I stammer because I'm unsure what to say to either. "Give the girl more than a minute to think about it, Brett." Garret pats Brett's shoulder and smiles at me. I spend the rest of the visit with the guys and get to make a guest appearance on the show. My pick for who will win it all may be evident when I bring up KC as the only choice. I may also hype the performance a of certain sexy shortstop.

Chapter 47: Loving Her Enough

-*Drew*-

August

I love baseball, I remind myself every day in early August, because I do, but I love her more. Missing her sucks. We talk every day that she is away, but it's not like waking up to her by my side. We have more phone sex, but again, it's not as good as the real thing. How did I go years without her? I have no idea how I did it, and I also have no idea what I will do when she is in LA all season and I'm here. It is killing me to keep it a secret, but I never get another really good chance to tell Annie about what Dom told me. So, I do the only logical thing left, and I t ell Craig.

"What do you mean you KNOW she is getting an offer?" He clarifies when I finish my confession. "I know because Dominic told me before she flew out there." Craig looks at me with a serious expression. "Remind me never to cross Dominic: he knows way too many things. You told Annie what Dominic said, right? What did she say?" I don't meet his eyes when I answer. "Nope, I went to tell her, and she got called for boarding. We've mostly been texting with our schedules since she got into LA and our video calls are reserved for other things." Craig rolls his eyes at me and lets out an annoyed sound, followed by an equally annoyed look. "Why the hell not?" I push back, "Well, for one," I say, putting up my middle finger. "I don't know that the information is true. Two." I put up my second middle finger. "I didn't want to get her hopes up, and then it was something else." "One and two back at you, but I guess it makes sense not to say anything." He is still flipping me off as he agrees with me.

"What do you think she is going to do?" He asks as he puts his hands down. "Take the job. It's an amazing opportunity. She'd be great on that show. She will be able to establish herself as a key baseball commentator." Craig seems surprised by my answer. "Doesn't that mean she'll have to move?" I cringe at his question, but I try to recover before answering. "Yeah, to LA." He asks the question with a look of concern. "How does that work? Y'all just got back together. You're locked into a ten-year contract here in KC." I take a deep breath and run my fingers through my hair.

Why does Craig have to ask all the hard questions? "We do long distance. She was willing to do that for me once. Why can't I now do the same for her?" The concerned look is still on Craig's face, which isn't making me feel better. I thought he would jump at the chance to agree with me. "I love Annie, you know I do, but it didn't work out so well last time y'all tried the long-distance relationship." He is right, but we've grown up, and I have my dream career now, and she should get hers, too.

"It's different. We are different. It didn't work last time because we didn't communicate our fears and we let bumps in the road turn into mountains. This time we will talk, we'll make it work." Craig slides me my smoothie and nods his head. "I hope so, for both of you. I watched both of you live life in half measures when you broke up. She did it in college, you did it in Arizona. I've seen you each become whole again here in KC, from just being around each other." Craig is a great friend; that is 100% a fact. "Wanna know another secret?" I think it's time to bring Craig into my plan for the future.

"Tell me it's a good secret." He grumbles. "Maybe?" I play it up. "Fine, yes you know I am great at keeping secrets." He laughs at himself, and I can't help but join in. "I am going to ask Annie to marry me." He comes around the island and gives me a hug and pats me on the back. "About time, man. About damn time." I tell him about Annie's dad and brother coming into town, so I can get his blessing. I tell him I asked Meg to come into town to help me design a ring. His face only reflects back the enjoy he feels for us. You'd think I told him I won the Series, because he is vibrating with excitement when he replies, "I'm going to be the best best-man ever!".

***

Meg, Miles, and Mr. Campbell got into town last night and are staying until the game on Saturday. I have a lunch date with Meg today, followed by ring shopping. I scheduled a reservation for dinner with Mr. Campbell and Miles to talk about asking Annie to marry me. My day is all about securing our future and Annie's will be about furthering her career. She has her meeting at the corporate offices today. Her move to LA will not change my mind about asking her to marry me. I want her forever; regardless of the distance we'll have most of the year. I can't wait for her to be my wife.

I pick up Meg at her hotel, and we have a fun-filled lunch catching up. "Did I ever thank you for introducing Annie to lingerie?" I mock toast her. To anyone listening, I'm sure it sounds like a weird question, but this is Meg. Meg laughs and grabs my free hand on the table, overcome with her laughter. "OMG, Drew! No, you haven't, but I'll take that as a thank you." She releases me and grabs her own glass and clinks it against mine. "Tell me which one is your favorite?" It's nice to know that Meg is still the same, no filters. "I still like the birthday special." I laugh. "Oh, that was a great one, perfect birthday set." I can feel Meg bouncing on her toes under the table. We talk and laugh, enjoying our time together, catching up.

From the original friend's group, Meg is the one I lost when we broke up. I understand why, but it is nice to have her back now. We get lost in our conversation before I notice the time and get our check so we can make it to our private appointment at the jewelry shop. Meg is wearing heels, of course, and she trips right before we get into the store. I catch her before she falls on her ass, and we share a laugh about how ridiculous her fashion choices are. "You know they make normal shoes, right? She rolls her eyes as she responds. "I'll wear those to the baseball game. Fancy jewelry store equals fancy shoes. We want them to take us seriously." Meg isn't wrong, everyone in the store looks similarly dressed. The woman assisting us is great, and she loves that I've brought my girlfriend's best friend to help get the ring right. Meg and I spent a few hours creating what is going to be a beautiful ruby and diamond engagement ring. We even have a concept for a wedding band to show Annie after I propose.

***

I drop Meg off at her hotel before getting ready for the dinner of my life. What will her dad say? Will he think we haven't been back together long enough? Will he have other objections? I worry and plan for all of the things he could say. I'm nervous as I wait at the table in the back of the same steak house we visited as a group last time they were in town. I want to make this easier and more comfortable in a private place, but not my apartment. They don't make me wait, arriving at the time of the reservation. I stand up, shaking both of their hands, and they slide into the booth on the other side of the table.

We make small talk and order our meals. I am about to change the subject, but Mr. Campbell does it for me. "Davis, go ahead. I think I know what is coming, but the floor is yours." Miles looks at his dad with a raised eyebrow. The look screams *What the hell was that, Dad?* I almost laugh, but this is serious, and I need to focus. "Mr. Campbell, I love your daughter. I know we haven't been back together long, but I'd like your blessing. Like you said before the draft: when it's right for us, I can ask her to marry me."

Miles looks amused, and Mr. Campbell doesn't miss a moment. "I think you should start calling me Will, Drew. My family doesn't call me Mr. Campbell." Has her dad ever called me Drew? I'm sure he has, but it's rare, and the fact that he wants me to call him Will is entirely new. "Love my Annie like it would kill you to lose her. I saw my daughter's pain after you all broke up. I understand that was a choice she made but she never really got back her shine until the last few months." He looks at Miles before looking back at me. "A Father only wants to see his kids happy, and I know that she is with you." His voice is soft, and I can see the emotions in his eyes. "I will, Mr.—Will. I've never stopped loving her. I promise to love her for the rest of my life."

Her dad offers me his hand over the table. "Then you have my blessing to ask her to marry you." I take his hand, relaxing. Miles has been quietly sitting and taking it all in, but he captures my attention. He interjects, "But remember, Drew, I'm not afraid to hurt you if you hurt her." He sounds serious but is wearing a smile. "I'll never forget Daniel's face. But while we are making it clear, I don't plan on hurting her either." I tell him and he responds by offering his hand and saying, "Welcome to the family". We go back to safer subjects like sports. I listen to Miles talk about his students and he tells some hilarious stories. I swear that we were never that stupid. Mr. Campbell laughs and then regals us with a few of our teenage missteps that sound very much like Miles's students' stories. After we leave the restaurant, I realize that I'm going to look forward to all the times we come together as a family.

Chapter 48: Family In The Ball Park

-Annie-

August

I get home late from the airport after my flight got delayed by two hours. I am mind-boggled by the possibilities and worries. I don't call Drew because of the time and the fact that he has a game tomorrow. I make it inside my apartment to find a pretty pink box on the kitchen counter with a note. I open the card and read. *'I knew you'd avoid waking me up, so I got your spare key from Craig. (hope that is ok!) I think you should get comfortable and come to bed. Love, Dimples.* I smile as I open the box to find a little red nightie.

My guy was listening when I told him I didn't normally sleep naked. I change into the nightie in the living room and quietly walk towards my bedroom. There in my bed is my man. He is doing that adorable snore, which means he is clearly in a deep sleep. I tiptoe to what has become my side of the bed, slipping quietly into the covers. I try not to touch him, not wanting to wake him up. I am turning my back to Drew when I almost scream as a strong arm wraps around my waist and pulls me into his large chest. "Go back to sleep," I whisper. "It's late." I whisper again as his lips meet my neck. "I'm having the best dream." His voice is deep and sleepy as he starts to kiss along my neck—his hand slides down the silk fabric, dipping between my legs. I should but I can't help lifting my leg over his, opening to his touches.

"Best wet, wet dream ever." He grumbles against my body. He slides his fingers through my wetness. "Mmm" is the only sound I can omit. He works me over, getting me to burn. As much as I'm enjoying his fingers inside my body, I know I want more. I roll myself over and on top of his body. Face to face with him, I kiss him hard and deep. I feel how hard he is under me, and I want more. I push down his boxers enough to slide my body down his shaft. "Oh, wow." He groans. He is fully awake now. His hands are everywhere on my body. I line him up and then grind my hips down his shaft. It's been too long apart; we rush towards our shared climax. When we finish, I snuggle into his warm arms and have the best sleep I've had since his birthday.

***

I wake up wrapped in a warm human blanket. I snuggle into his large chest, and he is already awake when I tip my face back. "Good morning, Angel. You know, I thought I had a sex dream last night. One where the sexiest woman rode me." I push up from his chest, blushing, before I kiss him. "Good morning, Dimples. I had a similar dream but got to ride a sexy baseball player." He laughs and pulls me back into a kiss, which doesn't end until my lips are swollen. He doesn't push for more, and neither do I. "It's good to have you home." He says when we break our kiss. I snuggle my head back onto his chest. "Yes, I'm right where I belong." We stay snuggled in my bed in a comfortable silence. Eventually, I think about the offer and the fact that I need to talk to him about what happened at co rporate.

He must be a mind reader because he breaks the silence first, "So, tell me about your visit with Corporate." I don't want to build up to it; I want to get to the heart of the offer. "I got offered to be a co-chair on *The Baseball Show*." I am watching his face: storm clouds are clear in those dark blue depths, but I also see how proud of me he is. "I'm so proud of you, Annie." He says but I hear the worry in his voice about what that means for us. "Thank you." I hear myself say but can't help the feeling of dread in my body. I don't want to leave him and move to LA, I want all my mornings to start like this.

"So, when do you start?" His question is so simple, but I hate that he thinks I'd make this decision alone. "I didn't say yes. I wanted to talk to you first." I confess. He sits up, looking at me now with concern. "Annie, you have to take it. It's a huge opportunity and something I know you want." I hear the desperate sound in my own voice, "But I'd have to leave KC." I want to say 'I'd have to leave you' but I can't form the words looking at him because I don't want to leave him. My heart hurts thinking about leaving him. I told him I wouldn't leave, and I me ant it.

"Annie Campbell, I love you." He takes my face in his calloused hands, tipping my face to look at him. "We can do long distance. You don't have to choose. I refuse to make you choose." I see how sure he is that we could make it work, but my mind pushes the fact that it would be months apart. We would only get small breaks to see each other. How can you have a relationship when you're always apart? I don't want that. I want mornings snuggled together, I want nights of making love, I want life with him here. "I love you, too much to leave. I appreciate you supporting me, but I'm still going to turn it down." I expect him to be happy with my revelation, but he doesn't; he looks frustrated.

"I will not cost you your career." He lets me go and gets out of bed, creating distance between us. "I didn't say you were costing me my career." I can hear the frustration in my reply. "Annie, be honest with yourself. If the club hadn't happened, we would have just kept up the flirting. You'd be taking this job without a second of hesitation." He is pacing my room, and I can't stay sitting and watching him. I get out of bed and interrupt his path. "No, Drew, your wrong, I had a plan. I was over being friends—I wanted more. Ask Meg if you need to, but I was done flirting with you. I wanted this, I wanted us back." I am mad at him for reducing this to a moment of lust in a club. I feel it in my blood, boiling, because this is so much more than that. How dare he try to push me to pick my career over him? I will not do it. *Oh shit, I think I'm having a moment of clarity.*

I sit down on the bed, feeling sick to my stomach. This scenario feels so familiar, but I was on the other side of it last time. I did the same thing to him at nineteen. I pushed him to pick his career. I gave him no chance to change my mind before I walked out. I feel my tears before I can stop them. His hands are on my cheeks, brushing them away as he kneels before me. His lips join his fingers, kissing my tears away. "Annie, please don't cry. It kills me to see you cry." I look up into his eyes and say with all the emotions I'm feeling, the thought that is driving the tears. "Please don't leave me, like I left you. Please." I feel desperate. I know I sound like it, but he can't end this because of a job offer.

"Annie." He says my name quietly as he looks at me with concern etched into every inch of his face. His thumbs continue to brush away the tears that I can't stop. "I choose you. I've wanted you since the moment I saw you celebrating a fake goal in your backyard. I wanted you when you wanted Daniel, and I wanted you when you left me. Annie, I will always choose you. But what I won't do is hold you back from being everything you ever dreamed. So, you have to say yes: you have to go to LA. You have to go be Annie Campbell, expert baseball reporter, because you are great at what you do." I go to speak, but he places one of his thumbs over my lips. "Please let me finish." I nod my head, agreeing to listen, and he continues. "I'm contracted for ten years here in KC. But don't misunderstand me. I'll be in LA every chance I can. I will sleep on flights and be the king of frequent flyer miles. We already proved that we are good at phone sex, and we can become experts at it." I can't help the smile that comes to my face , and he returns it.

"We can do this together. I don't plan on us ending over this, but I can't be the reason you don't get your dreams. We will have to be good at managing calendars that's all." He removes his thumb from my lips, but I don't speak. I throw my arms around him and fuse my body with his. I mumble in his arms, "I will think about the offer. I told them I needed time to make this decision. My hesitation isn't just about how to make us work, but about what I want for my future too." I pull back and look at him, taking in every detail of his face from his dark blue eyes to that dimple just peeking out from under his five o'clock shadow.

"I want you to understand that this is our decision. We both get a say in the yes or the no. I get a vote in what will make us happy too." He nods his head in agreement. "I'm 100% in on what makes you happy, Angel." I give him a look, "No, Dimples. You didn't hear me; it is 100% about what makes us happy—" I draw my hands in the air between us "—because there is no I in US." He laughs at my sorry excuse at a sports pun. He pulls me into a kiss, and I'll take that as his agreement to the deal. Eventually, he has to prepare for today's baseball game. He leaves for his apartment, and I head into the shower to get ready for my return to the sidelines.

***

"The fact that you didn't say yes, still shocks me!" Emma confession as I re-cap the offer for her and Meg at lunch. Meg looks completely unfazed by my confession. We are in our normal seating area for lunch, which gives us a level of privacy. "Drew wants me to take it. He gave me a whole *we can do this* speech." I tell the women, one looking at me like 'duh' and other looking at me like 'he better!'. "He sounds smarter every time you quote him." Emma looks completely in control of her emotions again as she praises Drew. "He loves you, Annie. I don't know why this surprises you." Meg says it like I should have seen this coming. I need them to understand why 'yes' isn't going to be my answer to corporate. "I like it here in KC. I wanted to come to this city and this team before I even knew there was going to be this second chance with Drew. I took a three-year deal here for a reason. I also left LA for a reason. It was killing me being there, I'm so not an LA girl." I watch the faces of my friends; they both give me support with only the nodding of their heads. "Facts, facts." Meg adds, a greeing with me.

Emma looks at me, and I see the pieces she's trying to put together, the problem she's trying to solve. "Is living in LA the only thing keeping you from saying yes?" She asks and I think about her question for a minute as I eat my lunch. "Yes. I liked the guys, and the show is amazing. But I don't want to live in LA again." Emma eats her own lunch, I can tell she's thinking about my answer. "Why not give them a counteroffer?" She asks making it seem like a logical next st ep.

"A counteroffer? Do I get to make counteroffers?" *Do I really have that* option? I think to myself. "Yeah. You do, Annie. What do you want?" Emma is not mincing words today, not that she normally does, but today she's been on fire with them. I list what I want. "I like being on the sidelines, but I also like to voice my opinions about baseball in general." Emma nods in agreement. She looks like she's solving the world's problems and then makes eye contact with me. "Why not counter that? You can do the broadcasting work from the booth here or at the away stadiums we visit. Do some side commentary while covering the games for the Griffons. You could set a new standard for being a co-chair who offers game time interviews. Offer them an olive branch agreeing to travel to LA for cover of the Series or to hype Spring Training." Emma looks satisfied that this solution solves my problem. I reach out and grab Emma's hand, "Emma, I love you and your big producer brain."

Meg gives her a big hug that seems to surprise Emma. I change the subject away from me and to the other ladies at the table. "Enough about me and my work problems. I think you both have things to spill about non-work-related topics.

I want to hear about your men and what is going on. Do we label them as hookups, arrangements or more?" Emma looks like she is about to bolt at my change in conversation, and surprisingly so does Meg. Interesting indeed that my question has them both on edge. "There is not anything to label. It was kissing, I'll give him credit that it was good kissing but still just kissing. That doesn't mean I want anything more with Mr. Muscles." Emma shrugs as she takes a sip of her drink.

I can't hold back my laugh at her review. Meg looks at Emma with a puzzled look. "Who is Mr. Muscles? That nickname makes him sound hot." Emma starts talking before I can answer. "He's Drew's trainer. He's ripped, with all those delicious muscles and those surprisingly sexy curls." Emma looks all distracted, describing Craig. "Oh... OHHHH," Meg laughs as the pieces fall into place. "You think Craig is sexy? Our Craig Mitchell?" Meg looks at me, and I nod my head yes. "Oh, this is great! I've only heard good things about his ability to please women; I have no personal experience because gross. He gets good reviews from what I've been told, if you know what I mean." Meg gives Emma a little nudge with her elbow. "We aren't headed in that direction." Emma counters, but Meg cuts her off. "Oh, my dear Emma. Your freakin' face full of lusty eyes says you want some of Craig's body in and around some of your body." Meg and her sex talk. She talks about sex and lust so easily and always has. "Is she always so straightforward?" Emma asks me. "Yes, yes, she is. Until this new guy in Oklahoma," I pointedly direct at Meg.

Meg wraps her arms around Emma's shoulders. "One situation at a time, Annie. We need to focus on getting Emma's NEEDS met." Emma doesn't look convinced that she does. Meg is unfazed and directs her scheming powers on how to get Emma and Craig naked in the near future. I should call her out, but Emma is actually smiling listening to Meg. For all her nothing more comments before, it appears that Emma could me be interested in something with our Craig. Maybe Meg's right to focus us on one thing at a time, but I will call her out soon about this mystery guy. I still have no idea what he even looks like, which is so unlike Meg and her over-sharing ways regarding men.

Emma separates from us before we head in the direction of the suite. Meg is watching the game with Dad and Miles in the suite tonight. "This is seriously impressive," she says, walking around the room and looking out over the field. "I'll come to more baseball games if you put me up like this each time." Of course she would think I could pull this off, "Oh, no, this has everything to do with the power that Drew wields and nothing to do with me." We laugh as she responds, "I think of you both as one person when it comes to things like this." Meg turns and freezes, looking at something over my shoulder.

"Hello, ladies." I turn and see that the something is actually Miles and Dad. Miles gives me a side hug. Dad comes over and hugs me. "Annie, my girl, it's good to see you before the game." I hug him back, "Yeah, I thought I'd sneak in to say hi." I pull back, and Dad notices the bruises on my arm. I haven't put on my jacket and its still slightly visible. "Your mom has a few words about that." "I called her while I was in LA and I heard." Which makes the room laugh, because my mother, I'm sure has talked to us all about how she feels about what happened with Camden. I notice that Miles has looked out the window a few times while Meg is enjoying the outdoor seats. "You can go out there with Meg. It's nice out there on the deck seats." He looks from her to me and then back out the windows. "Oh, yeah, it looks nice out there. I'll wait until you leave. I don't get much time with my kid sister these days." He wraps me up in a hug.

"You and Meg are working on that project, right?" I realize that I can get dirt on Meg, and Miles can help me get some information about this secret guy of Meg's. "Yeah. Why do you ask?" He doesn't look phased by my question; he is more curious about what I want to know. "There is a guy at work that she's into. I think really into, because she won't tell me anything about him." He looks again at Meg and then at me with a look of mischief. "Oh, it's not like she tells you everything about her hook-ups." I scowl at him, "Actually, she normally sends me photos so I can rate them. In all the years we've been friends, the only ones she's kept secret have been this new guy and the guy she was with after Tom in college. I think his name was Calder or Conor, I don't remember. I was always so curious about the guy in college because it was the first time she was limited with details and refused to introduce me to him at the senior night party at your guys' place," I explain to my older brother.

"It's happening again with this new guy, and I'm curious. Back in college, she confessed to me that part of it was that she really liked the guy but didn't think she should because the relationship was just friends with benefits. She told me he was clear about only being casual, so she'd kept it casual and let it burn out when she moved to Dallas. She didn't want to tell me more about him because it would have made her feelings real. I could tell she really liked him, and I wonder if that is the reason for all the limited information this time. I bet she is keeping this one secret from me because she likes him and wants to make sure it's real before giving me all the details. I want her to be valued for everything she has to offer someone. Meg deserves to be more than a hookup, you know." My brother takes a big swallow of his water, looking out at the ballpark. "Yeah, that's an interesting theory, and you're right, she does deserve to be valued." He looks back at me with a serious expression. "I'll see what I can find out when we return to Oklahoma. I'll make sure she's being valued." "Thanks, Miles, I appreciate it." I hug him before saying my goodbyes to the group and head down to take my place on the field.

On the field, I get my mic set up, talking to my camera guy for the night. The team comes out of the dugout ready to do warm-ups. I spot number 17 without a problem; he is my guy after all. I'm chatting away with my camera guy when I get a tap on my shoulder. To my surprise its Alex Christopher. "Good to have you back, Blondie." Alex is wearing his signature cool guy smile. "Alex. It's great to be back." Carlos jogs over to join us. "Glad you didn't forget about us." He says also wearing a smile. "Never. We are family, you can't forget family." They both laugh at my reference to us being family.

As we catch up, a woman in the crowd shouts in our direction. "He's a cheater!" *That is random,* I think but I am standing next to Alex. "Wonder what that is about?" Alex looked into the stands, curious about the outburst. "Davis is a cheater, run while you can." The woman shouts at us again. Carlos keeps surprising me because he shouts back, "We know that's a lie. Davis is head over heels for Annie." Carlos winks over at me. The woman will not drop it, "Maybe check social media before you defend a cheater." She walks off like her good deed for the day is done.

Chapter 49: Trending in the Wrong Way

-*Drew*-

August

Carlos runs over to me after I see him talking to Annie. "Good to have our girl back." He tells me. It feels fantastic to have her home. "Some lady said, and I quote, 'Davis is a cheater, run while you can' to Annie while I was over with her. I told her it was a lie, but the fan said to check socials. Any idea what that is about?" Carlos looks as confused as I know I must look. "Not a fucking clue, man. There isn't a woman on this earth who would tempt me away from Annie." As I tell Carlos, I can't help but look in her direction. "Yeah, I know. You only see Annie. Just wanted to tell you before I get distracted." He laughs and takes off for his position in the outfield. I return to warmups, and when I head over to Annie, she looks weird. "What's going on, Angel?" I walk towards her instead of heading to the dugout. Coach is probably going to give me a word about it, but I can't not check in with her.

"It looks like you're trending for all the wrong reasons right now." She handed me her phone so I could see what she was looking at. The hashtags on the screen are harsh: #Daviseheater and #DrewandCamdenBothDeserveAKneetotheBalls at the top of the list. "Why do they think I've cheated?" She takes back her phone before showing me photos of me and Meg at lunch. Meg's hand is on mine in the first photo, and my arms are around Meg outside the jewelry store in the second photo. I have a momentary panic that Annie will know what Meg and I had been up to that day, but the store name isn't visible.

"It's just Meg. Why all the hysterics?" I look to Annie for an explanation. "Yeah, I know it's Meg, but they don't." She points at the screen, implying that "they" are the people on the internet. Annie continues, "They don't know that she's a friend; they say you've cheated on me with your normal type." She sounds annoyed as she completes the thought. "Shit, I didn't think about anyone mis-understanding a lunch with my friend." I want to wrap her in a hug and kiss her, but I know we are both at work. "I bet Dominic is on it and will get this all cleared up," Annie says confidently as she steps up on her toes and kisses me in front of everyone. She clearly shows everyone paying attention that we don't have a problem. "Go get a home run to remind them that this crap is stupid." *She's my perfect* woman; I can't help thinking to myself.

✳✳✳

I do get the home run that Annie referenced in our pre-game talk. Coach tells me to skip the interview and post-game tonight. It appears that the social media thing is spinning now, and I listen to his advice. I head into the locker room and hang out with the team. Eventually, I check my phone to find a voice message from Dominic. When I listen to the message, I hear him tell me that his team is, in fact, already working on this. I hit the call button to check in, and he answers after only two rings. "We already have a statement ready to post. Do you think Annie would also post a statement?" I ask him why we need to do a statement. I was out to lunch with a friend from high school who is also a friend of Annie's. I tell him, annoyed that I have to explain this to everyone.

"Ok, that is an important detail—we can work with that." He covers the phone, but I still hear his muffled summary to his team. "I will draft a new statement, and then we can push it out on social media. Let me know if Annie will comment also; it would help this run its course faster." This is the only downside to professional baseball: I have to comment and defend myself on things that everyone who knows me already knows. I know fame is part of the price for my career, but it sucks. "Fine, I'll talk to her when I return to the apartment." I get dressed and head to my car, where the most beautiful blonde waits for me.

"So, this is a shit show," Annie says it so matter-of-factly that I can't hold back the laugh. "Yeah, agreed. Dominic asked me if you'd make a statement, but you don't have to if you don't want to." I pull her into my arms, and she wraps hers around me. "Of course I will, I know the woman in the photos is my best friend and your friend. I'm not going to let people say that stuff about you." When I pull back, Annie looks so serious and protective. I guess if this had to happen, getting to see my girl's protective side is a positive.

Annie's expression changes as she asks me. "I'm just curious, what was so funny over lunch?" I think back on the lunch, "Oh, I think we talked about her helping pick my original birthday presents wrapping paper, and that it was my favorite until recently." I laugh as I think about the conversation. Annie is blushing and lays her head on my chest. "At least the person taking the photos didn't get that sound clip." I feel her say laughing against my chest. "Yeah, there's some good news for the day." We release each other and get into the car to head home. We both post the statements on social media and then turn our phones on silent. We shut out the world and make love the rest of the night, oblivious to what anyone else says or thinks.

Chapter 50: Counteroffers

-Annie-

September

These stupid pictures have a life of their own online, and it doesn't end there. People have started linking Drew's photos with other beautiful women from his days in Arizona. I need to stop looking, but as the saying goes, you can't take your eyes from a train wreck, and this is a train wreck. I'm totally along for the ride with him. I've had a few more female fans approach me at games, telling me I deserve better and should leave him. I try to be nice, only saying the standard scripted replies we talked about with Dominic. "He didn't cheat," or "We are all good friends."

They all do the whole *oh, poor girl* routine. Meg has apologized a million times, and I keep telling her to stop. She had lunch with a friend that she hasn't seen in years, and it's lame that the world is trying to spin it into this cheating scandal. I'm having trouble getting over all the images of the other women. I look at them when he's gone and try not to compare, but some of these women are busty and luscious in ways I'm not. Ok, correction: all of these women are busty and luscious. I know I'm attractive, but I also know my breasts aren't a D cup, and my ass isn't that curvy.

I'm lost in thought in the booth before today's game when I hear someone out of nowhere. "Stop torturing yourself." Craig appears from behind me looking less than impressed. "What are you doing here?" I try to steady my racing heart as I shut my phone screen. "I came to talk to you as all good friends do, and then I find you looking at that shit." He points at my phone with a look of disgust on his face. "They are all so, you know…" I move my hands to make huge breasts over mine. He makes a face at my action as he sits beside me.

He sighs in annoyance before he starts to speak. "I will tell you this once and only once, and if you ever repeat it or tell Drew I said it, I'll deny it. I saw your photo from his birthday of your, well, you know." He isn't looking at me, but he waves his hands in the general direction of my breast. "From the very quick view that I got, I can tell you that Drew is a lucky guy, and more importantly, it seems like Drew prefers them." Craig does that little wave thing again, as he still doesn't look at me directly.

We are both blushing from the knowledge that he has seen that photo and from the fact that we are talking about my breasts. I can't help but wonder why or how he saw that photo. Drew has always been so careful with the older ones. Craig is a mind reader, I swear, because then he answers my question without having me ask it. "I accidentally saw it when I took his phone after the flowers. I was making fun of all his photos being of you or the two of you, and well, I kept scrolling. He told me to stop multiple times. You know I have trouble following directions." He shrugs his shoulders and, finally looking at me, giving me his best smile. "Now that we are clear that you have nice tits, can you please stop the scrolling?" He asks me, and I feel how much he cares about me and also how much he hates this conversation.

"Thank you, Craig." I hug him to express how much it means to me that he wants me to stop spiraling. "We add this to the vault of things we never bring up again," he says while I am still hugging him. "Agreed." It's the easiest agreement we've ever made. Then, because I can, I release him from the hug and point him toward Emma's office. "Here's a tip. You want to know what is behind that door." He smiles at me, and I leave the area because I don't want to hear whatever they say or do in that room.

***

I am enjoying lunch alone, listening to a sports podcast, when Emma slides into the chair across from me. She looks relaxed, flushed, her hair looks like someone's been messing with it. *Good for her*, I think. I don't know what they did, but I know that look can only mean it was good. "I was told to quote, 'We are even,' whatever that means." Emma doesn't elaborate, but I know who the message is from. "My dear Emma, that means you got some form of lucky with my best guy friend."

She smirks but doesn't deny it. Then she looks at me and rolls her eyes, "Fine, Mr. Muscles knows what he's doing with his tongue. Tell Meg, her intel was spot on about his abilities to please." Since I've known her, I've never heard Emma sound so lusty about a guy and I realize since I've known her talk about a guy. Unless you count talking about Camden and I don't. Craig really must have been good for her. "I'll let her know her source is good." I can't help the laugh that escapes me before I scoot over my half uneaten sandwich. "Changing the subject because I don't think I'm ready to hear more about Craig and his tongue. Can you help me with my formal counteroffer?" Emma is all ears, and we talk about what I want out of the deal and for my future, both personally and professionally.

With Emma's feedback, I will have a formal counteroffer by the end of the day. The main point is that I want to appear on the show, but I'm saying no to LA. Emma's helped me put together a proposal to appear virtually from the booth in the stadium locally or the one on location as I travel with the Griffons. If the

Griffons aren't in the playoffs, I'll be on set for all the games and available for the Series. I'll take time during my sideline reporting to interact with the guys about other games or the game I'm covering. I'll commit to talking about the other team just as much as I do the Griffons. It's a solid counteroffer, and now it's about how to deliver it.

"How do I deliver this back to the network?" Emma sits in silence for a few minutes thinking about it before answering. She is so good about giving herself time to think it all out. "You schedule a meeting with the show exec and then fly out to give your counteroffer in person." I think about it and Emma's right; the only way to do this is in person. "How do I thank you for all your help?" Emma gives me a look before answering. "You don't need to thank me. I get to keep my best reporter, and it's a win for us both."

She takes out her phone and makes a call before I can react. "Can you do me a favor?" she says to the person on the phone. "I need you to get Annie in front of the team tomorrow at the network office. We don't have a game here, but I need her back to finish the regular season." I hear the person talking but can't determine what they are saying. Emma nods in agreement and then tells them, "I'll make sure she's on the plane right after the game tonight." She ends the call looking triumphant. "Looks like you have thirty minutes tomorrow to pitch the network on your counteroffer." I wrap her in a hug, "You are the absolute best Emma."

***

I drive home after the game and pack my bag of just-in-case items. I plan to take a flight that leaves at 4 a.m. for LA and then a return trip to get home all the same day. It will be a whirlwind trip, but I want to be back before the last games of the regular season are played. I head up to the guys' apartment with my key. Drew gave it to me the moment I got in town in August. It's quiet when I enter the apartment, as both guys must have already headed to bed. I walk towards Drew's room, feeling completely comfortable. As I near the door to Drew's room, I can hear him talking to someone. "Yes, I have the questions prepared, and I'll try to be nice to him even if he did kiss her. Yes, DOM, I heard you. I'll be nice, and I'll try not to be a jealous asshole." I cover my mouth to hide the laugh trying to break out. Hearing Drew's side of the conversation makes it sound like his agent is scolding him.

I open the door, and he smiles at me, but then he notices my travel bag, and a frown crosses over his face. "I will talk to you before and after the interview. Good night, Dom." Drew hangs up the phone and puts his phone away. "I hope that bag means you're moving in, Angel." I feel bad about getting his hopes up, but it isn't like he's asked me to move in. "Not until you ask me, Dimples." Before I can say anything else, he steps right in front of me, wrapping his arms around my waist. "Move in with me, Annie." I know I'm wearing a shocked expression–I was joking. "Drew, be serious." He kisses my nose, "I'm not joking. I'm being serious, Annie. Move in, or better yet, let's start looking for a house. We have waited long enough for this. I don't want to spend any of our time a part."

He looks so sure, so happy at the thought of us moving in together. I agree; we've been apart for too many years. I want to come home to him after a long day and sleep next to him at night. "Yes, I'll move in with you. Maybe let's start with the penthouse and then think about the house at a later date." He kisses me, but I pull back before this gets too heated. "I have to go to LA tomorrow to tell them 'yes' on their offer." His face expresses his mixed emotions: worry, happiness, and love. "I'm proud of you for taking the job, Annie. We can look for a house here next season and get a nice condo out there."

I go to tell him about the counteroffer and that there is no need for a place out in LA, but he kisses me again and runs his fingers along the hem of my shirt. I get lost in the touch, and before I can regain my thoughts, he is undressing me. "You are the sexiest roommate I've ever had," Drew says between kisses over my skin. I'm in total agreement with him, too. We get lost in bed, and before I know it, I'm getting up early and get dressed quietly while he's still asleep. I wish I'd covered the details of my counteroffer, but we have time to discuss it when I'm home. I write him a note and place it over his phone before leaving to make my pitch and secure our future.

Chapter 51: Rapid Fire Round Two

-*Drew*-

September

I wake up to an empty bed, and it fucking sucks, but I'd better get used to it because she's taking the job. The job that I pushed, the job that will have her in LA and me here in KC. *What the fuck was I thinking, pushing her to take it?* I should have been selfish and told her to pick me, just me. I should have told her I love her and then asked her to marry me instead. I should have told her to build her future here with me, offered to build her the house of her dreams and give her kids and the white fence. I'd give her the world, if it means that I get to keep her. That is the hardest part of feeling all of these should-have moments. In reality, giving her the world is doing it this way. Letting go of her for the majority of the year with this new job. I reach out to grab my phone; I need to go over the topics for today's interview. To my surprise, I find a note on top of my phone. Interview questions forgotten, I sit up to read the note that could only be from one person. The handwriting that matches the words on my skin helps clear all my doubts about my choices.

> I'll be home tonight.
> Love you Dimples.
> PS: I can't wait to take over the closet with all

my stuff!

This woman! I'll make room for her here in the penthouse immediately. I grab my phone and notice an email from the jeweler telling me the ring is ready and to call to schedule a pickup. I don't waste time and call them and ask if I can pick up the ring today. As I get ready for my day I can't help thinking about the next part. The Proposal. I think of how I want to get down on one knee and ask the woman of my dreams to be my wife.

***

I show up at the studio of the KC local sports show hosted by Nick Jackson and Martin Smith. I agreed to do this interview because I know it's a good show and they both are big supporters of the Griffons. I was told it was laid back, so I wear jeans and a Griffons polo. Nick has on a Griffons T-shirt, and Martin is in a similar Griffons polo. I shake hands with them before they run me through the different segments that I'll be a part of today. "Any questions?" Nick asks me as we start walking towards the stage. "Nope, I got it," I tell him.

"Anything off limits?" Martin asks, looking from me to Nick. "Let's not bring up that Nick dated my girlfriend, and I think everything else is fine." My response gets a laugh from Martin, though Nick looks a little pale. He's quick to jump in, "I'd never do that to Annie." I choose to believe him and we move on. We take our places, and then we go through all things Griffons baseball. It's actually fun to talk baseball with them; it feels more like just talking with the guys about the game and less like an interview. I don't even realize it, but we burn through all the segments pretty quickly until Nick turns to me. "Ready for our tradition of Rapid Fire questions?" "Yeah man, I think I can handle it," I say, laughing at the of nerves I get remembering Annie doing this.

Martin:

"Favorite food?"

Drew:

"Pizza."

Nick:

"Beach or mountain vacation?"

Drew:

"Beach."

Martin:

"Summer or Winter?"

Drew:

"Summer, it's baseball season."

Nick:

"Something you can't live without?"

Drew:

"Annie."

Martin:

"Isn't that the reporter that we had on the show back at Spring Training?"

Nick:

"Yes, Martin, the very one I think. Drew, you mean Annie Campbell?"

Drew:

"Yes, the one and only love of my life, Annie Campbell."

Martin:

"Glad I made sure to ask for the clarification."

"Favorite ice cream flavor?"

Drew:

"Well, I could talk about Annie more, but I'll stop before my buddies give me a hard time."

"Favorite ice cream flavor is mint chocolate chip."

The guys both thank me, and I thank them for having me. When I hear "Cut" from behind the camera, Nick leans over. "I thought you didn't want to talk about Annie?" He is all smiles. "It was your stupid question, man." He laughs. "We get the best stuff during that segment." I nod, "Yes, you really do." They fill me in that the show will be on tonight as part of the evening news, and the media team will release the video online around the same time. After I leave the interview, I get the ring, and I can't wait to see it on Annie's finger for the rest of our lives. She is still in LA, and I'm trying to be patient and not send a million text messages. As I sit watching a game in the living room, I feel my phone vibrate, and I don't hesitate to check it.

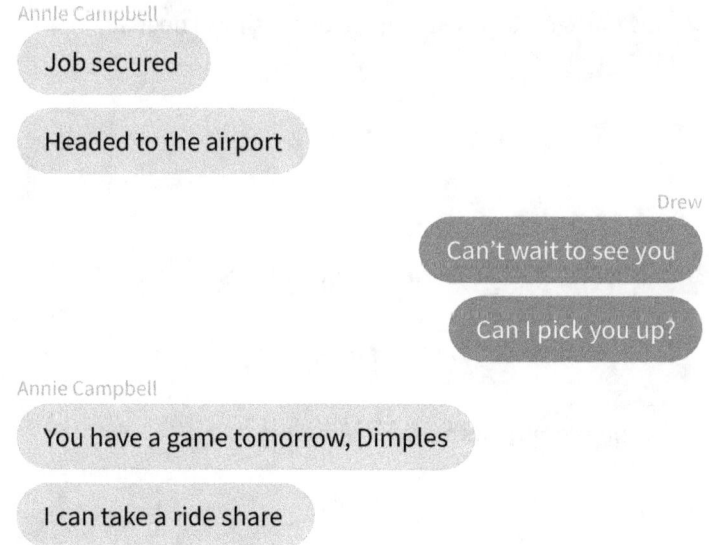

Annie Campbell

Job secured

Headed to the airport

Drew

Can't wait to see you

Can I pick you up?

Annie Campbell

You have a game tomorrow, Dimples

I can take a ride share

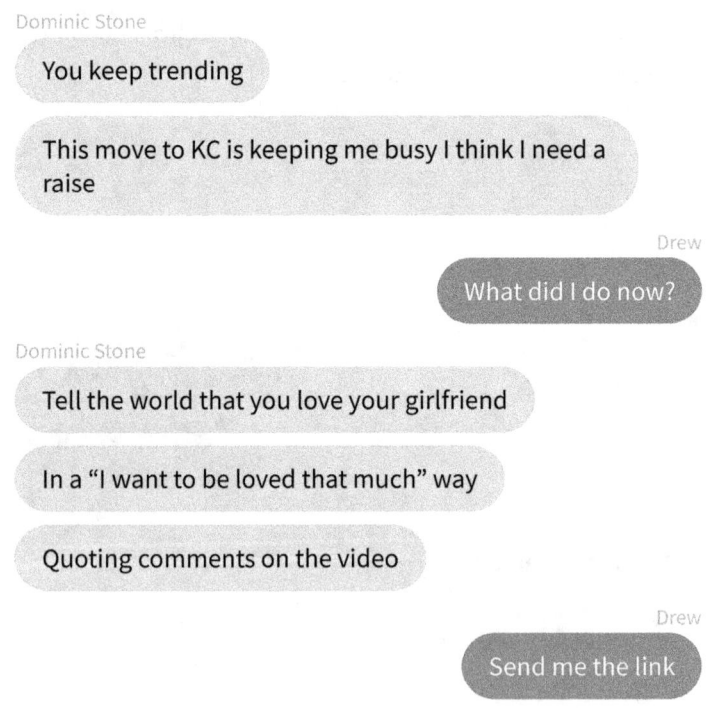

> **Drew**
> Let me pick you up Angel

> **Annie Campbell**
> Pick me up! Love you!!

> **Drew**
> Love you more

I'm counting down the hours until her flight lands when I get a text from Dominic.

> **Dominic Stone**
> You keep trending
>
> This move to KC is keeping me busy I think I need a raise

> **Drew**
> What did I do now?

> **Dominic Stone**
> Tell the world that you love your girlfriend
>
> In a "I want to be loved that much" way
>
> Quoting comments on the video

> **Drew**
> Send me the link

Here look at the comments lover boy!

I open the video link but don't immediately hit play on the video, going instead to the comments. They range from 'this guy is lame,' to 'at least he is playing great baseball,' to comments like 'I want love like this.' The remarks on love are growing, and I keep scrolling. 'If Annie doesn't work out, please hit me up, I'll love you.' 'I love, love. How do I get on the list to get this type of man?' Who knew that people love being in love? It's not something I have focused on personally, people being in love, people finding it, and those trying to keep it. It's clear from the comments though that people want to see it.

I eventually stop scrolling the comments and get in the car to get Annie. I'm driving when her name comes over the car system. I hit the button to answer. "I'm home!" she announces, and I hear how happy she is. "Best news I've heard all day!" I tell her before I hear someone in the background and Annie's muffled reply. Her voice comes back over the speaker louder, "Any idea why someone would tell me 'You have a good one' as I get off the plane?" I feel the smile on my face. "Well, I got us trending again while you were flying." I hear her sigh, "What did you do now?" She asks me, sounding nervous. "I may have said in my rapid-fire interview that I couldn't live without you, no big deal." I can hear the smile though the phone when she says, "Oh, Dimples, I can't live without you ei ther."

I hate that this will be the new normal, getting to hear her feelings but not *seeing* how she feels. How do I do this? How do I not lose my mind and just jump on an airplane to visit her every other day? When I pull up to her at the airport, I park the car, jump out, and grab her in a vice grip of a hug. "Missed me, did you?" She laughs as she holds me just as tightly. "Understatement of the year." I whisper into her ear. I want to hold on to her and never let her go.

Chapter 52: Communication

-Annie-

September

The counteroffer wasn't simply accepted at first pitch. I'm so glad Emma and I prepared, because the execs don't make it easy. We go back and forth; they want me in LA, and I don't want to return. I finally say, "I'm not leaving KC, so if you can't get behind this plan, I'll return to my job." I think I shock them all. I know they didn't expect me to push back, they had expected me to jump at their offer. I tell them I appreciate the opportunity and want to make this work, but I'm a Midwest girl, not an LA girl. If they want the woman from the pro-game and all my coverage in KC, they want me around the people I call my family, they want me to be around the people I love.

They ask me for ten minutes to discuss privately. I understand and go out into the hallway. I am pacing when Vinny comes down the hall and joins me. "You don't look like 'yes' is your answer to our little offer." I look at him and see the nice guy he is. "Well, I said yes but with terms." Vinny pinches his eyebrows together. "What was the problem with the original terms, if you don't mind me asking?" I can tell Vinny is trying to understand me, and I appreciate him asking. "I will not leave my home," and because it's true, I add, "I will not leave him."

I should have left the last statement in my head, but I think I'm running on pure nerves and want to be honest. "He is a lucky guy, if you're so determined," Vinny tells me, and before I can respond, he holds up his hand, "Hold on, I'll be right back."

He leaves me in the hallway as quickly as he appeared. Before I start thinking too hard about why he disappeared so quickly, he walks around the corner with Garret and Brett. "Campbell, I hear we have a counteroffer to approve." Brett doesn't mince words. "Give us the quick versions." Garret gets straight to the point. I fill them all in on my proposal, and they share a look when I finish. "Where are the suits?" Garret looks between the conference rooms. I turn and point toward the conference room I just left minutes ago. No sooner have I pointed before all three of them, Vinny, Garret, and Brett, headed in that direction. Vinny turns towards me, "Campbell, let's go." Who am I to argue with a legend?

The execs are surprised to see the team with me when we enter the room. "How can we help you, gentleman?" The most gruff guy of the group addresses us. Brett sits down at the table like he belongs here. "You can accept her great idea to update our show." "What is so updated about it?" The gruff-looking executive asks Brett. "She'll be reporting from around the country and in KC, she can highlight what's great about each city and team." Brett says. "Exactly, but he still isn't getting it." Garret sits beside Brett. "You're not thinking about the behind-the-scenes feeling that she gave us at the pro-game. She can do a lot of things being on location with the clubs, get guest interviews, exclusives with the clubs, you name it," Garret explains with his enthusiastic hand gestures. He isn't saying anything I haven't already pitched. Still, his excitement, drives the point home. "America loves her, and did you see the comments after she did her guest appearance?" Vinny steps into the conversation by taking his seat next. "Our ratings jumped. The coverage demographics show that we had more younger consumers than we've had in years. Bet if we did a deeper dive, we'd see an uptick in female viewership, too."

I'm so impressed with the way they are pushing for me. I know that even if I don't get the job that I'll speak the praises of these guys to everyone. "So, let's get this done and get her on the show," Brett says, looking around the room. "It's about to be playoff season. We want someone like her on the team," Garret says, tipping his chin in my direction. "You all want this? You want some young reporter to come in and change the show?" one of the execs asks. "Yes," they say in unison. He looks at me, nodding his head. "It's a deal, then. Annie Campbell, we lcome to *The Baseball Show*."

He reaches out his hand to me. I shake it. He then looks around the room before saying, "Looks like we have ourselves a new virtual anchor." The execs tell me to look for my formal contract in the next few days. They file out of the room. I'm left with my co-anchors and my personal heroes for having my back. "Thank you all—I can't thank you enough." I give each of the men a big hug. "Campbell, it's not every day we all agree: take the win," Brett says after I hug him. "Yeah, don't get used to us agreeing." Vinny laughs as he releases me next. "I wouldn't dream of it." We all laugh, and I go with them to the studio. I watch them record the show, realizing I'll be part of this team via my virtual addition soon.

I text Drew as I'm boarding the plane, and he insists on picking me up. I want to fight him, but I'm also so excited to see him and tell him about what happened today. I quickly let him know that I got the job. On the plane, I start reviewing the teams going into the playoffs and what other analysts say about the odds of each top team to make it to the Series. I spend so much time working that I'm shocked when the stewardess asks me to put up my tray table. I apologize and follow the rest of their directions before landing. I open my window on the decent overlooking the lights of the city I call home. Walking off the plane, I turn on my phone and hit the call button beside Drew's name.

"I'm home!" I announce, and I'm smiling so big. Before he can answer, a middle-aged woman in the terminal calls out, "You have a good one." That was weird. I mean, I know I have a good one, but why did she feel compelled to tell me? "Any idea why someone would tell me 'You have a good one' to me as I get off the plane?" He chuckles, "Well, I got us trending again while you were flying." I can't fight the worry at what this is about. "What did you do now?" I say, knowing it can't be all that bad, based on her comment. "I may have said in my rapid-fire interview that I couldn't live without you, no big deal." That feels amazing to hear, and my heart tries to expand out of my chest at his words. "Oh, Dimples, I can't live without you either." I see his sports car, and he pulls in front of me and is out of it before I can even make it off the curb or end the call. I am wrapped in a hug. "Missed me, did you?" I laugh as I hug him back. "Understatement of the year."

I watch the interview on the drive back to the apartment building. Just like my own interview, you can see that Drew's answer is unedited but authentic. He doesn't try to cover it up or move on from it; he doubles down with the 'love of my life' comment, and I swoon at how sweet it is. I've never been more proud of myself for making the counteroffer to the network. "It's crazy how they can pull this out of their guests," I comment when the video ends. "Yeah, I was in the zone, just answering their questions, and boom, I'm on TV telling how much I love you." He squeezes my fingers over the console.

When we get to the building, Drew insists on carrying all my bags, and he hits the penthouse key on the elevator. Looks like we are going to his place—or is it our place? I have to work on that definition in my head. I want to take him up on our conversation about looking for a house together before I leave. The apartment is quiet when we enter, and I follow Drew to the bedroom. He sets down my stuff and turns, pulling me into his arms and kissing me until I have to pull back to breathe. "Is this the treatment I'll get when I come home?" I beam, looking at my guy. He has those dark storm clouds in his eyes, but he blinks, and I feel like I must have read the look wrong. "Let's take a bath and relax, you've been traveling all day." He pulls me to the bathroom and the tub I've secretly wished to soak in since I saw it. He quickly turns tabs and adds things to the water that fizz. "Now to get you undressed." He runs his eyes over my skin, and I know I'm about to be a very lucky woman.

He peels off my clothing, discarding them on the bathroom floor. When I'm completely naked, he picks me up and places me in the bathtub. I don't have to wait long before he joins me, and I slide on top of his wet body. I can feel his hard dick already at my core, and I push down, and I feel him enter my body, and it feels so good. He palms my breast as I ride him, and he doesn't take his eyes off me. I'm sure we are making a mess with the sloshing water, but that's a worry for another moment because I want to watch him come undone.

"Fuck," he says, and I know that he is getting close and he wants me to get there, too, because he slides his left arm down and rubs his fingers over my sensitive clit. I look down and see "I love you" on his muscular forearm, and it almost turns me on more. I love this man so fucking much. I feel the rush of heat and the pulse of pleasure as I tense, the onslaught of my orgasm hitting me. Drew removes his hand from my clit to hold me and guide me on top of him as he thrusts hard. I know the moment he finds his release, too, as his groaned "Annie" echo against the bathroom walls.

He's still holding me when I hear him quietly say against my ear. "I wish you didn't have to go." I am unsure if I say or think it, but what is he talking about? He still has his arms wrapped around me, and I can't see his face, but I hear his heart racing. "I don't know how to be happy here without you, Annie. I am so fucking proud of you, but I hate that we will have stolen moments. This will be the longest ten years of my life, and I'll live for the moments we get together. I hope you know that I'm calling dibs on all of those breaks from baseball." *Oh shit*, it hits me that I still haven't told Drew about the counteroffer details. I was so caught up working on it with Emma and presenting it to the execs. I hadn't wanted to get his hopes up, so I hadn't told him the details. The main, very important detail. He doesn't know that I've accepted this job on new terms. He still thinks I'm moving to LA. I try to pull back to look at him, and he holds me tighter.

Shit, I need to fix this now: I can't have him feeling like this a minute longer. I feel guilty that he's obviously been more worried about this than I thought. "Drew, I'm not going anywhere." He nods, "Yeah, I know we will be fine doing the long-distance thing. I don't have to like not getting to hold you like this or make love to you like that." He sounds so sad, and I know he doesn't get it. He doesn't get it, because I still haven't told him the news. "Drew, let me look at you." He loosens his hold but doesn't release me. I place my hands on his cheeks and make him look at me. I make sure I have his attention. "I made a counteroffer. I should have told you more about it, but I didn't want to get your hopes up if they didn't accept it. The offer I accepted means I'm not moving to LA."

I see the storm clouds burn off, and there is left only hope in his blue depths. "What did you counter?" He is rubbing my arms I'm not sure if to comfort me or himself that I'm here and that this moment is real. "The short story is that I'll be working like I do now, but with some additional hours and more studying of baseball overall. I want you to focus on the fact that you are my home and I'm not leaving. I'm choosing us, I'm choosing you." I put a thumb over his lips because I see him start to say something. "I'm also choosing to further my career under my terms. I'm choosing to take on more work, but it is worth it, because I'll be with you almost every day." I move my thumb from his lips. "Ok, you can say something." He doesn't say anything at first; he just smiles that heart-pounding, earth-shattering, dimple-producing smile. When he finally speaks, it isn't what I was expecting. "Marry me, Annie."

"What? You're crazy!" My words echo around the bathroom in surprise. He has completely caught me off guard. My head is spinning. He is joking, right? He can't be serious. I want him to be serious, but it's crazy: we are naked in a lukewarm bath right now. We've only been back together a few months. "Marry me, Annie," he says again, then continues, "Let's not waste any more time apart. Let's choose us for the rest of our lives. I want forever with you. I had a whole plan to ask you, but fuck, I don't want to wait. It feels right for it to be now, for it to be here."

I laugh before asking, "So naked in the bath is the right time to ask me to marry you?" He smiles that dimple producing smile. "Is there a wrong time to ask for forever?" I melt at his words, because I don't care about a fancy proposal. I care about a forever with this man. "Ask me again. I promise to answer this time." He runs his hand up my neck and pulls me into a deep kiss, then pulls back just enough for us to be looking at each other. "Annie Marie Campbell, will you marry me?" I know I'm smiling as I answer, "Yes!" And before I can say anything more, his mouth is covering mine in a kiss so full of love I'll remember it for the rest of my life.

Chapter 53: I Have A Ring

-*Drew*-

September

I can't fight the shadows that come over me after we make love. I haven't been able to shake the storms in my head, thinking about her in LA. I know that we only have to do it for a month until the end of the season and she finishes her time covering the Series, which, if I'm being honest, I hope to be playing in. We will have three-ish months of time that we can be together without interruption. I'm already making plans on how to spend the time with her. However, before my brain can go through all the fun ideas, I remember that baseball season will start again and we'll spend almost every day apart for seven to eight months. I wrap her into me, leaving no space between us. "I wish you didn't have to go." I hear her muffled "What?" against my wet skin.

My heart hurts, but I say the hard thing that needs to be said. I feel her flinch in my arms, but she surprises me with her statement of not going anywhere. I'm fucking this up, and I try to recover the moment and my train of thought. I can feel her move under my arms. I want to hold her close, but when she asks me, I let her pull back to look at me. I keep my arms around her waist to keep her close as she'll let me. I don't want to stop holding her for a moment. She slides her hands into my hair and gives a small smile. "I made a counteroffer. I should have told you more about it, but I didn't want to get your hopes up if they didn't accept it. The offer I accepted means I'm not moving to LA."

Wait, what? My brain isn't keeping up. Did she just say she isn't moving? But how does that work with the new job? I think I may also voice my 'how' because she quickly fills me in on her counteroffer. I'm reeling, she figured out a way to keep us together this time. She fought for me—for us. God, my heart is going to pump right out of my chest. "Ok, you can say something," she says and removes her thumb from my mouth. I smile; fuck I can't stop smiling. She just gave me the most amazing news. I know that she is mine... Well, she's almost mine.

I want her to be mine forever, just like I'm already hers, and I want everyone to know that we are each other's for the rest of our forever. I don't think about my words, I just let them run out of my mouth. "Marry me, Annie." This was not my plan, but do I regret asking this question, here naked in the tub? Nope: no, I do not, because the look on her face is something I'll never forget. Her first response is one that I'll enjoy telling our kids, and maybe I'll be lucky enough to tell our grandkids, too. She makes me ask again, and on my third attempt, I get her answer of 'yes.' I pull my fiancée into a kiss, and we don't come up for air until the water in the tub is freezing.

When we make it out of the water, it's almost midnight. I can see that Annie is sleepy, and I have to admit I am too. We dry each other off, and we go to bed wrapped around each other. In the morning, I wake up first and listen to her breathe. I look at her, realizing that I have forever with her, and if that isn't the best way to wake up, I don't know what is. I slide out of bed and then go into my closet. I may have asked her to marry me last night, but I didn't think about giving her the ring. I dig out the box from the back of my sock drawer.

As I walk back to the bed, Annie sits up. "I don't like waking up without my Drew-shaped pillow." This woman is beautiful even when she is half asleep and with messy hair. "I had to get something." I slide back under the covers and pull her to my chest. She snuggles against me, seemingly forgetting I said I had to get something. "Not going to ask me about what I had to get?" This version of Annie is familiar, she clearly wants to go back to sleep. She yawns, "Oh, sorry. My brain is still in wake-up mode. What did you need to get?" She finishes with another yawn that punctuates her point. "I told you I had a plan of sorts. I wanted to show you I wasn't completely full of shit." I set the box on my stomach where she can see it.

"Oh, Drew, is that..." She sits up and pulls the sheet around her naked body. "I think you are supposed to give that to me on one knee." She smiles as she indicates that I should get up. "Is that so, Angel?" I get up, taking the hint, and get down on one knee. "What's next?" I ask her sarcastically. She swings her legs over the side of the bed. "I think we already did that part," she says, nudging me with her foot. I open the box, and the look on her face is exactly what I was hoping for. "Like it?" She nods her head but isn't making words. "Meg helped me design it. My requirement was that it should have some red, because as we both know, it's your color." She holds out her hand, and I slip the diamond and ruby ring on her finger. "It's amazing, Drew."

She looks at it and then at me. "Can we shout our news from the rooftop yet?" she asks me before throwing herself into my arms. "Maybe get dressed, and then we can go tell everyone we are engaged. I don't want to share my fiancée's naked body with anyone else." She releases me and then the sheet she had wrapped around her body. "Maybe first we should take this—" she shakes her left hand in my face "—on a test drive to make sure that it doesn't affect our sex life." How did I get so lucky to find her, not once but twice? "I think that I can handle a test drive with my fiancée." I stand up and then pick her up, throwing her back into the bed. We spend the next few hours test-driving our engagement and the sex— is so much better.

317

***

We must fall to sleep after the last set of orgasms, because it's late morning when I open my eyes again. I can hear the blender going in the kitchen, which means that Craig is up. I start to slip out of bed, but she must wake up, too, because she pulls the covers from her body and jumps out of bed first. She goes to the closet and comes out in one of my shirts that looks like a dress on her body. "Let's go tell Craig our news!" Her excitement has me jumping out of bed and grabbing a pair of pants before following her into the living area. "Good morning," Craig announces from the kitchen. "You two took long enough to wake up on a game day." He is pouring the standard three cups full of smoothies. He passes one to Annie, and she purposely uses her left hand to reach for it. At first, I don't think it registers, and I'm going to have to spell it out for him. As Annie takes her first sip of her smoothie with that ring sparkling, I see his eyes go wide, and he looks over at me and then back at the ring.

"Annie Marie Campbell, or should I say soon-to-be Annie Marie Davis!" Craig practically shouts into the quiet room. She looks from me to him, smiling. "Davis has a nice RING to it, doesn't it?" We all laugh at her corny joke. Craig moves around the island and gives us a group hug. "I declare now in front of you both as witnesses that the first one of your sons will need to be named in their uncles honor for all my efforts and FYI—I want to be called Uncle Craig." I laugh and give him a good nudge. "I thought I just had to ask you to be my best man? I don't remember signing up my future children to be stuck with your name." Craig gives me a nudge back. "I updated my terms, and I think a Michael Davis or a Mitchell Davis could really work." He walks back around the island, laughing. "I do like the Uncle Craig part". I look at Annie, and she nods her agreement, "I think we have some time before kids, but I agree Uncle Craig is really the only option". We celebrate over breakfast smoothies.

"Are you two going to surprise us all with a shotgun wedding next?" Craig asks us, looking directly at Annie. She looks at me and smiles before answering Craig. "I think I'd like to try the traditional wedding, or a destination wedding, but I think for right now I'm going to enjoy this." She shakes her left hand in Craig's face. "Who have you told?" He asks. "Just you so far," I tell him, and he places his hands over his heart. "Oh man, I'm the most important friend. I knew it, I feel touched." I roll my eyes, "Or the one that is living in the same apartment," I laugh back at him. "Speaking of telling people. We need to call our families," Annie says getting up from the table and giving me a kiss on the lips as she heads back to our room. "I'm so happy for you guys, seriously," Craig says before he heads in the direction of his room. "You next?" I ask, and he pauses and grins. "I'm working on someone, but don't hold your breath: she's playing hard to get. But I think you gave me just the card I need to get her to cave." He gives me a wink before disappearing.

Annie returns to the kitchen with her phone in hand. She pulls her chair over to mine and climbs back in, snuggling against my side. "Who first?" she asks, trying to play it down, but I know she wants to call her parents next. "I think your parents, then mine, then our brothers." Before my suggestion is even complete, she hits the call button on her mom's name and sets the phone down so we are both onscreen. "Annie, my girl, how are you?" Mrs. Campbell starts and then stops, noticing me on the call, too. "Oh, Hello Annie and Drew." I wing it, "Hello, Mom," I say, and it feels less weird than when I attempted to call her Kim.

Mrs. Campbell smiles but also looks confused by my comment. Annie smiles next to me and then very strategically holds up her left hand to cover her smile. "OMG," her mom yells over the phone, whooping and cheering in her excitement. Annie's dad comes into the living room, breathing heavy with a look of concern on his face. "What's wrong Kim?" "Nothing, nothing is wrong, our daughter is engaged! Will, she's engaged!" I watch her go over and give him a kiss. They congratulate us, and when her mom starts asking a million questions

Annie tells her that we have more calls to make but she'll call back soon to answer all her questions. We hang up and then call my parents from my phone. "Drew, Hunny, it's so good to hear from you—and on video, I'm impressed," Mom says as she answers my call. "Mom, I need to introduce you to someone," I tell her, b eing all dramatic.

I purposely am the only one on the video call at the moment, with Annie trying not to laugh just off camera. "Mind grabbing Dad so I can make the intro-ductions?" I see Mom moving around the house, and then Dad is in the video window. "Drew wants us to meet someone: it better not be a new woman," I hear Mom telling him before they both appear on the phone, looking happy and as calm as ever. "So, I'd like to introduce you to the soon-to-be Mrs. Davis."

At that, I pan the camera in Annie's direction, showing off that ring on her left hand. The video on my parents' end shakes from my mom jumping up and down in excitement. Comments from "Thank God" to "Finally" to "Oh, I'm so happy for you both" are shared before my mother settles and exclaims, "I have work to do on an engagement present." Annie whispers, "I think we need a new Jennifer Davis original. We need to add to our love story collection." Mom beams over the phone, having heard Annie. "I think I know just what I'll do, and I look forward to future additions to the collection." Annie looks from the phone to me, and I turn to look at her, too. "I can't wait to have a wall full of them." Annie smiles at me and gives me a kiss. "Ditto, Dimples."

Annie scrolls through her phone, trying to determine the next call to make. "Let's try Meg next. I know she's at work, but I want to tell her, or at least try to tell her." "Works for me, I mean she got involved in a mini-scandal trying to help me pick out that ring." Annie laughs as she hits the call button. "Best reason for a scandal in my book." "What about a scandal?" asks Meg from the phone. "Oh, you know that cheating scandal between you and Drew to get me this." Annie waves the diamond and ruby sparkler in front of the camera. "Drew, you caved," Meg says, laughing on the phone. "Guilty as charged, I couldn't help myself."

"Megan, I..." There is a guy's voice on the other end of the phone that cuts through our conversation. Annie gets a look on her face as her brother appears on the phone.

Annie gets a thoughtful look before almost screaming. "MEGAN ANN PATTERSON and MILES JAMES CAMPBELL." I look at her. Why is she calling them by their full names, and so loud—what have I missed? "We are focusing on your engagement," Meg says from the other side of the phone. "Annie, you got engaged?" Miles asks as he moves closer to Meg and her phone. "Congrats, you guys." Before Miles has the chance to say another word, Annie cuts him off. "You both have some explaining to do." I could be wrong, but Meg's cheeks are red. *Have I ever seen Meg blush?* I wonder, but I can't find a memory of it. Miles looks a little sheepish, but then runs his hand through his hair. "Not the time, but we'll talk. Love you, baby sis, and congrats again to you both." Meg jumps in, "Today, let's focus on the engagement. I promise to tell you everything," Meg looks worried. "How about you give me the, like, PG-13 version this time? I DO NOT want the normal X-rated version," Annie says, shaking her head. "Ok, fair, fair—only PG-13," Meg agrees.

I point at the time, as we still want to call Daniel and Luke. "We have a few more calls, but you aren't in the clear, you hear me?" Annie says, and they both shake their heads in agreement. "I love you both." She disconnects the call. "What was that about?" I ask, still confused. "It looks like my best friend has been hooking up with my brother, and I don't think it's since she moved back to Oklahoma," Annie responds, and yes, she sounds a little annoyed, but that is definitely a smile on her face. "Well, that is an interesting development for sure." I change the subject to the task at hand. "Who's next? Daniel? I don't think he is hooking up with anyone we know." Annie laughs next to me, and I know I said the right thing.

Daniel answers, but not on camera. "Sorry man, I'm doing PT. What's up, or can I call you back later?" I jump in knowing how busy he is and later I'll be busy at the game, "No problem, man. I'd say yes to calling back later, but I think the news will break before then, and I wanted to tell you. I asked Annie to marry me last night." He is breathing heavily for a second before I hear him. "That is great news, brother—you've always looked at her like she was your forever. Wish I hadn't been an asshole in high school, but I guess I'll just have to be the best fucking brother-in-law." I chuckle and agree with him, "Yeah, I'll let you get back to PT, just didn't want you to hear it from someone else."

"Let me know when and where, and I'll make sure that I'm there for the wedding. Looks like they want my unit stateside for a while after the last tour anyways," he says, sounding both excited and annoyed. "Well, I'll take it: come take some vacation time to KC soon, or meet us at the beach after the season ends." I offer because I do want to see my brother and he deserves some time to relax. His job isn't easy. "Yeah, I will see about sometime soon, gotta come see my brother play some ball, and a beach sounds relaxing." I can't help making the suggestion, "Book time in late October to watch the Series. I'll make sure you get tickets." I hear Daniel laugh on the other end of the phone, "You're a cocky motherfucker, but I've known that since you were born." We say our goodbyes and disconnect the call.

I get off the phone and check the time; we have just enough time to get one more call in. I select Luke's name from the screen, and he answers me in what looks like a office. "Why the hell are you calling me before a game?" Luke answers. "Nice to talk to you too, ass," I say, laughing. Luke smiles on camera, and I pull Annie next to me. "We have some news." Before Annie or I can speak, Luke says, "You didn't get her pregnant, did you?" Annie flips him off with her left hand at just the right angle to see the ring. "Oh shit, is that what I think it is?" He is wearing a big smile, and I hear someone 'Shhh' him in the background. "Give it up, Alexis, my best friends just got engaged."

He returns to looking at the phone, smiling at us. "I'm the best man, right?" I give him a look, and then from behind us is a loud "Nope, that's me. I got

322

them both to the same city." Craig has joined the conversation. He walks over, standing behind Annie as he talks to Luke. "Well, I'm wounded," he says before continuing his whine. "Why did I go to law school again?" A female voice in the background says something that sounds like, "I'm not sure how you graduated." Before Luke can answer, Craig cuts in. "Whoever that was, I like her: bring her to the wedding." "When is this wedding anyway?" Luke asks. "No idea yet, but we'll let you know." Annie pipes in, and we chat some more before d isconnecting the call.

"So how long before we can take this global?" I ask Annie. "Why wait? All our friends and family are in the loop." She shows me a photo of her hand in mine with the ring slightly out of focus. "When did you get that?" I have no idea when she took it in the whirlwind of this morning. "Should have been paying attention, Dimples." She says before winking at me. "Hate to break up the happy couple, but it looks like you both need to get ready for the game tonight, or some people aren't making it to work," Craig interjects, giving us much-needed focus to get ready for tonight's game. With that reminder, we head in different directions to get ready for our jobs, which are now both solidly in th e same city.

Chapter 54: Home

-*Annie*-

Mid-October

I'm busy but completely, overwhelmingly, all-consumingly happy. I have started my new role on *The Baseball Show,* and the guys are great. I love that they give me hell but also give me my credit. Tonight is a huge game for the Griffons, as they are in game four of their series with New York, and if they win today, they will make the Series for the second straight year. Drew has been a machine in October, in fact, the whole team has been on fire. They want it, and they want it bad. Drew had happily announced to me that it would be bad luck if I slept anywhere but with him for the rest of his career.

I've moved into the penthouse. My old apartment only has the furniture I left behind for Craig. He tried to pay me for it, but I told him no. He insisted on moving to my apartment to give us personal space. He even sometimes knocks before using his key to the penthouse. He does loudly announce himself with his favorite, "Anybody Naked in the living room?" when he forgets to knock.

My favorite thing about the penthouse is that our paintings are together on the wall. After Drew and Craig had carefully secured it to the wall, Drew had wrapped me in his arms to admire them. "Angel, this was how it was meant to look." I'd agreed with him. The two of us, like our pictures, together was always meant to be. I'm now in the booth studying for the game, I close the article I've been reviewing. I feel like I'm as prepared as I can get, and I shut the tablet in front of me and take in a deep breath. The game is still hours away, but I need to walk around to burn off my excited energy. I text my fiancé to see if he's here yet or if he is still at our apartment.

Annie

You still home?

Drew Davis

Nope, walking from my car actually

The parking lot is already almost full

Did I get the game time wrong?

Annie

Yeah, KC shows up

Drew Davis

Best fans in the league

Did you need anything, Craig is still at his apartment?

Annie

Nope, just wanted a minute with my fiancé

Drew Davis

Meet me at the locker room

Annie

I'm not having sex in the locker room, Drew Joseph!

Well, damn! I could have locked the door, but have it your way, fiancé.

Seriously, please meet me at the locker room. I promise that I'll keep on all my clothing.

I know I'm smiling as I make my way to the Griffons locker room. I have no idea why I need to meet him here but I'll play along. I waved to the team staff as I make my way to the locker room. The Griffons are a family thru-an-thru, and if I didn't already feel like part of the family as the team reporter, as soon as we announced our engagement, the team hosted a mini post-game celebration for us. They even put a picture of us from prom on the screen with a big congratulations at the first game, after we'd announced our engagement. Drew appears, and he's not dressed in his uniform yet, but in his suit. *Damn, does he look good in a suit.* We meet in the middle and share a sweet kiss. Before I can ask what, I'm doing here, he takes my hand and leads us in the direction of the dugout. He leads us out on to the field. "What are we doing out here, Dimples?"

He continues to walk us over to his spot on the field. "Taking it all in. Do you feel that energy?" He says with awe in his voice, spinning me to look at the stadium. Its empty, all the seats waiting for the fans to fill them in the next few hours. Drew wraps his arms around my shoulders, standing behind me. "It's going to be a great game, I can feel it," Drew says against the shell of my ear. "Yeah, I trust your feelings any day." I soak in the feeling of being right here with him on the eve of his biggest start.

He pulls back, unwrapping his arms from around me. "Ok, follow me again." He offers me his hand and walks me to home plate. He smiles as he looks at me, "Annie, we need that home run. Do you have one in the tank?" He laughs and flashes me that dimple. I laugh too but take up my position at home plate. "Yeah, I got this." I smile and position my pretend bat. Drew in a mock announcer voice says, "It's bases loaded, and Davis steps up to bat."

Drew sets the stage, and my heart skips a beat when he refers to me as 'Davis.' God, I can't wait to be a Davis. "If she delivers the home run, this is over. The Griffons will go on to the Series. Can she do it?" He announces in that cheesy announcer voice. "There's the pitch," Drew shouts, and I swing my pretend bat and point to the back wall. "That's it, Griffons fans she's done— it's in the fountains. Home run, Davis!" I round the bases and at third I point at him and make our little heart shape. He gives me one back as he waits for me at home base, and when I reach him, he pulls me into a deep kiss, and I've really made it home.

THE END

Epilogue: Friendsgiving Davis Style

-*Drew*-

November

The last year has been the best of my life. An outsider would say it's because I moved to the Griffons and won the Series, but that is only half of what made this last year so important, so special. The fact is that I got my life back by joining the Griffons because that decision led me back to Annie. I understand how blessed I am to have both things happen in the same twelve-month span of time, but I'm not taking a second of it for granted. The Series was a massive career highlight, and I love that my fiancée was there to celebrate it by my side. I'd gotten to kiss her after we'd been announced as the world champs, the photo went crazy and got us trending again.

We've done the interviews and celebration events in the city, and KC displayed its ability to throw one hell of a party. They'd closed down most of the local schools, because so many people wanted to come out and celebrate with us. The team appreciated their support, and we loved the city's excitement around the parade and celebration events. I'm sure it will be the highlight of my career and will live in my mind as a core memory to talk about and share with others.

Now that we are a few weeks removed from the whirlwind of the win, I can't wait to enjoy quiet time with my fiancé. I've been pulling a few strings and can't wait to surprise her with the 'Davis Thanksgiving' I've planned. We all deserve a much-needed vacation from the fall weather, and I've set up a fun little trip for everyone, including our parents, to Hawaii for the week of Thanksgiving.

Annie has zero idea of the location change. Everyone has been acting like we are still on for the traditional Friendsgiving in Oklahoma. One day we will do that, but this year was too big of a year, and it's because it's my first-year attending, I thought I'd make up for missing the last few years with a bang. "Annie, are you almost ready?" I shout from the living room in the penthouse.

"It feels weird that you packed my bag for me. How do I know you packed what I need? Did you even pack underwear?" She comes out of our room with a look of nerves. "I can tell you that I packed your underwear. I will also tell you that they are all my favorites." My comment earns me her sexy smile, and I can't wait to see her in what I've packed. "Drew Davis, we are going to a family event—I can't just wear lingerie the whole time." Annie walks over to me and wraps her arms around my waist in a hug. "I have a few things for you to wear in front of other people, promise." She looks up at me with apprehension. "I guess I can go shopping if I need to." I kiss her before we make one final sweep of the apartment and head out.

Annie is texting her mom about ingredients and doesn't seem to notice that I've driven north to the airport instead of going south on the highway headed towards Oklahoma. She finally notices when I pull off the highway at the airport and park the car in the garage. "Did you book a plane to get us to Oklahoma? It's only a four-hour drive, Drew." Annie is giving me serious side eye as I turn off the car and look at her.

"We have a change of plans. I'll give you more details after we get to our gate, but I'll give you this fact. Everyone is in on the change." Annie narrows her eyes at me. "When you say everyone, do you mean family or friends" I kiss the back of her hand, "Annie, I mean everyone, all friends and family." Annie gets out of the car with me and stays quiet as we go through the process of getting through TSA and walking through the airport. She doesn't seem upset, just calm. I can't stand it any longer. "Angel, are you angry with me and the change of plans?"

Annie looks at me as we walk with a smile. "Not angry, but annoyed that none of my so-called family or friends even hinted at anything. How did you get them all to cover this change in plans?" I wrap my arm around her waist as we walk. "Angel, I just told them I have years of memories to make up for. Also, it helps that the destination is pretty amazing, and I told them that if you found out about the trip, the destination could be modified."

She laughs hard at my last statement. "So, you pretty much said free vacation to all those who can keep a secret?" I shrug, "Yes, Angel, I did. I have no shame in guilting our friends and family." We are almost to the gate, and Annie still doesn't know that nearly all our group is leaving from KC and is already waiting for us to arrive. I pause on the side and pull her into me a few gates before ours. "Want to know our secret destination?"

She looks up at me with a smile. "Yes, Dimples, tell me where we are going." I kiss her lips prolonging the moment. "I booked us an exclusive hotel in Hawaii. I told you it was one of my favorite places, and I want to see if it could be one of yours, too." Annie looks shocked, "Drew, please tell me you packed me for a Hawaii vacation instead of the one we originally had planned to Oklahoma." I kiss her again before answering. "Yes, Annie, why do you think I insisted on packing for you? I got you covered for a beach vacation. I have a few people I'd like to see at the gate if you're ready." Annie narrows her eyes on me, "Drew Joseph, are you telling me our family and friends are already here?" I laugh, "Yes, Angel, we have a group waiting on us. Act surprised." Annie kisses me. "I don't think I'll have to act surprised. I'm shocked you got this organized and I had N O IDEA."

At the gate, we meet everyone in our friend group except Luke, who is flying from Texas. All our family has joined us here in KC; even Daniel has made the effort to be here. I've told everyone that this is an all-events celebration. I have a lot to be grateful for, and I want to celebrate with the people who have supported not only me but also Annie. I can't think of a better start to Friendsgiving: Davis Style.

Epilogue: Friendsgiving Hawaii Style

-*Annie*-

November

Looking out over the ocean from our private room in Hawaii and I'm beyond relaxed. I didn't know I needed to hear the ocean to help me disconnect from the world, but I did. Drew really did a great job organizing this secret vacation for our family and friends. I didn't even get a hint at his change in plans; the man is good. I was 100% preparing for our traditional Friendsgiving at my parents' house. I will miss our tradition, but I think I'm going to enjoy this new version, especially if it means that I'll have Drew by my side for all our future Friendsgiving's. He isn't the person I miss anymore; he is the person that I get to experience life with every day.

As if my thoughts have conjured him, I feel his strong arms wrap around me. "Angel, what do you think of the place?" I continue to take in the waves as I tell him how beautiful it is here. "Still like the idea of getting married here?" He asks. We'd looked at the website when we'd been playing around with wedding locations and it was available during the July break. It had felt right, so we'd booked it over the phone. Seeing it now in front of me, it was perfect. "Yes, I think, marrying you here is going to be amazing."

Before I say anything else, I feel his lips against my ear and feel them running down the side of my neck. I lean to give him better access to kiss further down. "You are distracting me from the ocean," I tell him as he continues his path, and he hums his agreement. His hands have found their way to my waistband and are inching down my skirt. "I think you have too much skin covered by this outfit." Drew pulls my skirt and underwear from my body before working on removing my tank top and bra. Before I realize it, I'm standing naked, and he lays me down on the lounge chair on the balcony. We are secluded, but I'm not focused on that at the moment, because Drew has pulled me to the edge of the lounge chair. "Open those legs for me, Angel."

I open my legs, and before saying another word, Drew is sucking my clit. I let out a moan of satisfaction. He has learned my body and what makes me burn. He sucks and licks me as I continue to bask in his actions. I can feel my body responding to his efforts, growing wetter and hotter with each motion. When he pushes two fingers into my core, I moan again. "Angel, that is the sexiest sound, but I want to remind you that someone could hear you out here." He doesn't wait for my answer before sucking my clit back into his mouth. I grab his hair and try to keep my moans inside my body. Drew continues to lavish me with attention until my legs are trembling, and my release takes over my body. I moan his name on my release, forgetting where I am. I only know that I'm wit h Drew.

When I blink back into existence, he is lying next to me on the lounger. "Dimples, I think Hawaii is going to be my favorite vacation spot." Drew laughs before kissing me. "Angel, that was just the beginning of our trip. I've got so many things I want to do with you naked while we're here." I laugh at him because I can't wait to see what comes next. I'm about to start undressing him when there is a knock at our door. "You better go get dressed, Angel. I think we have to spend time with other people." Drew helps me up from the chair, and he grabs my discarded clothes. I take them and head to the bathroom. I can hea r muffled sounds from the room, but I'm not sure of the context. When I come out fully dressed again, Drew is waiting for me alone. "Who was at the door?" "It was the coordinator for our Friendsgiving dinner. They wanted to give me an update on the location and let me know that they are ready when we want to head down."

***

Drew has outdone himself with what he is calling Friendsgiving: Davis Style. In front of me is a full table setup with all the decorations for Thanksgiving. There are nametags for each of the guests of our party with a menu of the items that will be served. He has traditional Thanksgiving foods on the menu as well as what appear to be local offerings. It all sounds and looks amazing. I am in awe of all the effort he put into this surprise. "Drew, this is amazing. You know you are setting a crazy standard for Friendsgiving, right?"

He smiles as he wraps me into a hug. "This Friendsgiving is special. It's my first one, plus we are celebrating so many things." I kiss his neck. "Yes, like you winning the Series." Drew kisses the top of my head. "Or celebrating your new job." I answer with a kiss to his jaw. "Or celebrating our engagement." He gives me that dimpled smile before responding. "Or celebrating that I love you." I go to make up another reason to celebrate, but we are interrupted. "Or we can celebrate that I made this happen by tricking you both." Craig laughs and wraps us both in a bear hug. No sooner has he let us go than Luke is replacing him. "I think of this as my reward for graduating from law school and passing the bar." Our friends and family continue to filter in; until the table is full of laughter and joy.

Drew clinks his glass to get everyone's attention. He stands up, looking over the table. "I never thought I'd get to attend a Friendsgiving. I spent years avoiding it because I was worried about seeing Annie with someone else. Looking over this group, I've never been more appreciative of how surprising the last year has been. Thank you for letting me change a few things this year." The group laughs because this is completely different in the best ways. "I can't wait to create these moments as a group of friends and family for years to come." He raises his glass, and we all do the same. I can't wait to see what happens for us all, the big life events, and the additions that will come. I look at Drew, my future husband. They don't know it yet, but we'll all be back here in a few months. Our destination wedding feels more real seeing it with my own eyes, but my forever has already started, because he's right in front of me.

THE END

...at least for this couple, we still have friends in our group that need their happy ending...

What is Going on Between Miles and Meg?

Take a deep breath and buckle in because Miles and Meg are the next couple in The Friends Group Series.

What is the history between Annie's older brother and her best friend?

Glad you asked because the first book in their two-part love story is The Roommate Situation.

Keep reading for the preview of The Roommate Situation!

The Roommate Situation

The Friends Group Series Book 3

Chapter 1: Settled In

-Meg-

September

I feel like I arrived at college as a bright-eyed, smart ass of a freshman yesterday, and yet here I am at the start of my senior year, still a smart ass but a little less bright-eyed. The adult world is on the horizon, and it feels overwhelming. *Did I get all I needed out of this college experience?*

I enjoy my graphic design minor, but I love architectural design and can't wait to use it to make eye-popping art with buildings. My summer internship validated that I can be both creative and functional in what I design. As I sit here at the second-hand table we inherited from the last tenants of our apartment, I realize I will have to start looking for a real job in less than ten months, not just internships.

Where do we want to end up? Will we stay in Texas or move back to Oklahoma? I vote for staying in a bigger city here in Texas first, but eventually moving back to a small town. I love the small-town vibes for when we are ready to start a family. Maybe I need to research both options to see what the job market offers for us both. I take a deep breath. I don't need to spiral down this rabbit hole yet. Tom and I will figure it out over the next few months we still have in college. This topic requires further development, but I think one area will be resolved soon

.

I've been with Tom for five years. We started dating the summer before senior year, and my high school boyfriend became my college boyfriend, and I hope he soon gets the upgraded label of fiancé. I hadn't wanted us to go to different colleges, so I'd compromised at eighteen when we were both accepted here at the University of Belmont. Tom was set on coming here and didn't even consider alternative options. Personally, I'd always dreamed of going to Norman with my best friend Annie, but love led me down this road and here I am. Belmont has grown on me, and I love my professors, so I guess following the guy has worked out for me.

We stayed on campus in the dorms the first few years but we both wanted to get out of there and get our own place. We got lucky in May and found this two-bedroom apartment. I'd stayed in Texas for the summer working at a firm in Dallas. The drive was a little long but I've loved getting to live on my own knowing that it would be our place when Tom came back after the summer for our senior year of college.

For that reason, we'd both signed the lease on the apartment. We were being smart about our futures, thinking about student debts, and setting ourselves up for success. My parents liked Tom but had expressed concerns about us moving in together before we were engaged. I'd tried to reassure them that I thought an engagement was approaching then and I think I'm going to get to share some good news with them soon.

Tom has been hinting since he moved back in August about focusing on our futures. I know it's going to be a proposal. I'm so confident that he is planning to propose on Friday. He made us a dinner reservation at the fancy restaurant in town for our makeup fifth Anniversary. I went shopping for a special dress, even video called my best friend, Annie, to make sure it checked the boxes for both sexy and future-hottie fiancé vibes. Now I just have to wait two more days to wear it to my engagement dinner.

As if I've summoned him by thinking of our future engagement, Tom appears at the apartment's front door. He looks tired as he comes into the apartment. "How was your business marketing class?" I ask him as he drops his bag by the door, not on the hooks I installed over the summer. "It was fine, nothing special." He mumbles in reply.

I walk over to him, wrapping my arms around his neck, and pull him into a kiss. It's nice that we are almost the same height. All I have to do to kiss him is step into his arms. He kisses me back, but he breaks the kiss sooner than I like. I move my hands to the hem of his shirt but before I can make a move, he grumbles, "Meg, I just got home. Can't a guy relax before you jump his bones?" There is a spark of annoyance in his green eyes. I feel annoyed with his response to my welcome home. "My bad for wanting to touch my boyfriend."

I step out of his arms and walk over to the table where I'd been thinking about the future. "Meg, don't be mad, it's been a full day with my internship and classes." He steps up behind me and pulls me against his chest, for a hug. "You have the sex drive of a teenager, and I love that, but can we do it later?" Tom says and kisses my neck before releasing me and walking into the kitchen.

He runs his hands through his short brown hair, clearly annoyed but trying to play it off. He starts rummaging through the fridge for something to eat. He goes from pushing me away, to holding me, to trying to eat, in record time. The man jumps from one thing to the next so easily, sometimes I think I'm going to get whiplash from how quickly he changes gears. It's just Tom, he is always changing his mind, lately. In fact, he almost missed graduating with me in the spring because he went back and forth with which business degree to major in. He settled on Management since he thought it would be easily applied in the job market.

I try not to be annoyed. I like sex, I enjoy giving and receiving orgasms. Once sex found me, I was all in and my sex drive hasn't changed. I'm not ashamed of it and I don't remember Tom complaining about it over all the years we've been together.

That is, until the last few weeks after he returned from Oklahoma. When he first got back it was like nothing had changed, we jump back into bed without complaint or issue. In fact, we didn't even make it to the bed; he didn't hesitate in getting me naked and we barely made it to the couch before he was inside of me.

Over the weeks since then, we've had sex, sure, but Tom feels different; distant. He hasn't been making much of an effort to surprise me or to prolong the experience like he did before he left. I am trying not to overthink it, but in reality, I'm totally overthinking it.

We spent three months of summer break apart, and I guess it throws us off our game in that department. So, yes, I've been horny for my boyfriend since he moved into the apartment. As much as my B.O.B (Battery Operated Boyfriend), does the job, I want the real thing, now that he is back. *What's so wrong with having the sex drive of a teenager anyway?*

***

I wake up horny and alone. We didn't end up having sex last night before bed. Tom's version of relaxing is video games, which he started playing with his buddies, shouting out directions and locations like it was life or death. I moved my studying to the extra room we set up with a desk and a bookshelf. I could still hear him but at least I had a sound buffer.

When I had all I could take of editing my capstone description, I called it a night and headed to bed. I slipped into my sexy nightie and assumed Tom would wake me up when he came to bed. Yet here I am, in a sexy nightie, waking up in bed, alone. I check my phone and see a missed text from him at 6:00 AM. I'm not even sure why he would be up that early, as classes don't even start until eight.

Tommy

> Study group early

> See you tonight

I checked the time, and it reads 7:40 AM. *Who the hell schedules a study group so early at the beginning of the year?* I would get it near midterms or finals, but a few weeks into the school year seems harsh. I make a note to ask Tom about it when he gets home tonight.

I wonder if it has to do with the subject or the professor; a challenging class for me always comes down to one of those two factors. Either I didn't get the material in the way I should, or I couldn't connect with the professor's teaching methods.

I shower and get extra personal with the shower head, trying to burn off my frustration in the way available to me. A girls got to do, what a girls got to do. I always focus better after a big O. I consider it my superpower. After my shower, I'm able to focus my mind on the tasks ahead.

I put on a mauve dress that complements my black hair and olive skin. It's September in Texas, and there isn't even a hint of cold weather to be thought of.

I'm anxious for fall, which normally starts to make an appearance here in late October. I can't wait to transition to all the layers, cardigans, sweaters, and vests. Until then, I plan on looking good in all my summer dresses.

I've always believed in showing up fashionable, even just for class. I take the short walk to campus from the apartment. It's one of the reasons we couldn't pass on the apartment. Getting something so close to campus was a huge perk. I love walking around campus and getting to save on gas.

As I enter campus, I grab a coffee on the way, even deciding to grab one for Tom. He seems overwhelmed, and I want him to know I am thinking about him. Mind made up, I order a second coffee. I even sweet talk the barista into adding a heart around his name.

When I get to the library with two coffees in hand, I realized I should have texted Tom to ask him where his study group is meeting. The library has lots of options depending on the size of the group. With luck, I find an outdoor table and set down our drinks. I pull out my phone to text him about the coffee.

Meg

I brought you coffee!

Where in the library are y'all studying?

Tommy

Oh, thanks but we already headed to class. I'm already on the other side of campus.

Meg

I guess that gives me a second dose of caffeine today!

Enjoy!

I put away my phone, frustrated at myself for not texting him earlier. I hate to waste money on a second cup of coffee I don't need. I take a seat and pull out my computer. I may as well get some work done on my capstone project. I open my project submission form and see the assignment description: create a sustainable sports facility.

I read over the task details again for the billionth time. For the sake of the project, I need to determine which sports would benefit from increased facilities and how to optimize them for both athletes and spectators in our local area. We've partnered with the business school to get marketing data from the community. I still have a few areas to think about for the project, so I set an alarm on my phone, so I don't miss class and get to work. I've been known to get lost in my ideas.

I easily burn through two hours reading the materials and making notes on what I find essential from the business school's data. I feel like I've settled on a few good ideas and a focal point for completing my capstone submission form. I add my notes and save them to review one more time before submitting them to my advisor by the end of the week.

As I start packing up my stuff, I hear a deep male voice say my full name, in only the way he does. It sends my pulse racing, I wish it didn't but it does. I have no idea why hearing my full name from him makes me feel this way. No, that's a lie, I totally understand why it makes me feel this way, because it's him. I know it's him because everyone else calls me by my nickname Meg and only he calls me Megan.

"Megan, I haven't seen you around this semester. How are you?" I look up and make eye contact with a similar set of blue-gray eyes belonging to none other than Miles James Campbell. Miles is my best friend Annie's older brother by a year. He is the starting quarterback at Belmont, and everyone here knows him and loves him.

He's the All-American football player with his blue-gray eyes, blond hair, and tall muscled body that goes on for days. Never mind, the fact that he was my first crush. I still can't help but take in all of Miles Campbell with appreciation. There's just something about him that sucks me in.

I've only seen him a handful of times over the years. We don't have similar degree programs or friend groups. I do cheer him and the team on every home football game, which I count as seeing him. I've been watching him play football for what feels like my whole life.

"Miles, you are the only person who calls me Megan. You know that, right?" He flashes me a quick smile. "Yes, MEGAN, I do. It's our thing, me calling you Megan while the world calls you Meg. You'll always know it's me when you hear it." God, he isn't wrong, I do always know it's him when I hear Megan. I briefly wonder if I'd know it was him if he called me Meg. His smile is infectious, and I catch myself smiling back. "You going to graduate eventually, old man?"

"Ouch, that hurts, Megan. I'm only a year older than you; old man is a harsh label. If you must know, I'm graduating in the spring. Thank you very much". I've always enjoyed messing with Miles; we push each other's buttons in a good-fun sort of way.

That is what happens when you've known someone since elementary school. We started off pushing each other's buttons, and it never stopped. Annie has been a referee in our ongoing button-pushing antics on more than one occasion.

"Then, look at us, Okies graduating at the same time." He laughs at my Oklahoma reference. Here in Texas, it's almost thought of as 'shameful' to be from Oklahoma. I think they are just jealous of our ability to keep up on the turf, if you ask me.

Football is as much a force of nature here as it is back home in Oklahoma; the only thing they have that we don't are the pro teams. Miles and I make small talk for a few more minutes, and I realize it's been nice to catch up with him. We probably could have talked longer, but my alarm reminds me to get to class. We wrap up the conversation and I shout over my shoulder as I leave, "See you around, old man". Miles never lets me have the last word, and shouts back at me. "Until next time, MEGAN".

The day goes by quickly, filled with classes and group discussions about upcoming projects. I get back to our apartment later than I expect and Tom is already in the apartment. I can hear his voice through the door as I'm about to slide my key into the lock. "I'm going to talk with her tomorrow. We already have dinner planned, and then I figured that's when I'll bring it up." I hear Tom's words, and my heart races with excitement. So, he really is planning on asking me to marry him after dinner tomorrow.

It's great to know that I have it figured out as I slide the key into the lock and open the door with a little more noise than usual. "I gotta go, talk to you later." Tom ends the call as I enter the apartment. "Everything ok?" I ask, trying to play like I didn't hear the end of his conversation. "Yeah, everything is fine. Sorry, I missed you this morning." Tom comes over, hugs me, and kisses me on the for ehead.

"No problem, I should have texted you sooner, but I was trying to surprise you. That is one early study group." He releases me and heads in the direction of the kitchen. "Yeah, Meg, it's crazy early, but it was the only time we could fit it into our schedules with everything going on this semester."

Tom changes the subject, "You interested in some dinner?" I give him the out, "I could eat." He laughs, and I follow him into the kitchen. "What about the Tom Special?" I ask and he gives me another hug before releasing me to dig through the fridge. "Sure, I'm game for fried chicken and mashed potatoes." He looks over the fridge at me, "but you have to make the gravy." I smile as we go about making a meal that we've perfected. It was one of the staples at the diner we met at in high school, and it is our running joke that it is the only meal Tom can actually make that is worth eating.

Chapter 2: Not What I Was Expecting

-*Meg*-

I wake up excited and anticipating what today means for our future. I checked my calendar and confirmed that I have two classes and a nail appointment before our dinner plans later tonight.

I almost didn't schedule the nail appointment, but since Tom confirmed it last night. I feel like I'll be glad to have a fresh set of paint on my nails for all the photos I'm preparing to take with a ring on that finger.

Tom left early today to do a half day at the bank, where he has an internship, before his class. I can't help but think cheesy thoughts as I get ready. They range from ridiculous to more ridiculous, but I don't care. *'I'll soon be Mrs. Williams'* to *'I'll be calling Tom my fiancé'* to *'what are good boy and girl names that go with Williams'*.

I need to work out my emotions as I am bubbling over with them. I swear I'm bounce-walking to campus, I'm so excited. I need to get out some energy before class, so I call the only person who will understand my excitement.

The video call rings twice before I see a close-up of a single blue-grey eye. "Meg, I answered because I love you, but it's too early for video calls." I don't hold back my laughter at the single-eyeball image and Annie's random comment.

"First, it's after nine in the morning, wake up, and stop being a baby. Second, I have NEWS. I have news, like big, big, BIG news!" I sing song say to her. She sits up, and now I see her whole face in the video with her blonde messy bun tipping to one side of her head.

"Did he pop the question before you all made it out of bed?" Annie half screams into the phone, looking both excited and impressed. "Get your mind out of the gutter, Annie Marie. But no, not yet, but I overheard him on the phone saying he would talk to me after dinner." Annie deflates a little before asking, "You booked a nail appointment, didn't you?"

She shakes her head, giving me a look. "You are totally giving it away, and you know it." My best friend knows me too well. "I am not!" I respond defensively. "Anyone who knows me understands I have standards for these big events. Even without the possibility of a proposal, I'd have gotten fancy for our fifth Anniversary makeup dinner."

Annie shrugs, "Ok, valid point. You have that sexy purple dress ready. The one you purchased a few weeks ago?" I can't help rolling my eyes. "Annie, I thought I told you it was lavender mist." Annie rolls her eyes at me. "Whatever, it's too early to remember the exact color of purple of your dress. At least I remembered it was a variation of purple, and you looked amazing in it."

I beam at her over the phone. "Ok, fine, it is too early for you to remember 'Miss I hate mornings'. I just needed to tell someone before I explode with excitement." Annie smiles at me. "I'm so excited for you, BFF, and you can wake me up with good news any time." We continue our conversation, moving on to other topics before we both need to get on with our days. Before we disconnect,

Annie tells me she'd better be the first person I call to show off my ring. I promise her I will make her my first call later tonight.

***

Tom and I are having a nice dinner at the fancy restaurant in town. We talk about our futures and the possible careers we hope to have. We joke and laugh about the teenagers we were when this relationship started. We both agree that sneaking around at the lake had been both a rush and crazy. We also agree that sex in a room without the fear of being found is so much better.

It's always been easy to talk to Tom. We started as friends first, after all, working at the diner back home. It had morphed into something more over the summer between junior and senior year of high school. He'd been on the edge of nerdy but cute, which wasn't my style of bad boys and jocks.

He'd caught me off guard by asking me out. I'd surprised myself by saying 'yes,' and we've been together ever since. On the drive back to the apartment, Tom holds my hand, and it's comfortable and relaxing, listening to the radio.

I feel good about my outfit and have my makeup looking good for pictures. The French-tipped nails will look beautiful in the dozens of photos I'm sure to take with the ring. True to his conversation, nothing happened during dinner, and I think I enjoyed it more knowing it wouldn't happen. I didn't get distracted by thinking it was coming.

I am not the nervous type, and it feels completely foreign to be this nervous right now. I notice Tom is starting to look anxious, too. I step into his arms as we enter the apartment and kiss him. He only holds the kiss a moment before pulling back and asking me, "Do you need a drink or something? I could use a d rink."

350

I can feel the nerves coming off him, and I don't think a drink will help. "Tom, why don't we sit down?" I suggest. He nods his agreement and sits down on the couch. "You look nervous. Everything ok?" I throw him a bone; I don't want him to back out on this proposal due to nerves. I sit down on the second-hand couch next to him and go to retake his hand, but this time he pulls back. "Meg, it's not working?"

What? I think, *what isn't working? I couldn't have heard that right.* I guess maybe I blocked out part of his words. "What?" I ask him, hearing my confusion in the one-word question. Tom looks at me now as if it should be easy to understand. He looks uncomfortable as he starts to speak.

"We aren't working. Meg, I don't know when it changed for me, but it has changed. I care about you, but I'm not in love with you like I used to be. I think it's time to end this relationship." Tom runs his hands through his hair as he speaks. I feel numb. This isn't what I was expecting at all. I feel blindsided. *Didn't we have a great dinner? I could swear we talked about our futures and he'd held my hand and kissed me only moments ago.*

I ask the only thing that comes to mind as a reason for this crazy turn. "Is there someone else?" Tom pales and runs his hand through his hair again. "No, Meg. No. I just realized over the summer that I didn't miss you as much as I should. I should have needed to talk to you, but I didn't."

I feel my heart racing and try to focus on what he is saying. "We've been with each other for so long that I should have missed you in every way, and I realized it was nice to be by myself. I want to make decisions for myself and only myself. I didn't have to text to stop by a friend's house on my way home or to ask if we had plans. I thought my feelings would change when I moved into the apartment, but they didn't. I felt like I had to answer to you again and I don't want to answer to you, I want to answer only to myself." The numbness I've felt up to this point in the conversation starts to churn into anger.

How the fuck does he get off acting like I control his life? Yes, I plan dinners and date nights because it's part of being a couple living together. If anything, I'm pretty laid back with our relationship. I don't care about much, and I'm always really flexible with our time.

I don't even know if I've ever been mad about him showing up, telling me he's already eaten. I didn't even call him every day over the summer because we'd both been so busy. I'd reached out to talk to my boyfriend, but not in any way that would make it feel as if I'm controlling.

He can have his feelings, but I want to call bullshit on him acting like I was someone who made him answer to me. Tom interrupts my anger by continuing his justification for this breakup. "In my mind, this relationship has run its course." His words snap me back into focus and back into my body. "Don't you want to see who else is out there?" He gives me a pleading look, and all I can think is *Fucking wrong question, Tom'*.

I don't think, as I start speaking, I let the thoughts roll out of me. "Well, since you are done, there isn't any point in begging. Good news for me is that I can find someone who can fuck me like a teenager now."

Tom looks at me with sadness and pity. Fuck him and his pity look. "Meg, I don't want to hurt you. I've known it was over since I got back." The more he speaks, the worse this gets. He really needs to shut up.

"Tom, that doesn't make it better, you know that, right? What did you want to get in a few more fucks with me to make sure that breaking up was the right decision? To hold you over until you can find someone else?"

I am pissed, and I can't stop myself. "You moved into our apartment and slept next to me, and what realized one night, 'Meg isn't the one for me'? Why let us celebrate our anniversary? Was it for old times' sake? Why not wait to have this conversation after fucking me one more time? Better yet, why didn't you break up with me when you got back from Oklahoma? Why wait for weeks to do this?"

Tom stands and starts pacing in the small living room. "Meg, I was torn when I moved back in. I thought it was a phase, and if we spent time together, it would return to how I felt when I left. Then, after I realized I wouldn't change my mind, I tried to find a new place. I didn't like any of the options, so I gave it more time. I thought I might have been rash, so I tried again to see if being here with you would change my mind. All it did was make me realize we aren't on the same path anymore."

He stops pacing to look at me. I feel like an idiot. Here I was thinking our futures were aligned, and he had been working up his courage to dump me the whole time. He's been trying to change his mind about breaking up with me, and if I didn't misunderstand his last few sentences. The ONLY reason he didn't do this earlier is due to his inability to find a suitable living arrangement.

I close my eyes and cover them with my hands. I take a few deep breaths to keep my emotions in check. I will not let him see me cry. "Tom, I can't live here with you." Before I can say more, he interjects. "I thought about it, I'll move into the second bedroom, and you can keep the main bedroom. I'll even move the desk and bookshelf if you want them in your room. We can stay friends and have our own bedrooms. We can be adults about sharing the living spaces after all these years together."

I can't believe he just suggested we stay living together. I know I give him a look of 'absolutely the fuck not' because he runs his hands through his hair again in frustration. He goes to talk again, and I interrupt him this time.

"Ok, Tom, that sounds great. We can be adults about this, sure, sure. Do I leave a sock on the front door when I'm having sex like a teenager?" He stares back at me with a surprised expression, like he didn't think about us having over new p eople.

"There is no way that works. We aren't really friends, Tom, are we? I would never treat my friend like this, and I don't want to be friends with someone who treats me like this. We aren't anything anymore other than exes."

I will not give in to tears; I chant in my head as I finish speaking. I feel them at the back of my eye sockets, but refuse to let them fall. I refuse to let him see me cry. "Meg, the semester has already started. The possibilities aren't great in town for a new place to live. I looked and finding a new apartment is nearly impossible. Like I said, I tried and didn't like the choices." I scoff. "I don't think you wanted to leave bad enough then."

I need space from him, I need to cry, and most of all, I need Tom to leave. I won't beg him to want me or stay with me. Even if I didn't see this coming, I know my worth, and I don't want someone who doesn't want me.

"I need you to leave Tom. I need to be alone to think and process." Tom stops his pacing to look at me. "Are you ok, Meg? I feel bad leaving you like this." I look at the man I thought I was about to spend forever with and don't see that version anymore. I see a man I don't know, and it's another heartbreaking blow.

"Tom, I need space. Leave this apartment." He nods his agreement. "Let me grab my stuff, and I'll stay with a friend for the weekend. We can talk about this, but it can wait until Monday after classes."

I don't reply because he heads toward the bedroom. I stay on the couch, trying to stay numb, trying not to think about my feelings. I will not let the tears fall until he closes the door behind him. He makes his way back through the living room and gives me one more glance before he heads out the apartment door.

I'm unsure how long I stay on the couch, lost to the silence and the darkness, still not allowing myself to cry. Then out of nowhere it starts. I feel the cold, wet tears streaming down my face. I don't just cry, I break apart into sobs, my breath catches, and I can't get enough air.

I am sitting on the edge of an endless abyss. The only thing that keeps me here is the sobs racking through my body. As if realizing my body exists again, I know I'm going to be sick, and I barely make it to the bathroom before the anniversary dinner empties from my body. It's my body's way of getting all remnants of this night out of me. When it's over, I go to the sink and rinse my mouth out.

When I look in the mirror, I'm a disaster. Or better yet, a fucking hot mess. My makeup is smudged or completely gone, and my eyes are swollen and red. My beautiful lavender mist dress looks wrinkled, and I may have vomited on it after my exorcism.

I want out of this dress as soon as humanly possible. I yank it over my head and throw it in the trash. I may even burn it to cleanse my body of this night. I change into a Belmont football T-shirt and lazy-day sweats. I climb into bed and realize it smells like him, and I hate it.

I get up, change the sheets, and throw the blanket in the corner by the laundry hamper. I get back in, and all I can smell is spring flowers. I spiral for hours, and I have no idea when I finally succumb to sleep, but eventually, I do.

Chapter 3: Beginning of the End

-Miles-

It's only taken five years, but I am finally in my senior year and my last football season. The five years were intentional, as I was redshirted my freshman year. I needed that year to grow both as a leader and physically to be ready for this level of football.

The extra year allowed me to get in all the hours I needed for my degree under my full-ride scholarship without being weighed down during the football season with credit hours. I know this is the end of my football journey. I'm good, I wouldn't have made it to a division one college if I wasn't, but I'm not good enough to go pro.

It's been a great run, I have enjoyed the hell out of being on the field under those bright lights. I've been on a football field for so long that I don't remember not being on one. I've reached my mountain top in the sport and want to go out with as many W's as possible.

We've completed three non-conference travel games with all W's on the board. We kick off our last non-conference game here at home this weekend, and then it's all conference schedule for the rest of the season. I know the games will only get harder and L's will happen, but I want them to be few and far between.

The only pressure I feel is to give the guys the best chance possible for the season. I know a few guys, like my roommate Jamal, want to add to their stats to help their chances at getting drafted. I've played with guys already in the pros, so I get the pressure to make every game count.

My old roommate Dax comes to mind as he is the most recent one of my teammates to get drafted. He's also why I have to pay more in rent this year. The asshole decision to enter the draft left us a roommate down, and we've been stubborn in our requirements to replace him. We should have offered it to one of the other guys, but we had both been stubborn about it.

Finding a random roommate who wants to live with me and Jamal is hard. Jamal Arthur is the team's starting wide receiver, and we are both part of the same recruitment class. Looking at him, most people would notice his 6'4 height and muscles and see a tough-as-nails football player.

In reality, the guy is a jokester and giant teddy bear; if he isn't smiling, something is very, very wrong. He almost went into the draft last year with Dax, but his mom asked him to graduate first. He refused to let his mom down, so here we are together in a house that has an empty bedroom.

He told me all summer to make him look good this year, and I plan to get him his highlight reel. The house we rent is close to the campus and has been housing some form of football players for years. The landlord, Harry, is middle-aged and a huge football fan. He loves us and doesn't care if we party as long as we don't trash the house and the police don't get called. We love him for keeping the rent the same since we moved in and giving us freedom.

We've had a crazy number of people interested in the open room upstairs next to mine. At first, we both showed up to give the tours, but I got sick of the process. Now Jamal is in charge of filtering the requests, and I show up to the ones he can't.

I'd been the one available in August when Tom Williams took the tour. I knew the guy from Oklahoma. I had been surprised to see him because I thought he was living with Megan, my sister's best friend and his longtime girlfriend. But I must have mixed up my facts from my sister.

He'd asked how many people we had over and if we had an agreement about parties. After he left, Jamal vetoed him right away. His direct quote was, "No, he would be a major buzz kill." I don't know Tom well enough to disagree with Jamal's statement, so we didn't offer him the room, and he didn't reach back out.

Maybe he also felt it wasn't a good fit. We've kept the search for a new roommate open and posted on the school website. I told Jamal that if no one takes the room by October, we should call it and ride out the rest of the year, splitting the rent two ways. I'd rather have no roommate than one who doesn't fit in. I have no interest in bringing drama into my life with two semesters left in my collegiate career.

***

On Saturday, I get a text message from my sister. This isn't completely unheard of, as she normally sends me a good luck message on game days, but it's not her normal good luck message. Those are to the point and the message I'm reading is frantic.

Baby Sis

I can't reach Meg. I'm worried

Can you check on her?

Miles

Why? What happened?

Why are you worried?

My heartrate picks up at my sister's concern about Megan. Annie can be dramatic but in all the years I've lived here she's never asked me to check on Megan before. Something is wrong. I try to keep calm and watch as the ... flash on my screen as my sister types.

Baby Sis

I guess Tom broke up with her last night.

I'd drive down but I'm covering the game for the news department. I can't skip it.

Miles

You guess he broke up with her?

What does that even mean?

You know I also have a game today?

Baby Sis

Yes, I know you are hot stuff but it is a night game, so I'm not asking you to miss your game.

You're probably still in bed if I was a betting person.

> I called him after she wouldn't pick up and he said he left her alone after breaking up with her.

> He said I should check in with her. That she seems upset. No FUCKING duh, asshole she'd be upset, she thought he was going to propose.

> This is as big deal Miles.

> So... please Miles, it's Meg, please for me!

Miles

> That's all kinds of fucked up.

> For you and for Megan I'll go check on her

> Address?

I'm not sure why, but I'm the only one who calls her Megan; everyone calls her Meg. Maybe it has to do with the fact that the first time I met her, when she'd been over to play with Annie in elementary school, she'd introduced herself as "Megan Patterson, but everyone calls me Meg". I didn't want to be like everyone else, so I called her Megan. She'd blushed, and I like that so I never stopped calling her Megan.

Annie texts me the address to Megan's apartment. All the puzzle pieces click in my mind. I understand now why Tom was looking at apartments? I feel guilty; I should have brought it up when I saw her at the library, but I wasn't sure and I didn't want to start shit if I wasn't sure.

Yet, I feel guilty, especially if she thought a proposal was coming and not a breakup. I was surprised to see her at the library this week, and I was more focused on her than thinking about her dickhead of a boyfriend. Well, I guess now her ex-boyfriend.

I know enough about him now to have an opinion about him. He's an idiot for breaking it off with Megan. She's feisty and beautiful, a lethal combination, I've actively avoided for years. I grab my sweats and head out to check on my sister's best friend.

I have no idea what to expect when I arrived at Megan's apartment, but it wasn't this. I knock on the door once, twice, but there is nothing. I keep knocking on the door and knocking on the door. I think it's starting to sound more like banging on the door versus knocking.

At some point, I wonder if she isn't home, and I feel ridiculous for continuing to bang on her door. *Did my sister get the facts wrong?* I swear, if she sent me on a wild goose chase, I will find a way to get back at her. I wouldn't put it past my sister to be dramatic about a situation that Megan would laugh off easily.

I'm about to head home when I hear a noise on the other end of the door. "Megan, you there? It's Miles." I hear the sound of feet near the door and then she says through the door, "Miles, what are you doing here?" Before I can answer, she continues, "Annie. Did Annie send you?" I go to answer but she keeps talking. "Tell her I'm alive and I'll call her later. I just need..." Her voice breaks and it sounds like she is going to cry.

I fucking hate it when Megan cries. I don't know what to do. I know that I want to hold her until she stops but what does she need me to do? Do I try to solve her problem, or just wait it out? There should be a manual or playbook that tells guys how to respond to weeping females so we don't make it worse.

"Megan, I'm not leaving until you open the door. Consider this a big brother move if you need to, but I promised Annie I would check on you. I don't think she's going to count me talking to you through a door as fulfilling my promise."

I must get through to her because I hear the bolt on the lock turning. "I warn you, Miles, do not comment on my appearance. I'm opening this door because I know your sister, and she'll skip her game if you don't report back soon." Megan is right, Annie is stubborn, and she would totally skip her game and drive here if she doesn't hear from me soon.

The door flies open, and I'm greeted with the saddest version of Megan Patterson I've ever seen. Megan's raven hair is up in one of those messy bun things, but it's falling out in all directions. She is in oversized sweats and a t-shirt, which wouldn't be surprising on most college girls, but Megan isn't most college girls.

She always looks put together, even when relaxing at my house growing up. The kicker about her appearance is her red, swollen eyes. I want to kick his ass for hurting her. I don't think, I react. I step into the doorway, wrapping my arms around her in a hug.

Megan must need it because she doesn't fight me. She wraps her arms around my waist and her head against my chest. Neither of us moves for a long time, we stay in this moment. For her lack of her normal style, she smells nice, like sugar cookies. Then my guy brain kicks on in full force and I realize Megan's not wearing a bra. I don't mean to notice, but what guy wouldn't notice the feel of hard nipples pressed against their chest? I have to mentally pull my brain away from thinking about Megan's hard nipples against my stomach and back on the reason I'm here.

"How are you feeling?" I expect a smart-ass answer because this is Megan, but I don't get it. "Awful, Miles, I feel awful and really, really stupid." She pulled out of my arms slowly as if she'd rather stay, but she didn't want to burden me with continuing the hug. "You know you are anything but stupid, a smart-ass comes to mind as a better description."

She smiles at my comment, but a small, reluctant smile. "Can I come in? I do bear the gift of breakfast." Megan moves out of the way then waves me toward the kitchen. I lay out a spread of items from the local bakery Annie aggressively suggested that I must stop at before checking on Megan. "How did you know I love these?" Megan says as she picks up a cherry pastry. She rolls her eyes and answers her own question, "Right, Annie."

I agree with her that it is Annie's doing. "She would have come herself, but she has an early game to cover in Norman. But I wouldn't put it past her to drive here right after its over since it's only a three-hour drive, give or take." Megan nods her head in agreement, then gives me a look. "Don't you have a game today?"

A look of alarm passes over her face with the thought. I can't help it, I laugh. "Don't worry, it's a night game. I have to leave in about 15 minutes, but you are on the way to the stadium, so I'm all good." "I totally forgot what the game time was. Thank goodness Tom didn't ruin both our weekends. Or senior years." Meg finished her outburst by taking a big bite of the cherry pastry.

I don't give in to Megan's pity party. Maybe I should, but I'm not that guy. "You have all your senior year to enjoy. Don't let fucking Tom ruin it. He was an asshole anyway." I feel good with my choice of description because, looking at her broken, all I can think of is that the guy is an asshole. She's one of a kind, that I know to be true. "Did you even know him well enough to call him an asshole?" Megan asks me, and I smile. "There you are. Glad you're still my smart-ass Megan."

We talked for a few more minutes, and she tells me she will call Annie after I leave. I give her another hug. It feels right to hug her, and she lets me hold her for a moment before we both step out of it. "Call me if you need anything, even if it's just another round of pastries." She smiles at me as she holds the door. "Miles Campbell, my personal food delivery service. Thank you, and I'll be sure to text if I get any cravings." I walk away laughing. Megan may be down, but she's not broken, and that difference feels important.

***

At the stadium, I arrive and head back to the locker room. I throw on my headphones and listen to some punk rock to get myself hyped. I don't raise the volume when guys come into the locker room. I enjoy the music mixed with the loud and rumbustious atmosphere of the team.

I run myself through the game strategy. Mentally checking my log for all the plays for today and go through the hot takes to remember about the upcoming defense. I review the play calls for today's game at least ten times and make sure that I know a few of Coach Will's favorites just in case he wants to throw in a conversion or trick play.

I'm dialed in and ready to get on the field. There isn't anything better than a home-field advantage. It's the familiarity, but it's more about the fans and atmosphere they create. We enter the field at warm-ups to the loud sounds of the crowd.

The music is going, and the team is pumped as we stretch and run through a few drills. I make my rounds with my starting guys. It was something I learned early in my football career. Appreciate the guys protecting you, and they'll give it their all to watch your back. I will get hit because it's football, but it will be much less likely with these guys holding the pocket. I slap pads and do special handshakes with all my guys. I return to the quarterbacks, and our coach reminds us it's about timing, not perfection.

We return to the tunnel and wait for the big announcement and the game to start. When we next enter the stadium, fireworks, the band, and fans are on their feet. The sounds are deafening, and the best hype material. Guys yell "let's go" and "bring it on" as we run to our bench.

I love this feeling that rides the line between excitement and nervousness. As the starting quarterback, I have a team relying on me to do my job. Tonight is no different from the other games I've played; however, tonight I know the countdown to the end is coming. I have a limited number of times left to enjoy all of this.

Today's match-up is a non-conference game, but it's still my first-last home game in this stadium. My mom must have gotten in my head about savoring the moment because I've been trying to document it all mentally. I even enjoyed two-a-days this preseason, and that felt insane to think because two-a-days suck for a reason.

When it's our turn for the offense to take the field. I huddle the team and call the play. As soon as I get the ball, I'm locked onto my target, good old Jamal. I step up and throw a spiral and know it will hit my guy. He doesn't have to slow down as the ball lands in his waiting hands. The feeling is right and I know tonight is going to be a good night.

***

"We put on a great performance tonight, gentlemen, but this is only warmups. Conference games start next week, and that will be the real test." Coach Will, ever the motivational presence as he delivers our post-game wrap-up, then officially releases us from the facility. I checked my phone and see I have missed a few calls and messages. I listened to my parents' voicemails letting me know that I looked great on TV, and they can't wait to make it to the game in October. I'll call them back later, as the locker room is too loud. I opened the messages app and see I have messages from both Annie and Megan.

Baby Sis

You are my hero thank you

PS: Meg gave me a lecture about distracting you on game day

PSS: Great Game!

Miles

That is hilarious

Didn't realize she was still so into football

Baby Sis

Don't let her fashion choices fool you

Megan is a football girlie

Miles

Noted

You in town?

Baby Sis

Yes, of course

Miles

Drive safe home and let me know if you want to grab food before you drive back.

I leave my conversation with Annie and move to the messages from Megan. I knew Megan loved football, but I have a running habit of downplaying how much attention I've given her over the years. I pretend to both of them that I'm clueless when it comes to all of their actions over the years but the reality of the situation is I've noticed everything about Megan Patterson.

Megan Patterson

Thanks, Miles for the food

This is Meg if you don't have my number and if you needed this message to tell you than well shame, shame, shame...

Miles

Megan, I have your number in my phone

no need for the shaming

Also no problem regarding the food

Megan Patterson

Really, I bet you have me saved as Megan!

Miles

Obviously do you have another name?

Megan Patterson

Nope. It's my name.

Good game today. I skipped coming in person but I'll be there at the next home game, so repeat the effort.

Miles

Plan on it. I'd say I'll see you there but unless you let me know the section there is no chance, I'll find you

I don't get another message and assume Megan and Annie are both done with messaging me for the night and doing the girl sleepover thing they do. Jamal comes over, showered and ready to go. I've waited thirty minutes for him to get his ass in the showers because he has to joke around with everyone in the locker room.

"We got that thing tonight, right?" Jamal is giving me his best nonchalant expression. We don't say the word 'party' in the locker room to avoid the staff overhearing. "Yeah, man, we have that thing tonight. You sure took your sweet ass time in the shower. See anything interesting?"

Jamal gives me a big smile and a wink. "Fuck off, Camp, you know I stay for the gossip, not the dicks. However, I bet a lot of people would have stayed for the dicks. We have some impressive teammates." I can't help but laugh at him, and it doesn't break his stride. "I heard that blonde I've had my eye on broke it off with her boyfriend. Could be my night to make a move."

I can't help laughing again at my friend. Jamal Arthur has a type, and it's blonde and curvy. I've never seen him break his type in all five years of hanging out with him. I'm surprised he can even find a blonde in a twenty-mile radius that he hasn't hooked up with. "You finally ready to head back to the house?" I ask as I put my phone away.

"Dude, it was an asshole move to leave me this morning. I thought we had an unwritten rule about carpooling." Jamal gives me his best feel bad for me expression. "I told you I had to check on my little sister's friend this morning." Jamal's smile morphs to the one he uses for women.

"I like little sisters and their friends, Miles." I give him a shove as I get up from my locker and grab my stuff. "Fuck right the hell off, Jamal. You don't get anywhere near Megan or Annie." His laugh is the only reply I get. We have had this conversation before. I know he wouldn't try anything with Annie. Even if every time she's in town, he puts on a show of flirting with her. I grab my stuff so we can get to the house and finalize a few things before it's overrun with partie rs.

I want to say the party has the same effect as the game on my system, but it doesn't. I've enjoyed myself at college, make no mistake, I'm a playboy like Jamal. I was good my freshman year, because I had a girlfriend from back home, but then she broke up with me because she felt like she wasn't getting the whole college experience with us at different colleges. We had only been able to see each other on breaks, and those were short.

After I was let off my hook, I enjoyed the rest of my time here in Texas. That is, until recently, I've been on what Jamal calls my drought. Maybe the truth is that I was a playboy, but right now I've benched myself from hooking up. I have found it harder to enjoy the random girls who want to be on the arm of the starting QB.

I don't know why, maybe it's because I know that I'm not going to be QB1 next year, I'll be an English teacher back in my hometown. My teammate gives me hell that I'm going from the 'king of the jocks' to the 'home room teacher'. I'm no reporter like Annie; I don't have any interest in being the center of attention unless it's on the football field in my pads.

I much prefer to blend into the crowd and watch the drama unfold. Tonight, I'm having a good time watching the freshman guys try to hit on girls and getting turned down. I overhear a group of sorority girls discussing who on the team is worth a one-night stand.

I make a note to tell Jamal that he came in second to me. He'll love that. I don't take any pride in the fact that they all thought I would be a great one-night stand. *What does that say about me?* I have no idea, but I'm not going to find out tonight. I'm playing the role of the sober-ish guy and making sure that the house doesn't get completely trashed.

We have a standing party rule to close with the bars, so at 2 AM, we close the party down. Anyone who isn't trashed gets a trash bag and helps pick up the discarded cups and bottles. The house empties quickly, and what's left is a mostly clean space. Jamal and a blonde head back to his room at the end of the main floor as people leave.

I do a final sweep of the house, wiping down the kitchen counters and returning the pillows and blankets to the couch. I look around and figure it's good enough, so I lock the door and make my way upstairs alone.

It feels empty up here without a roommate. Dax had been loud and messy, with an equally loud girlfriend, so usually this was the time of night I was subjected to moans. I don't miss having to share a bathroom with them. At this rate, I'd better get used to it, as I think we've missed the window to get a roommate this semester.

Chapter 4: Best Friend Therapy
-Meg-

I wake up to a nonstop knocking on my front door and I feel like death. So, I don't answer it. I think it will stop but it only gets louder, like someone is trying to knock the door off the hinges.

I'm annoyed, I want to stay in my bed and give myself at least one day to feel like shit before I try to figure out my life. When it continues, I make myself get up. *There better be a good reason for this.* I'm in the living room when the knocking stops and I'm debating going back to bed when I hear the person on the other side of the door speak.

"Megan, you there? It's Miles." I would have known it was Miles by just the use of my full name in his deep voice. I make my way to the door and speak through it, maybe I can get him to leave without opening it.

"Miles what are you doing here?" I don't let him answer because my brain clicks, I never called Annie last night after my not proposal. "Annie. Did Annie send you? Tell her I'm alive and I'll call her later. I just need...." My words catch and I realize I may cry again when I think about telling Annie what happened.

I'm saved from making new words by Miles' voice through the door. "Megan, I'm not leaving until you open the door. Think of this as a big brother move if you need too but I promised Annie to check on you. I don't think she would count me talking to you through a door as fulfilling my promise." Miles has always been a good guy and this proves it. I know very few guys that would drop anything at their sister's request.

I warn him that he better not comment on my appearance. I don't think Miles would but it's the ice breaker I need to start unlocking the door. I also realize if I deny him, I'll have Annie at my door and I don't want her to miss an opportunity at her own university. She's been looking forward to getting to report at the game today with the possibility she could be on the network national coverage.

When I open the door, Miles does a head-to-toe scan and before I can make a joke or smart-ass comment, I'm enveloped into his strong arms. I didn't know I needed it until I'm in his arms and I lay my head on his chest and wrap my arms around his waist. I can't help registering again how good he smells as he holds me. I feel safe and protected. Miles has always been my protector. I've witnessed countless times his brotherly protection has kicked in with me and Annie.

I can't help that I start to compare the body against me to the last male arms that held me. Tom wasn't an athlete like Miles, his body wasn't like Miles at all. Miles is all hard muscles and is so much taller, he's over a head taller than me at my 5'6. I'm not sure how long we stand in the doorway with his arms wrapped around me. At one point Miles even hugs me a little tighter.

Eventually, he clears his throat before breaking the silence and I can hear his words through his chest. "How you feeling?" I want to be my sassy self but I'm not feeling it and the moment feels too real to play it off as anything but genuine. I answer Miles's question honestly. "Awful, Miles I feel awful and really, really stupid."

I reluctantly pull out of the hug and Miles releases me slowly. I should thank him for it but that feels weird to tell him that his hug was so important. I look into his blue-gray eyes when he response to my comment. "You know you are anything but stupid, a smart-ass comes to mind as a better description." There is the Miles I've grown up with, the one that doesn't let me get away with self-pity. I can't help the smile that comes to my face.

He continues by asking to come in and bends down grabbing a bag from the ground that I hadn't noticed when I opened the door. I take a step back and point in the direction of the kitchen. He makes quick work of laying out the spread of food from my favorite bakery down the road. He's even got the cherry pastry that's my favorite. I pick it up and ask, "How did you know I love these?" But I answer my own question again. "Right, Annie."

Miles nods his head in agreement. "She would have come herself, but she has an early game to cover in Norman. But I wouldn't put it past her to drive here right after its over since it's only a three-hour drive, give or take." Now I'm the one nodding my agreement.

I think about what day it is and realize that today is the home opener for Miles. "Don't you have a game today?" Shit, I hope him coming here isn't going to throw off his pregame rituals. He shrugs his shoulders and laughs at me. "Don't worry it's a night game. He looks down at his watch.

"I do have to leave in like 15 minutes but you are on the way to the stadium so I'm all good." I take a deep breath and relax. I know Miles is the key for the team to have a great season. I don't want to be the cause of him having a shitty game. "Thank goodness Tom didn't ruin both our weekends. Or senior years."

Miles shakes his head like he's disappointed with my comment. "You have all your senior year to enjoy. Don't let fucking Tom ruin it. He was an asshole anyway." *Tell me what you really think of Tom*, I think. Miles's comment does make me smile a little more. "Did you even know him well enough to call him an asshole?"

Miles breaks into his full smile at my question. "There you are. Glad you're still my Megan." I can't help liking the way he says 'my Megan' like he has some claim on me. Middle school Meg is having a happy dance in my brain. He stays until I've finished my pastry and taken a few drinks of the water he grabs me from the fridge.

I'll have to thank Annie for letting me borrow her brother for the morning. Miles is just what I needed to not wallow the day away. He looks at his watch and lets me know he has to head out to go to the game. He gives me a quick hug and shows himself out the door but tells me to call him if I need anything and I know he means it.

Miles wasn't wrong at 6 PM I get a knock on my door and it's Annie. She wraps me in a bear hug to the point that breathing is hard. It's so unlike the gentle hug that I got from Miles. Both Campbells have come through for me today.

"You didn't have to drive all the way here" I tell Annie. "Like hell I didn't. You need me and you practically moved into my room when I ended it with Drew. You and Tom have been together for five years, I'm not letting you sit here alone."

Now I'm the one bear hugging her. "Thank you". She makes me take a shower and change. I do feel better after the shower and I grab a pair of leggings and my lucky university football shirt reserved exclusively for football season. The team doesn't always win when I wear it but it's my superstition that if I don't, I could be the reason that the pass is missed or the defense doesn't stop the run.

We snuggle up on the couch turning it to the local station to watch the game. We see the team enter the field to the roar of the crowd. I look for the number 10, it's a habit I formed in middle school, I find Miles as he races on the field.

He is near the end with number 5, which is one of the standout wide receivers from last year. Annie hits mute on the sound.

"I'm happy to watch football with you Meg, but I want you to know we can talk too." Having said her piece, she unmutes the sound and we watch the football game. At half time the team has it locked in with Miles and number 5 leading the way. The announcer reminds me that his name was Arthur. I have it locked in now so I can yell at him to run faster or remind him that its his job to catch the football. They have connected on two touchdowns and then the running back got the third.

The defense has held them to one field goal. At the half I realize I should take this opportunity to talk to my best friend about everything and I reach over and mute the sound. Annie looks at me but doesn't speak. "I feel so stupid thinking he was going to propose. I thought all his secret conversations since he got back had to do with it. I took them as planning for a proposal but it was really him planning to end it."

I look at Annie and she's watching me and I know she's giving me the floor. We've always been able to understand when the other person has more to say and she gets me, I have more to say, so much more. "I should have realized it was off when he got back. We always had a great sex life but when he come back it was different.

He jumped back in bed with me the first week but then it slowed down quickly. The same things seemed to happen around our conversations. He was around for breakfasts and dinners. Eventually, it slowly faded to the random meal he would be home. I thought it was because we were both busy adjusting to classes, and internships. Now I look back and realize I should have asked more questions."

I pause having burned out the main thoughts running through my head. Annie wraps me in another hug. "You are anything but stupid. You loved Tom and you gave him your trust, which is what you should be able to do when you love someone. He's the asshole for not being honest with you from the start. He should have called off the anniversary dinner and been honest with you. I swear if he tried to come into this apartment while I'm here, I'm going to wound him in a way he won't forget."

I laugh hard imaging all the ways in which my feisty best friend could cause a man pain. Looking at her you wouldn't think she could with her girl next door thing but she has mad defense skills thanks to years with an older brother. "I don't want to live here with him but we are both on the lease, I can't kick him out."

We break the hug and Annie looks around. "I get that the living spaces are small and you will run into him often. Plus, you don't want him here when you bring home his replacement. Or wait, maybe that is what you should do. Make it uncomfortable for him." Annie has an evil plan brewing and I like it, we've always been great at making plans.

We both get distracted by the TV, I notice the game score. The team has added more points to the board. I watch Miles step up in the pocket and throw a ball perfectly to his tight end. I think that I should thank him for this morning. He's taken time to check on me and make me feel a little less alone. I pull up his name on my phone and text him a message that I know he won't see for hours.

Annie takes a moment to get on her phone too as the game winds down to the final minutes. "Want to order from that Chinese food place we had last time you were in town?" I ask Annie. She agrees telling me to order extra egg rolls. I call in the order as we finish watching the end of the game and when the reporter talks to Miles, Annie watches with interest taking notes on her phone. Miles does a great post-game interview, spinning every compliment of his play into the efforts of his teammates. After the interview is over, we turn off the TV and I realize I want Tom's crap out of my bedroom. "I think before we get to the plan around rebounding, I need to get the assholes stuff out of my room. Want to help me throw Tom's shit in the spare room?"

We are attempting to move the desk to my room when we get message notifications, we both consider that as a sign for a break. Annie looks happy as she responds to her message. "A new guy? Please tell me it is?" She looks up with disgust, "Nope, Miles being a big brother. He told me to drive safe since he pretty much knew I'd drive here."

I laugh because he called it and the look makes 100% sense now. I check my phone and see Miles has also responded to my message. We send a few messages back and forth and I make a mental note to text him my section before the next home game to see if he keeps his word to try to look for me.

There is a knock at the door and I check it finding the delivery driver with our dinner. Annie and I continue our break to have dinner. After we spend a few hours moving the desk and bookshelf into my room and haphazardly throwing Tom's stuff into the spare room.

We do draw the line at not damaging anything but it doesn't bother me for a second that he'll have a room full of unorganized items to figure out when he comes back. "I think I need to get a different doorknob for my room so I can lock it. I still plan on trying to find a new place to rent but since the semester has started it's going to be a hard thing to come by and I don't want to move into a dump." Annie agrees with my approach. I couldn't ask for a better friend and I hug her. I swear Annie Campbell is the best thing to ever happen to me!

Chapter 5: Finding a New Place

-Meg-

I wish Annie could stay around for Tom to come by the apartment. I would have loved to see her nice personality turn hostel, but she went to lunch with Miles before heading back to Oklahoma on Sunday. She invited me to lunch with them but I didn't want to intrude on family time and both Campbell siblings have already helped me out this weekend.

I spend the time after she left reorganizing my new space and going to the hardware store to get what I needed to add a new lock to my door. Thank God for Dad forcing me to understand tools and how to be self-efficient. I even got the one that has a code you can enter, giving me a backup if I forget my keys. I kept the old one so I could replace it when I move out.

I work on homework the rest of the night, with football playing in the background. My hearts not into it and the football keeps pulling my attention. Eventually, I have to turn off the TV and open my music app to listen to my top hits playlist. My project management class is both interesting and boring at the same time. I know I'll need this course someday but right now I find it is the last one I want to work on. I would rather be lost in my design for my capstone but I need to talk to my advisor about the written project description before I get into the actual drawn design phase of the project.

My brain is numb from the work, so I close the documents. I determine that it's time to call Mom. I don't waste time and give her the news about me and Tom breaking up. She's upset for me and asks me multiple times during the phone call if I need her to visit or if my parents need to make a visit to Texas. I tell her I'm fine each time but it makes me feel better to know they are always there if I need them. She reminds me that I need to come home more and I let her know I'll try.

Monday morning the reality sets in as I make my new routine alone. I don't have to think about Tom and his schedule of activities, no coordinating of meals. That is, until I get a message from him asking to talk. I would rather not but I have to face this reality and unfortunately him.

I send him back a time we could meet outside of the apartment in public. I don't know why but I don't want to be here with him. I want to avoid us being in this apartment alone as often as humanly possible. He lets me know the time works. I don't respond and I walk to campus.

Today I'm back in 'Meg mode' I got ready in a flowing dress which complements all my curves in a beautiful shade of cornflower blue. I pulled my hair up today in a braided style because it's functional. I head to the indoor cafe grabbing a coffee and a table. Opening my computer, I go to the campus website and select the classified section. I used it to find the apartment I'm currently in and I want to see what options are available. There isn't much available which doesn't surprise me. I don't want to be picky but I do rule out a few because they are way too far away from campus.

There are a few options I'm interested in based on the location. I sent out three messages asking if the rooms are still available and a few comments about myself. I feel like myself again because my emails feel like me, sassy.

> *Female from Oklahoma, yeah get over it. Senior at the university graduating in the spring. Easy going unless you eat the last of my chocolate during that time of the month. I'm laid back, bring over your hot date and I'll be a great wing woman, giving you all the hype. I'm looking to move in quickly as my previous roommate is a pig and I refuse to stay in that environment unless it is completely necessary. I would love to come tour the room posted as soon as humanly possible.*

I make my way from the coffee shop to class running into the same familiar faces. Once you make it to senior year, there seems to be a small familiar group of people in each class. I grab my seat by my friend Jane. We'd agreed to be class buddy's sophomore year and from there our friendship has blossomed.

We are the kind of friends that talk before and between classes and we group up for every project we can. We used to hang out a lot in the dorm common spaces with Tom and his friends. I tried to hook her up with Tom's roommate sophomore year but they didn't click.

Last year I gave into Tom wanting to hang out with his friends more and I started to ask Jane along with the group. I even invited her to our new apartment party back in May. Jane attended and it had refreshed our friendship and we talked most of the summer. We've been having the great debate all summer if you could turn a summer fling into a relationship.

Jane is shy and she told me she liked this guy but thought it was bad timing. In late July, she texted me and asked me if it was weird to have phone sex with someone you haven't had real sex with. I give her my best response of empowerment. Something along the lines of 'if you enjoy it, then why not?'

Now she's been trying to figure out how to turn phone sex into real sex. She told me they have hung out but agreed to take it slow in person. I was happy for her because she really did seem to like him. As I get closer, I notice Jane giving me a worried look. "What do I have something on my dress?" I look down and inspect myself but there isn't anything out of place.

"No, you look great. I guess I'm surprised you look normal today." I give her a puzzled look. "Why wouldn't I look normal today?" Then I remember, I told her I thought Tom was going to propose and I'm not wearing a ring today. I shake my left hand. "I read it wrong; he broke up with me instead of a proposal."

She goes to say something at my off handed comment but is interrupted by the professor starting the class. I mouth to her that we will talk about it soon. I open my computer to take notes. I also open my email to check to see if my advisor has commented back on my request for a meeting this week about the capstone. I'm pleased to find a message from two of my room inquires instead.

Room for Rent
From: Jamal Arthur
To: Megan Patterson

Megan,
I could always use a wing woman! I'm off today, so feel free to come by at the address on the listing. My roommate is busy but I'm happy to give you a tour. I'm up front, we host parties often, so if that's a deal breaker totally understand.
Jamal

> *Room For Rent*
> *From: Kate Jones*
> *To: Megan Patterson*
>
> Megan,
> The room is open. I am open tomorrow from 1 PM to 3PM if you want to tour the room. I do not like a lot of noise and would appreciate notice if you plan to have visitors. Please let me know by tonight if you have interest in booking a time to view the space.
> Kate Jones

I reply back to Kate that I am open tomorrow at 2 PM. I am concerned with her visitor comment but anything is better than being Tom's roommate. I also reply back to Jamal, he already seems fun and easy going. I comment back to his message, interested in a tour today after I get out of class and I let him know that in addition to my wing woman skills I make a great party host.

After I finish my emails, I focus back on my professor and get to copying down the notes he's already started on the board. The problem with senior year is that each professor has a whole grade consuming project. They all give the same excuse that in the real world all we'll be doing is projects. I beg to differ that I'll be working on five different major projects at the same time but what do I know?

I have lunch with Jane and fill her in on the drama with Tom. She looks worried and concerned all rapped into one person. I do cut our lunch early to go view the room, before I leave, she grabs me into a big hug and tells me, "Your so brave, I mean it." I give her my best smile when we break the hug and I do feel brave.

I walk back to my apartment dropping off my backpack before walking the few blocks to the house with the room for rent. It's a little farther from campus on cold weather days but I can drive to campus if I have too. The house looks pretty normal with is brick exterior and average landscaping but I realize I should have told someone I was going to a random house to look at a room for rent.

I ping my location to Annie and tell her if she doesn't hear from me in two hours to call the authorities. I make sure she knows that I'm looking at a room for rent as a reason for the location ping. After completing my messages, I walk up the front steps of the house and ring the doorbell.

The man that answers the door bell is sexy as hell. I have no idea how guys get away with walking around shirtless but I'm not going to complain about it because he's all toned muscles and ebony skin tapering down to black athletic shorts.

He chuckles as I bring my eyes back to his face noting that his green eyes and his easy-going smile. *He must get a lot of girls.* "Hello beautiful, what do I owe the visit? I'm not complaining I'm interested in whatever you're selling." He follows with a wink as he leans on the doorframe, and I can't help the laugh that comes o ut.

"I'm hoping you're selling me on a room, sorry stud to disappoint showing up empty handed and fully dressed." I wink back resulting in him laughing. I realize I didn't introduce myself or get his name before our flirty exchange. "I'm Meg Patterson, I really hope your Jamal Arthur or this is going to be really awkward."

He laughs again and it's deep and real. "Yeah, I'm Jamal Arthur but call me Jamal. I pause, "Wait are you on the football team?" I ask and he gives me another grin. "Yeah, but less about me and more about you. When I got your message, I didn't imagine Megan Patterson to be a knockout. Come on in beautiful and I can show you the place."

He steps back holding the door for me as I enter the house. "What did you think

Megan Patterson would look like?" He smiles as he says, "Let's say someone less temping and far from the description of knockout." "Nice to know" and it really is nice to know after the events of this past weekend. I make sure to let him know he can call me Meg and then he takes me on a tour of the house.

The space is surprisingly big and open and thank goodness clean. Jamal points down the hall, "I'm down the hall in the master, which I do pay extra for. Your room would be upstairs with Camp." I interject, "I'm going to guess he is also a football player?" Jamal winks as confirmation and we head upstairs.

I realize that I'll be sharing a Jack and Jill bathroom with Camp. Each side has its own toilet and sink, only sharing the shower. When I go in to inspect it's very clean with a towel on the hook and bottle of body wash and shampoo in the shower. I turn around asking "Is Camp ok with a female roommate?" Jamal chuckles, "Yeah I don't think he'll find sharing with a female difficult. If it helps, he's got a sister, so he at least has some experience with females."

That is a good fact to know about Camp, guys with sisters at least have some common sense and it makes me think of Miles. On more than one occasion he'd yell at Annie from their shared bathroom about her having too much shit on the counter referencing to her makeup and hair products. "Good news for Camp, we don't have to share a sink."

Jamal is standing in the open room and laughs at my comment. He shows me a good size walk in closet that would hold all my stuff. "This is great" I smile around the space. "Should I take that as you're interested in moving in?" He watches me as I look around the space again, I should wait to see what the apartment looks like with the girl but I like this space and I've always gotten along great with guys. They seem to enjoy my ability to talk about football and sex with ease.

"Yeah, I'm interested" I look at him again. "And you're sure you're ok with the

parties? We have them often on weekends and there will be lots of girls over."
Jamal is eyeing me expecting this to be a problem. "Jamal, dude I told you I was
fine with the parties as long as I'm invited. I don't have a problem, and I'll tell all
the girls that you and Camp are the best. I told you I'm a great wing woman. I'll
tell them y'all asked me how to make a woman orgasm with just your tongues.
It's a valuable talent and us woman are into guys that have functional tongues,
it's sure to help your game."

Jamal starts laughing so hard he has to bend over. "You are amazing Meg, but I'll
let you know that I can do that already and I've never had complaints about my
tongue skills". He winks at me again. "Oh Jamal, my hopefully new roommate,
I'm sure that's true but I'll wait to hear the moans of your next female visitor to
validate."

Jamal smiles at me. "When do you want to move in Megs?" I bounce up and
down on my toes in excitement. "Can I move in this Sunday?" Jamal smiles
"Works great for us as long as it's not early, we'll get back late from the road
game". When I question if I should meet Camp first, he tells me that Camp said
he trusted his judgement.

We exchange phone numbers and he hands me a set of keys. "Don't you want
me to pay a deposit?" I question looking at him and the keys in my hands. "We
already paid September, let's call it good and you can start paying your part
starting in October." I thank him and leave the house with hope for the rest
of my senior year. I make sure to text Annie as I walk back to campus to meet T
om.

Meg

I got a room at a house!

Also, this is my check in that all is good!

385

Glad you are alive

Great News! When do you move in?

Sunday!

That is amazing. Do you need help moving?

I do but I'll ask around here

You can't visit again two weekends in a row

Fine but I'm visiting in October for the family game. How many roommates will you have?

Two guys. The first one is hot as hell and he knows it. I didn't meet the second one as he was at some school thing.

Interesting…

Yeah, I'll send pictures after I move in

Find The Roommate Situation on Amazon or at www.anable ssing.com

Also by Ana Blessing

The Friends Group Series

Book 1: Should Have Called Dibs (Annie and Drew: Part 1)

Book 2: Making It Home (Annie and Drew: Part 2)

Book 3: The Roommate Situation (Meg(an) and Miles: Part 1)

Book 4: The Forever Plan (Meg(an) and Miles: Part 2)

Acknowledgements

First and foremost, I would like to thank my Heavenly Father for all the opportunities. I know without him, none of this would be possible.

To my original, from day one, biggest supporter, Mom—Thank you! When I need someone to help my brain from spiraling into self-doubt, you've always been the safe place I can go to quiet the storm. Thank you for believing in me, my dreams and being the best BETA reader, I could ask for. Dad, thank you for pushing me to think bigger and to not settle for less. I couldn't have gotten here without your voice in the back of my head telling me I can do anything I set my mind too. Little brother, thanks for laughing with me and telling me to make sure to write good smut, if I was doing this. Kayla, thank you for being the best friend I needed for all these years. Thank you for supporting me and this crazy wild dream. I'm already looking forward to our future adventures. To my Instagram family, thank you for humoring me when I only had book reviews to offer and humoring all my random writing updates.

To my family, my support group; my husband and two boys. Thank you for being my favorite second chance story. For proving that Love finds a way. You all gave me the grace to follow this crazy, amazing dream. I wouldn't be here without you. Thank you for supporting me and for being proud of me, even if you can't read these books until your over eighteen. I love you the most, the end, I win!

And finally, to all of you—the readers, thank you for taking the time to read this book. As a reader myself, I know how many options you have in your endless TBRs. Thank you for joining me in this journey. I appreciate you and hope to see you again with the next one!

About the Author

Ana Blessing has always had a passion for reading, devouring hundreds of books over her years of reading. A fan of the phrase, "I'm only going to read one more chapter" but really meaning 'I'm finishing this book at 3AM'. Her passion for reading led to her writing her debut novel *Should Have Called Dibs*, the first book in *The Friends Group Series* in 2025.

She loves to watch football, baseball and tennis, cheering loudly in person or from her couch.

She has been married to her leading man for over fifteen years. She is a mother to two wild boys, who keep her busy when she's not writing. They happily call the Midwest home along with their family cat.

Join The Friends Group either on the website www.anablessing.com or on Instagram @authoranablessing.

www.ingramcontent.com/pod-product-compliance
Lightning Source LLC
Chambersburg PA
CBHW071143100726
47908CB00002B/233